THE TALES OF
IRYVALYA:
HORIZONS

LeAnn Kelley

The Tales of Iryvalya: Horizons

This book is a work of fiction. Names, places, and events are all fictitious with no tie to any past or present person, place, or event.

The Tales of Iryvalya: Horizons
Copyright @ 2025 LeAnn Kelley
All rights reserved

Published October 2025 by:
LeAnn Kelley Enterprises, LLC
www.LeAnnKelley.com/LAKLLC

ISBN-13 (paperback): 978-0-9975352-6-6
ISBN-10 (paperback): 0-9975352-6-1

Edited by:
Lisa Gilliam

Cover design by:
Deranged Doctor Design

To My Readers,

This book exists because of you-and so, it is rightfully dedicated to you. Your encouragement, your love of stories, and your belief in the world of Iryvalya breathe life into these pages. Without readers, countless tales would be left untold, and so many worlds would never have the chance to live.

Thank you for stepping into my world of Iryvalya, for walking beside these characters, and for becoming such an important part of my journey.

Be the spark!
Volnyri,
LeAnn Kelley

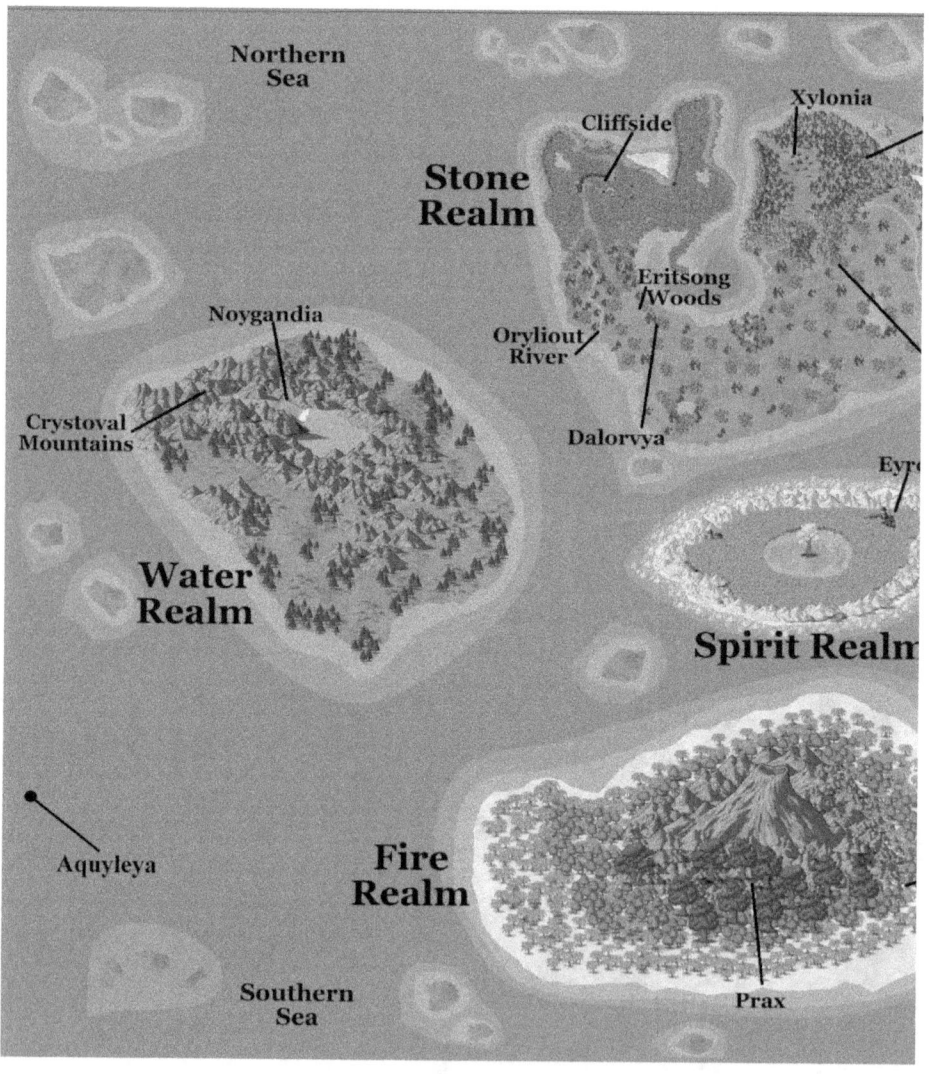

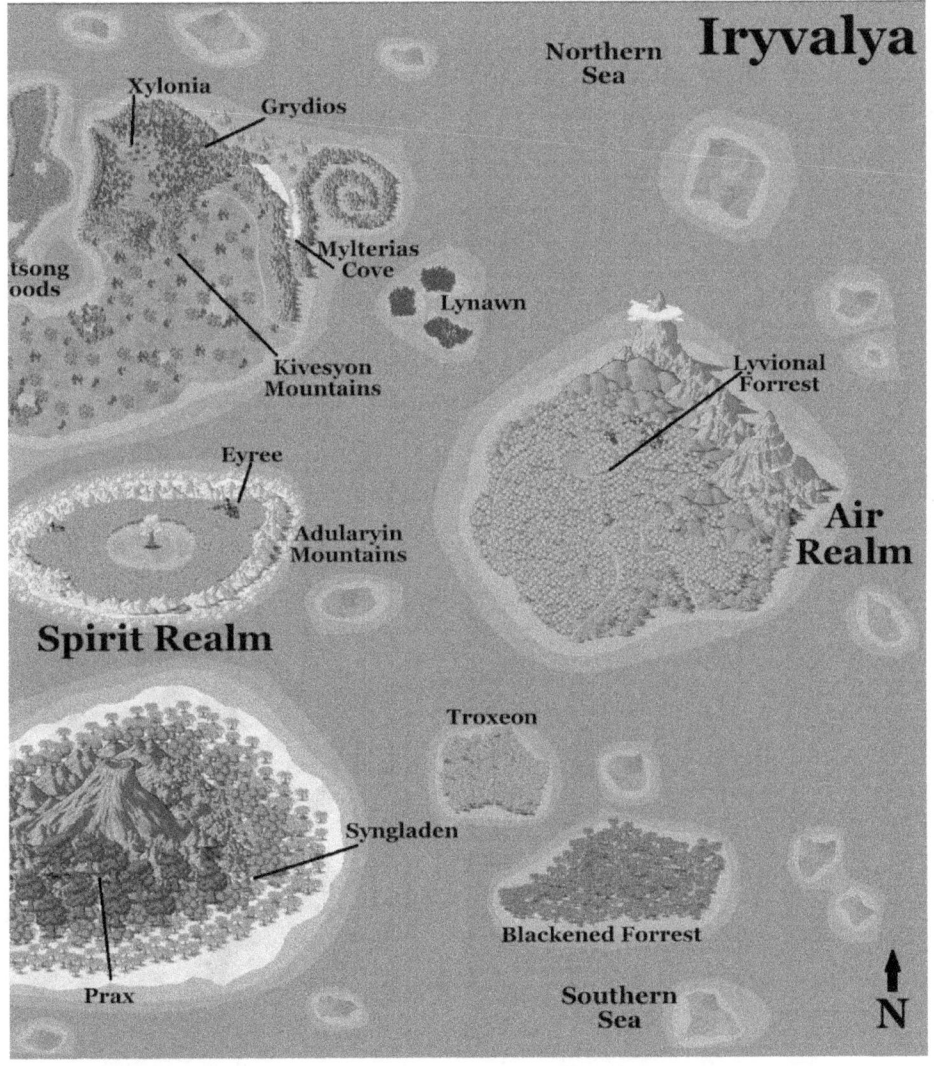

↷1↶

STORYTELLER

"The people of Iryvalya were without hope while everyone believed that Nyrieve was dead… Most people couldn't believe she could have survived falling into the volcano… but as she often did, Nyrieve surprised them all…"

"But, Gramzy, why didn't she rescue everyone right away?" Nykirys asked as he brushed the dust off his pant leg, only to get more on it, as most young elves did. The dust and rubble of the long-since-destroyed home still seemed to spread to everyone it touched, even so many years later. It was as if it missed what it once was and was reaching out from long ago, almost as if to say, "I am still here."

I looked around the room that was crumbling apart. It was softly aglow by the candlelight. I watched the light dance along the edges of the walls and imagined it once was home to a family who dined near the hearth to keep warm when it was cold and who might have sweet-smelling flowers in a vase when warm. The room might have been once filled with the laughter of children who could never imagine what this would turn into one day. Something unrecognizable as a home or barely as a building. There were even scorch marks along the top of the walls where the thatching once was to protect the people from the elements. Now all I see above is the stars shining brightly in the turquoise light of the Nydian moon.

"Did I ever mention that I was born under the Nydian moon?" I asked.

"No, but it doesn't surprise me with your hair having the same color in it," Nykirys said, smiling. "What made you think to say that?"

"Besides it shining down on us now, it is reminding me of a story about Nyrieve after she recovered from the fall into the volcano. Once she was healed enough, she had walked outside with a companion, trying to figure out what her next step should be, and stood out in the forest of the Spirit Realm watching the Nydian moon's light shine down over everything. She was scared and didn't know what she should do at first, and then she saw a sign that the choice she was ready to make was what

1

Iryvalya herself wanted her to do."

"What sign was that?"

"Irybugs…"

I could see Nykirys's eyes open wide and a smile starting to cross his face. "She saw the irybugs?"

"She didn't just see them. She watched them come into the forest towards her and then they danced all around her."

"That would have been amazing to see."

"Yes, it most certainly would have, Nykirys," I said with a smile. "Not many people are lucky enough to see irybugs in their lifetime, but Nyrieve was not just anyone, was she?"

"No, she wasn't."

"Should we stop for the night?" I asked, wondering if maybe it was too late to keep telling the story.

"No," Nykirys begged.

"Please, Gramzy," Fyleeza added as she batted her eyes at me. "I love hearing your stories about Nyrieve."

I smiled at them both. They reminded me of myself when I was young and couldn't ever get enough of hearing the stories about Nyrieve and her adventures, battles, triumphs and defeats… I frowned for a moment, thinking again about this destroyed home I was sitting in. While not every home in the village was as destroyed as this one, it wasn't an unusual sight. I remember as a young child walking past roads with nothing but rubble, no house frame even left to the imagination. Nyrieve had wanted to save the whole of Iryvalya, but even with the best of intentions and attempts, you can't be in every place at once. Even some of the places she loved the most were not able to be saved.

"Okay, you two, I will tell you some more…"

They smiled up at me. I could see the dust and dirt in their hair from just walking around this old building. I could only imagine how much it filled the air on the day of the attack here. But there wasn't anyone left here who could tell us about it firsthand. Anyone who had survived either had passed, moved away, or understandably did not want to talk about it. Most people did not want to remember those days or the ones that followed shortly after. But if we did not remember our past, it would come around again to remind us. That was why I kept telling these stories, to make sure things would not have to go this way again.

"Could you tell us about the dragons?" Fyleeza asked. She was thirteen leaf years old, but this is what she had asked about every time I told stories to her and her younger brother.

"You always want to hear about them." Nykirys laughed. "I love the dragon stories too, but you ask for them each time Gramzy tells us stories."

"I love hearing about them, and how everyone thought they were gone, but they were smart enough to hide and be ready to help Iryvalya when Nyrieve needed them," she said with a smile.

"I enjoy the dragon stories too, children," I said with a smile. "My brother and I loved hearing the stories from my *Gramzy* as well. I do not think a single visit from her happened without her telling us a few stories, and they always had dragons in them in some way."

"I wish we could have heard them from her too," Fyleeza said with a sigh of disappointment.

"I'm sorry I am not as good as she was with telling their stories," I said with a chuckle.

"I didn't mean anything bad by that, Gramzy, I just meant…"

"I know what you mean, my dear, and it's okay. I wish she was able to tell you the stories herself to you all."

"I'm just glad she told them to you so you could then tell them to us," Nykirys said.

"Me too," I said, thinking of my Gramzy and how she could tell stories better than anyone else I knew. The stories were so detailed, I could picture myself there with her. One of the drawbacks to growing older is losing those who meant so much to you. I was just glad that my brother and I were told all the stories and were able to pass them down to others and keep the memories and stories alive.

"I can tell you about how Nyrieve first discovered the dragons in the Air

3

Realm," I said.

"Yes!" they both said in unison.

"Nyrieve had been in the Air Realm trying to figure out her next steps…"

I told them about how Nyrieve found the secret entrance and path that led up to where the dragons hid from everyone and were able to be free. I told them about how she even learned how to ride one on her great journey to the Spirit Realm.

I would never tire of telling these stories to the children, or even any adults who wanted to learn them. I remember as a child I would feel almost embarrassed to repeat the stories, because they were not mine, but then I learned with each generation who learns about Nyrieve and what she tried to do for Iryvalya, the closer I felt to Nyrieve and like I was a part of those adventures with her.

The Nydian moon had past the midpoint over the Northern Sun. I hadn't realized we had been out so long.

"It is time to head to your rooms and get some rest before the Nydian moon sets away from the Northern Sun, children. Besides, if I keep you up too long, your parents might not let me keep taking you on these walks!" I said with a laugh, knowing their parents loved hearing the stories when they were young just as much as the children did.

With big sighs and heavy feet, they got up and dusted themselves off the best they could. As they left to go back to their home nearby, I said to them the phrase I'd heard my whole life growing up and that I make sure to tell everyone, "And don't forget, in Iryvalya, the smallest spark of hope can change the world… Be the spark!"

When I said "Be the spark," they both chimed in and said it with me. We all laughed, because they knew it was something I would never stop saying.

I took one more look around the ruins of the building, just wishing Nyrieve would have been able to save it. I could only imagine what the house Nyrieve grew up in looked like walking through what was left of it. There wasn't much left, outside of the foundation. People took everything they could when the village was sacked. That never stopped me from roaming through the house trying to find something from the past, even when my mother swore to me she had checked it thoroughly herself when she was younger.

Perhaps one day I would find something myself. As I stood to go, I noticed a faint glow from the hearth. I stepped closer to see what it was, and to my surprise, it was an irybug flitting about. All I could do was smile.

☙2❧

BAYSIL

I was finally able to stop the wound on Kaleyna's head from bleeding, but I didn't know how much more of this she could take. It had been many weeks since Nyrieve fell into the volcano and died… I could hardly process that she was now forever gone or that I was trapped here in this jail Fyra put us in. I had no idea where Rowzey was, or even if she was alive at this point. The only thing I could force myself to focus on was helping Kaleyna and trying to keep us both alive.

The room we were being held in was dark and hot. I couldn't be sure where we were, or if we were even still in Prax, but I knew we still must have been inside the Fire Realm somewhere, since we never boarded a boat or anything else to travel far. It looked almost like we were in a cave of some sort, but I couldn't really tell. Whenever they took us out for anything, we had a hood placed over our heads and could not see out.

"Baysil?" she whispered hoarsely.

"It's me," I said, trying to reassure her. "You're going to be okay… We're going to be okay…"

"I don't think we are going to be able to get out of here…"

"You can't think like that. We have to get out of here," I said as I stroked her matted blue hair back away from her face. I took a strip of cloth I had torn off my shirt and poured a small amount of water on it, using it to wipe some of the blood off of her lacerated face. She winced as I gently went over some of the newer cuts. I wished they would take things out on me instead of her, but for some reason they wouldn't. They hadn't even talked to me much or asked me questions. They knew she was her best friend, so they thought she knew more than me, I was guessing, but what difference did it make if Nyrieve was gone?

"I think they are going to kill me," she said quietly.

"Then maybe you have to answer whatever it is they keep asking you," I said.

6

"Ny would not have wanted you to die too."

"But they keep asking me things I cannot answer, even if I wanted to," she said.

"What do they keep asking?"

"They want to know where Nyrieve is. It's like they don't believe she is dead, as if she could survive falling into a volcano. They aren't questioning me if Jehryps is still alive, so why would they think Ny is? Do they honestly think the two of them somehow orchestrated this? She hated him."

"How could she have survived that? No one could…" I said sadly.

"I don't know, but it seems like they have reasons to believe that she is still alive…"

"If that was true, she would have tried to save us already, Kaleyna."

"How could she?" she asked.

"I don't know," I said, hoping she was somehow alive somewhere and could save us.

"If she was alive, she might be hurt or not even know if we are alive," she said. "Either way, I cannot answer their questions when I don't have any answers."

"I am going to make them talk to me next time," I said. "You need to rest and heal."

"I don't want you going with them," she said.

"You cannot go back out there, Kaleyna. If you keep going out, you will die and then I will have let Nyrieve down, not to mention Prydos."

"And I can't take it if you die…" she said softly. "If both you and Ny die, then everything we have done was for nothing…"

I hugged her as close to me as I could without hurting her. "Don't say that… The things you have done have helped so many of us, and you gave Nyrieve's life more purpose. You have been there for her, and I cannot tell you how much it meant to me that you two had each other growing up. I know you meant so much to Ny too… We just can't give up… We have to try to keep going and get out of here."

The door slammed open, and light poured in, blinding my eyes. A large figure stepped in front of me and tossed a black hood at me. "It's your turn," they said to me. "Put it on or I'll put it on you."

7

I quickly and carefully moved Kaleyna aside, shushing her protests. "It's okay, you rest. I'll be back," I said. Once I was standing, I carefully placed the hood over my head. Again, the world went black and I couldn't see anything. Not even faint lights coming through any worn threads.

I walked as slow as the guard allowed, but they were pushing me to go faster. I couldn't keep track of the different turns we took or the stairways going up and down. Finally, after what felt like thirty minutes, the guard stopped me and shoved me down into a chair. The chair was nothing like I would have expected. It was soft and cozy. I didn't want to take the hood off. I wanted to sit in this chair for a few moments and not think of what was about to happen.

The hood was ripped quickly and sharply off of my head. I knew a bunch of my hair went with it. The light was low in the dark room, so it was easy for my eyes to adjust and glance around. There was no one in front of me, so I had to assume the person who took the hood off was behind me. There was nothing remarkable about this room. The walls looked of wood and floor as well. There was a large chair across from me, and I could sense the person behind me moving slowly and calmly, different from how it felt having the hood removed. I didn't want to be the first to say something, so I sat in silence as the person slowly walked towards the chair and sat down. They leaned over and lit a tall candle inside a thick candle holder on a table beside them, and then I could see a face I had seen before.

"Hello, Osidya," I said flatly.

"You remember me, do you, Baysil?"

"How could one forget someone as…"

"I would be careful with the next words you choose, for you never know if those could be your last," she said with a grotesque smirk.

"Why would I ever say anything bad about the person who had a part in creating one of the greatest people I had the privilege of knowing?" I asked with as much fake flattery as I could muster.

"Is that all I am? The creator of the 'Bringer of Peace'? It seems that is the only thing people want to acknowledge me for these days… Well, being her aunt, as she told everyone," she said, sounding bitter.

"What would you prefer to be acknowledged for?"

"Prior to everyone learning about my *sister's* quanta'mu, I had been helping control the Fire Realm... Fyra would come to me for counsel about the happenings here, but now..."

"Now no one wants to talk to you?"

"Oh, they'll talk to me, but they seem to question every action or inaction I take. How can they think I would ever betray my people for—"

"Your daughter?" I asked with a smirk of my own.

"She is not my daughter. She is merely a child I birthed."

"That wasn't always the way you felt about her, was it?"

"It doesn't matter what I had felt at one time. The only thing that matters now is finding out what you might know about her whereabouts."

I shook my head in disbelief. "Everyone saw what I saw, her getting thrown into the volcano."

"And yet not everyone believes that she was destroyed in it..."

"Do you?"

"No, I don't."

"Why?"

"Call it a mother's intuition if you must, but let's just say the day she was born I felt something different in the world, and that feeling hasn't gone away just yet."

"Could it be more along the lines of being hopeful that she is still alive?"

"That it cannot be."

"I know there was once a time you were happy to have Nyrieve and you wanted to keep her."

"Oh, was I?"

"At least that is what Arnayx said." I could see something flash across her face. I couldn't tell if it was sadness or anger.

"What would he know about how I felt?"

"I imagine because those were things you said to him once upon a time."

"Your imagination is wrong. Those were things that he thought I felt or wanted. When we met, he knew who I was and what was expected of me, yet he still pursued me and didn't stop until I couldn't think straight and fell for his lies of love and a future together."

Bitterness, that was what I was sensing from her. But was it bitterness over what she thought was done to her or bitterness that it didn't come true? Either way, if Kaleyna and I were to survive this, it might be best to try to keep Osidya from thinking I wasn't sympathetic to her.

"I am sorry to hear that... It must have been a very confusing and dark time for you."

She leaned in to look me in the eyes. "I am not sure if you mean that or not, but either way, it was both a confusing and a dark time, a time that has lingered with me ever since."

"I didn't think most people knew about Nyrieve until just the past year or so..."

"I lost more than just that child when she was born, even if people didn't know about her. People knew my sister was gone and always questioned if I did it just to get ahead with my family and the Klayn."

"Oh..." I said, not sure what I should say to keep her talking.

"Oh?" she asked. "That is all you can say to someone whose world was turned upside down and never made right-side up?"

"I am sorry," I said. "To be honest, this is the most interaction I have had with someone other than Kaleyna in... I honestly don't know how long it has been since... since Nyrieve was pushed into the volcano."

"Yes, the dark caves do make it hard to keep up with time passing," she said with a look of actual understanding.

"Have you been in those before?"

She tipped her head to the side and smiled. "How else do you think they punish an elf who runs away to be with the enemy and comes home with a dead sister?"

"I didn't know... I am sorry... How long were you in there for?" Maybe if I keep trying to sympathize with her, she might give me more information to help get Kal and me out of here.

"No one knew, really, except for my parents, who put me in there, and a couple of council members who are long since dead," she said with a look of joy, "and while I cannot be exact on the time, I believe it was more than a year… I remember not being able to be there when my sister was laid to rest… That is one I never forgave my parents for… I was the only daughter now, and it looked horrible that I chose not to be there as support for my parents."

"I can only imagine that it felt horrible and disorienting being down there for a year," I said, "especially with me not even knowing how long—"

"It has only been a few weeks," she snapped at me, rolling her eyes. "You cannot even begin to understand how hard everything has been for me. It took years to get my parents to accept me again, and with some… persuading of sorts, get me to be the representative of our family within the Klayn and council."

The smile she had when she said that made me not want to ask her what she did to persuade them. I had thought I might be able to reason with her to get her to let us go, but I didn't think reasoning was possible with her.

"I am sorry you had to endure so much, Osidya," I said softly while looking down at the floor.

"Good, it is nice to hear someone recognizing what I have gone through…" she said. "Now let's get onto the business of why we are really here, shall we, Baysil?"

"I would tell you more information if I had it, but once Ny went into the volcano, Kaleyna, Rowzey and I were surrounded and taken away. I have no idea where Rowzey—"

"No one knows where that silly old fool is…" she interrupted.

"She disappeared?" I asked, wondering if Rowzey found an opportunity to change into her dragon form and fly away.

"Yes, they took her back to the rooms you were all staying in, and while going through everyone's things, she managed to escape. I will never understand how those guards ever lost her. She is an old woman. It isn't like she could just jump out one of the windows and fly away."

"Oh no, hopefully she didn't fall or get hurt…"

"If she had they would have found her by now… I think she used a potion or spell to hide herself long enough to escape, and if I had been the one watching her,

11

she would have never gotten away with it."

I thought about how shocked Osidya might have looked if Rowzey would have changed form in front of her, and maybe even picked her up in her mouth and tossed her into the sea as she flew away. Maybe Rowzey somehow saved Ny and they were hiding in the Fire Realm trying to figure out a way to save us… That is, if Ny somehow survived the fall. I knew it was crazy to think she didn't die, but I had to hold on to hope that all we had worked on and done for so many years wasn't to end like this.

"Either way, Baysil, what I need to know from you is what was your plan for after the party?"

"Plan?"

She rolled her eyes. "Yes, the plan! What were you all planning on doing once you were done in Prax? Were you going elsewhere or did you have plans to attack or what? Kaleyna refuses to say anything about what we don't already know, and to be honest, I am tired of seeing her face and watching her bloodstained tears run down her cheeks. How my daughter ever picked such a whimpering friend is beyond me, but I assume she has some good qualities… like keeping her trap shut. However, in this case it is making things worse for herself."

"All I knew was a day or two after the party, we were supposed to leave Prax and regroup with some of the other members of the Nomydrac."

"Where was that supposed to happen?"

"That I honestly do not know. There were a few options, but Ny did not want to tell anyone which place until we left," I lied.

"Which places did you know of for the options?" she pressed.

"The only two places I had overheard her mention were Troxeon and the Blackened Forest," I said.

Osidya's eyes widened. "Troxeon?"

"Yes, she said something about wanting to see the place she was born and the place where…"

"Where what?" she snarled.

"The place where her aunt gave her life to save hers," I said, hoping to provide

12

enough detail for her to think I was telling the truth.

Osidya started pacing back and forth. "How does she know about that?"

"I believe Rowzey explained information about her Leaf Day…"

"Ahhhhhhh," she yelled out to no one, then grabbed the candlestick from the candle that she lit earlier and walked straight to me and slammed it into my head.

Everything looked black and almost red at the same time. She kept hitting me as I put my hands up to protect my head, and began shouting, "That is my sister… Rowzey had no right… Ny should have been the one who died…"

I didn't know how many hits she landed on me before everything went black.

❦ 3 ❦

NYRIEVE

"It is your fault, Ny. She wouldn't be stuck there if it wasn't for you!" Prydos yelled at me.

I couldn't argue with him. It was the same thing I had been telling myself over and over again for the last few weeks. I just stood there as Prydos's spit hit my face as he continued to yell at me.

This was not how I expected my arrival in Aquyleya to be. I had hoped that I would be able to talk to Prydos myself and let him know what had happened, but somehow, he knew... and by the stares of everyone around us, it seemed everyone knew.

"Prydos!" I heard Kylyan shout out as he grabbed his friend's shoulder to turn and face him. "She would have never left Kaleyna there if she had a choice, and you know that."

Prydos let Kylyan pull him into a hug. "I don't know anything anymore," Prydos said through tears. My heart was breaking even more than it already had been. I was devastated that Kaleyna, Rowzey, and Baysil were all left behind in Prax. At least I was still hoping that was where they were. Also hoping that Fyra did not harm any of them on account of me. I kept telling myself if they were gone, I would feel it. I would feel it if I had lost them forever, wouldn't I?

I stepped towards Prydos, and Kylyan quickly signaled for me to stop. He gently shook his head. I felt a tear slide down my cheek. I wanted to be the one to tell Prydos what happened. I wanted him to understand I didn't mean for this to happen, but now all I could do was watch Kylyan lead Prydos away.

I stood for a moment to collect myself and finally looked around. Aquyleya was nothing like I could have ever imagined. I wasn't sure what I pictured the underwater city to look like, but it definitely wasn't anything like what I was seeing.

Above me was all the blue of the sea and sunlight passing through in beams. I didn't know how the water wasn't crushing down on me or what was holding it back. It looked as though if I could have reached up high enough to touch it, my hand would return wet. I could see so many creatures swimming about, as if the craziness of our world was as it always was. Maybe for them it was. It only seemed to be creatures like me that wanted to ruin this world. Why couldn't we learn from other creatures and live together in harmony?

I looked back at the pathway I had followed down for a few days to get here. It was dark and felt like it'd never end at times. Domi had brought me to a small island filled with tropical trees and nothing else, or so it seemed. After following Domi through the trees, we came across two trees that were twisted up together towards the sky. This was where she said we'd find the hidden way to the underwater city. Near the base of the trees, we dug about three feet down until we found the hatch. She handed me a bag with food and candles inside. I begged her to come with me, but she said she needed to cover the hatch so no one would find me. She promised me that she would come find me as soon as she could. I asked her why she couldn't just portal us to the city and the only response she'd give me was that it wasn't safe. Safe for whom? Her or me or both? More questions and no answers.

Outstretched before me were small huts made of what looked like grass and wood. They weren't anything fancy like the homes in Prax, and they weren't simple like the homes in Noygandia. They were warm and inviting. The pathways were made of what looked like crushed seashells. There were paper lanterns along the pathways ready to be lit when the darkness came. Each home was on a platform, some only one level high and some two levels. The windows looked to be covered only by cloth curtains on the inside. The temperature here was not hot or cold. It just felt comfortable and safe. I couldn't understand how I could be underwater like this and still be dry and breathing, but I was appreciating the beauty before me.

It had been at least two fortnights since I left the Spirit Realm with Domi. She had been able to get in touch with Sudryl and arranged for me to come here to Aquyleya to figure out how I would proceed. I had felt so confident back in the Spirit Realm surrounded by the irybugs when I decided I needed to forge a new path. Standing here now, all I wanted to do was run away. I knew in my heart I wouldn't, but knowing what might lie before me, I was scared.

"Nyrieve!" I heard my little sister Dymma shout out as she pushed past the few people who were just staring at me.

I smiled as she rushed towards me and pulled me into a strong hug. I held her so close, feeling my face wet with hot tears. "Dymma, I'm so sorry."

"Shhh," she said, holding me as we both went to the soft ground on our knees. "You did everything you could. We know that."

I cried harder, letting myself let go of everything I had been holding in. I felt more arms around me. "We love you," my father said. "It'll be okay," Clyo said. I felt my heart breaking again, knowing that it was her daughter I left behind. Why wasn't she yelling at me or hitting me? That's what she should have been doing. No one should have been trying to make me feel better.

I didn't know how long we all knelt on the ground, holding each other and crying, but by the time we finally stood up, everyone else who had been there was gone. My father took the bag Domi had given me, Dymma took my left hand, and Clyo took my right and led me through the pathways to their house.

We didn't say anything else the rest of the way there. What else could we say in that moment? They took me to a room with a bed and gestured for me to lie down. I slumped into the bed and cried myself to sleep.

I slowly woke, remembering where I was and those I had left behind in Prax. I could hear the hushed voices of my father and Clyo talking in the next room.

"Should we wake her?" Arnayx asked.

"She'll wake up when she is ready," Clyo responded. "She's been through more than you or I could imagine. What she needs now more than anything is to feel safe and loved."

How in the world could she say things like that when I left her child behind with a hateful and cruel elf like Fyra? Maybe she didn't understand the dangers that I left Kaleyna in or how it was because of me that they thought Kaleyna was me. I wanted to just pull the blankets over my head and go back to sleep, but couldn't after

I heard Dymma speak.

"She's awake, you know," she said to them both.

"How do you know?" her mother asked.

"I just know," she said simply.

I took a deep breath and stood up. There was a looking glass next to the door and I looked for a moment at my tear-stained face and the wrinkled clothes I'd worn for a few days, before taking a deep breath and stepping forward through the door.

"Good morning, Nyrieve," my father said, walking to me and pulling me into a big hug. It felt so good to be held and I didn't want him to let go, but I released him as soon as I felt him start to pull back.

"Morning, everyone," I said in a raspy voice, sitting down at the table with them.

"Oh, Ny," Clyo said, "all that crying is hurting your beautiful voice."

"I deserve worse than a strained voice and puffy face from crying," I said quietly.

"Why in Iryvalya would you say that?" she asked with her head tilted to me as she got up and poured a hot cup of tea.

I just stared at her, blinking and looking to everyone else in the room. They all looked at me with blank faces. "It's my fault Kaleyna is not here, or Rowzey or Baysil. And it is my fault that Ghily is dead."

Clyo walked over, setting down the steaming mug on the table, and put her arms around me. "You would never harm someone like that, Ny. Everyone who knows you knows you put others before yourself."

I felt the warm tears starting to fall down my face again. How could someone have so many tears? I should have run out of them by now, and kind of wish I had.

"It shouldn't have happened this way," I said, clearing my throat.

Clyo stepped back and gestured for me to sit as she walked over and grabbed the hot tea and placed it in front of me. I took a long slow sip out of the hot mug. I could feel the heat burning my tongue just a little, but I didn't care. It tasted so good and I could feel it soothing my throat.

Dymma placed her hand on top of mine and said, "Everything happens for a reason, Ny..."

"So Ghily was killed and Kaleyna is being kept by a crazy murderer for a reason?" I asked softly.

"I don't know what the reason is, Ny, but there has to be a reason for all of this... Otherwise..."

"Otherwise what, Dymma?" Clyo asked her daughter curiously.

"Otherwise, it was more cruel to get to know my sisters than not... because if Kaleyna is never returned, Nyrieve will never forgive herself and it'll be as it was before, just me."

Both my father and Clyo stood to hug their youngest daughter and comfort her, as I just sat there realizing everything she said was true. If Kaleyna was killed or never found, there was no way I could ever forgive myself. Kaleyna was my closest friend. I would not give up on finding her and bringing her back to those who love her.

"Dymma..." I said quietly.

They all turned to look at me. "Yes?" she asked through her tears.

I took a deep breath and thought very hard about what I was going to say. I couldn't just tell her what she wanted to hear, but I couldn't let her think there was no hope anymore either. "Dymma, I don't know what is going to happen. I don't know where Kaleyna is or how I will find her. But I promise you, I will do everything to find her and bring her back so we can be a family all together."

"But I need you too, Ny," she said in a whisper.

"I need you as well... but I cannot just hope Kal will be found... I have to try to find her too," I said. "There is just one problem..."

"What's that?" my father asked, sitting next to me and placing his hand on top of mine.

"I have no idea how to find her," I said. "I doubt they will keep her and the others in the same place, because they will know I will come looking for them."

"Well..." Clyo said.

"Well what?" I asked.

"Most of Iryvalya believes you are dead," she said nervously.

"What do you mean? Why would they think that?" I asked, confused.

"You fell into a volcano, sweetie," my father started. "Most people cannot survive that. Even the Bringer of Peace has her limits."

I hadn't really thought about it. I knew after it happened that everyone would think I was dead, but I figured it wouldn't be long before the world would hear that I was still alive and it'd eventually get back to Fyra.

"If the world thinks I am dead, how did everyone here know I was alive and when I'd be arriving?"

"Sudryl had told us once he heard from Domi that you were alive. He knew we were going crazy thinking you were dead and not knowing about Kaleyna," Clyo said, "so he had a meeting of everyone in Aquyleya to let them know what was going on and also to put a lockdown on anyone leaving here for a while. He didn't want it out that you were alive, as it was figured that you could get here safer if no one was looking for you."

"That explains how Prydos knew…" I said.

"He is taking it the hardest," Clyo said. "He's been coming over to see us every day to see how we are doing, and before his reaction to you yesterday, he had expressed his fear for both Kaleyna and you. I think when he saw you, all his worries and fears for Kaleyna overwhelmed him."

"That doesn't make it okay," my father interjected.

"No, it doesn't," Clyo agreed.

"Yes, it does," I said. "He loves Kaleyna, and he has every right to be angry at the person who left her trapped in that place with those horrible people."

"You didn't just leave her trapped, Ny," Dymma said, taking my hand and looking at me with tears slowly flowing down her reddened cheeks. "We all know you love Kaleyna and Rowzey—"

"And Baysil," I said quietly.

"And Baysil," she said. "We know it, and we know you wouldn't have left them if you had any choice in the matter."

I could feel my throat tightening again from the tears I was fighting back once more. I had been struggling with this since I realized what happened, and I knew she

19

was right. I would have never just left them behind, and I know I needed to figure out how I was going to save them.

"Ny," my father started, "I know you are upset and blaming yourself, but you have something that I don't think you realize yet."

"And what is that?" I asked quietly.

"You have us. You have your family and you have friends here, and we all want to help you."

"I don't know how you can help me..."

"Neither do we, yet," he said, "but we will figure out a way together."

"Exactly," Dymma said, "we are a family and we'll figure this out together."

For the first time since I woke up after falling into the volcano, I felt something... hope.

❧4❧

NYRIEVE

"It has been quite some time now hasn't it, Nyrieve?" a familiar voice asked me as I stepped outside the door of my family's home.

"Iclyn?" I exclaimed as I turned quickly to see Iclyn standing in front of me with a faint smile. Her snow-white-tipped gray hair was pulled back into a braid that lay across her shoulders and reached down to her hips.

"It is good to see you," she said as we embraced.

"It is so good to see you too," I said. "What in Iryvalya are you doing down here?"

"It's a bit of a long story, but one I would love to tell you and hopefully catch up on you…"

"Me? I assume everyone knows what has been happening to me, and maybe know more than I seem to." I sighed as I stepped back.

"I am sure you know a lot more than you think, and I would be honored to help you… The Nomydrac is still here for you and expanding with more supporters by the day."

"It is? I… thought with everything that has happened the Nomydrac was more or less just a word for those of us who originally came together to fix… whatever this world is…"

"Just because one might not hear about someone or something doesn't mean it isn't there thriving in the shadows," she said sheepishly.

"I'd love to hear more," I said.

"Well then, let us walk together and perhaps get you some food… You look as though you haven't been eating much."

I smiled, remembering Iclyn telling me similar things when I was young. The small phrase reminded me of the simple time that was, and the safeness I had felt as a child growing up in Cliffside. It felt like that time was so long ago, much longer than it really was. It felt like the last time I was in "my" room was a lifetime ago, and made me think there really hasn't been a place where I had felt like I was "home" since.

"What is it?" Iclyn asked as she took my arm and began to lead me to another house.

"Just thinking about Cliffside…"

"Me too… It isn't the same, sadly," she said.

"What do you mean?"

"Without Lydorea, it is just another village, another house… She is what made that place my home…"

"I am sorry, Iclyn," I said, thinking of Lydorea's warm smile and caring eyes.

"Thank you," she said as she pushed open the door to a small home and stepped inside. I went in behind her.

The room was cozy and welcoming with plenty of places to sit.

"Would you like something to eat?" she asked with a grin.

"Yes, thank you," I said, not feeling like I could refuse her if I had wanted.

"Good, I made something I thought you might like," she said. "Have a seat and I'll bring it out to you."

I looked around the room. It looked plain in the sense that there didn't seem to be many touches that would have told me this was Iclyn's home. I remember the rooms that her and Lydorea shared, and there were blankets on every seating area, pillows even on the floor, and little trinkets.

"I didn't decorate," Iclyn said, breaking my thoughts. "Here, hopefully I remembered correctly you like this."

She handed me a hot bowl and I took a deep breath, holding in the delicious aroma. How did I not notice the smell before when I came in? It was one of my favorite soups Rowzey would make when I was sick. It was chicken, noodles, broth and spices.

"Iclyn, you made Rowzey's soup!" I exclaimed.

"It is close to Rowzey's," she said, carefully holding a bowl of her own as she sat down next to me.

I took a spoonful of the hazy soup and let it dance on my tongue as it brought me more memories of years gone by. "This tastes almost exactly like Rowzey's," I said, taking another spoonful.

"I am glad you like it," she said, enjoying hers as well.

"How did you ever get Rowzey's recipe from her?"

"I didn't." She chuckled. "Lydorea watched her make it and wrote it down. She tried to make it a few times, and it wasn't bad, but it wasn't the same. We never told Rowzey we had it, but one day Rowzey came to our rooms and gave us a jar. When we asked her what it was, she said it was the spices we needed to get the soup just right."

"She knew?"

"Doesn't she always?"

"She always seemed to."

"And I am sure she still knows…"

"Knows what?"

"How much you want to help her and the others…"

I sighed and stared into my bowl. "I hope so."

"Rowzey is one of the most intuitive people I have ever met, Ny, and I have met a lot of people throughout my life so far. I believe that if Rowzey ever had felt like you were going to do the wrong thing, she would have been one of the first to say something to you."

"True."

"And I am pretty positive if she is able to, she is telling Kaleyna and Baysil the same."

"I didn't want to leave them."

"Anyone with any sense knows that, Ny. You loved them all and would have given up your life for them, I know it."

"I just don't know what to do."

"Yes you do. You know what you need to do is figure out a way to get them back safe… The hard part is how to do that."

"If I just go back to the Fire Realm, they will kill me and them, I fear."

"You're right about that. What you need is a plan."

"Do you have one?"

"I have some ideas, but as most things go in life, we need more than just one idea. Before you arrived, I called for a meeting of the Nomydrac… Well, as many as we could get here before it went into a lockdown city."

"If it went into lockdown after they found out I was alive, then how did you know to try to get everyone together?"

"Lydorea made sure to leave me many messages so I'd know some of the things I needed to do. She didn't always know what the timeline was, but she knew what things would likely come to pass. When I learned you were going to both realms to meet with the leaders, it made me realize that this was one of the things that Lydorea had warned me about, so I decided to be proactive and try to get as many people as I could to Aquyleya while I could without rousing too much attention."

"Who all did you get here?" I asked curiously.

"You'll find out tonight."

"What is tonight?"

"We have made arrangements with Sudryl to get us a place we can meet and work on a plan. He has some amazing talents, and he has done very well with helping me procure all that we need to figure out what your next steps should be."

"Do you honestly think we can figure out a way to somehow save them and all of us not die?"

"If anyone can, it is the Nomydrac," she said, hopeful.

CRSO

I walked into a cave-like entrance, thinking it would be dark and wet, but was again surprised with all that lay beneath the seas. The ground was a firm sand and above was the sea. I don't know what magyc held it at bay, but whatever it was, I was enthralled with what I could see above me. We had to be a long way from the surface, but there was still light above. It took a while for my eyes to adjust and finally be able to figure out it was sea creatures swimming and crawling above us that lit up as they moved. I remember Baysil once telling me about something he called bioluminescence. Somehow the creatures' movement in the water had a reaction that caused them to light up. I had almost thought it was make-believe, but Baysil wasn't one to make things up. I wished he was here right now to see this beautiful place. It reminded me of the irybugs when they swarmed around me in the Spirit Realm. The lights were everywhere above, getting brighter as others dimmed and then switched. I could stay here forever just watching them dance above me.

"Ny?" a strange and yet familiar voice called to me, snapping my gaze away from the lighted dance above me. I turned and looked at a face that seemed familiar and yet strange. I tipped my head to the side, studying the person's face, trying to place where I knew them from.

"Don't tell me you don't remember me?" they said and then busted out laughing.

"Emryleia?" I exclaimed. That laugh. I could never forget the laughter of one of the dearest people I had once known in Cliffside.

"So you do remember me," she said as we rushed towards each other into a hug.

I took a step back, still holding her, and asked, "What are you doing here? I haven't seen you since…"

"Since I left Cliffside when we were what, fourteen?"

"Yes, where have you been and how did you end up here?"

"Well, those are both very different and long answers, but I will give you the condensed version for now. I left when my grandmother had found out where I was. As you know, my parents had been killed during one of the raids from the Pyrothian Elves shortly after I was born, and no one knew if I had other family, so I was sent to Cliffside. Eventually my grandmother found me. She learned how the fairies were taking care of orphaned elves and hiding them for safety. She traveled and found me there. I wish I could have said goodbye to you, but my grandmother feared for our safety and everyone in Cliffside if it was heard that an elf came to collect her granddaughter. I wanted so much to let you know what happened or where I was, but Lydorea said it would put all of us in danger."

"Lydorea was always smart and protecting everyone," I said. "She had told me you left with family, but... Wait, that means you're an elf too?"

Emryleia smiled a beautiful wide grin at me, with her emerald-green-and-silver swirled eyes sparkling in the light. She pushed back her now deep-amethyst-and-cobalt straight hair, showing me her elf ears like mine. I looked at her again with a smile that started to hurt my cheeks. I was so happy to see my friend. I never thought I would have the chance to again.

"I love it. You look beautiful!" I said, feeling the first real pings of joy and happiness since long before falling into the volcano. Then with that thought, I could feel my face falter and tears brim again, knowing I shouldn't be feeling joy like this when I didn't know if Baysil, Kaleyna and Rowzey were safe or even alive.

"Now you stop, Nyrieve," Emryleia said. "I know you are worried about your friends, but it is okay to be happy to see an old friend too!"

I smiled. "I know, Em, it has just been such..."

"A whirlwind?" she asked.

"Exactly."

She smiled and said, "It feels like its been forever since I heard someone call me Em. I missed it!"

"No one calls you something shorter?" I asked.

"My grandmother said that because my name was given by my parents, she wanted to make sure to use it in full."

"That makes sense. I can call you Emryleia then," I said.

"No, I like it, makes me feel like a kid again."

"A kid? You are like two inches taller than me. How is that possible? I thought I was older than you," I asked with a chuckle.

"That is true, Ny, but only by a couple of months!" she said and winked at me.

"So, the other important question, what in the world are you doing here?" I asked.

"When I heard about you and who you really were, I decided I needed to help."

"Why?"

"Because you are supposed to bring peace to Iryvalya, right? My parents' lives were taken because of all this war, and I think that if there was any way I could help honor them and their memory, it would be to help you so this doesn't happen to another child."

"You have always had a kind and caring heart, Em. I am so happy that you are here."

"Me too," she said, squeezing my hands. "So, I have been here in Aquyleya for about six months. I had come across Sudryl while trying to find the Drayks in the Air Realm, but everyone was gone. He was in the sea, I think waiting for me to get back to my little old boat so he could take me to the Drayks. He said he thought I could be of important help and brought me here."

"What did he say he thought you could do?"

"Be here for my friend." She smiled.

"How do you think he would have known I would need a friend?"

"I think it wasn't just that, but I do have a couple of talents that he thought could be helpful."

"Like what?"

"I am guessing you have learned you have some powers, and I do too."

"What is your power?"

She smiled and gestured to the ceiling of water above.

"You did that?" I asked in shock.

"Yep, my grandmother helped teach me ways to manipulate the water and the ability to suspend it. Sudryl said he only knew of other merpeople that could do that. Makes me wonder if merpeople and Lumaryia Elves have ancestors in common..."

That made me think for a moment. Could all the different races be connected to one race, and as we moved apart and changed environments, we changed how we looked and powers we had?

"Don't think too hard on this, Ny. We don't have time to try to figure out the origins of Iryvalya."

"How did you know what I was thinking?" I asked, now wondering if Emryleia had other powers I didn't know, like reading minds.

"Because I remember that is how you would think often when we were kids. I remember in one lesson Iclyn was teaching all of us, you couldn't get past how far back or deep the subject could really go and she had to keep telling you that it was a question to work on later."

I chuckled. "I guess some things never change."

"And I am glad for that. It will take someone who looks beyond the surface of something to help bring this world to peace."

"No pressure, right?"

"I think that was a question you would have asked, and probably did, a long time ago!"

"You are not wrong."

"While I am sorry you have to do all this, at least you do not have to do it alone."

"I just don't want anyone else to be hurt, Em."

"Everyone who is here, or has been here for you, already knows that. We all know the risks that come with trying to bring this world together, and we all know that the biggest risks come to you. And yet here you are, still doing what you can to help everyone else."

"I guess…"

"Ny, you could have walked away from this back when you found out about who you really are. You could have walked away when you learned the truth about your parents. You could have walked away when Lydorea died. You could have walked away each time people have tried to kill you. You could have even walked away after what happened in the Fire Realm… and yet here you are. You know the risks to yourself better than any of us. You are here, Nyrieve. You keep stepping up to try to help our world. Us being here to support you is honestly the least we could do."

I smiled and accepted the hug Emryleia offered, took a deep breath, and let it out feeling just a little bit of my stress and fear leave my body. She was right. It was important to have friends by your side and friends who can remind you that you are not alone in everything, even when it seems that way.

"Thank you, Em," I said, squeezing her tight before letting go. "I am very happy and grateful that you are here."

"Keep those happy thoughts in mind. I have a feeling that this is going to be a long and overwhelming evening," she said softly, "but it isn't anything we can't get through together."

I smiled. "Thank you, Em."

"Any and every time!"

ଓ5ଯ

NYRIEVE

The table for everyone to sit down at was large, round and made completely of what looked like old coral. There were enough seats for all thirty of us. I recognized most of the people standing around, but some I had never seen before. I was excited when I looked over and saw Louv here. I hadn't seen him since we were in Xylonia, but he didn't look any different. I gave him a big hug. He was in person form, so I knew it had to be nighttime, otherwise he'd be in his stone shape.

"Louv, I didn't think you would leave the Stone Realm. What are you doing here?" I asked.

"Nyrieve," he said in his gruff voice with a large smile on his face, "it is good to see you again, Your Highness."

"Please don't start with the 'Highness' stuff," I said. "I think we are well beyond formalities by now."

"As you wish, Nyrieve," he said, making a small bow with his head.

"So what is it that made you come here?"

"You, of course," he said with an almost blank look on his face.

"Me?"

"When we heard you might have been killed in the Fire Realm, I reached out to the Nomydrac and heard that some of us were meeting here to figure out the next steps and also try to locate you if possible."

"Oh," I said quietly, "I am sorry to have made you leave your home…"

He smiled and said in his deep gravelly voice, "I haven't left Xylonia in a long time. It is nice to see other parts of the world, and I had to win a bet."

"A bet?"

"Yes, I had bet that you were still alive, and the only way to prove it would be to find you… and yet here you are, finding us."

"Who was the bet with?"

"With us, of course," said two familiar voices in unison.

"Well, if it isn't Leyhroi and Jynkins," I said with a smile, "my favorite twin satyrs."

They both laughed and rushed up to give me hugs.

"While it is great to see you both, I must say I am quite disappointed to hear you bet against me being alive."

"We weren't betting against you, Miss Nyrieve," said Jynkins.

"It was more we were betting on the volcano," said Leyhroi. "I have never heard of someone being able to beat a volcano before."

"And I told them both that Your—I mean Nyrieve is not like any other elf we have known, and the world needs her too much to allow a small thing like molten lava to take her away from us all."

"Yes, such a small thing," I said with a smile yet remembering the burns I obtained before I could portal out of there.

"How did you do it, Miss Nyrieve?" both satyrs asked together.

"It is a secret," I said, "but perhaps when this is all over and done, I can tell you more."

"I am sorry to interrupt," said Iclyn to me quietly, "but if we could get started, we will have some time to catch up more afterwards."

"Of course," I said. "I am sorry to be wasting time."

"It's never a waste, Ny," she responded. "I just know some people have traveled long and are quite tired, but we want to get some information together while it is fresh in everyone's minds."

"I understand."

"Nomydrac," Iclyn said loud and clear, "thank you all for coming from all corners of Iryvalya. We have a lot to go over and need a lot of help with things to come, so if we could all come and sit at the table, we'll get things moving along. Nyrieve, if you could come here and sit by me, we will get things started."

I glanced at Em and she smiled. "No worries, I'll be sitting right next to you!"

I smiled back and walked quickly to where Iclyn directed me and sat to the left of her, and Em was now seated on my right. I looked around the table at everyone

31

and felt both sadness and hope. It was a strange thing to feel such opposite emotions at the same time, but while I was sad about things not having worked out exactly as planned and everyone here had to travel to help me once again, I felt the hope that maybe with the help of everyone, we could get back Rowzey, Kaleyna and Baysil.

୧୫ଞ

"I don't care what you think, Iclyn. Saving those people is important, but it isn't the most important thing we need to do."

"I hear what you are saying, Tycori," Iclyn responded, sounding calm and collected, "but we do have to remember that Nyrieve is the one who gets to decide what she wants to do at the end."

Tycori sighed deeply and looked at me for what felt like the first time. Their eyes had constantly darted around the room but never made eye contact with me until now. "Your Highness, I know you love these people and that they have been there for you, but we need to think about more than just their safety and return."

"I am listening. What do you suggest?" I asked.

Tycori leaned forward in their chair, their short hair shifting slightly on top of their head. From what I could see, it was shades of dark red, and their skin was dark tan, but with what looked like shades of green when caught in the candlelight just right. Their eyes were swirls of a dark and lighter red, making them look almost menacing against their soft-looking facial features. They couldn't have been much taller than my waist, but their presence was bold and powerful.

"Your Highness—"

"You do not need to address me so formally," I said simply.

"I'm sorry, but my father always taught me to talk to those of royalty with respect."

"And while I appreciate the sentiment, I am honestly royal in name only. I do not live like I am above anyone else. We are all the people of Iryvalya, and we can talk plainly to one another, especially here and now with all we are trying to accomplish."

"My father was right about you," they said.

"Your father?"

"He said he met you on a journey and that you were most kind and humble."

"Draykorian?" I asked.

"Yes, my... Nyrieve," they said, "that is my father."

"He is a very kind person. We had some great conversations in the Spirit Realm."

"He said as much as well."

"I am glad he felt the same. Now please continue with your suggestions."

"I feel it is important to get your friends and members of the Nomydrac back, I truly do. However, they cannot be your priority."

"Oh?" Prydos said, speaking up for the first time. "And whose priorities should they be?"

"Truly, I believe they should be yours, Prydos."

"Mine?" he said, annoyed. "Of course no one wants to have the Bringer of Peace take any risks to get my Kaleyna back, right?"

His words stung. I knew he was angry, and I didn't blame him for that, but I did not want to leave her or anyone else behind. I wondered if he would ever be able to understand... I also now wondered if that was how Kylyan felt about me too. I tried not to look directly at him, but my eyes constantly wandered to him, missing his arms around me and feeling secure in his presence.

"No one said that," Iclyn quipped, "and talking like that will not get us anywhere, Prydos."

He just sat back and rolled his eyes as he crossed his arms over his chest.

"I believe," continued Tycori, "that it would be wrong to let anyone know that Nyrieve survived the volcano just yet."

"Why is that?" Kylyan asked softly.

"If she goes back to the Fire Realm, they will know she survived, and they already tried to kill her once. Do any of you think they wouldn't try again?"

There were murmurs around the table and heads shaking no.

"Then we need to keep them wondering and worrying. When people are afraid, they make mistakes. We cannot be the ones who make those mistakes and give away what advantages we have," Tycori said. "I think it would be wise to send someone as a diplomat to the Fire Realm to try to negotiate the release of our people, and treat the situation as if Nyrieve did die in the volcano. This way, they might believe that she is gone, and we can work towards a way to reach our final goal of bringing peace to Iryvalya."

"And how do you think we can do that? What do you think will make the Klayn leaders want to work together?" Kylyan asked.

No one said anything. I sat there and thought about each place I had visited and the people there. Not the leaders, but the elves and their few children… "Their children," I said out loud.

"What about their children?" Iclyn asked.

"I can't believe I didn't put this together before…" I said, still trying to process it in my head.

"What is it, Ny?" Em asked, lightly touching my arm and bringing me back from my thoughts to the table.

"If they want their children to have a future and the possibility of more children, they would need to come together," I said, everything making sense to me.

"Can you explain more?" Kylyan asked. My heart felt like it skipped a beat hearing him talk directly to me without anger or sadness.

"Yes, it might take a minute though. I was thinking, when I went to both realms, I met with the people, not just the leaders but the actual people of each realm. I had noticed that there were not many children in either, and it didn't really click to me until now that it is because they are poisoning their own bloodlines. They are having children with people who are not far enough apart in relation to one another, and that is causing them all kinds of medical problems and the inability to have healthy children or even get pregnant in the first place," I said, taking a deep breath. "Their leaders must know this, but keep lying to them so they don't revolt. They need to know the truth, that if they aren't being held hostage from all the other elves in Iryvalya, then maybe their families could continue to grow if they so wish, and maybe with that, the magyc that has been depleting within the Klayns could come back. Look at me and… Kaleyna… She and I are of both Klayns, and we are

34

healthy and have some abilities. Our bloodlines were strengthened by coming from different families, not weakened by it. If we could get word to the people of the Klayns about this, then maybe they would stop supporting their leaders and help us overthrow them and become just the people of Iryvalya, not Lumaryia or Pyrothian Elves."

It was quiet for a lot longer than I thought it would be. I started to think maybe this was a dumb idea. Maybe I was not thinking big enough. Maybe I needed to give up on any hope of a more peaceful way to bring our world together. Maybe—

"How is it no one has figured this out before?" asked Iclyn, looking around the table. "How is it that Lydorea didn't know this?"

"Maybe she did," I said, "and maybe that is why she wanted to help me find Clyr. Maybe with Clyr, I would be able to tell all the elves of Iryvalya about this and they would believe me."

Iclyn's eyes widened at the thought. "She always told me you would need Clyr for something, and it would be important. But she never told me why."

"Perhaps she didn't know for sure or she didn't know if I would ever figure it out."

"Now we just need to make a plan," said Tycori.

"A plan to do what exactly?" asked Prydos.

"Two plans actually," they responded. "One for you to go get your lady back along with Rowzey and Baysil, and the second one for Nyrieve to get Clyr."

"I know Lydorea told me once about how important Clyr would be to you," Iclyn said, "but I don't know where to find it."

"If I had my pack from the boat that took us to the Fire Realm, I might be able to—"

"I have your pack," Kylyan said softly.

"What?" I said, surprised.

"The captain of the boat had reached out to Sudryl and thought we should keep it safe for you. I honestly didn't remember I had it until you just mentioned it. I am sorry. I was not trying to keep it from you."

"That is great news," I said, not even caring that he forgot to tell me. "If you could get it for me, let me go through it and see if there is anything in it that might help. Lydorea told me that things in the pack would come to me as I needed them, and maybe there will be something in it that can help us find Clyr and help get our people back from the Fire Realm too."

"I will bring it to you once we are done here, my lady…" he said, in the way he talked to me that felt like so long ago.

"Thank you, Kylyan, for taking care of it and… everything else." Tears started to sting at my eyes, but I closed them tightly shut to fight them back. Right now wasn't the time to think about anything other than what was in front of us.

"I think it is time for this meeting to end for the evening," Iclyn said. "We've been here for hours and finally have a lead on what our next steps should be. Let us all go back to our houses and get some rest. I will get with Nyrieve tomorrow and figure out the next time for us to meet again. Does anyone have any questions?"

No one spoke up, so Iclyn continued, "Then Volnyri, everyone."

"Volnyri," everyone said in unison.

☙6☙

NYRIEVE

The knock on my door was soft but persistent. I took a breath, looking around the small house Iclyn provided to me. It was simple but quiet... almost too quiet. She thought that it would be better for me to have a place of my own, so if I was needed for meetings or anything else, the rest of my family would not be awoken or interrupted. I agreed with the idea, but I was already feeling lonely, and being in this house made me feel it even more so.

"Coming," I said and crossed from the small kitchen to the door and opened it quickly.

Kylyan stood in front of me alone, with my pack in his hands. He stared at me with his cobalt blue and orange eyes. They looked the same as they had before and yet different. They seemed more hardened and weary.

"Would you like to come in?" I asked nervously.

He nodded and I stepped back so he could come inside. I closed the door and turned back to face him, shocked to see him drop my pack on the floor and pull me into a tight and warm hug. Tears started to pool in my eyes. I had missed his arms wrapped around me and the feeling of safety I felt in his arms. How could I have forgotten how much I wanted and needed him around me? I had missed him every day, of course, but being alone in the room with him now and feeling the strength of him holding me close reminded me of how much I had missed him.

I held him back as tightly as I could and wanted to never let go. I don't know how long we stood there together. It could have been for an hour, but when he lessened his hold and stepped back, taking my hands in his, it felt like it had only been for a second. I looked into his eyes, slightly covered by his now shaggier-than-I-remember hair of the same color as his eyes. It looked as if his eyes had tears forced to the surface but he was able to hold them back better than I could.

"It is good to see you, Kylyan," I said softly, feeling his rough fingertips tracing the back of my hands.

"I have wanted to hold you since the moment I saw you walk into Aquyleya," he said, his voice hoarser that it had been at the meeting earlier today.

"Why didn't you?"

"I was honestly afraid of what Prydos might have done to me, but more so what he might have done to you..." he said in almost a whisper. "I am ashamed that I would do that to you, but I just—"

I interrupted his words when I pushed up on my toes and softly kissed his soft full lips. It was chaste and gentle at first and then became stronger and fevered as we held each other as close as we could as we kissed. I could feel his hands at the small of my back, trying to keep me balanced on my toes. My hands had gone to his face, feeling the warmth of him in my hands mixed with the roughness of the stubble on his cheeks. I then wrapped my arms around his neck and nuzzled my face into the side of his neck, breathing in the spicy citrus smell mixed with the salty air. I didn't want to let go, but I was beginning to lose my strength to hold myself up to reach his height. I slowly lowered back onto my heels and looked up at Kylyan.

"I have missed you so much," I whispered.

"And I have miss you, my lady..."

"I am sorry I left you back in the Air Realm." I sighed. "I was just worried that—"

"I know what you were worried about, Ny, I really do. I know why you pushed me away. I've always known deep down. I just didn't want to admit it. I know I am a weakness for you, and that those against you could use it to their advantage. I just didn't want to admit that it was probably safer for you without me there."

"I don't know if it was safer or not. Look at all those I have left behind to be..." I took a deep and shaky breath.

"They are alive."

"What?" I asked, shocked. "How do you know that?"

"The same way when I heard you were killed in a volcano I knew it wasn't true."

"How?"

"Prydos. He knows Kal is still alive. They are as much a part of each other as you and I are."

"I hope you both are right... I hope she and Rowzey and Baysil are alive..." I said. "I don't know if I could live with myself if anything happens to them..."

"Ny," Kylyan said, taking my face gently in his hands, "you and I both know all three of them are very capable of taking care of themselves, even Rowzey, as old as she is."

I forgot, he didn't know what Rowzey was. He didn't know Rowzey was a dragon, and even as old as she must be, she was probably more capable of taking care of herself than most of us.

"What is it, Ny?"

"What is what?" I asked.

"Something went through your mind, something you are keeping from me."

"I..." I stammered. I couldn't think how to respond, so I decided to be as honest as I could. "There is something you do not know, about Rowzey. And I want to tell you, I wanted to tell you in the Air Realm, but..."

"But you don't trust me..." he said, looking at the floor.

"I do trust you... I just... If it gets out too soon, it could cost lives."

"Whose lives? Rowzey's?"

"Yes, her life and others..."

"Then don't tell me."

I looked at Kylyan with shock. He always wanted to know. Why was he backing down now?

"Don't tell you?" I asked. "That doesn't sound to me like the Kylyan I knew."

"The Kylyan you knew was stupid and pushed you to make choices I wanted you to make, instead of keeping you close to me, I ended up pushing you away and into the arms of another."

"Another what?" I asked, confused.

"I don't know who it was, Ny, but Miaarya told me that there were... others."

My eyes widened and a disgusting look crawled across my face. "Of course she did. I am sure she told you so many things about me that left you wondering if you ever really knew me, right?"

Kylyan looked a little surprised at my reaction. "To be honest, yes. She said that you were putting your best side forward with me, but that it wasn't who you were and that you were a more… free spirit with others, unlike I had thought."

"That stupid, lying, no good, freaking—"

"It was untrue what she said?"

"I don't know if she has told the truth once in her life, unless it was for her own gain."

"What do you mean? She said she raised you and tried to help you along the right path."

I took a deep, calming breath. "She was there as I grew up and *guided* me; however, it wasn't guidance as much as it was grooming me to do as she had planned since my arrival in Cliffside."

"To do what, be the Bringer of Peace?"

"More like the Bringer of Peace for the Pyrothian Elves."

"What?" he asked, looking confused and dumbfounded.

"It wasn't until after leaving the Air Realm and going to the Spirit Realm that I started putting things together about her and also seeing memories of things she did."

"Seeing memories?"

"Domi, she is a Valya, a watcher and recorder of Iryvalya. With her and some others, I was able to see memories and events that had happened as if I was there in them. I learned more about Miaarya then and even more in the Fire Realm. She is working with the Pyrothian Klayn and tried getting me to forgive Jehryps and even wanted me to start pairyn with him."

"I'm sorry, what?" he asked, tipping his head to the side, looking angry.

"It didn't work, obviously. I knew better and there is nothing in Iryvalya that would have ever made me want to be with him in any way. Even though I know he became the way he did because of his family and being groomed himself to be as horrible of a person as he was, I could never get past things he had done."

"You said *was*. What do you mean *was*?"

"Jehryps did die in the volcano in the Fire Realm."

"Good."

"I don't feel it's that simple anymore."

"Oh no?" he asked with his eyebrows raised, confused.

"The things he did were wrong... so many things. But he was raised to think that is how he should be, and at the end, he told me he was sorry for the things he did and wished he hadn't. I can't forgive him for those things, but after watching how his family is—well, his sister Fyra at least—I don't know if he had much of a chance."

"Did you push him into the volcano?"

I looked at him with shock. "Do you honestly think I would throw him into a volcano?"

"I could have..."

"Really?"

"After what he did to you, Ny, and Lydorea, he didn't deserve to live."

"How do we get to determine that, Kylyan? How do we get to decide who deserves to live or die?"

"He hurt you. That is enough for me."

I thought about it. Was it that simple? If a person hurts someone I love and care about, do I get to decide to take their life away? Does anyone have the right? Was that what I was doing by being the Bringer of Peace, deciding to be an executioner when it fit into how I felt? No. I would not be like that, even if everyone around me said I could, I would always try to value life first over emotions. It was a promise I only needed to make to myself, because in the end, I was the only person I should be able to control.

"Either way, he is gone now."

"Who shoved him in?"

"He jumped."

"What?"

"It was his choice. His family was not very happy about it either and blamed me."

"I can't believe he did that. Is it crazy I almost respect him for doing that to himself instead of hurting others?"

"I don't know, Kyl... I don't know."

He stopped pondering and looked at me with a smirk. "I haven't heard you call me Kyl in... a long time... I missed it."

I smiled back at him. "Me too."

He hugged me close and tight. I stopped thinking about everything else going on and enjoyed this moment, feeling safe and protected.

"Would you like to sit down?" I asked as he let go of me, and gestured to the couches and chairs spaced throughout the room.

"Of course," he said with a smile. "You first."

I sat down on an overstuffed white couch. The cushions were filled with something that was both soft and firm. It looked like I would sink when I sat down, but I didn't. It wasn't hard like a rock either, just comfortable and practical.

Kylyan sat down right next to me and, as if he could read my thoughts, said, "The furniture is strange, isn't it?"

I laughed. "Yes, I was thinking about that. I have never felt anything like it. I'm comfortable, but not too comfortable. I don't think I could ever fall asleep on it if I wanted to."

"It is the same in the house Prydos and I are in. Although, he does sleep often on one of these. I just don't know how he does it."

The mention of Prydos made me think about how Kylyan and I ended things before I left for the Spirit Realm and the moment I shared with Aurilya. I felt like I needed to tell Kylyan about what happened, while it wasn't more than kissing and we weren't together, I didn't want to keep things from him.

"I need to tell you something, Kyl," I said softly.

"You were with someone else, weren't you?"

"I was..."

"You twyned with another?"

"No, no, I didn't do that. We kissed... and while I enjoyed it and know it could have been more... you were always on my mind."

42

He looked down at his hands. "We were broken up, Ny. You didn't cheat on me."

"I feel like I did."

"You can't cheat on someone when you're not pairyn with them anymore."

"I never wanted to break up with you, Kyl. I just didn't…"

"I didn't give you much of a choice, Ny. I know that now. You were doing what you thought was right and I was being selfish and not wanting you to leave. Or at least not leave me behind."

"I didn't want to leave you behind either, but I also didn't want for you to come and get hurt just because I love you."

He picked his head up and looked at me from an angle with a small smile. "You what?"

"I know you heard me, Kyl. I love you. I have always loved you, and even broken up, I always will."

"I love you too, Ny. I have never stopped, nor will I ever stop loving you."

"But we are broken up, aren't we?" I asked with a chuckle.

"Let's just say we *were* on a break of sorts."

"Were?"

"Nyrieve Vynlync, will you please take me back and pairyn with me until I can convince you to get tyed one day to me?"

"Tyed? Asking to get tyed already?" I laughed.

"Not today, but one day when it is right, I do have every intention of asking you to get tyed to me. Until then, I will follow you wherever you go, with your permission, of course."

"Kylyan, you are the sweetest person I could have ever wished for," I said, taking his hand in mine, "and if you are willing to put up with me and my stubbornness and the idea that I am supposed to somehow bring peace to our world above all else, then it would be my honor to be pairyn with you again."

Kylyan pulled me close to him and kissed me passionately unlike he ever had before. It was so pure and full of love and intensity all at the same time. It filled me with an excitement about a future together, even if we didn't know how long it would be. I had someone I could look to for comfort and be there to support as well. I had my person and I did not ever want to let him go again.

"If we are really going to do this, Kylan, we need to agree to a few things I think."

"What is that, my lady?"

I smiled at his response. I didn't think anyone else could address me formally like that and still make me feel comfortable and secure as he did.

"I think we both need to listen to each other, so if I tell you I have to go and do something, even if you do not want me to or you can't come with me, I need you to hear me and understand that it is just what needs to be done. It isn't because I don't believe in you or trust in you, it is because it is how I truly feel it needs to be done. I will listen to your suggestions, but I need you to trust in me."

"Trust without any information at all?"

"No, of course not. That is not fair," I said, taking a deep breath. "If you can promise to listen to me and trust in me, I will do the same. I will listen to your counsel and trust you with things as well, but that doesn't mean we both have to obey one another, but we need to trust each other."

"If that is all we need to do, then I will do it. I will trust you, hold your counsel when you want and need it, but I will trust you know the right decisions. Doesn't mean I won't complain about things, but I will trust you."

"Are you sure you want to know everything?"

"I can handle anything you can throw at me."

I smiled at him as I snuggled up closer to him. "Are you positive?"

"Try me, Ny!" he said, looking as if there was nothing I could say to shock him.

I felt a huge grin start spreading across my face as I whispered, "The dragons are still alive."

His face dropped and he looked at me in disbelief. "Are you serious?"

"Yes, I got to ride them to the Spirit Realm."

"You've ridden a dragon? There are dragons and you have ridden a dragon and I have not?"

"That's not even the biggest secret."

"Oh, what is that, are you a dragon too?" he asked, laughing and keeping me close to him.

"No, I am not a dragon," I said, getting quieter, "but Rowzey is."

"Wh-what?" he stammered as I laughed.

∞7∞

JOYNOX

"Do you truly think I would believe you have had no word from Arnayx after the death of his child?" Hyorda asked as they slowly paced in front of my desk.

"I wish I had heard something from Arnayx," I said, trying to sound disappointed.

"But you haven't, is that right?" they asked with a side glance.

"I have not heard anything from him since he left Noygandia."

"That was months ago, Joynox. You and Arnayx were always inseparable, even as sniveling children, but now you don't know where he is, and he never reaches out to you?"

"To be honest, I am very hurt by his decision to leave the Water Realm without talking to me or even leaving me a letter explaining where he was going."

"You mean *they*."

"Yes, they," I said. "I do care and worry about Clyo and Dymma—"

"And Nyrieve?" they asked after turning and placing both their hands on my desk and staring deep into my eyes.

"I'm not sure what she has to do with Arnayx, but the last we had heard on her was she fell into the volcano in Prax. No one has seen her since, so it is assumed that she perished inside the volcano."

"You do not know what the one has to do with the other, Joynox?" they asked, still staring at me.

"I do not."

Hyorda took a deep breath, pushing themself off of my desk, and took a seat in the chair directly across from me. As they sat and brushed off imaginary dust from their clothing, they made a tsk-tsk sound. I decided to not respond but just sit in wait for more information. Hyorda did not usually ask questions about things they didn't think they already had the answers to, especially not to a lowborn, as I was considered to most.

"Joynox, I have been around for… well, a lot longer than most here, and I have an excellent memory. Including the memory of a time when the Water Realm went into quite the frenzy of trying to locate your friend when he was missing for some time. Now there have been many stories as to where he could have gone or whom he was with, but in the end, it never seemed to matter and it was mostly forgotten. I, however, do not forget things and timing. He disappeared almost seventeen Leaf Years prior to that mixed-blood elf's Leaf Day. I recalled this when everyone went up in arms about the prophecy about the Bringer of Peace being found in the Stone Realm. Do you think that is a mere coincidence?"

"I would think my best friend would have told me if he had a child other than Dymma."

"Do you now?" they asked softly.

"I do," I said as confidently as possible.

"I do not," they said, "because if they even breathed a word of it to someone, it would be possible for others to find out. The most important part of keeping a secret is not telling others. The less who know, the more guarded your secret is."

"I understand that, Hyorda, and I am not doubting your insight or sources of information, but I cannot agree that Arnayx would ever keep something so big and important from me."

"You are smarter than the council gives you credit for, Joynox," Hyorda said with the slightest of smiles.

"I am not sure what you mean…"

"It proves to me that you are in fact trustworthy, for you to keep the secret of your friend's whereabouts and the fact that he is the father of the Bringer of Peace, Nyrieve Vynlync."

I stared at them, blinking slowly. I did not want to confirm or deny anything, as either would make me look guilty, so I decided to continue to play dumb.

"That is quite the theory, Hyorda," I said flatly.

"Oh, is it really going to take so long for you to admit to me what you know?"

they asked, and I responded with silence.

"Fine, Joynox, I do not like having to be the one to foster an equally trusting relationship with anyone," they said, slowly rubbing their temples. "Do you know I have not needed an ally in over one hundred years? Needing to make one of you is both annoyingly uncomfortable for me as well as necessary."

"What are you trying to say?"

They rolled their eyes like a teenager and let out a deep breath. "Look, Joynox, I am not as everyone thinks. Most assume I am old and conniving… Well, I am both of those things, but they are not for the betterment of the Water Realm. They are for the betterment of Iryvalya."

My eyes widened at their statement. Memories of Hyorda flew through my mind, trying to determine if times I thought they were being evil was that or, perhaps, something more.

"I can see you still do not want to trust me," they said. "Look, I have known about Arnayx and Osidya's child since before she was born. I know about Rievenya's role as well. She was supposed to kill the child but instead gave her life up for it. It took me a long time to figure that one out, but I did, as I always do. I know I sit on the council and agree with them wanting to 'kill the quanta'mu' and keep our Klayn pure from those 'disgraceful Pyrothian Elves,' but the truth of it all is I am like the Bringer of Peace. I am a quanta'mu myself."

"What?" I asked, dumbfounded.

"You are the first person I have shared that information with in many, many years."

"That cannot be true, Hyorda. How would you get on the council if you were mixed-blood?"

"It is amazing how time seems to make people forget things they once knew. My family, at least my Lumaryia side, were already on the council when my Leaf Day arrived. It wasn't quite as shocking as it is now to have a mixed-blood child; however, it wasn't talked about as much either. It really wasn't until Fyra's family joined the Pyrothian Klayn council that it was a shameful thing and forbidden. Since that time, I haven't talked about my mother's side of the family. The majority of them live on the outskirts of the Water Realm. We used to meet up on a small island in between the two realms for many years. Sadly, as time moved on, those who knew of me became fewer and fewer, until the last time I went to meet them and no one was there. So I am either to assume they have all perished, or no one knows about me anymore."

"Wh-why are you," I started, my mouth getting dry. I took a sip of water from the glass in front of me. I did something I would never usually do. I looked Hyorda in the eye and asked, "Why are you sharing this with me, if it is true?"

"I love that you still question my sincerity. It makes me more sure of choosing you as an ally in what is to come."

"You still didn't answer me, and what do you think is to come?"

"Oh, sweet child," they said, "I am telling you because I need help. I need help making sure Nyrieve is successful in her quest to fulfill the prophecy of uniting Iryvalya. And what I believe will come is either peace in our world or the destruction of all the elves in Iryvalya."

I sat back in my chair, letting my thumb rest on my jaw and my fingers lie across my mouth. I had so many things I wanted to say and to ask, but I didn't know if I should trust Hyorda. I had never trusted them before and believed they were one of the strictest rule-following elves I had ever known. But was it all an act? Was it the same as what I had done for Arnayx and Nyrieve?

"I want to trust you, Hyorda, I truly do," I said softly, "but there are many reasons to believe everything you are saying is only to get information from me I may or may not have."

Hyorda stared at me for only a moment before they closed their eyes and mouthed something I couldn't make out. Suddenly fire engulfed them completely, and as I rose up to grab the water pitcher near my desk, they snaped their fingers and the flames disappeared.

"Have you ever seen a Lumaryia Elf have that much control over a fire spell?"

I was still standing with the pitcher in my hand ready to toss it on them. I placed the pitcher on my desk and sat back down with a thud.

"I can't say that I have," I replied, knowing that having that much fire magyc and control of it couldn't be done by someone without bloodlines from the Pyrothian Elves.

"Will you trust me now?" they asked. "You could easily turn me in for being mixed-blood, and who knows what the council, let alone the Klyan, would do to me."

"I will trust you, Hyorda," I said, still in a state of shock. "How do you know you weren't the Bringer of Peace?"

"Do you honestly think there are so few mixed-blood elves out there?"

"I don't imagine there are many."

"Maybe not many, but there are plenty of us. It wasn't just an elf of mixed blood that was set to bring our world to peace. It was exactly Nyrieve who was supposed to help us. She will help us."

"But she is dea—"

"She is not dead, Joynox. That is one thing I know for sure."

"And how do you know that?"

"I have friends in, let's say, very high places," they said with a gentle smile. I didn't know they were capable of a kind smile. It was almost more distressing than the scowl they normally wore.

"Who are the friends?"

"How about you answer my questions and I will answer yours."

"What do you want me to tell you?"

"Where is Arnayx and his family?"

"They went to an underwater city. I do not know the name or location of it. They wanted to tell me, but I thought it was best I didn't know."

"That is very smart, but somewhat unhelpful. I know a few merpeople I can talk to and find out where they are."

"You know merpeople?"

"You'd be amazed at the people I know," they said almost sheepishly. It was very strange to see any emotion coming from Hyorda, but it really felt genuine. "I also need to know if you have heard anything more about Nyrieve."

"I was told of her falling into the volcano."

"She didn't fall. She was shoved in."

"What?"

"My sources were there and observed what happened."

"But if you know she was pushed in, then you know she can't have survived. It's impossible for someone to survive falling into a volcano."

"Yes, and if it was anyone else in our world, I might not give it a second thought. However, it is Nyrieve, the Bringer of Peace, and I do not believe she is gone. Nor do most of the Pyrothian Elves."

"Why is that?"

"They had some elves go down as far as they could to find her, and they found nothing of hers."

"Everything could have burned up."

"True, but there were traces of Jehryps, so they believe there would be some trace of Nyrieve."

"Possible, but not overly likely."

Hyorda took a deep breath. "Joynox, I am going to share with you something I didn't intend on sharing. I have never told another elf what I am about to tell you. You need to promise me that this information will not leave this room."

"I promise."

"One of the people who was there ended up on the shores of the Water Realm, and they happened to find someone to come get me. When I went to see them, they were badly hurt. I do not have the necessary skills to help heal someone like them, so I did what I could and secured them an escort to a place that should be able to provide them assistance. They told me that Nyrieve survived, and when I asked how they knew, they said when she was shoved into the volcano, they rushed to the edge to try to save her, but it was too late. They could only stand by as they watched her fall deeper into the volcano, but right before she should have landed in the lava, she disappeared."

"Disappeared or disintegrated?"

"I might be old, child, but I am not confused," they said, giving me a look I was more used to from them: disappointment.

51

"I'm sorry, please go on."

"Nyrieve did not fall into the bottom of the volcano. She was able to portal herself out."

"Portal?" I asked, confused. "I thought only Valya could do that."

"Unless one thought to teach our Bringer of Peace how to do it, in case of a situation like the one she was in."

Is it possible? Could the Bringer of Peace be alive? That would mean there was hope for Iryvalya and all of us who want the world to be a better place for everyone.

"Who is the person who told you this and how could they have escaped to the Water Realm to tell you?"

"They escaped because no one, for the most part, knows what they are. If they did, this would be a much different conversation."

"You still haven't answered my question."

"It was Rowzey," Hyorda said in a whisper.

"How would she get here? She is old and frail like…"

"Like me?" they said with almost a snarl.

"No, just no one knows how old she is or what she is."

"I know both things, actually. Rowzey was a friend of mine when we both were young. My family liked exploring Iryvalya during my childhood. We traveled to some of the other realms, and once, in the Air Realm, I had gone on a hike up a mountain and stumbled across her…"

"Her what?"

"Her nest."

"Nest?" I asked, even more confused. "You're saying Rowzey is a bird?"

"Keep your voice down," Hyorda snapped, "and I am not calling my friend a bird. I believe she would find that either quite insulting or possibly so hilarious she would never stop laughing."

"Then what is she?"

"Rowzey is one of many who have been long since forgotten, and ones that have aligned themselves with the Bringer of Peace."

"This isn't telling me anything."

"Rowzey, sweet child, is a… dragon."

My eyebrows rose up and I stared at Hyorda, trying to see if there was anything on their face that would betray them and prove they were lying to me. But I saw no change.

"Dragon?"

"Yes."

"Really, a dragon?"

"Really."

"If that is true, which I am not saying I believe, then why in Iryvalya haven't they helped keep the world from turning into the mess that it is today?"

"Same as us, we all have free will. For many centuries, dragons tried to keep out of the affairs of elves, fairies and the like, mostly because they felt they were better than us and didn't want to deal with our day-to-day drama."

"They could have put an end to this long ago, and yet they let this destruction happen."

"Yes, the elders could have stepped in and put an end to it, but they feared repercussions and the threats from the elves of figuring out a way to remove them from the Leaf Day tree. A truce of sorts was made. They stay out of the affairs of the elves, and the elves wouldn't remove the dragons from Iryvalya."

"Couldn't the dragons have threatened the same in return?"

"No creature in Iryvalya has been quite as cruel as the elves have been, and the dragons would never do anything against Iryvalya and the Leaf Day tree."

"They ran away out of fear?"

"Yes, but they are tired of hiding and the destruction we all bring with us."

"Does Nyrieve know about Rowzey?"

"Yes, Rowzey confirmed that with me."

"Let me get this straight, you want me to somehow help you because there are dragons and Nyrieve is somehow alive?"

"That is correct, Joynox."

I shook my head and looked around my office. This was just too much. How could this be? My normal plan would be to take time and think things out and weigh

53

out the pros and cons of everything. But this was my best friend's daughter, and the only person who could bring Iryvalya peace.

"I'm in."

"I haven't said yet what I need from you."

"I don't care, I am in."

Hyorda smiled at me and said, "We are going to make a great team."

∾8∾

NYRIEVE

"What is this?" Iclyn said, looking down at her name familiarly scrolled across the envelope.

"It's a letter I found in my pack from Lydorea. It wasn't there before, but it was last night when I went through the pack," I said softly.

"Did you read it?"

"No, I haven't even opened it. I was just glad we happened to be in the same place when I found it."

"I don't think that was by chance, Ny," she said. "Lydorea seemed to know so much more than we believed she was capable of."

"I guess so…" I replied, thinking about the letter addressed to me I found in the pack.

Iclyn carefully broke the seal on the envelope and opened the letter. I watched her eyes darting quickly across the page. I could see tears threatening the corners of her dark and light gray eyes. I sat silently as she read the page multiple times. I even made sure to look away as she brought the letter to her face. It seemed like she was trying to see if it smelled like Lydorea or something.

After a few minutes, Iclyn set the letter down and looked at me. "Thank you for bringing this to me."

"Of course. I couldn't keep anything like that away from you."

"I know, it's just… I miss her so much, and while I am so happy to get this, it just makes all the sadness and loneliness come back full force. I know that isn't what Lydorea would have wanted, but it just is how it is."

"I wish there was a way I could bring her back."

"Me too…"

"I guess there is no point in holding it back. Lydorea gave me information on how to help you."

"She did?" I said, wondering if it was similar information to what she wrote to me.

"Yes," she said, handing me the letter to read.

Iclyn,

I know it has been so hard on you since I left, but your strength and determination is needed now more than ever if Nyrieve is to be successful in this next step of her journey.

Do you remember the place we always talked about visiting? The one we said we'd see before we get too old and just sit in rocking chairs together. I need you to help Nyrieve get there. I also need you to bring the amulet, the one I told you to keep hidden but close by. When you get to the place, there will be more information to come. I cannot risk putting it down on parchment just yet. The things we need to know will come to us when the time is right. Luckily I know when that will be. At least I hope so.

I know you miss me, Icy, but know I am with you. Part of me will always be with you. Our love is more than just the time together on Iryvalya. It is far beyond that. I feel we will be together again one day, though I do not know how exactly. But like most of my visions, I am not usually wrong. Perhaps we will live in another realm together or we'll come back as irybugs or me as a tree and you a sangrynaw with your nest secured in my branches. No matter how it happens, I look forward to being near you again.

I know you will argue against this, but please do not close yourself off to finding love again. Nothing will change or lessen the love we have for each other and the memories we made. I know there is another out there who can give you comfort and love, and I truly want that for you, but only you can allow yourself to be open to it.

I love you, my Icy beauty.

Love Always,

Lydorea

I looked up at Iclyn. She was staring into the fire burning in the hearth.

"That was a beautiful letter. Thank you for sharing it with me," I said softly. Iclyn just nodded. "Do you know the place she was talking about?"

"Yes, I remember the place."

"Where is it?" I asked.

"If Lydorea was worried about even writing it down, then I am not sure how

56

safe it is to speak it."

"I think I know where it is," I said, thinking back to the walk Lydorea and I shared in Xylonia when she told me about Clyr and where we'd need to travel to find it and break the curse.

"You do?"

"Lydorea told me of the place she had wanted to take me to find Clyr, and that she could break the curse with her blood for us to be able to use it."

"That is what is in the amulet she mentioned, her blood."

"It makes sense. Then I know where we need to go, but you don't need to say it aloud. It's best to keep this a closely guarded secret, then."

"Looks like we are off on another adventure from here," she said, sounding worried.

"I don't want you to feel like you have to go with me, Iclyn. That isn't fair to you."

"Lydorea said I needed to go, so that means I need to go."

"Are you sure?"

She smiled up at me. "If Lydorea asked me to set all of Iryvalya on fire because she believed it would have made it a better place, I would not have hesitated."

"Then why do you look and sound so nervous?"

"You have never been to this place, Nyrieve. You do not understand what it is capable of."

"You make it sound like the place itself is alive." I chuckled.

"Not far from… Just believe me, Lydorea and I had researched this place for many years in preparation for going one day. I had always thought it would be her and me together, but I guess it'll be just me."

"I'll be there with you, and I am sure we could get a few more people to come and help."

"I think that would be wise of us. This is not a place to go without backup of some sort."

"How dangerous could this place be?"

"Depending on who you are and your intentions, it can be deadly. But because

57

we are going with the best of intentions and the belief that what we are doing will help Iryvalya, I think we'll be okay."

Her wording made me wonder about how different the Blackened Forest was from anywhere else in Iryvalya. At least, I hoped we had the same location in mind.

"What should we do now?" I asked.

"It will take me a little time to prepare for this journey. I know most of what we will need, but there are some things I will need to talk to Sudryl about to see if it's possible to obtain them from here, or maybe on the way there. I also will need to secure travel to the location…" Her voice trailed off as if she was trying to remember many different things at once.

"What should I do?"

"If you can gather a few people to travel with us, that would be great. Make sure it is people we can trust and have the right intentions."

"What would the right intentions be exactly?"

She took a deep, cleansing breath and said, "If anyone is with us who is not there to help Iryvalya but only to serve their own desires, then they will not survive the—" She stopped herself from saying the location. "The place we are going. I honestly do not know how many people we will need. I'll have to figure that out. At least three I think, maybe more…"

"We will need three people besides us," I said.

"How do you know that?"

"I received a letter from Lydorea too, with some information as to what I should do and prepare for."

"Did she say anything else?"

"Yes, she did… but it was mostly information regarding a possible locator spell and different areas where we are going to search. She requested that I do not speak of some of those details until we are on our way from Aquyleya."

"Then I won't ask any more questions about it… You do the things she told you to do, and I will do everything I can as well."

"How long do you think we have before we need to leave?"

Iclyn sat in silence for a few moments, thinking, before she answered, "I do not like that it will take so long, but I think we should be able to leave here within a fortnight."

"Okay, what do we tell the others, those who are not going with us?"

"Nothing."

"What do you mean nothing?" I asked, confused.

"If they are not traveling with us, then they won't know we are leaving until we are already gone."

"But I can't just leave my family without telling them I am going, or Kylyan either."

"I understand, Ny, but I don't think that is a safe option. If the person is not going with us, then we should not tell them. There are reasons for this, and I promise I will explain them, but until then, please trust me."

"I trust you…" I said, even though I didn't understand.

附

"What are we going to tell him then?" I heard my father say gruffly.

"I don't know, but I don't think it is safe for us to tell him the truth," Kylyan said, sounding tired and stressed.

I stepped inside the house and closed the door quietly behind me.

"Nyrieve!" Dymma exclaimed as she rushed over to me and wrapped me in a hug. I would never get tired of getting hugs like this from my little sister. I squeezed her back and held her until I felt her arms start to loosen and then she took a step back. She had a huge smile on her face. "I am so glad to see you. I didn't know if you would be too busy to come by."

"It's good to see you as well, Dymma…" I paused, looking around the room. Both my father and Kylyan were sitting at the table as Clyo stood, bringing them something to drink. "What did I walk in on?"

"It is Prydos, Ny," started Kylyan.

"More like Prideful!" my father said under his breath.

"Okay," I said, walking over to the table and sitting down. "Fill me in."

"He is being unreasonable," my father started. "He expects everyone to hate you and take his side about Kaleyna."

"I don't think he wants everyone to hate her," Kylyan started.

"It doesn't sound very different from that, Kyl," Clyo said as she set a hot cup of tea in front of me with a smile.

"Thank you, Clyo," I said, holding the hot cup between my hands. I wouldn't have thought being under the sea would be chilly, but on a day like today where there didn't seem to be much sunlight reaching down to us, it was.

"You're welcome, my dear," she said as she patted my shoulder and sat down as well.

"Prydos wants everyone to hate me?"

"I don't think it is that simple, Ny," Kylyan started. "We all know he is upset and wanting Kaleyna back, and he just isn't thinking clearly about this."

My father let out a sigh of derision as he stated, "He flat out told us we should shun Ny and not speak to her again until Kaleyna is safe."

"He feels because they are both your daughters you should…" Kylyan trailed off.

"We should cut off one daughter to what, hope she can save the other alone?" Clyo asked.

I took a sip of the tea and felt the warmth go down the back of my throat and the heat spread though out my chest. "Would it do any good for me to talk to Prydos myself?" I asked.

Everyone stopped any movements and looked at me blankly.

"What?" I asked, not understanding why things were getting so out of hand with Prydos. I knew he missed Kal, I knew he would be upset with me, but this seemed like it was going far beyond that.

"Ny," Kylyan chimed in, "Prydos doesn't seem the same. Not since…"

"Since he learned about Kaylena?" I questioned.

"No, it was before that," he replied. "It seemed like sometime after we heard you left for the Fire Realm, he began getting more and more paranoid and angry with you."

I thought for a moment. "Who else was with you during that time? Right before or after learning about where we were going."

"Just people with the Nomydrac."

A thought crossed my mind. Could it be? Could she have done something to Prydos to make him get this upset with me? It would make sense, she was a traitor and could not be trusted.

"What are you thinking, my dear," Clyo asked gently.

"I think I know who caused him to change."

"Who?" Kylyan and my father said in unison.

"Miaarya."

"How could she do it, and why would she?"

"I am only now realizing how much about my time in the Fire Realm I haven't filled you in on. It is important, but it wasn't the most important thing to fill you in on right away. While we were heading to the Fire Realm, we encountered a boat with a passenger on it. It was Miaarya."

"Miaarya?" Kylyan asked. "I knew she had left when we headed here, to Aquyleya, but she said she was going to go back to Cliffside."

"She isn't who we all thought she was… I had trusted her completely growing up and for so long afterwards… I know it is hard to believe, but she has been working against me since before I arrived in Cliffside. She has lied to everyone about everything. She is working with the Pyrothian Elves, and from what I could tell, directly with Fyra."

"But she talked on and on about how much she loved you and wanted to help protect you… I mean, she even made Prydos wonder at first if she even cared about Kaleyna, because you were all she ever talked about," Kylyan stated.

"Trust me, I saw her making deals with the elves when I was an infant."

My sister's eyes widened. "How did you see that if you were just born?"

"I had some help with a Valya."

"A Valya?" my father asked. "I have heard of them but thought they were only a story to make sure kids behave."

"They are very real and have been quite helpful. They document everything. For all we know, there could be one here documenting this moment. They are not good or bad. They just are."

"But I don't understand," Kylyan said. "How would Miaarya cause this issue with Prydos?"

"I don't know exactly how, but I am sure she would know of a way to poison him against me with a potion or spell of some kind. And if we don't know how she did it, we can't know how to reverse it."

"Couldn't you ask a Valya to see what Miaarya did?" Dymma suggested.

"I don't know… I don't know when I will see Domi again, and she is the only one I know who would likely help me with this."

Kylyan took my hand gently. "Isn't there a way to send her a message somehow? I cannot bear to hear the things Prydos says about you. I don't agree with him, but if I say anything close to it, he starts getting angrier. I am honestly afraid to tell him about us again."

My father's eyebrow rose up. "Us? What do you mean us? Because since we arrived here, you have made it clear in no uncertain terms that you and Ny are no longer together, that she left you and broke your heart."

I felt pangs of sadness and embarrassment to be having this conversation with everyone here.

"I know, sir," Kylyan said, "and I was angry at Ny, uncontrollably angry and mad and I couldn't fully understand why. It was like I knew for a while she was leaving and doing what she felt she had to, and I was mad about that, but I wasn't angry. And then over time it turned more into anger and at times even felt like hate. When I would write a letter to her, I would try to control my thoughts and not let it skew the overall goal of doing what is best for Iryvalya. But then it would just eat at me and I would get more and more angry. I think Prydos and I just fed off each other and blamed Nyrieve for everything bad that had happened to us and taken away Prydos's love and breaking my heart…"

"What changed?" I asked, feeling saddened to know for so long both Kylyan and Prydos hated me.

"I don't know exactly what it was… The day you arrived here in Aquyleya, it seemed to shift. When I saw you, I was still mad at first, but then I remember seeing

Prydos come at you and it was like something hit me, and even though I was mad, I didn't want you hurt. I had to stop him. He yelled at me all that evening about why I was protecting you, and I couldn't fully come up with an answer. But after that meeting with the Nomydrac, I listened to you and watched your every move. I began to remember why you left in the first place. It wasn't to hurt me or get Kaleyna hurt. It was to do what you thought was right. In that moment, it was like someone removed this curtain that had been around my head, and I could see things clearly again. I wasn't mad at you anymore. I was just so happy to see you and know you were safe."

Clyo took a deep breath. "There is nothing we can do to fix this problem with Prydos... The only thing that will stop this is when he sees Kaleyna."

"What do you mean, Momma?" Dymma asked.

"Someone, and from what you said I am imagining it was this Miaarya person, placed a curse on both Kylyan and Prydos. The only way for the curse to be broken is for the object of their love to be seen or proven somehow."

"You're saying," I started, "until we are able to save Kaleyna and bring her home, Prydos will just keep getting more and more angry at me?"

"Not just at you," Clyo replied. "He is getting more and more angry with anyone who likes you or supports you. He could very well end up being the undoing of the Nomydrac. As much as I know my daughter cares for Prydos, he is not going to do any good by being around you or anyone who doesn't hate you as much as he does."

"Then what can we do?" I inquired.

"The only two things I could do," Clyo said, "are either make a sleeping potion to put him to sleep until we wake him, or a forgetting potion. He would forget most everyone and everything for a while, but he wouldn't be a threat until his memories start to come back."

"Kylyan, he is your friend," I said. "What do you think we should do?"

"I don't know... He is no good to us if he will be working against us... but he is strong and smart, and we can use him to help us... I just don't know, Ny. In the end, I think you should make the decision."

"Is it possible to make both potions? We can try the forgetting one first, and if it works, great, but if it doesn't, we can use the sleep one as a backup... maybe even try to make a couple of the forgetting one, in case it begins to wear off..."

"I will get started on it right away," Clyo said. "Dymma, can you help me find the ingredients we'll need?"

"I'm on it," she responded as she started to rush into the back room.

"I hope this works," I said.

"It has to, Ny," Kylyan said, squeezing my hand. "I cannot lose you again."

༺9༻

NYRIEVE

"How are you feeling, kiddo?" Arnayx asked me as we watched the bioluminescent creatures above swim around.

"Kiddo?" I responded with a smile.

"It is what I called Dymma often when talking about her or to her, and you are my daughter as well, so it seemed to fit," he said, looking a little nervous about my response.

"I like it," I said truthfully.

"That's good… How are you feeling about everything else going on?"

"It depends on the minute you ask me… Sometimes I am doing okay and thinking about the next steps, keeping it logical. Other times I feel like a complete mess and can't stop crying with worry about Kal, Baysil and Rowzey. And between both of those, there is a huge variety of feels all across the spectrum of possible feelings."

My father put his arm around me and squeezed. I didn't think I would ever get over how good it felt to have him care about me and give me hugs and even just smile at me. I had had many hugs, but nothing compared to hugs from people who actually cared about how I was and wanted me to know they cared.

"Now I am going to ask the uncomfortable 'Dad Questions,' okay?"

My left eyebrow rose in curiosity at what might be the next thing he'd ask. "Okay, what is that?"

He took a deep breath and started. "I know you and Kylan have… rekindled your relationship—"

"To a degree," I corrected. "Until Clyo can finish the potion, we aren't spending much time together outside of the public gatherings, where it would look strange if he wasn't there."

"I know, I just want to make sure you are making the right decision with him."

"Do you not like him?"

"He is… fine."

"Fine?"

"When we first met him down here, he wasn't mean-spirited about you, but as time progressed, he was."

"I believe that was because of Miaarya."

"I know, I know," he continued, "and over the past few days when he and I have been around each other, we've talked and I do believe he genuinely cares about you and would do anything he could for you."

"I think so too," I said with a smile.

"But…"

"But?"

"But you are my daughter, and I don't know if anyone is good enough for you."

I laughed. "Are you being serious?"

"Yes and no," he said with a smile. "I just want to make sure you are happy and have someone by your side who not only will protect you but will listen to you and wants the same things as you."

"I think I understand what you're getting at."

"I know the interactions you have had with your mother, Osidya, haven't been the best, but before you were born, she really convinced me she loved me and you. I believed we would somehow be a family for a long time, even after Rowzey hid you away. For many years I tried to meet with Osidya, and during those times, I thought we wanted the same things, but as time went on, she changed what she wanted and how she viewed me. I don't want that for you."

"I don't think it could be like that with Kyl," I said. "We both seem to know who the other is and what we want."

"Beyond what you want for Iryvalya?"

"What do you mean?"

"What happens after you save Iryvalya and the world is at peace? Where do you want to live? Do you want a family of your own? What does he want?"

I sat there thinking about it. I didn't know if we really ever talked about the

66

future beyond trying to save Iryvalya. There had been too much other stuff going on to really think about it, even just what I wanted. What did I want?

"I don't know... any of it."

"It is hard when you are young in general, but you are the Bringer of Peace, so I imagine it is much harder yet to think about what happens after everything is done..."

"I worry that if I think too far ahead, I might lose sight of what I need to do next."

"I understand that," he said, "but maybe... maybe you should sometimes allow yourself to imagine the future you want. Because hopefully one day, you'll get to work towards that."

"I do know something I want in my future," I said.

"What is that?"

"You," I said, looking at his softened face in this light. "I want you and Clyo and Dymma all in my life."

He had a big wide toothy grin on his face and pulled me to him into a big hug. "I am happy to hear that, but you do not have a choice anyway. I missed way too many years of your life and I don't want to miss another."

"Thanks, Dad," I said.

"I love hearing you call me that."

"It is great and strange at the same time."

"Why strange?"

"I never called anyone names like Dad or Mom. I always wanted to but never did."

"You don't have to worry about that ever again. You will always have me and Clyo as parents."

"Couldn't ask for better ones!"

"Am I interrupting?" Iclyn said softly.

"No, Iclyn," I said. "Would you like to join us watching the bioluminescence?"

"I would, but I have a couple things I needed to talk to you about."

My father side-squeezed me and stood up. "I can give you some time to talk. I need to go check in on Clyo and Dymma anyway. See if they need me to help with anything."

"Thanks, Dad," I said, smiling at him.

As he walked out of the room, Iclyn silently walked over to me and sat next to me and looked up. We sat in silence for a few minutes before she said, "It really is beautiful, isn't it?"

I nodded. "Yes, it is. I have never seen anything quite like it."

"I don't think we could anywhere else in Iryvalya."

"What did you need to talk to me about?"

"Have you made your choices for when we leave?"

"I haven't yet."

"Do you need help deciding?"

"I could use some suggestions on who you think should go."

"I think it would be good to have Koyvean come with us, for one."

"Koyvean?" I asked. "I thought she would have gone back to the Spirit Realm after learning about me falling into the volcano."

"She did," Iclyn said, "but apparently she talked to a friend of yours, Domi, and made her way back here just a couple of hours ago."

"She's here now?" I said excitedly and also worried how upset she might be with me for everything that happened in the Fire Realm.

"Yes, she is currently resting in my house here."

"Well… as soon as she is awake and would like to talk to me, let me know and I'll come right over."

"Thank you, Ny," she said. "Do you think this Domi person might be good to ask as well?"

"Uhm," I hesitated, "Domi isn't a Nomydrac technically… She is a—"

"A Valya, correct?"

"Yes," I said, surprised. "How did you know?"

"I interrogated Koyvean for quite some time until I felt she was being completely honest with me, and one of the things I made her explain was who Domi was."

68

"Interrogated? 'Made her' tell you? Do you not trust her anymore?" I asked, concerned.

"I do... now..."

"Is she okay? Is that why she needed to rest?"

"Yes, most likely. I didn't torture her or anything, just used a truth potion..."

I stared at her, knowing there was more she wasn't saying.

"I used the truth potion after I stuck her with an—"

"Enchanted stick?"

She looked at me, surprised. "How did you know?"

"Lydorea gave one to me as well in the pack. I think it is still in there... I didn't see it, but I didn't search very deeply in the pack either. Still hard to do."

"You will find what you need in the pack when you are ready and have a need for something in it."

"Do you think it might have some of the herbs Clyo needs?"

"It might. Lydorea was always one to pack much more than needed... and in the pack she gave you, it might not look like it, but it can hold so much more than you could ever expect."

"I think the pack is enchanted to hold so many things and still look normal in size and weight."

"That sounds right to me. She is... was, always prepared and wanted everyone to have anything they might need."

"If you don't mind, I am going to go check the pack and see if maybe I could help Clyo."

"I don't mind, but if you could please decide who is going to go with us, we need to start preparing to leave as soon as we can."

"I will, Iclyn, I promise," I said as I stood up and rushed out to the house I was staying in.

As I opened the door, I became quickly aware someone else was in here with me. Then a hand quickly covered my mouth and another wrapped around my shoulders to hold me still.

"Don't say anything," the person said in such a hushed voice I couldn't place them.

I stood there quietly, not knowing what was going to happen next, but I knew as I slowly slid my hand over Klaw and grasped it in my hand that I wouldn't go down without a fight. I have too many people that need me. This is not where I will end.

"Ny," they continued, "leave Klaw alone. I am not going to hurt you."

They slowly released me and allowed me to turn around with Klaw still in my grasp.

"Jyngy?" I whispered, surprised.

"Shhh…" she said and walked around me over to the small kitchen area and looked around. She then picked up the mug I cleaned earlier on the counter and stared inside it. After a few moments, she straightened up and looked over at me. "Come here and see this," she said in her normal voice.

I quickly walked over to her and looked inside the mug. I couldn't see anything. "I don't understand, I don't see anything in the cup."

"I think someone might have put something into your mug… or mugs, I don't know for sure," she said.

"How can we check?" I asked.

"It is not *my* mug, but since it is yours… you can cast a spell to reveal if there's something hidden…" she said as she walked over to a small bag she had on the counter. She rummaged through it until she found a small book with many different written spells and enchantments from what I could see. "Here, this one," she said, pointing to the page.

I read the page over, and it looked like a spell Lydorea would have cast. "Where did you get this, Jyngy?"

She smiled at me. "I think you already knew this was from Lydorea."

"How did you get it?" I asked, starting to wonder if maybe Jyngy wasn't really on my side anymore.

"She gave it to me, back when we were in Mylterias Cove. She gave me a small bag with a bunch of different items. She told me I would find uses for these as they became needed. I genuinely didn't believe it was more than an empty bag, but over time, items would appear in it, and while I couldn't always understand why, they mostly seemed helpful at the time."

I took a deep breath and decided that if Jyngy had wanted to harm me, she could have hurt me right away. I needed to trust in Lydorea that she wouldn't have provided these things to someone she thought might harm me. I read the spell over again and repeated the strange words out loud. I saw a faint glow come from inside the mug. In the bottom it looked like small dusting of powder that I had never seen in any of the cups before.

"What is that?" I asked.

"It is poison, I believe."

"What?"

"It comes from a shellfish creature. After it is dried out, it gets ground up into a powder and can kill in high doses. This isn't quite high enough to kill someone but would definitely make them sick for a while."

"How did you know it was here?"

"I have been watching your house here for a few days, I wanted to make sure it would be safe for me to come see you. Today I saw someone leaving your house, but I didn't see them enter. I wasn't sure then if there was someone else in here, so I snuck in to check. I had just started my search and noticed something off about scent in the room and that is when you came inside."

"But how did you know it was poisoned?"

"Once you have been poisoned by this, you would always recognize the smell coming from it, even from far away."

"I don't smell anything."

"Count yourself lucky. It smells of rotted fish to me."

"Do you know who it was who left?"

"No, they had a cloak on covering their face from me. I could tell they were a little taller than you and had a more muscular build."

"Hmm," I said, thinking about who it might be.

"Do you have any idea who it could have been, Nyrieve?"

"I do, actually," I said, frustrated.

71

"Whoever it is, I can get rid of them."

"No, Jyngy, you can't do that. He is under some sort of spell, and we're trying to help him."

"Who is it?"

"I think it is Prydos."

"Prydos?" she asked, shocked. "He's a Drayk. How could he do that?"

"We believe he was cursed or has a spell put on him. Until we can remove it, we are going to try to make him sleep or something."

"I can help with that."

"Thank you, Jyngy," I said, "but can you first tell me what you are doing here?"

"I followed you when you left the Spirit Realm," she said softly.

"Why would you follow me and not tell me?"

"I had to be sure."

"Be sure of what?"

"That the Pyrothian Elves didn't do something to you and you were working for them."

"Why would you think that?"

"You escaped. They never let anyone escape, at least that I have ever heard of, so I was concerned."

"I didn't escape exactly."

"I know… now."

"Wait, what do you mean they don't let anyone escape?"

"From what I know of the history of the Pyrothians, there hasn't been anyone that survived being held captive by them."

"That means Rowzey, Kaleyna and Baysil have no chance to be free from them?"

"Not exactly."

"What do you mean, Jyngy?" I asked, getting more worried.

"I don't think anyone has tried to rescue someone who was being held there. No one would take the risk to become captured themselves."

"Great, that makes me feel better," I said sarcastically.

"You are not like anyone else, Ny. You are the Bringer of Peace for Iryvalya. If anyone can rescue them, it is you."

"Do you want to come with me to get some supplies to my family and let them know about what Prydos seems to have done?"

"No, I will stay here and look around, if you don't mind. See if there is anything else askew."

"That is fine... I am really overwhelmed with everything, but I need to finish what I was doing."

"I understand. It will be okay," she said.

I ran over to my room and grabbed my pack and walked past Jyngy. "I shouldn't be long," I said as I walked out the door.

I ran all the way over to my parents' house and walked inside without knocking.

"Nyrieve?" my father asked from the couch as I closed the door behind me. "What's happened?"

"I am not sure," I said. "Either Prydos tried to poison me or Jyngy is lying to me and trying to make me think she is trying to help me and trying to poison me or it isn't Jyngy at all."

"I have never met this Jyngy person," my father said with a scowl.

"I have," Kylyan said as he walked into the front room from somewhere in back.

"Kyl," I said, feeling some relief in him being there. He walked over to me and gave me a hug.

"Why do you think someone was trying to poison you?"

I explained to them what had occurred when I went back to my house, and same as me, they didn't know what or who to believe.

"Why didn't Jyngy come here with you?" Kylyan asked.

"She said she wanted to check the house for anything else out of place. I knew I needed to come here and get my pack out of that house, just in case."

"How about you stay here with your father? Clyo and Dymma are collecting some items from the storage rooms and should be back soon," he said. "I will get Iclyn and Koyvean, and we will check in with Jyngy to see what we can figure out."

73

"Thank you, Kyl," I said, giving him a tight hug. I knew he needed to go, but I just wanted to hold on to him longer.

"It's okay, Ny," my father said. "Kylyan can take good care of himself. He will be fine."

"Thank you, sir," Kylyan said as he let go of me and stepped back. He gave me a chaste kiss on the cheek and bolted out the door.

I looked at my father and he gave me a half smile as he walked over to hug me. "Since you arrived, things seem so much more..."

"Chaotic?" I asked.

"Yes."

"Calm and serene doesn't seem to follow me as much as I would like it to," I said, holding him close.

"Perhaps one day it will, my dear," he said, placing a light kiss on top of my head.

"I hope so," I said back to him. "But I don't know if I would even know how to relax and not have to worry about everyone everywhere all the time."

The door to the house opened, with Clyo and Dymma laughing as they stepped inside. Once they looked at me, they quieted and asked what was going on. My father filled them in the best he could and I filled in any of the gaps I could.

"Do you really think it was Prydos that tried to poison you?" Dymma asked with a scowl on her face.

"I don't know. I am not sure how far the spell on him could push him," I said wearily.

"I can tell you one thing," Clyo said. "Whoever it was, they might have cleared out much of the storage rooms, because when we went in there, it was practically empty of anything that could have been useful."

"Does anyone keep records of who goes in and out of them?" I asked.

"I don't know. No one seemed to know we went in there today, so I am guessing it works on the honor system," Clyo replied.

"But, Mom," Dymma said, "there was someone there watching us."

"What?" Clyo asked. "Who and where? I didn't see anyone."

"One of the Valya where there in the distance."

"How do you know that, Dymma?" I asked.

"I have always been able to sense when they are around, and sometimes I can almost see them, but it is usually seeing something out of the corner of my eye. If I try to look closely or focus on it, they disappear."

"Maybe I could send word with Sudryl to let Domi know we need her help," I said, thinking out loud.

"Sending a message to Domi will prove quite pointless," Domi said, appearing clearly as she stepped away from the back wall.

"Domi?" I asked. "What are you doing here?"

"I have learned some things that I felt were too important to wait to tell you," she said. "If the Valya found out I left like this, they would be most displeased, but I believe you have the right to know. Though it seems like you might have put a lot of it together by yourself already."

ଓ10ଞ

STORYTELLER

As I reached the bottom step in my home, I looked around at all the different trinkets and mementos strategically placed around the living room. Along the many bookshelves were journals, books, viewing crystals, carved wood and stone items. I ran my hand along the old worn journals. I took out a dark blue leather-bound journal. I knew every inch of this book and all the stories it contained by heart. I slowly opened the pages, looking for the ones I had read more times than anything.

Being alone in the house tonight felt quieter than it normally did, especially as of late. Recently the house had been quite busy with people wandering around or someone cooking in the kitchen. Everyone seemed to be asleep by the time we got home. After making sure Nykirys and Fyleeza were in their beds all tucked in, I decided I couldn't sleep just yet. My mind raced with the stories of Nyrieve, the Nomydrac and even the dragons. A smile crossed my face, wishing I could have seen it all as it happened.

"What are you doing up so late?"

I spun around to see my brother walking in through the kitchen door.

"What are you doing up?" I asked back.

"I was hungry, so I found something to eat. You want some?" he said with a smile.

I looked at his plate and saw different cheeses and bread.

"Is that all you're going to eat?"

"It is now. I had some of the leftover stew from dinner while I was cutting up the cheese."

I laughed at him. "It really is good to have you home for a while, brother. I have missed you."

"I have missed you too, my favorite little sister," he said as he walked up to me and gave me a one-armed hug.

"Your only sister," I reminded him playfully.

"Oh yes, that's right, it was just the two of us," he said with a wink. "You know my memory isn't what it used to be."

"Yes, we are getting older but still have many more years ahead."

"I hope so," he said, "but you never know... the Klayns could always, you know..."

"Yes, I know," I said with a sigh. "As we were constantly reminded growing up, *anything and everything can change in the blink of an eye*."

He smiled at me. "You sound just like her, you know?"

"Who?"

"Mother."

I smiled, "I take that as a compliment."

"As it should be."

"Thank you."

"So where have you been all this time? You are covered in dust and rubble... You were out at the manor, weren't you?"

"You know me well."

"Even as a child you always liked to sneak off to the manor, even when Mother would get upset with you for it."

"I love seeing it and always hope to find something new," I said as I looked at the journal in my hands.

"You have collected more historical items about Cliffside and Rowzey and the Bringer of Peace than anyone else," he said with a soft smile. "I think they would all be proud to know someone cares so much about the past to keep it alive for new generations."

"I hope so... but I have to admit, part of my hoarding of all these items is because when I read the journals or see the trinkets, it makes me feel like I was there with them."

"I know."

"I just wish I could have been there and helped the Nomydrac and..."

"And what? Do you think you would have been able to do better?"

"I can't say I would have made things better in any way. I just wish I could have helped and been a part of it."

"I know, me too."

"Really? You've never said that before."

"Not out loud to you, at least. I remember telling Father once that I thought if I had been around during the rise of the Bringer of Peace, maybe I could have been a protector and maybe kept one more person alive."

"What did Father say?"

"He was logical for the most part, explained how it couldn't have been possible when I wasn't even born yet. Then he told me, 'I wish fewer people had died, but it is how it had to be, and those who fought alongside Nyrieve knew the risks they were taking and chose to take them anyway.'"

"That sounds like Dad."

"You still didn't answer my question."

"What was that?"

"What are you still doing up so late?"

"With the anniversary of the Battle of Ash and Air being close, my mind is always racing with thoughts of the past and some of the future."

"Same, it makes me remember the celebrations we had in the past for it growing up."

"Do you remember the years when Mother and Father tried to ignore it and trick us so we wouldn't talk about it?"

"I do, I always imagined it was because while many celebrated the anniversary of the Battle of Ash and Air, they remembered the losses more than the wins."

"Nothing is ever just an all-around win, is it?"

"Nope," he said, "but this cheese that was brought in for the festival is amazing."

I laughed as I reached over and took a piece, shoving it in my mouth. Instantly I could taste the salty sharp flavor and closed my eyes and smiled. "You know what this reminds me of?"

"I do, sis," he said, handing me his plate. "I'm going to go upstairs and get some sleep."

"You don't want the rest of this?"

"Nah, I filled up on the stew. Besides, I knew you would need a snack while you reread Rowzey's journal for the what, millionth time?"

"Thank you, you're the best brother I could have hoped for."

"You're welcome, and you are the best sister I could have hoped for… except those moments as children when you would follow me around everywhere and wouldn't give me back my stuff."

I giggled and gave him a big hug. "I'm sorry I was such a pain."

"Was?" he asked as he stepped back and winked at me.

"Am."

"There you go," he said as he started up the stairs. "Don't stay up all night reading. Lots to do tomorrow."

"And don't forget," I said, and we both replied in unison with a chuckle, "be the spark!"

"Good night, sis."

"Good night!"

I took the plate of cheese and the journal over to the couch to get comfortable. The hearth was burnt down to just a few pieces of wood and embers glowing bright red. I figured I would read just until the fire went out, then get some much-needed rest.

I quickly found the page I wanted and then took a few minutes to eat the bread and cheese first. I didn't want to get any crumbs or oils on the journal. These had been preserved for so long, I would hate to cause them any damage or marks just because I was lazy. After I finished my food, I wiped my fingers off on my skirts and started to read the pages in the accent I knew Rowzey spoke in.

I's need to start by saying what a beautiful little elf Nyrieve is. She has been very calm and quiet so far on this journey we's are taking to Cliffside. I's have some potions I's could use to help her stay asleep and quiet if we's find that we are being followed. I's originally planned to fly there quickly, but if I's am found out by someone in the Stone Realm or Cliffside itself, they might wonder more about who this little "fairy" is.

79

We's have taken a boat from Troxeon to Lynawn. The ride itself wasn't very eventful. Ny slept most of the time, except one night, she just kept her eyes open and wouldn't go to sleep. I's took her up on the top of the deck and she looked up at the moons and stars in amazement. I's decided to make sure she was able to look up at the skies at night anytime I's could.

When we's arrived in Lynawn, I's came across a pair of satyr brothers, Jynkins and Leyhroi. They were helpful with getting us to shelter and yet quite annoying. I's couldn't get them to stop asking questions about Ny. Eventually I's explained to them if they couldn't just help me, then I's would be forced to turn into a dragon and eat them. They must have found it to be a good joke or knew who I's really was, because after that they seemed to just do what I's asked. I's will need to talk to Knarfy about them and have him make sure they protect our secret.

The last night on one of the islands in Lynawn, Ny was again not wanting to fall asleep, but just lay quietly in my arms as I's rocked her. I's took her outside into the small forest and sat on a long-ago-fallen tree trunk that was covered in soft moss and ivy. We's sat for what felt like only a few moments when the most amazing thing happened.

Suddenly we's were surrounded by irybugs. There must have been hundreds to possibly thousands of them. They mostly just danced around us, but at one point some began to land on little Nyrieve. She just lay there watching them dance around her, and as she watched the one walk up her chest and over her cheek, she just smiled and giggled. I's imagine part of the giggle was because of the feet tickling her face, but it was one of the sweetest and most innocent laughs I's have ever heard.

How in Iryvalya am I's supposed to tell this sweet child one day that she is going to have to risk her life to save all these people and creatures that might not do right by her? I's am not sure if I's am doing the right thing. I's won't admit that to anyone else, but I's am worried. This sweet little girl deserves so much more than what is likely in store for her.

One thing I's can at least promise, I's will be by her side for as long as I's am alive and able to. I's will never turn my back on her or abandon her, even if she hates me for helping hide her away. I's will still do the right thing by her however I's can.

And as for yous, the person who might be reading this one day. I's hope I's kept to my promises to help Nyrieve become the Bringer of Peace we's all hope her to be. And also, shame on yous for reading a journal that wasn't meant for yous eyes."

The last part always made me laugh. I always thought that it was funny how Rowzey knew that this would be read. I wonder though if she had any idea when writing it, how much insight it provided for so many of us about the beginnings of the Bringer of Peace? How it made so many feel much closer to her and maybe even understand more of her reasoning behind some of her actions and inactions. I'd like to think so.

I stood up and gently placed the book back in its spot on the bookshelf and let my gaze move across the line of books to the viewing crystal. I gently picked it up, looking at the image frozen inside. It was an image I had viewed a million times or more. Standing together was a tall elf with cobalt-and-orange hair and a medium-height elf with different shades of green hair intricately styled on top of her head. They were arm in arm with big smiles on their faces. Both dressed in fancy clothing and looking a little stiff.

I knew the image well. It was described to me many times in my life. It is amazing it somehow survived being moved around Iryvalya for years and all the destruction and rebuilding of different villages. I remember the day it was given to my mother. She looked at it and cried. I couldn't understand for the life of me what about this image made her cry so many tears. I would have thought she'd be more happy than sad about this being located and brought back to be saved and on display with so many other mementos. But I was a child then and didn't understand as much as I like to think I do now.

I placed the viewing crystal back carefully on the shelf, just as my mother showed me to do many times. I took the stairs slowly and quietly up to my room. As I walked down the hallway, I noticed no light seeping out from under anyone else's rooms. It was calm and peaceful knowing I was the only one awake right now. It felt like time stolen away that was mine and mine alone to enjoy.

After getting changed into my sleeping gown and climbing into my soft cozy bed, I took out my portable pen and jotted some things down in my journal to remember.

- *Tell the kids about Ny's trip to the Spirit Realm next.*

- *Remember to thank Aurilya's granddaughter for the cheeses she brought.*
- *Check with the baker to see if everything will be ready for the celebration.*
- *And if you are reading this and you're not me, shame on you!*

I chuckled out loud as I wrote the last part. After reading it in Rowzey's journals, I liked to end my entries with something similar. It made me feel a connection to her.

I placed the journal on my night table and blew out the candle. I slid deeper into my blankets and let sleep take me over.

ᏚᎢᎢ 11 ᏗᏗ

NYRIEVE

"How do we know we can trust her?" my father said sharply.

"Dad," I said, "Domi was there and helped me when I ended up in the Spirit Realm. She didn't have to help me in the ways she has, but she chose to."

"All I know of the Valya is that they don't help or pick sides, they just watch, like a fly on the wall."

"He is not wrong," Domi said.

"You are not helping, Domi," I said as I looked at her with frustration.

"I don't lie, Nyrieve," she continued. "For centuries, the Valya have done… well, nothing to help the people of Iryvalya. Well, that is not exactly true. There have been a few who have, but typically when that happens, they are banished from the Valya and the Leaf Day Tree."

"Typically?" I asked.

"Yes, but there have been some whispers among many of us who are tired of watching Iryvalya come to ruin over and over again."

"Are you referring to the Koneyotta?"

"The what?" my father and Clyo asked in unison.

"The Koneyotta were what came before the elves and fairies," I answered.

"You are correct, Ny," Domi said simply. "We are tired of seeing this world destroyed by deceit and power-hungry creatures."

Dymma spoke up. "Why is it I can see you when others can't?"

Domi smiled kindly at her. "You have a special gift of sight. Do you usually know when someone is lying or telling the truth?"

"Usually," she said.

"Yes, you definitely seem to have the ability to see through the haze that surrounds most people. Many don't even realize they are lying or hiding the truth. It is just protection they put up. But you, Dymma, you have the ability to cut through that haze and see things for what they really are. Which would explain why you can see us, but because we are pretty good at hiding most of the time, we only appear in the fringe of your vision."

My father and Clyo hugged their daughter close to them. "How did I not know any of this?" Clyo asked.

"I didn't want to worry you or Dad," Dymma responded.

"Worry us?" our father asked.

"You have always had so much to worry about with the Klayns and your other daughters, I didn't want to give you more to worry about."

My father just shook his head and said, "I have failed all my girls."

"No," Dymma and I said at the same time.

"Ny and I have not been failed, and I believe if Kal was here, she would agree," Dymma said, hugging them both back.

"I don't mean to interrupt," Domi said, looking at me, "however, there are some important things we need to discuss, Nyrieve."

"I'm sorry we got off track," I said to her. "Please fill me in on… everything, I guess."

"One of the things I was coming to inform you about, you are already aware of, the curse that was put on Kylyan and is currently on Prydos," she said in a monotone voice. "The other thing I came to tell you is that I believe I have figured out where Alabynes might have gone after leaving the Spirit Realm."

"Where?" I asked.

"The next place you have already planned to travel to," she said.

"What?" my father asked, giving me a confused and disappointed look.

"Oh, you haven't told them," Domi said with a small frown. "I am sorry, I didn't mean to overstep."

"It's okay, Domi. Dad, you all need to understand I have to leave to get something to help us and Iryvalya. It might be the key to getting the people of the Klayns to listen."

"When are you leaving and where to and for how long?" Clyo asked, looking equally nervous.

"I… I can't say yet," I said. "I trust you all, but I don't know if anyone is spying or could hear us or… I don't know, I just don't want you all to get hurt for knowing where I am heading."

"Then who is going with you?" Clyo asked.

"Only a small group of people. We can't be sure who is safe. Since Kylyan and Prydos were cursed, we can't know for sure who else might be."

The room was silent for a long time. Dymma finally spoke up softly but confidently. "Ny is right."

"Right about what, dear?" Clyo asked.

"She can't tell us or anyone else that isn't going. There is too much uncertainty here with those of us hiding out in Aquyleya."

"You do not think we can be trusted either?" my father asked, looking heartbroken.

"No, that isn't what I am saying, Dad," she continued. "I think it is more a way to keep you safe. If none of us know where she went, we can't be forced to give up her location and it's less likely that someone will try to press us for answers we cannot give. Right, Ny?"

"Yes," I said, "I cannot leave here knowing you are all at even more risk of being harmed than you already are just by being my family."

My father stood up and walked over to me and hugged me. "I don't like this, Nyrieve. It has been too many years without you in my life and now… now I have to just let you leave without protecting you. I am failing you as a father."

My eyes stung with the threat of tears. "Dad, you are not failing… Right now, you can't keep me safe or keep me from doing what I need to do for Iryvalya."

"That is how I am failing."

"No, because that is not what I need you to do. What I need you to do is keep our family safe. Keep Kylyan safe for me. If I know you are doing that, then it is one less thing I need to worry about when I leave here."

"I promise you I will, Ny," he said, squeezing me tightly.

CRORO

"I am sorry, Nyrieve," Domi said after closing the door to my house.

"Sorry?"

"I didn't mean to say something to upset your family. I should have waited until it was just us."

"It's okay, I would have likely told them anyway at some point, because I trust them."

"I understand that, but… I am still a bit new at interacting with people and not just watching what they do."

"I can imagine it is a difficult thing to navigate. I have been talking to people my whole life, and half the time I feel like I am doing it wrong."

"That is interesting, Nyrieve. I will need to think on that more."

I sat on the couch and gestured for Domi to sit as well.

"I am glad I had the missing herbs Clyo needed for her potion to work. Lydorea definitely was very prepared for me… Do you know who Lydorea is? I don't want to assume you 'watched' her," I asked.

"Yes, I know who Lydorea was. I very much enjoyed watching and recording her. I wasn't the only one who did, but when I had the chance, I liked watching her interactions with people and the way she talked to herself when no one else was around. Sometimes I think she was speaking to me and telling me things I needed to know and record, but I never talked to her myself."

"That is amazing," I said, imagining Lydorea at the manor in Cliffside moving about with things to do and helping everyone she could. "I appreciated Lydorea when I lived in Cliffside, but I feel like I didn't appreciate her or her talents enough."

"Usually people do not appreciate one another until it is too late," Domi said thoughtfully. "At least in my experience."

"I can see that," I said, thinking if maybe I should be making better use of the time I had with people instead of thinking one day things would go back to normal and I could spend more time with them. "Things will never be normal for me, will they, Domi?"

"It depends on what you regard as normal."

"Normal… When I say or think normal, I think of Cliffside and days of just

86

walking around the village or helping Rowzey make food for everyone. I even think of the simplicity of going to bed at night with no thoughts or concerns about tomorrow."

"That does sound like a simpler life. I don't know if you will ever have normal as you once knew it to be, but I imagine after a while a new normal begins to play out."

"I just wish I knew what was to come…"

"I cannot tell you about your future. Even if I could, I wouldn't, because futures can always change."

"What do you mean?"

"Most of the Valya that can see future events, they don't know it exactly. It is a glimpse of what might happen. Often, it's similar to how the Valya saw it, but it isn't always exact."

"Why do you think that is?"

"People change each day, just a little. Every piece of new information plays into who you are. Today you heard your father say that he thought he failed you. This information can play into how you do something next. You might want to take fewer risks so he doesn't have to worry so much, or you might choose to disregard it and trust in your own instincts. These might not seem large, but each thing shifts the way we continue down our paths."

"I can kind of understand that."

"The biggest thing I have seen is those who are unwilling to take in new information and realize they were wrong about something. Being wrong about something doesn't make them unintelligent, but choosing to not learn and make better choices… Well, it is up to you to decide what type of people they are, but from my experience, those are the same people who keep making the same poor choices over and over again. With them, the future is clearer, because they don't change, so their path keeps pretty clear. Those who are open to new ideas or viewpoints, their paths change more frequently. It doesn't mean the path is drastically different then their original, but it usually means their path and future is more fulfilling and intricate, but not very straight."

87

"What kind of path do you think I have?"

Domi smiled softly. "You have the spiral path, Nyrieve. Always learning and growing."

I laughed lightly. "So I never know where I am going?"

"Not at all," Domi replied. "While your path isn't exact, it is always moving forward."

"I'll take that as a good thing," I said, hoping it was.

"Would it be okay with you if I take one of the spots on your journey?"

"I am more than okay with it. I just don't want you to get hurt or in trouble."

"It is too late for that concern."

"What do you mean?"

"When I found out where Alabynes went, I didn't get the information in the way Valya are supposed to."

"What way is that?"

"With permission. I researched everything I could find inside the Leaf Tree and couldn't find anything of use." She paused looking at me. "When Jagula was gone, I went into her quarters and searched through her things. I felt bad to do it, but I needed to know about Alabynes."

"Go on," I said, getting more curious.

"In there I found many records that were hidden away. Some were about the Koneyotta, others about Valya who went against their nature and integrated themselves with the people of Iryvalya, and Alabynes was one of them."

"Why would he do that?"

"That is what I asked Jagula when she returned to her quarters," Domi said. "She was at first not upset with my trespass of her quarters, until she saw the records about Alabynes in my hands."

"Did she explain it to you?"

"At first, she commended me on my thorough research into helping you, but when I showed her that not only was it believed Alabynes was still alive, but how I could find him, she said that it was okay to help out elves, dragons and fairies from time to time. This was something that I had always been told was forbidden for

Valya to do. When I asked why, she would give me no answer, but took the scrolls and kicked me out of her quarters and said I needed to get back to watching and not helping you."

"She must have changed her mind if you are here now, right?"

"She did not. The following night, I went back into her quarters and took the scrolls, all of them, and left the Spirit Realm to find you."

"But can't she 'see' that you are here with me?"

"I also took an enchanted ring from her room, one that blocks me to all Valya."

"Why would you take the scrolls and risk everything like that?"

"I love being a Valya, but us standing by while all these negative things are happening, just because 'we are the watchers of Iryvalya,' doesn't make sense to me anymore. No one minded me teaching you how to portal and how that saved your life, but I do not know if there is more insight that Alabynes might provide to me that could cause issue among the Valya."

"Then I guess we'll need to go find him and ask him directly."

"That is in part why I wanted to go with you to the Blackened Forest. I can help you with finding Clyr, and then we can find Alabynes and ask him the questions you have as well as the questions I have."

"Then we have all but one person ready to go with us," I said.

"Who are the others?"

"You, me, Iclyn, and Koyvean, and I need to ask someone else."

"Do you know who you are going to ask?"

"I do, actually. It is someone who I feel we can trust but that no one in either Klayn really knows about. That might give us an advantage if we come across anyone who is against me and the Nomydrac."

"Who is that?"

"Emryleia."

ᏟᏚ12ᏚᎧ

NYRIEVE

"Shut up, Ny, you can't be serious?" Emryleia said with a wide grin on her face.

"I am quite serious, Em," I said with a smile.

"I am in. When do we leave?"

"You don't have any questions on where we are going or why?" I asked my old friend.

"Look, I already know you can't likely tell me any details while we are here in Aquyleya," she said, "but I trust you and I want to be able to help. Sitting here under the sea is beautiful and all, but it can get a little boring."

"I want to believe that it should be a relatively simple trip, but every time I think that is the case, I am proven wrong."

"Good, when do I need to be ready by?"

"You are eager!" I laughed.

"You don't have to answer. I'll get prepared and be ready to leave whenever you tell me. Is there anything in particular I should pack?"

"Do you have any weapons, by chance?"

Emryleia walked across her living room and picked up a long straight walking stick.

"What can a walking stick protect you from? Other than falling."

Emryleia just smiled at me as she took a few steps away and began to spin the stick around in front of her and around her head. She tossed it in the air a little ways and spun around, catching it while standing in a strong defensive stance.

"I get the feeling you have done this before?" I asked with a smirk.

"I might not have been fighting as the Bringer of Peace," she said, straightening herself up, "but living away from Cliffside allowed me to be exposed to many different types of people, and creatures for that matter. And it might not be a surprise to you, at least, but not all those we came in contact with were what you might call… friendly!"

I smiled. "I don't remember you being a fighter when we were growing up."

"I wasn't… Learned the hard way pretty quickly that even if you're a good person and don't want to harm anyone, others do not care. I was shocked to learn that many people will hate you without cause, only thinking you might want what is theirs or because you are not like them."

"I was sad to learn that as well, Em."

"I can imagine, at least from all the stories I have heard of you and your adventures."

"What have you heard?"

Emryleia's eyes shifted with what seemed like embarrassment.

I laughed to ease her tension and said, "Come on, Em, I am sure it is nothing that isn't either true or completely fabricated."

She looked at me and half smiled. "I just don't want to offend you with things I have heard. I don't know if they are true or not, so I don't repeat them, but I always listened to hear about what might have happened to you."

"It's okay, I won't be offended, at least not by you telling me about them."

She took a deep breath as she sat down on her couch and gestured for me to do the same. "The one that I heard more than a year ago is that your mother was one of the people who was trying to kill you."

I chuckled. "That one might be true, actually… but I don't know for sure. She isn't the kindest person I have ever met, let alone for a mother. I know she is angry with me, and likely herself for having me in the first place, but truthfully I don't know if she has or is trying to have me killed."

"That is really sad… I couldn't imagine a mother being like that."

"I am glad to hear that. No one should have to hear such ugly things from a parent."

"I'd like to think that my parents would not have been like that, but my grandmother definitely wasn't. She always made me feel wanted and loved. She would tell me stories about my parents so I could feel like I knew them, even just a little bit."

"That is wonderful."

"I know your father is here in Aquyleya. Does he treat you well at least?"

"Yes, Arnayx is my father. He and Clyo both have treated me better than I could have hoped... Sometimes it feels strange. I mean, most everyone in Cliffside had been good to me, but it is... I don't know the right word. We are 'family,' but I haven't spent much time with them, and while I want them safe and protected, I don't know how things will be if danger isn't around each corner and we can actually get to know each other."

"I can understand that. Finding new family can be tricky to navigate. You want to wholeheartedly trust them because they are part of your bloodlines, but at the same time..."

"You know not everyone is capable of being trusted?"

"Exactly."

"I don't know how to fully let my guard down. I don't think I have been fully relaxed and calm since..."

"Cliffside?"

"Yes, and that was... I don't know even exactly how long it has been since I left..."

"I heard about you being the Bringer of Peace around my seventeenth Leaf Day, and if I remember correctly, my Leaf Day was around half a Leaf Year after yours."

"I know I celebrated my eighteenth Leaf Day in the Water Realm and then went to the Fire Realm... but how much time passed between those I can't fully recall... Time doesn't seem to move like it used to."

"My eighteenth Leaf Day was just a couple months ago, and remembering yours was during the harvest season, your nineteenth Leaf Day should be coming up in a fortnight or two."

"Can it really have been that long?" I asked.

"Your family arrived in Aquyleya around four months ago."

"Really?" I asked, confused. "I didn't realize I had been in the Spirit Realm for so long recovering. I know it took time to fully heal and be able to travel again.

Domi had said to me that there were things she needed to do before we could leave to ensure that no one would be looking for us, but I just never pieced it together that it had been so long..."

"I don't know if it is as important to keep track of time with everything you have gone through. You have a lot to figure out each day, so I'd imagine they begin to blend together."

I nodded to her, but still felt confused. I know I had been in the Spirit Realm for a while, but I never thought it was so long. Why didn't I remember more time there? I would need to ask Domi what happened while I was there and why I couldn't remember more.

"Either way, maybe while we are on our... adventure? Or whatever you want to call it, we can celebrate your nineteenth Leaf Day."

"I guess," I said flatly. "After my seventeenth, I didn't really expect many more..."

"Then we definitely need to celebrate you, Ny," she said with a smile.

I smiled at my friend. I knew she was trying to be positive and help. "Thanks, Em, sounds good. I am going to let you pack. I don't know how long before we will leave, but it shouldn't be many more days. Just please don't tell anyone."

"Never," she said as we both stood up. At the door, I turned to say something, but Em was right there and gave me a big hug. "Thank you for trusting me, Ny, I won't let you down."

"I know," I said as I hugged her back. I smiled, turned and stepped outside her house.

I walked slowly back to my house, watching the water dance around above me. It was beautiful to watch and see all the sea creatures above and around me, but without the wind moving across my skin and making my hair dance in the breeze, it seemed almost unreal. I did not like having my senses as limited as they were here. The bubble that protected the people here was wonderful to keep everyone safe, but it didn't feel like this was a way to truly live, at least not in the long term.

CRELO

"Domi?" I said after I entered my house.

"Yes," she said as she walked out of the back bedroom.

"I have some questions," I said.

"Of course," she replied.

"How long was I in the Spirit Realm?"

"Altogether or—"

"After I fell into the volcano and portaled in front of you."

"Ahh," she said with more thoughtfulness than she normally had. "I was wondering when this might come up. I had thought your family would have questioned the time outright, but when they hadn't, I just wanted to wait until you were ready."

"Ready for what exactly?"

"Do you remember when you woke and I took you outside? You decided that you were at a crossroads and not at a fork in the road and you had the irybugs flying around you and landing on you?"

"Yes, I remember that like it was yesterday," I said.

"After that moment, the irybugs kept swarming around you. I had never seen anything like it in all my years as a Valya. I didn't know what was happening, but you began to almost glow like the irybugs and you started to lift off the ground with them. I thought they were going to fly away with you somehow, and I ran towards you and grabbed your hand. When I touched you, the irybugs just flew away and you landed back on the ground in front of me unconscious."

"I don't remember any of that," I said, trying to recall being pulled off the ground.

"For a while I thought perhaps you were levitating up with them, but when you were unconscious, I didn't think that was it."

"I don't think I levitated either," I said sullenly.

"Why?"

"I tried in the volcano, and it didn't work… I don't think I have that power anymore."

"Have you tried since?" she asked.

"No, and I don't want to… It already failed me when I needed it the most, I can't do it again only to be reminded of how I wasn't able to get back to my friends and save them."

"I don't think that is the case," she said, "but that isn't the point. After you fell back to the ground, I took you back into the Leaf Day Tree and we did everything we could to revive you, but nothing seemed to work. Then we did the only thing we could do."

"Wait?"

"Yes, we waited until you awoke on your own, and you didn't recall how long you had been unconscious or that you were at all. I wanted to talk to you about it, but Jagula insisted that it was best for us to keep out of it, as she felt it was the work of the irybugs and they know more about what is best for Iryvalya than any of us do."

"Your saying I slept for what, over a month?"

"It was about a month and a half actually."

"You should have told me sooner, Domi," I said trying to remember anything during that time.

"I know, and that is in part why I am here now."

"What do you mean?"

"I… I don't think…" Domi stuttered, which was nothing like what I knew of her. She had always been so sure and collected in her responses or comments anytime I heard her speak.

"Domi, what is going on with you?" I asked, concerned.

"I do not believe I am a Valya anymore," she said, looking at me with her head tipped and her brow furrowed.

"How do you figure that?"

"I have gone against the rules. Our rules. The rules the Valya have always lived by."

"What rules have you broken?"

She looked all around the room, as if she was trying to figure out how to explain this to me. She took a deep breath and looked at me. "I have chosen sides. I have chosen to help you, and the Valya are to remain neutral at all times, and I

95

cannot do that any longer."

"Domi," I said, shocked, "you cannot give up who you are for me."

"Valya is not who I am," she said thoughtfully. "It is who I always thought I was, but I do not think that any longer. I have watched the people of Iryvalya my whole life. I have seen things I could have prevented. I have seen things I could have fixed. While I have known my whole life that I am supposed to be only a recorder of time, I can no longer just watch Iryvalya keep falling into the destruction of the past over and over again."

"The past?"

"Do you believe you are the first Bringer of Peace this world has needed?"

"I hadn't really thought about that," I said, feeling a little dumb that thought hadn't crossed my mind.

"Iryvalya has had the rising and falling of good people and leaders as well as the rising and falling of bad people and leaders. It is always different and yet always the same. One group gets it in their heads they are better than others, that their ideas and ways are the best ways, and they think everyone should follow them and do what they do. It is the elves now, but before that the Koneyotta, and before them another and another. It is a circle that just keeps going around and around, never seeming to cease.

"I am tired of watching so many good people try to do the right thing, only to watch them fail and see Iryvalya fall again into darkness. I am not the only one, either. There has been talk for many years among the Valya that we should do something, we should find a way to help, but the response from our elders is always the same. That it is our job to document, not intervene. I was almost fine doing that, recording everything, believing we should not interfere in what happens. But that night, the night the irybugs tried to take you away... I couldn't let them. I have heard of it happening before, the irybugs coming to take someone away... but I couldn't let you be one of them."

"Where would they have taken me, Domi?" I asked.

"There isn't a word for it in your language that would make sense," she said, gesturing her hands in the air. "What I have been told is that you would have been taken to a place in Iryvalya no one would have ever found you."

"But I thought the irybugs only came to those who were doing their best for Iryvalya."

"That is true, but… if you are close to dying, they want to reward you by bringing you to the place you love most to pass peacefully."

"Why was I about to die? I was fine, I was standing there in the forest with you."

"I wasn't sure, to be honest. When I brought you back inside the Leaf Tree, I worked for days trying to figure out what was wrong with you. The only thing I could figure is you must have been poisoned somehow, but I couldn't figure out by whom. While you were recovering from the fall from the volcano and portaling, we checked and tested you, and you were fine. There is no reason the irybugs should have thought you were close to death, unless you were poisoned sometime after you arrived and before you woke up."

"Do you know who poisoned me?"

"I cannot say for certain, but I narrowed it down to a few people. The two fairies who attended to you were on the list, but I do not believe they had anything to do with it. They were very adamant about helping you recover."

"Who else could it have been?"

"There were only two others who checked in on you while you were initially recovering and again after I saved you from being taken away."

"Who is that?"

"One was Takyri. You met them while—"

"I remember them. They showed Baysil and Kaleyna the archives in the Leaf Tree."

"That is correct," she said. "I have known Takyri for my whole life. They also feel similarly as I do about wanting to help Iryvalya and not always stay in the shadows."

"And the other?"

"Jagula," she said quietly.

"Why would Jagula want to harm me? She helped us," I said. "She is friends with Rowzey too."

"I don't know why, Nyrieve, but she is the only other person who was around you. She has also been quite adamant that I stay away from you and stop helping you in any way. She was most angry that I told you how to portal, telling me that it wasn't your destiny to survive that volcano, that by me telling you how to do it, I caused change in the way Iryvalya is supposed to be. But, Nyrieve, when I saw all those irybugs light up the forest for you and want to take you to a place for you to pass in peace, I knew I had to save you and I have to help you in any way I can."

"Does Jagula know?"

"I am sure she has figured out I am here by now and that I am helping you. But it doesn't matter anymore. I am not going to go back to just recording life, I am going to help you save Iryvalya."

ᎤᏛ13ᏕᎤ

BAYSIL

I couldn't breathe. There was water all around my head. I hit and grabbed at it, making no progress. I looked around the best I could and all I could see was Kaleyna sitting on the floor staring at me. I rushed to her to try to get her to help me, but that was when I could see her hands moving. This was her doing. She was killing me. I tried to shake her but nothing happened. She wouldn't stop. I couldn't think of anything else to do, so I pulled my arm back and slapped Kaleyna across her face as hard as I could.

Suddenly the water fell to the ground and I was gasping for air. I was down on my knees in front of her. She was curled up on her side holding her face crying loudly. I kept coughing up what water had made its way into my lungs. After the coughing stopped, I crawled over to Kaleyna to see what was going on.

"Kal?" I asked, softly at first. When she didn't respond I shook her and started to yell, "Kaleyna! Wake up. Look at me."

Finally she seemed to snap out of whatever daze she was in and looked at me in confusion. "Baysil? What, what is going on?" She looked all around us and then at me, reaching out to touch my face. "Why are you all wet? And why does my head hurt so bad?"

"You were just trying to kill me, and you don't remember?" I asked in disbelief.

"Kill you?" she said, shocked. "What are you talking about?"

"I woke up to a… a… water bubble of some kind wrapped around my head and I couldn't breathe. I saw you moving your hands in a circular motion, and until I hit you, the water wouldn't leave me."

"You hit me? Is that why my head hurts?"

"That is your question, really? Why were you trying to kill me?"

"I wasn't, I mean, I don't remember doing that. And how could I have? We never have much water in this room, let alone enough to drown someone!"

I looked around the room, and just inside the door was an empty bowl. Kal's eyes followed mine to the bowl.

"Who put that there?" she asked me.

It didn't make sense, the bowl, the water, and even more so how Kaleyna didn't seem upset with the idea she almost killed me. It was like she was there but not there. I knew for the last couple of weeks she had been getting more quiet and distant, but I had thought it was because of being locked away here.

"Kal," I said, sitting down next to her. I took her hands into mine and looked into her eyes. They didn't look different and yet they seemed distant. "What is going on? When they have taken you away lately for interrogations, you don't come back with injuries anymore, but you don't seem yourself either."

She pulled her hands away from me and looked at the doorway. "Nothing is going on, Baysil. Just because I do not want to talk to you any more than I have to doesn't mean something is going on."

"Really?" I asked. "Because you changing the way we have always been able to communicate does lead me to think something is going on with you. Are you trying to protect me from something?"

She turned her head towards me quickly with a fire burning in her eyes. "Protect you? Did you really ask me if I was trying to protect you, Baysil?"

"I did," I stammered, not used to hearing Kaleyna talk like this. "What is going on with you?"

"Look, I don't know what you think you know about me, maybe you did know me pretty well once upon a time, but that isn't me anymore. That person, the one *you* promised to protect and keep safe, she is gone. I have been beaten and screamed at and burned and starved, and you know what it was all for? It was for NOTHING!"

"Kal, what are you talking about?"

"You can't be serious, Baysil. Do you really think we are here for some grand purpose? Do you really think that we are still supposed to help that dead elf that got us here in the first place?"

"We don't know if Ny—"

"Do not say her name. I am so sick of hearing her name, saying her name, remembering her name."

"Kal, this isn't you. She is your best friend, your sister even."

"She is nothing. She is dead. And when you are dead, you no longer matter. She doesn't matter. The sooner you figure that out, and maybe the guards here figure that out, they could let me go. I have told them everything I know, everything I have ever known, everything I had thought and hoped for. I broke promises and gave up secrets, only to make the pain stop, and you know what it has gotten me? More pain."

I couldn't believe what I was hearing. Did they break Kaleyna and I didn't see it coming? They still took us each for days at a time and then brought us back to this dark and dank room. At first we would tend to each other, wrapping wounds and providing comfort. Now, we mostly just sat in silence. It had been so long since either of us were brought back to this room bleeding, I just thought they had given up with the beatings. When they took me, they usually brought me to a room full of food and tied me to a chair at the table, and they'd all feast in front of me, not letting me have anything to eat. I had assumed that was what they did to Kaleyna too, but what if they were doing something worse?

"Kal, what have the Pyrothians been doing to you when they take you from here?"

"Nothing," she said flatly.

"What do you mean, nothing?"

"They take me to the sleep chamber. Some days, I am able to take a bath and sleep in a bed. I don't know how long I sleep, but when they wake me, it's just to drag me back here."

"They let you take a bath and sleep?"

"Same as they do you," she snapped.

"They have never done that to me, Kal," I said, still shocked. "Do they give you anything to eat or drink before they let you sleep?"

"They started to give me food when I told them about what our next steps were going to be."

"What next steps did you tell them?"

101

"About going to find our parents in the underwater city. They were mad when I couldn't remember the name, so they didn't let me have any desserts."

I couldn't believe what I was hearing. "Did you really give up your parents' location?"

"No, because I can't remember it. Sometimes I can't remember the village I grew up in. I remember the roar of the sea when I close my eyes, but nothing else."

"Kal, I think they are doing something to you to try to get you to tell them things, messing with your mind somehow when they let you sleep."

"They aren't doing anything but letting me rest. I just don't want to wake up because all they do is bring me back in here with you."

"Why didn't you tell me this was going on?"

"I figured you were doing the same," she grumbled. "They said you already told them how we were going to go find our parents afterwards and Prydos..."

"I didn't tell them anything."

"Liar," she spat. "They said you would start to lie to me too, now that you made a deal with Osidya."

"I made no such deal with anyone."

"Right, and that is why they knew about me and Prydos and how we were going to get tyed."

"I never said anything to any of them."

"Then who would tell them that?"

"Miaarya," I said quietly.

"She wouldn't have told them anything. She has been checking on me and making sure they get me the foods I like. She said you and her have been having"— she smiled coyly at me—"well, you know what you both have been doing."

"Miaarya has been visiting you?" I asked, still shocked.

"Almost every time I leave. She was so happy to hold me the one night and stroke my hair. It felt almost like I was back home in... in... ugh, I can't remember the name..."

They had to be doing something to her while she was sleeping. If Miaarya was involved, then I knew they had to be close to finding Nyrieve if she was still alive, but at the least the Nomydrac. I didn't know how I could let any of them know, since I was stuck in this stupid locked room.

"Kal," I whispered, "you didn't tell them about Rowzey, did you?"

"Tell them what?"

"Who and where she is?"

"I don't know where she is… She abandoned us too."

"She didn't…" I stopped myself. Maybe Kaleyna really didn't remember us making Rowzey leave when she had the chance. "Did you tell them who Rowzey is?"

"They know who she is."

"Who do they think she is?"

"They think she was this little old frail woman who liked to butt into the lives of everyone around her. Someone who makes some good food from time to time, has an accent no one can place, and someone trusted by the rebels."

She didn't say anything about her being a dragon. Did she forget or was it possible they were listening right now to try to break us into giving up secrets for them to hear?

"Kaleyna," I said, "I am going to do everything I can to get you out of here and back with your family."

"Prydos, that is who I want to see. Just him," she said, sounding sleepy. I helped her lie down on the matted straw floor and covered her with a blanket.

"Just rest, Kal…" I said. I didn't think I would be able to sleep again while alone with her. If she was trying to kill me in her sleep, I would need to be awake to protect myself. I needed to get her out of here and back to where she could recover her memories. I wished Ny was here to help keep Kaleyna from going down this dark path. I hoped Osidya was right and she was alive somewhere, and hopefully she would come rescue us before the Kaleyna we knew was completely gone.

CRBO

"Osidya," I said flatly, "we need to talk."

"I heard you asked for me this last time they took you out," she said, sounding bored. "I must say I didn't expect you would want to see me again after the last time

103

we met."

She walked over to me tied up in the chair, looked at the mark along the right side of my face and traced her finger down the crooked scar beginning to form. "I am sorry I did that. You had such a handsome face."

I steadied my nerves to not react to her touching me with all my might. "I would say thank you, but I doubt you truly mean it."

"Oh no, I do mean it. Nothing gives me more pleasure than appreciating beautiful things… in many ways," she said, drawn out. "If you were only interested in providing me with more information, maybe I could have found better uses for my… frustrations."

"Is that what you are doing to Kaleyna? Taking out your frustrations on her?"

"I have never once hurt that girl. Besides, I haven't had a discussion with her in over a month's time."

"Then who has been talking to her?"

"What makes you think I am going to tell you anything? You have not provided me with the information I need to secure my status here, so why should I help you at all?"

"Because someone is somehow extracting information from Kaleyna to find out if Nyrieve is alive, where she would be, and I am sure they are not sharing that information with you."

"And who do you think is doing that?"

"Miaarya."

"Miaarya?" She laughed. "You must be joking? That simpering little suck up of a bald fairy is somehow getting information from Kaleyna?"

"I believe so."

"Why?" she asked, her eyes narrowing at me.

"Kaleyna said that Miaarya has been seeing her and providing her with baths and allowing her to sleep in a bed. I think while Kaleyna believes she is just sleeping, Miaarya, or someone she is helping, is extracting information from Kaleyna somehow."

"Baths and beds? Is that how your people interrogate?" She laughed.

"Never," I said flatly. "What you all have been doing to me, starving me, beating me and more, that is what I have done and would do. But I do not know how to trick the mind to give up information, but Miaarya knows how. She has used some magyc in the past to trick people into trusting her, and I wouldn't put it past her to do it again."

"I am getting bored of this conversation, Baysil."

"So am I," I said, surprising her.

"Then why did you want to see me?"

"Because I thought maybe, just maybe, if you would help get them to stop destroying Kaleyna's mind, then I would tell you some things to help your... status."

"Really? After all this time, you will give up where Nyrieve is?"

"I cannot tell you something I do not know, Osidya, and you know that. But I can provide you with some information you might find useful."

"Why would you give up the information Nyrieve would have sworn you to secrecy to keep?"

I took a deep breath and said, "Because if Nyrieve knew what was being done to Kaleyna, she would tell you anything and everything you wanted to know to save her friend."

"Is my child really that simple, Baysil? She would toss her loyalties aside so easily?"

"That is what you do not seem to understand about your daughter, Osidya. She isn't like you. She doesn't do things to help herself get further in her station. She doesn't turn against people because she doesn't like what they think or who they are. Nyrieve is one of the most level-headed people I have met through my life, who doesn't let superficial things influence her and her decisions. She does what is right when she has the opportunity to do so, even at her own detriment."

"Why do you admire her so much?"

"Why don't you?"

"Because of her, I lost everything that mattered to me. My sister, my parents' respect, my—"

"That is your problem, Osidya."

"What is my problem, Baysil?" she replied with a pompous shake of her head. "You."

"Me what?"

"That is all… you."

"I don't understand."

"Of course you don't, because you are all you think about. You are all you worry about. You are the only one who has had all the worst things in Iryvalya happen to her. You are the one who should be revered. You are the one who could never do the things your amazing caring, giving, loving and selfless daughter does each and every day of her life."

"How dare you speak to me like that?" she said, slapping me hard across my face. I could taste the tang of copper from the blood in my mouth.

"Tell me this, Osidya. Am I wrong?"

"This is stupid," she said, turning to leave the room.

"At one point in your life you wanted your daughter. You loved your daughter. You would have done everything you could have to protect her. But something changed. I cannot believe for a moment that you just simply stopped loving her and wanting a good life for her. I have to believe that someone or something is forcing you to not see her for who she is or what she could accomplish."

"Why would you think that?" she said, slowly turning to face me. "Why would something stop me from caring about her?"

"Because all that you have done here to me," I said slowly, "and I still will not give up all her secrets to you."

"She isn't your child."

"No, she's not," he said, "but I love Nyrieve like she was mine and I would never do anything to betray her trust or harm her. I am not of her bloodlines, but you are, and I have no idea how you could despise your own child so much. The only thing that would make sense to me is you were brainwashed or cursed, because what creature in their right mind could ever turn their back on their child?"

She just stood there staring at me. I couldn't tell what she was thinking or feeling, only that she didn't move a muscle for the longest time. Finally, she walked over and grabbed a chair, set it right in front of me and then sat down.

"I cannot speak for why exactly I despise my quanta'mu like I do," she said, "and thinking on it only makes me more angry. However, as much as I want to believe you are crazy, I don't. Tell me what you can and what you know. I will try to make sure Kaleyna at the least is kept away from Miaarya."

"I have your word?"

"Surprisingly, yes you do, Baysil."

I took a deep breath and swallowed, hoping if Nyrieve was alive, she would forgive me for what I was about to reveal.

ɔ14ʍ

NYRIEVE

"Come in," I said, sitting on the couch with some of the items from the pack from Lydorea strewn about me.

The door opened and I saw Kylyan step inside the door. I felt my heart speed up just seeing him. I jumped up, dropping some of the items on the floor, and rushed over to hug him.

"Did you miss me or something?" he asked, squeezing me tightly.

"Or something," I said, holding on and trying to memorize the way I felt in his arms.

He stepped back, looking at me. He tipped his head to the side and asked, "What is it?"

"What is what?" I asked.

"What is going on, Ny? Something is," he said, sounding concerned.

I took a deep breath and stepped back. "Come sit and I'll fill you in the best I can."

I walked back to the couch and picked up the couple of items I dropped and pushed them back into the pack that never seemed to get full no matter how much I put inside it. Definitely one of Lydorea's best charms.

We both sat down next to each other and Kylyan nodded for me to start.

"You know I can't just stay here, right?"

"I know that," he said, starting to sound worried.

"At any time I am going to have to leave to try to get something I will need to help bring the people together, so they know I am honest and only wanting to help."

"What do you mean at any time?"

"It could be a few days from now or tonight, Kyl," I said. "I honestly don't know when Iclyn will have everything prepared, and when she does, we have to leave right away."

"How will you be traveling?"

"I honestly don't know."

"How long will you be gone?"

"I don't know that either," I said softly. "I wish I could say it would be quick and we'd be back right away, but there's no way to know how smoothly things will go."

"I know I can't stop you, but can't I go with you?"

"I wish you could, but I need you to make sure Prydos doesn't hurt someone, or himself for that matter. You seem to be the only one he will listen to. Clyo believes she has the right ingredients to give him a sleeping spell, but if it doesn't last as long as it's needed, we will need you to help keep him calm and safe."

He closed his eyes tightly, and then looked at me. "I understand, but I don't like this. We have split up before and it didn't go so well, did it?"

"No, it didn't," I agreed, "but maybe if we can get through this, then we don't have to be apart ever again. Well, unless you get tired of me and decide to find another elf or fairy or—"

"Or no one. There is no other for me than you," he said. "For the short time Miaarya kept pushing me to find someone else, I made a friend or two, but there is nothing like you, Ny. When I am with you, I can picture my future, see us growing old together and enjoying our lives, making a family if we decide to…"

"I can too, Kyl," I said, taking his hand and squeezing it. "I do have one more favor to ask of you while I am gone."

"What is that, my lady?" he said with a sweet smile that I couldn't help but meet with my own.

"Could you keep an eye out for Arnayx, Clyo and Dymma?"

"They will be my family one day too, Ny, so of course I will."

"If something were to happen to me…"

"It won't, but if it does, that will not change anything. I will keep an eye on them no matter what for as long as I live."

"Thank you, Kylyan," I said, squeezing his hand again. "I don't know if I could go do this not knowing they will be watched over."

"You don't have to worry about that, Ny, I promise… Now," he said, looking at the pack, "what is all in that pack? When I brought it to you it felt almost empty, but all the items you just shoved in could not have fit in that!"

I smiled as I showed him the pack. "Lydorea enchanted it or something, and it seems to be able to hold whatever I put in it."

"That is pretty amazing. I could use one of those," he said with a smile.

"Maybe when everything is done, I can let you have it."

"No, that is yours and yours alone, Ny, but you never know, maybe you could enchant one for me or find someone else to."

"I will make sure to look for one while I am gone." I laughed.

"Yes, I am sure you will find some shops wherever you are vacationing to, and make sure while away you make good use of your time to get a massage, a tan or something. I don't know what people do on vacations."

I laughed louder. "That makes two of us!"

"How about when things are… better, you and me go someplace, just the two of us?"

"I would really like that."

"Where would you want to go?"

"Uhm, I don't know… maybe Cliffside? Show you where I grew up… or the Spirit Realm, show you the Leaf Day Tree… Where would you want to go?"

"I have no place I want more than another to go to. As long as it is with you, I would be more than happy."

"Ditto!"

"Since you don't know when you are leaving, would it be okay to enjoy right now and just cuddle on the couch together?" he asked.

"There's nothing else I would rather do right now."

⚬

"Nyrieve," someone said quietly but urgently.

I opened my eyes, still in Kylyan's arms, and saw Iclyn standing in front of us.

"What?" I asked in a whisper.

"We need to leave in the next hour. Get everything together you need and meet me at the tunnel where you came into Aquyleya."

"Uhm, okay, okay, I can do that," I said, sitting up, trying not to wake Kylyan.

"I will get the others and meet you there. Just make sure not to attract much attention as you make you way."

"Do my parents know?"

"I have not told them," she said, "and they will be asleep I'd imagine. Perhaps a note that Kylyan could provide them? Just do not leave much information where someone else could read it."

"Okay," I said, "I will figure something out."

Iclyn nodded and rushed out the door silently.

I turned and looked at Kylyan still asleep on the couch. I decided I would gather my things quickly and then wake him to tell him I was leaving. That way there would be nothing on paper for someone to read.

I went into the small bedroom and gathered the few items I had and placed them in a large pack Iclyn provided me a few days ago. It held everything quite well, even the pack from Lydorea, with room to spare. I looked around, making sure I didn't forget anything. I looked myself over. I had my normal leather pants on and Klaw secured to my thigh. My boots were getting worn but were still so comfortable for traveling in. My green shirt was tucked into my pants and my hair pulled back in a braid that finally seemed to be getting longer after losing so much from the volcano.

I knew I was physically ready to leave, just not ready otherwise. I sat on the corner of my bed, just wondering if I would ever have a place again to call home. A place where I could have things on display and not only things I could throw in a pack to take off again. I remember as a child always wanting to travel Iryvalya and see everything there was to see. Now I realize that while I loved seeing all the places I had been, it didn't feel as great without a home to return to. More like I was just a single fluffy seed from a dandelion flying around without a place to land and put roots down. Maybe one day I'd be able to have a home and a family of my own, but unless we could get Iryvalya to a place of peace, it would never be safe for me to have children, because they would always have a target on their backs.

I heard Kylyan stir in the other room. I stood up, grabbing my large pack, and walked out of the bedroom.

"I was wondering where you went to, Ny," he said, the smile on his face falling when he saw my pack. "Are you leaving... now?"

"Yes," I said, feeling somber. "Iclyn was just here and said we need to leave."

"I knew you had to go, but I was hoping we'd have a couple more days."

"Me too... I can't even go tell my family I am leaving."

"I'll let them know, Ny," he said, walking to me and holding my hands.

"Thank you."

"I don't know exactly what to say, Ny," he said, furrowing his brow. "I know you have to go. I know I can't go with you. I want you to stay, and you can't."

"I am so sorry for this, Kyl," I said, squeezing his hands. "It can't be easy for you or anyone who cares about someone who is leaving and can't tell you where or what or when they'll be back."

Kylyan dropped my hands and pulled me into a tight hug. It seemed like forever and only a moment at the same time. He slowly released me from his hold and looked into my eyes. I wanted to say so much and yet I didn't know where to start. Luckily for me, he did.

"My lady," he said with a half grin, "don't worry. The last time we parted, things were not good. I was demanding you to do something you couldn't and I didn't trust you like I should have. I know better this time. I know you are only doing what you feel is the best thing, and in the end, I know you will always do what is right. I trust you, Nyrieve."

"Thank you, Kyl," I said, pushing through the sticky lump forming in my throat again. "I don't want to leave you, I really don't."

"I know that," he said with a smile, "but the truth is, you are not leaving me. You are going to go do something... magycal I think."

"Something magycal?"

"Yes, I think you will find what it is you need or what you are looking for, and then maybe something else. I don't know how to explain it, but somehow deep inside me I feel like this will change how things are going to move forward for all of us."

"I hope it is all good things."

"Me too. I know it'll be hard on you, because you will miss everyone here and you feel guilty about Rowzey, Baysil and especially Kaleyna. I just... I don't know, I just think this is going to help somehow."

"I truly hope you are right, Kyl," I said softly, almost not wanting to jinx myself with too much hope.

"I really think I am."

"I am going to miss you," I said, giving him a soft kiss, feeling the hair on his face lightly prickle my face.

"I know," he said with a smile. "I will make sure by the time you see me next, my face will be soft and smooth for you."

"I don't know, I kind of like it," I said, running my hands over it.

"Then maybe I'll keep it," he said.

"I wouldn't mind. As long as I still get to be in your arms when I come back, I'll be happy."

"When you come back, Ny, I want to maybe make things more official with us."

"What do you mean?"

"If it was safe with the Prydos stuff, I would have asked you already to vow each other to get tyed."

"What?" I asked, surprised, and felt my heart begin to race. "You would want to do that... like already?"

"The time we spent apart only showed me how much I miss you and want you in my life, each and every day. But I know that isn't how things work, especially right now. I would just be happy to know that even if you have to go and do things without me, we are tyed to each other forever. I love you, my lady, and want it to be known to all of Iryvalya."

My heart was pounding so hard I could feel it even in my fingertips. Part of me was asking myself, Isn't this too fast? But my heart already knew the answer, that it wasn't. What Kylan and I shared was real and true and the love would never go away. We might not always agree on things, but if we loved each other, were willing to listen to each other and trusted one another, then it would work. We just had to choose each other each and every day, and I knew that was what I would do.

"I love you too, Kylyan," I said, grabbing his face in my hands and kissing him hard on his lips, "and I would love to be tyed to you."

He smiled so widely that he looked like a child on their Leaf Day when they saw the presents laid out before them. "Then when we are together again, we can figure out if it still makes sense to you and with everything else going on, we will make it officially known our betrothal and plans to get tyed to one another."

"I can't wait."

"Me either," he said, kissing me again and again. I held him as long as I could before he let go and kissed me again and said, "You best be going, my lady. I will wait for you always."

"And I you," I said, grabbing my pack to leave before I could change my mind and just stay with Kylyan here forever.

"Volnyri, Ny," he said as I stepped through the door.

"Volnyri, Ky," I responded as the door closed behind me.

I quickly looked around and made sure I saw no one else. I silently took off back towards where I entered Aquyleya. As I walked, I noticed there were no houses lit with any light. The only thing I could see was above the bubble that kept the water from crashing down on us. There were many different things swimming around above, though I couldn't make them all out. It was beautiful seeing their movements light up as I rushed to meet up with everyone leaving.

"It is good to see you again, Nyrieve," Koyvean whispered as I approached her, Iclyn and Emryleia.

"It is very good to see you again as well, Koyvean," I said, giving her a quick hug. "I am glad to see you were able to get out of the Fire Realm safely."

"I technically never made it back to the Fire Realm. I wasn't happy being sent here to deliver your family, but I do understand their importance to you," she said flatly. "I was here a lot longer than I had expected to be, and by the time I had Sudryl bring me back to the ship, the ship was already on the move away from the Fire

Realm. When I reached it, they said the Pyrothians advised them to leave and they knew they had no choice. They didn't go far from where they were docked, but far enough for the Pyrothians to not see them as a threat. I waited with them until we heard you were killed and then I tried to get into Prax to find you."

"No," I said, "they could have captured you!"

"Someone did, though who, I am not sure. They did not provide me with their name, but she seemed to have much respect for you and told me you were alive. I wasn't sure I could believe her, but I really had no choice. I left to come here, but on the way back I ran into some interference."

"What did she look like and what kind of interference?"

"She had long, mostly black hair with some yellow in it, and far too many earrings for my preference. It isn't helpful to have things that can be ripped out of my body when I am fighting someone."

"I think that was Quwyst," I said. "She helped me see what was really going on with the people in the Fire Realm."

"Perhaps," Koyvean responded.

"She also is the one who pretended to attack me when we left Cliffside."

"That explains some of the things she said to me."

"Hey," Iclyn said, "if you two are done catching up, we need to get a move on."

"What about Domi?" I asked.

"She will meet us when she can, I am not sure what she needed to do, but I guess she felt it was more important than going with us."

"Okay," I said, worried that Domi might get caught by the other Valya, and who knows if they would let her leave.

"Let's get a move on," Iclyn said. "Do not let your guard down starting now. Make sure we watch ahead, behind and all around us. If something or someone feels off, speak up. We need to make sure this goes as smoothly as possible."

"Is there something that has you extra concerned, Iclyn?" I asked.

"Yes," she said, "I received word that someone in Prax is giving up information on you and where you might be. We cannot wait any longer to leave and get some distance between us and Aquyleya."

"Who would do that?" I asked, surprised.

"Baysil," she responded.

"But he would never…" I said, wondering if it could be true.

"You don't know what they are doing to him to make him talk," she said. "As of right now, we have to assume he has been compromised, and he might no longer be on our side."

᭒15᭓

NYRIEVE

"I just don't think Baysil would turn on me…"

"Ny, I understand you don't want to believe he could do that," Koyvean said, "but you have to understand, he has been held in the Fire Realm for months now. We don't know what they have done to him to get him to talk."

"I know," I said as we kept walking through the pathway leading away from Aquyleya. "I just… I guess I don't want to know what they could have done to him that would have made him break…"

"I can understand that," she responded.

We had been trekking along for a couple of days now. We stopped only to eat and sleep. Though sleep wasn't coming to me as easily as I would have liked. I was worried about Kylyan and my family in Aquyleya, hoping they would be safe and understand me leaving like I had to. When I wasn't worrying about them, I was having nightmares about Kaleyna and Baysil. I was especially worried that the dreams were more than just dreams and they were visions like I have had before. I hadn't had any since the Fire Realm, and couldn't help but wonder if that, like my power to levitate, was gone. I didn't want to tell anyone yet about either, but I knew it wouldn't be long before I had to admit something was wrong. I thought Domi would keep my secret for a while, but I was sure she'd encourage me to not talk to someone and try again. I just didn't know if I was ready to learn that I might have lost that ability forever.

"I think we are only an hour away from the entrance," Iclyn said. "We should probably stop here for a bit and rest up before we head out. There shouldn't be anyone at the entrance, but there is no way of knowing and we need to be well rested if we have to fight our way out."

Everyone agreed and sat down. Iclyn passed out some bread and cheese she had brought with her. I took the waterskin that she provided me when we started. I couldn't figure out how it could hold so much and yet seem so light. When I asked, she told me they were enchanted with a spell Lydorea had taught her. I didn't know how much was in it, but hopefully it'd last until we found a place to refill it.

No one talked while we ate. I thought we were all just tired of the dark and ready for some fresh air. I couldn't wait to look up at the moon, though I had no idea which one I would see. Time really seemed to be different under the water. I didn't seem to be able to keep better track of which day it was.

"Ny?" Emryleia asked.

"Huh? What?" I said, snapping out of my thoughts.

"I asked if everything was okay?"

"I'm sorry," I said, "I was off in my thoughts."

"What were you thinking about?"

"Time, honestly, and trying not to think about leaving people behind again."

"Ny," Iclyn started, "you know everyone will be safe in Aquyleya for now, and if anything happens, Sudryl has backup plans that will ensure everyone will be able to get out and get to someplace safe. He told me he knows a couple places he could escort them to."

"I am happy to hear that, but I still worry."

"I know," she said. "How about you all get some rest. I'll take the first watch."

I leaned up against the wall behind me. It was a bricklike substance of some sort pressed up against what I imagined was just water, but how it kept from crushing down on us, I couldn't figure it out. The floor was a hard sand, like it was wet, but it wasn't wet to the touch. I leaned my head back and tried to turn my brain off and get a little sleep.

CRBD

The fog was so thick in front of me, I couldn't see anything ahead. I looked behind me and that too was covered in fog. I couldn't tell where anything was. I started running but still couldn't find anything. Where was I? And then I heard something that made me stop.

I knew I heard footsteps, but now there was nothing but silence. I started to move again, and the footsteps began. When I stopped, they stopped.

"Hello?" I asked but was met with only silence.

I crouched and tried to see or hear anything that might help me understand what was going on. Somewhere off in the distance I started to see a glow of light. It was faint, but I knew I needed to head towards it.

I quietly took a long deep breath to steady myself. I stood up, and very slowly and quietly started to advance towards the light. As I moved I didn't hear footsteps anymore. There was nothing again. I kept focusing on the light ahead. But now there were more. More lights, and they were all different colors. At first I thought maybe they were irybugs, but there were too many colors and they were all on the ground.

I started to move faster, wanting to get closer to the lights. I felt like they were calling to me, wanting me to come closer. In the back of my mind I wondered if this was a trap, but I couldn't stop myself. I no longer just wanted to know what the lights were, I needed to know.

I was almost to the lights when they started to fade away. I began running, not wanting to miss seeing what they were. As soon as I reached where I thought the lights were, they were gone, but the fog began to lift in front of me.

I saw a pond only a few steps in front of me. Had I not stopped when I had, I would have fallen in. It was still hazy enough that I couldn't see everything, but I couldn't see anything lighting up anymore. I stopped and listened. All I could hear were bugs singing their songs and the water lightly lapping at the shore. I kneeled down to look for what could have made the light, but all I could see were tiny turtles playing around in the water.

I had never seen such small turtles before. I kneeled down next to the water to get a closer look. They were nothing like any turtles I'd ever seen. The ones I had seen in Cliffside were always colors of the environment around them. Usually they were the shades of grass, greens to browns, or if they lived closer to the water, sometimes they were even shades of blue. These turtles here, they were so colorful, like every possible color I'd ever seen. And it wasn't just one color on each. There were multiple colors on each one.

They looked so happy and playful splashing in the water. I couldn't believe how little they were, so I reached down to see if one would crawl to me. I held my hand there for a few moments, and suddenly one of the little turtles splashed over to me and crawled onto my hand. I slowly and carefully lifted it closer to my face to examine it more. It was no bigger than the tip of my index finger but didn't seem to be a baby. While it was hard to see the details, I could tell the shell's scutes had age lines on them, but it was almost impossible for me to count them all.

The little turtle crawled into the palm of my hand and just looked up at me. I would have almost thought it was smiling, but I wasn't sure if turtles could smile. I looked over its little body. It was mostly a deep shade of purple with some light yellow and green on its shell.

I didn't want to harm it, so I set my hand down by the water again and watched it jump back into the water to play with its friends.

There must have been at least a hundred of them in front of me. Were they attracted to the lights I saw as well? I wished I could ask them where the light went.

All at once the little turtles stopped moving. They were all turned towards me, staring at me. I didn't know what I did to attract their attention like this, but it was amazing to see all their tiny faces. I realized they were not looking directly at me, but above me. That was when I realized there was something slowly moving up behind me. I moved my right hand to Klaw and unfastened the strap silently. I gripped Klaw, ready to fight, when a hand grabbed my shoulder and I jumped up.

CꙄꙄꙄ

"Nyrieve!" a familiar voice shouted. "Nyrieve, put Klaw away. You were dreaming!"

I realized it was Iclyn talking to me. I opened my eyes and looked around. I had Klaw out and held at Koyvean's throat. I immediately pulled it back and put it away.

"I am so sorry, Koyvean," I said, looking around, trying to understand what was happening. "Where am I?"

"We are still in the tunnel out of Aquyleya," Koyvean said, her voice still flat but sounding slightly annoyed. "I was trying to wake you so we could continue out of here, and you decided to attack me."

"I am so sorry," I said, still feeling confused. "I was dreaming I was... I don't know where I was... and someone was grabbing at me from behind and I was trying to protect myself."

"You were dreaming, Ny," Iclyn said. "We had tried to wake you for a few minutes, but when you wouldn't, Koyvean shook your shoulder and you attacked her."

"I really didn't mean to do that. I just..."

"It's fine," Koyvean said flatly as she straightened herself up. "I am more upset that you had the upper hand on me, even when you were asleep."

"I don't think I had the upper hand. It was only a combination of luck and confusion."

"Ny," Iclyn said softly, "what were you dreaming about?"

"Huh?" I said reactively. "Oh, I mean, it was just me walking through fog and getting lost and finding pretty animals and then someone grabbed me..."

"I see," she said, pondering what I said.

"I know that sometimes my dreams mean something, but a lot of times they don't. Nothing in the dream felt familiar."

"Things you described just now sounded familiar to me," she replied.

"What things?"

"The fog... Was there a lot of fog? Did it disperse? What color was everything else?"

"Yes, there was a lot of fog. I couldn't see anything for the longest time until I came across a pond of turtles."

"Turtles?" Emryleia asked.

"Yes, they were so tiny and colorful, nothing like I have ever seen or heard of in Iryvalya, so that proves it had to just be a dream."

"I don't know anything about the turtles," Iclyn said. "However, the fog part, that I have heard of before."

"Cliffside even had fog," I said. "I don't think fog is unusual in most places."

"Perhaps, but I recall Lydorea telling me a story about the Blackened Forest and how there are times when it is completely engulfed in fog that could last for days."

I thought about it. Could it be this was a dream of something to come when we get to the Blackened Forest or just a dream of weird things because of all the stuff constantly running through my head? "I honestly don't know if it is a dream telling us of something to come, Iclyn, or just weird dreams from an overactive mind that won't shut off."

"I know," she said. "Don't stress on it, but we'll check with Domi when we see her. She might have more insight if she has been to the Blackened Forest or knows those who have. Maybe she would know if the turtles you saw were real or not. If we find out those are actually there, we'll need to proceed with this as a warning dream and make sure to watch our backs even more carefully."

"You're right," I said, thinking I would never forget about what those cute tiny turtles looked like and how I would love to see them with my own eyes.

"How about we get packed up," Iclyn said. "I think it'll do us all some good to get out of this tunnel and get some fresh air."

I bent down to grab my pack and slung it over my shoulders. After taking a moment to straighten myself up and downing a few large gulps of water, I was ready to keep moving.

Everyone else was ready too, so we started off again in silence.

After walking for only about twenty minutes, we could hear sounds coming from ahead. It was the sound of birds and trees rustling in the breeze.

"Wait," I said.

"What is it?" Iclyn asked.

"When I came in through the hatch, Domi had to stay behind to cover it back up."

"Okay?"

"If it was covered back up, we shouldn't be hearing birds or trees in the wind."

"She's right," Koyvean said. "Let me go first and take a look. If there is an ambush, lock the hatch behind me and make your way back to Aquyleya as quickly as you can."

We all walked behind Koyvean to the entrance. She silently began to open the hatch.

"No need to be quiet," a familiar voice said on the other side.

Koyvean quickly opened the hatch and looked up to see Domi standing there with her hand outstretched.

Koyvean took her hand to climb out, then turned around to help the rest of us up.

The sky was a beautiful turquoise, telling me it was the Nydian moon that was closest overhead. I had lost all sense of time in the tunnel and didn't realize it was night. I was longing for sunshine on my face, but it was probably for the best it was dark, not sure our eyes could have handled too much sun after so long in the dark tunnel.

"Domi," I said, "what are you doing out here?"

"Someone had to dig out the hatch for you all to get out easily."

"Thank you," I said.

"Of course," she responded. "I have some food and water for all of you on the beach. I figured you could use something before we leave this little island."

We followed Domi over to where she had some food set up for us to grab and eat. I took some cheese and fruit and sat down on a rock near the edge of the water. I listened to the sounds around me, trying to take in a moment of peace before the next leg of our journey began.

"Do you mind if I sit with you?" Emryleia asked.

"Of course not," I sat, patting the open space on the rock.

"So, your dreams happen?" she asked as she bit into some cheese.

"Sometimes," I said, enjoying some cheese as well. "It isn't all my dreams, but sometimes they seem to tell me something about what has happened or what will happen. Sadly I have no control over them or a way to tell if they are more than just a dream."

"Hmm," she said. "My grandmother told me once of someone she knew who had dreams like that, and over time she was able to start telling if the dream was past, future or nothing."

"How did she do that?"

"I don't remember exactly what it was, but she said it was something to do with the... sheen of the dream."

"Sheen?"

"Yes, she said that something looked different in those dreams. Like there was a coating to it. I want to say when it was a dream of the past, it was duller. Like it wasn't as shiny or something. Dreams of the future were more shiny or something."

"I never noticed that in mine," I said.

"It could be different for everyone," Em replied, "but next time you are in the dream or when you wake up, try to think if there was anything different with the way the dream looked than typical dreams. It might be for nothing, but it couldn't hurt, right?"

"No, it definitely couldn't hurt. It would be helpful if I was able to tell those things apart."

We sat in silence, eating and enjoying the fresh air, when I could hear the large flapping of wings in the distance. I looked towards the sky and saw a dragon approaching us. Emryleia was staring up at it as well with her mouth hanging open. I had to chuckle when a small grape tumbled out of her mouth and onto the beach.

"You okay, Em?"

"I knew dragons still existed, but..."

"It is always amazing when you see one, no matter how many times you have," I said, "or how many times you ride one."

"What? Ride one? You're not saying we're going to have to ride a dragon right now, are you?"

"I don't know what Iclyn and Domi planned for us, but I am sure we will be finding out pretty soon."

❦16❧

NYRIEVE

The world of Iryvalya always looked so much more peaceful from high up in the sky. I could see the beautiful blues and greens of the seas and the lush forests of the islands we flew over. I missed seeing all of these things. I wondered, if I were a dragon, would I ever stop flying? I could stay up here forever seeing the beauty of our world without all the fighting.

We'd be needing to land soon, but I just wanted to keep flying. The people of Iryvalya used to be able to fly, maybe not like a dragon can, but it must have been so hard when they started to lose that ability. I remember the feeling I had on top of the mountains in the Air Realm when I levitated myself almost off the edge. Before the scare, it felt so wonderful and freeing. I wonder if I will ever experience that feeling again from my own powers.

I didn't know the dragons we were riding this time, but the one I was on was a dragon from the Spirit Realm. It was long and slender, with a black back and silvery white underside, looking a lot like Rowzey did when she was in dragon form. As the sun shone down on us and I looked closer, the black scales along its back where not simply black. There was almost a halo in each scale that seemed to reflect a rainbow of colors. The beautiful plume of feathers that came off the top of its head danced around me in the wind. While they had the different colors in the middle of the feathers, the rest of the feather was similar to the scales. At a quick glance you could dismiss them as all black, but as the wind spread the feathers apart, there were hints of color all throughout them. Nothing like this was ever described in the books I had read or the stories I had heard about the different dragons.

This trip was much easier than the last time flying with the dragons, because Iclyn made sure we each had a saddle of sorts. When we flew the last time, I remember Kaleyna and I trying to adjust the blankets just so to make it more comfortable, but it never was as comfortable as this saddle. When I asked how she had them made, Iclyn said that long ago when the dragons weren't in hiding, there were many dragon riders who would travel all around Iryvalya and needed something better than just a blanket. When she learned of this, she requested to have some made for our journey. Apparently not all the dragons wanted to wear saddles while flying, but the ones taking us now didn't mind and understood how hard it was to ride so long in discomfort.

I could see in the distance an island ahead of us that we seemed to be heading directly towards and way off in the distance what looked like a black mass in the middle of the water. That had to be the Blackened Forest, but why would they be landing on a different island?

The island ahead looked thick with forest and plants, the only things that looked slightly sparce of any vegetation were the beaches. They were big and looked like nice warm places to land. I was expecting to feel colder now that we were getting further into the harvest season, and my Leaf Day, but it wasn't here. It was just sunny and warm. I wondered if it had to do with being closer to both suns equally that kept this area similar to the Spirit Realm.

We landed pretty smoothly. After I climbed down, I stretched for a few minutes trying to get my legs to move as they typically should. The saddles helped, but being on the back of a dragon for hours still made me feel so stiff in my legs and back. Once I was able, I walked to the front of the dragon I rode.

"I know you can't respond to me in dragon form in a way I can understand," I said, "but thank you so much for letting me ride on you."

The dragon nodded and brought their face down closer to mine and lightly nudged me with the top of their head, their feathers tickling my face. I laughed for a moment and gently patted the dragon's cheek area. I could see their eyes were a mixed swirl of soft silver and a moss green.

"I hope one day I will get to meet you again," I said.

The dragon again nodded and then slowly backed away from me. With only a few hard flaps of their wings, they were moving further and further up in the air, then started flying away. It was only a matter of moments before I could no longer see the dragon in the sky.

All the others had landed and their dragons had taken off. It looked like everyone was taking a few moments to move around and stretch out like I did. I wouldn't think riding a dragon would be tiring, but the whole flight I had to make sure to have my legs tight enough to keep me in the saddle and not fall off. I grabbed my bag and slung it over my shoulders and walked over to help everyone else collect their things.

"That was one of the most amazing things I think I have ever done in my entire life!" Emryleia said, excited.

"It does rank up there, doesn't it?" I asked with a smile.

"I knew there were dragons and dragon riders long ago, but I never imagined that I would be one of them!"

"I didn't think I would be either, Em," I said. "Maybe we'll get lucky and get to go again, but maybe it'll be for something a little more…"

"Less impending possibility for death?" she asked with her head tilted to the side and her eyebrows raised.

I smiled and nodded my head. "Yeah, that about sums it up!"

"Are you both ready for a short trek?" Iclyn said, bringing me back to wonder what we were doing here.

"I am ready," I said, "but if I was right in what I saw up there, why did we land here on this island and not a bit further away on what looked like the Blackened Forest?"

"I don't know, Ny," Iclyn said. "When I set everything up, that was where we were supposed to land."

"I can tell you," a faint voice said from the edge of the trees.

I looked over and saw a familiar-looking pixie hovering in the air, their wings beating and keeping them in place.

"Hello," I said as I walked closer, with my right hand resting on Klaw, still unable to place where I knew the pixie from. "Who are you?"

"I am Call," he said, tipping his head to the side. "You once knew me as Callya."

"Oh, that's right," I said, it dawning on me where I knew them before. "I had met you and your twin, Ayllac. I am so sorry I didn't not recognize you."

"It has been over a Leaf Year since you have seen me," he said with a deeper voice than I recalled.

"Yes it has," I said. "What are you and all of us doing here though?"

"This is my home," Call said. "My sister and I received a message and came back here a while ago and have been waiting for you to arrive."

"How did you know we would be coming here? That wasn't what we were planning on," Iclyn asked, and I heard the suspicion growing in her voice.

He took a deep breath. "I know this will be hard to understand, but when… a friend arrived on the island a while ago, my sister and I were contacted to come back and help them, as they had been hurt. When we heard of your movement from the underwater city, we had some pixies meet up with the dragons flying you to have you come here."

"But why?" Emryleia asked.

"Because we do not know if we can save our friend," he said.

"And you think we can help?" Koyvean asked.

"No," said Domi, "I don't think that is it, is it, Call?"

"It is not it," he said with sadness in his voice.

"Then what is it?" I asked.

"The friend," he said with his voice shaking, "the friend is Rowzey."

"What?" I said, almost shouting. "Rowzey is here? And she's dying?"

"She will be angry with us for bringing you here, I am afraid," Call said, "but we believe that you would want to see her before she passes on."

"Of course I want to see her," I said, tears streaming down my face. *Rowzey can't die, she just can't*, I thought.

"Then please, follow me," Call said as he turned and flew off down an overgrown pathway.

I rushed after him, not wanting to get lost. The path was hard to follow without tripping. I felt the sting of a branch as it hit my cheek. After a moment I could feel something dripping down my face. I reached up and felt something wet on my hand and when I looked I could see I was bleeding where the branch hit me. I didn't care though, I needed to get to Rowzey. She couldn't die, not now. She was the only mother I really ever knew. I will not lose her!

"Ny! Nyrieve!" I heard shouted out behind me, but I didn't stop. I trusted Call and believed him when he said Rowzey was here. He was here when I was born, and Rowzey trusted him and his sister with everything, so why shouldn't I?

It felt like I had been running forever when the pixie finally started to slow down and turned back to check and see if I was there. "Nyrieve, are you okay?" Call asked.

"I am fine. Where's Rowzey?" I asked, out of breath. I didn't remember the last time I had run for so long without stopping.

"She is just over this way, but I need to warn you…"

"Warn me what?" I asked, hearing my fellow Drayks starting to catch up.

"Rowzey… she doesn't seem fully herself right now, so you have to be easy with her. You don't want to overwhelm her with questions right away, just take your time. I know you want to know where she has been and what has happened, but just try to…"

"Thank you, Call, for the warning," I said as my breath started to even out again.

"Okay, follow me. We are almost there," he said as he turned and flew more slowly.

After a couple of minutes, we entered a clearing in the woods with what looked like a tiny village. It had a few larger houses, but there were hundreds of tiny houses that hung from the trees. Most of the buildings, my size and pixie-sized ones, looked old and abandoned. I could see a few other pixies flitting around to different houses or off to the woods.

Call stopped in front of the door to one of the larger houses and turned to me. "She is in here."

"Nyrieve," I heard Iclyn say from behind me, "you need to stop right now and wait a minute."

"I need to see Rowzey, Iclyn."

"I understand that, and I won't stop you from it. I know you trust Call, and I remember him too, well, as he was before. And I know Rowzey trusted him and his sister greatly. I just ask that you please give us a moment to check around outside and make sure it is safe."

I wanted to tell her no and just rush in the door, but she was right. I needed to have more caution, and these women had risked their lives to be here with me. "I am sorry, everyone, I shouldn't have run off like that."

"We get it, Ny," Emryleia said. "It's Rowzey, but you need to keep safe as well."

"I will do a sweep of the houses nearby," Koyvean said as she took off.

"I'll check the woods around here," Domi said. "I have read enough about this place that I have a good idea what I should and should not find."

"You've read about this place?" I asked Domi.

She tipped her head to the side and stared at me for a moment. "You don't know where we are, do you?"

I shook my head. "No, just an island near the Blackened Forest."

"Nyrieve," Domi said softly, "this island is Troxeon… the island where you were born."

"What?" I said, shocked, taking a quick second glance at everything. "I didn't realize… I mean, I knew I was born on an island, but…"

Iclyn looked around with surprise on her face. "I didn't realize this was that island either. With Koyvean checking the houses and Domi going to check the forest, I will stay outside the building to keep watch. You go in and see Rowzey. If you need me, just yell, okay?"

"Yes," I squeaked out. I was trying to process that this was my birthplace and that Rowzey was in the building in front of me.

"It's okay, Ny," Em said, patting my arm. "I'll come in with you to see Rowzey."

Call looked at both of us, and Em nodded to him to go ahead. He must have used some sort of magyc to open the door, because he didn't touch the handle at all. I took a deep breath and followed him inside.

The smell was the first thing that hit me as I stepped inside. It was sickeningly sweet and yet foul at the same time. I knew right then that whatever was wrong with

Rowzey wasn't good.

I followed Call back towards a bedroom, and lying on the bed was Rowzey. Her hair was laid about her all clean and had fresh flowers placed in it. I could only guess the pixies did that to try to help cover the smell coming off of Rowzey. Her face was so pale, it didn't look like she had much color left. Her eyes were closed and her cheeks looked sunken in, as if she had not eaten in months.

I stepped closer to the bed and sat down on the chair right next to it. I slowly and gently took Rowzey's cool hand in mine and her eyes opened. I couldn't help but smile at her, I was so glad to see her and be here with her.

"Rowzey?" I said.

"I's Rowzey," she said with a chuckle. "I might be in this bed, but I's still know who I's is."

"Of course you do," I said as tears started falling down my cheeks and I could feel the sting of the salt in my tears on my cut cheek.

"Now what did yous get into, Ny? Yous gone and gotten cut on yous pretty face."

"It's okay," I said, "I just lost a big battle with a small sapling."

She chuckled and squeezed my hand. "I's sure have missed yous."

"I have missed you too, Rowzey."

"I's knew yous would be alive. I's told Baysil and Kal yous would be fine, but not sure they believed it."

"You always know everything, don't you, Rowzey?" I asked, wanting to know more but remembering what Call said.

"I's usually do," she said. "I's know yous are worried about them, but when I's left, they were alive, Ny."

I felt my heart skip with joy knowing they both could really still be alive. "I am glad to hear that, Rowzey. How did you get here though?"

"Baysil told me I's needed to remember my promise to leave if something happened. I's didn't want to leave them, but a promise is a promise."

"How did you escape?"

"They seemed to be curious about me. They said they thought I's wasn't something they knew. And because I's was old, they kept me in that tree house yous stayed in. There was always a guard, at each door, except the balconies from the rooms."

"They didn't have any idea that you could just fly away, did they, Rowzey?" I said with a side smile.

"No, they didn't. Yous would think with yous just disappearing like yous did, they would have kept a better watch on me, but they didn't."

"How long before you were able to escape?"

"I's had to wait at least a fortnight. It seemed after that long of me just shuffling around the house, they didn't think I's would try anything or be dangerous."

"They were wrong, weren't they?"

"Yes, they were," she said with a laugh. "One night, after it became dark, I's went out on my balcony. I's had been going out every night, just to build a pattern and make everyone think it was normal. But the last night, I's went out and tried to turn on the balcony, but I's couldn't. There wasn't enough room to change and not be seen."

"What did you do, Rowzey?"

She took a deep breath. "I's jumped."

My eyes got wider. "You jumped that far down?"

"Yes, and unfortunately hurt my leg pretty bad," she said, "but once I's was on the ground, I's grabbed a branch to help me to walk. I made it to the clearing when I's hear a voice speak out to me."

"Oh no, someone saw you?"

"Yes," she said, "it was Quwyst, she helped me, Ny. She picked me up and carried me to that place we went before. They bandaged my leg but did not have any medicines to help. It was enough though. After I's was bandaged up, she took me to a clearing surrounded by trees, she told me I's could change there and no one would see me."

"She knew you were a dragon?"

"She must have. So that is what I's did. I's changed and took off to find yous."

132

"I am so sorry, Rowzey, I was back in the Spirit Realm under the Leaf Day Tree."

"I's knows that now, but I's didn't then. After a couple days traveling only by night, I's ended up on the shore of the Water Realm. I's was getting weaker by the day. I's could find some food and water, but nothing to help the infection. But one day, someone came upon me there in the Water Realm."

"Did they harm you?"

"Oh no, Hyorda and I's go back a long ways."

"Hyorda!"

"Yes, she was someone who know who I's really am, and though she couldn't help me, she managed to get me on a ship that brought me here."

"Why would she do that? I thought she hated everyone that wasn't Lumaryia."

"She knows how to play the long game, Ny," Rowzey said. "She is someone I's fully trust."

I couldn't believe this. Why didn't Rowzey tell me before that this person could be trusted? I thought it was a mean old evil woman, not someone who would help Rowzey and knew about dragons on top of that.

"I am glad she did what she could to get you here," I said.

"I's am too," she said. "I's know the pixies are doing all they can to help, but I's know this isn't something that they can fix."

"Why can't they?" I asked.

"When I's fell and got cut, there was dirt and other things that got into my blood. Without medicine to help, the infection has spread everywhere."

"Is there something they need to help you? Maybe I can find it."

She smiled softly at me. "I's don't know anymore, Ny. But I's got to see yous again, so I's am okay with this."

Call flew to the other side of Rowzey's bed with his twin sister, Ayllac, next to him. "We are not okay with this, Rowzey, and we haven't given up."

"I's know, my little friends, but everyone has to die sometime… Nyvilliry."

"What does that mean?" I asked.

Ayllac spoke up with her soft sweet voice, "It is an old Koneyotta saying. It means 'the only guarantee in life is death.'"

↠17↞

STORYTELLER

"Who's there?" I shouted, looking all around me. I knew I heard something moving in the distance, but now it was silent. I closed my eyes and began to scan the areas around me. I could sense the baby rabbit in its den about twenty paces to my right. To the left there was nothing more than the sap slowly moving through the trees. Then I sensed her. She was about fifty paces behind me, crouched down to the ground and smelling like wildflowers. As I pushed past the scent of the flowers, I could feel her aura. It was bright pink and had little zaps of yellow dancing around it. I knew who was there.

"Zozo?" I asked out loud excitedly.

"How did you know it was me?" she replied.

"Because you are you, and I could sense you."

"You could sense me, dear cousin?" she asked as she stood up and started walking towards me.

I smiled at my beautiful cousin. She was a similar height to me and had long wavy pink hair with dark strands of red mixed throughout. Her spiral eyes sparkled in the sunlight of the same pink as in her hair and eyebrows, as well as a bright yellow gold swirl.

"I have always been able to sense you, Zozinyal," I said, giving her a big hug.

"It is so good to see you, Cuzzy!" she said, squeezing me tight.

"It has been a while since I saw you last," I said, stepping back. "Where have you been?"

"I went on an adventure to see if I could find some more artifacts for the festival."

"And did you?" I asked, curious.

"I did, actually," she said, sounding distraught.

"What did you find?"

"It was some dragon bones… and a dragon skull," she said somberly.

"Where in Iryvalya did you find those?"

"It was on a small island I happened upon," she said. "It was very strange, Cuzzy. I was exploring throughout a forest that looked like it was burned to the ground, perhaps during one of the battles long ago, but in the middle, where the clearing was, I came across the bones. It didn't look like they were buried or anything, just left out for all of Iryvalya to witness. It looked almost like maybe it wasn't destroyed in any battle but purposely burned to the ground."

"That is odd," I said, thinking back on all my studies of the dragons. "It almost sounds like it might be the remains from a pyre funeral… but for a dragon perhaps?"

"It is possible. There isn't much that would shock me," she said.

"Did you bring it back here?" I asked.

"Yes, my children were with me. They helped clear the debris away and collect everything we could find. I think the forest might have been inhabited by pixies once upon a time as well."

"Why would you think that?" I asked, curious.

"My eldest said while they were surveying the area around the forest, they believe they saw what might have been an old pixie house up in the trees."

"That is interesting. It is too bad there were no pixies there to ask what happened."

"That was my thought as well."

"You'll have to show me the island on a map when we get back to the manor. I think my parents had at least a hundred of them of all of Iryvalya."

"Sounds good to me," she said with a smile. "So what is it you are doing out here exactly?"

I laughed. "Would you believe me that I was waiting for you?"

She laughed even harder. "Oh, Cuzzy, I know you can sense me, but even you are not able to see into the future like that!"

"You're right, Zozo, I am not quite that good… at least not as good as I was in my youth!"

"You are full of it," she said with a smile. "I know you used to get little glimpses

136

of what might come, but unless things have changed, you never had control over it like that."

"No, that part has not changed," I said. "The truth is, I was thinking about this old little island here, and wondering if it was time to…"

"To open it up for everyone to come see?"

"You know me well, Zozo," I said. "My parents loved turning this tiny island into their little house away from… everyone and everything."

"You wouldn't think it would have been such a safe haven with the village only a small bridge and a few steps away."

"True, but I think because of everything the people of the village went through over the years, they tended to just leave each other be. It is one of the few places that hasn't been seen or touched by anyone outside our bloodlines."

"What does your brother think?"

"He, like me, is torn. We want to ensure the remembrance of the places and people here, and it wasn't always our land. Long before us, it was a place where the children from the old manor would play, along with the village children. As my mom always said, 'Our family is only a small part of all those who tried to fight for Iryvalya, and it's our duty to help all parts be remembered…' but this place…" I said, looking around, remembering those moments in childhood where we would come to this little island and get to play without anyone bothering us or visiting the area just to explore old ruins, we'd just get to listen to my parents and Zozo's parents tell stories of people, many long since gone, and those who fought for Iryvalya and gave their lives to try to bring our world to peace. It was like them telling us about those people kept them alive somehow through the memories. I didn't understand it either when I was a child, but I do now."

"I know, Cuzzy," Zozo said. "I remember when my parents would come stay with yours in the village and we'd spend so much time out here playing just the two of us."

"Those were great times. We were safe and so far away from all the troubles in the world."

"Then perhaps it would be best, for now, to keep this place as it is, just for the bloodlines. Your parents worked so hard to rebuild a new manor for orphans and then this place, maybe it should be just a place for those of us who understand that the stories we were taught were so much more than just stories, they were people's lives."

"I think you are right, Zozo… One day this place will be something to share, but maybe not just yet."

"Yeah, just not yet, Cuzzy," she said, giving me a hug.

"Shall we go back to the manor and get something to eat?" I asked.

"You know it," Zozo said. "Hey, don't you have a recipe book from Rowzey still? I could have sworn I saw it here somewhere once before. I remember as a kid it was a light pink color."

"Of course I have it. Actually, I think I have all of them. They were found by my mother when she had gone through the old manor to draw the design to make a new manor. She wanted to see if she could get it as close to what the original one might have looked like. She always took such good care of the cookbooks. She knew they must have meant a lot to Rowzey, especially for her to have hidden them so well to survive so much destruction. My brother, I believe, has been using them all week to make different dishes that he thinks would be good for the festival. I have been sneaking samples whenever I can!"

"Oh, I haven't seen your brother in years. It will be good to spend this time with family, and if he can cook anything at all like your father, we will all be in for some full bellies!"

"Let's go find him, Zozo, and enjoy some food. We still have a few days until the festival," I said as we started heading back to the manor, "but I feel like I have nothing ready."

"Oh, you don't need to worry so much, Cuzzy. I am here, your brother is here, and I have a sneaking suspicion that there will be more help as the days go on."

I squinted at my cousin. "What do you know that I do not?"

She smiled back at me. "I have no idea what you are talking about. I am just figuring we should remember what your mother always would tell us…"

"I do not know how that would apply here," I said, confused.

"Cuzzy, just remember to be the spark." She giggled at me.

"I am trying to, but without more information I can't be the spark!" I said back, laughing at her, knowing she said all she was going to at that point.

"You'll get more information when you need it! Now let's go get some food!"

ᘓ18ᘔ

JOYNOX

"This is crazy," I said quietly to Hyorda.

"Sometimes crazy is exactly what you need," they said, "but it just might work."

"I understand that, but if we go to the Lumaryia council with this request, they will no doubt question my intentions and loyalties."

"Yes, they would. However, I will ensure that it won't look like your idea to go. I will not make it obvious. You will just need to trust me."

I cannot believe I am working with and actually do trust Hyorda, but for some reason, I do.

"Okay, I will do it."

"Good, the council is set to meet in a few minutes. I will head there now and wait for you inside. Just remember, no matter what I say, hold fast in our plan."

"I will."

Hyorda rushed out of my office and left me there to sit in silence trying to figure out how I could convince them of our plan. At best they'll think nothing of it and agree. Worst case, they'll think I am a traitor and have me executed.

It was now or never, and I didn't want to rush and attract any attention to myself. I checked myself in the looking glass and made sure I looked in order. I stepped outside my office and saw the worried look on Brydetor's face.

"Joynox, sir?" he asked.

"Yes," I said, trying to sound normal and not as stressed as I am.

"I don't know what is going on with you and Hyorda," he said softly, "but please, sir, whatever you are doing, be careful."

"I don't know what you—"

"Sir, I have worked with you for years," he interrupted, "and while I know you are blind to a lot of things, especially when it comes to others' feelings, I am not. I know whatever you are doing, it is either because you believe in it or you are being forced. I don't want to see you harmed."

I felt confused by what he said. What did he think I was blind to?

"Brydetor, I appreciate your concern for my well-being, I truly do, and would love to hear what it is you think I have been blind to, but—"

"To me," he said loudly.

"What am I blind to with you?" I asked, feeling truly confused and also wanting to move this along so I could get to the council without rushing.

"You have always been in love with Arnayx. It is plain for everyone to see, but have you never once thought that maybe there is another person in this world you could love?"

"What? I am not in love with— I mean, that is crazy. He has a family and I just… I just… I."

"You just? You just are too blind to see I have not worked for you just because it is a wonderful job and I enjoy everything about it. I do it because I am in love with you and have been for years… but you cannot see past him."

"Bry," I said, finally understanding what he was saying, "I am sorry if I have been blind. I didn't look at you, or anyone else, because I didn't want to be hurt again. It has just been easier to not… try not to love anyone. If I don't, then I cannot get hurt yet again."

"Maybe one day you would realize that not everyone would hurt you or turn you away."

I stood there, not sure what the right thing to say was. Had I thought about Brydetor in a loving way before, of course, but as I always do, I had pushed those thoughts away and kept my focus on my work and trying to do what was good for Iryvalya.

"Look, Bry, I… I want to continue this discussion with you, I truly do, but I have to go to the council's meeting now. Please do not think this is because of you or a sign that I am not interested in you, I just… I have to focus on what is next right now and maybe… don't know, maybe once things, I don't know, settle, we could finish this conversation?"

His face was somber and voice flat as he said, "Go do what it is you always have to do, sir. I will be here… working."

I closed my eyes for a minute and responded, "I hope you will be here." I quickly turned and walked out the door, heading to the council chambers. My heart was pounding so hard I could feel it in my eyes. I know Bry had no idea what I was about to do, but the timing of this couldn't have been worse. I didn't want him to think I didn't care for him, but right now I needed to do what was right, even if it was a risk to my own possible happiness once again to make sure Iryvalya might find happiness as a whole.

☙

"Welcome, Joynox," Hyleia said. "I thought you would have been here earlier when we started."

"Yes, I am sorry," I said, fumbling a bit. "I had an unexpected issue come up when I was on my way. My apologies to the rest of the council."

"It isn't much of a council today, Joynox," Hyleia replied. "Hyorda and I were just discussing the absence of you as well as our other two missing council members."

"Shall we wait for them?" I asked, catching a small smirk from Hyorda.

"No, no," Hyleia responded. "Apparently we three will be the only ones in attendance today. The others apparently have come down with an illness of some sort and cannot attend. Food poisoning or something, their assistants said."

Hyorda sighed. "That is why I try to prepare all my own meals. I know how to cook things to not get ill from them."

Hyleia almost rolled her eyes at Hyorda, but instead closed them and stated, "Not everyone is as talented as you are in the kitchens, Hyorda."

"No, they are not," Hyorda replied arrogantly.

"If it is just the three of us today," I said, "should we just cancel or…"

"No, no," Hyleia said, "there are a few matters for which the timing is important, so let's just try to get through it all as quickly as possible and then we can leave anything else until the next meeting."

"Okay," I said. "What is up first?"

The three of us had gone over about ten different issues, from people needing more food to others wanting us to do more about the low conception rates that were still happening. Finally the issue I was waiting for was brought up.

"The last thing I see on the list," Hyleia said, "looks to be there was yet another report of a—" Hyleia laughed out loud. "You won't believe it. A dragon!"

Hyorda and I joined in the laughter together.

"That is absolutely ridiculous," Hyorda said. "Dragons have been gone for centuries. I do not understand how people can keep claiming to see something that no longer exists."

"Yes," I said, "this seems quite silly. Where is someone claiming they saw the dragon this time?"

"Somewhere on the northeastern shores of the Water Realm, it says," Hyleia said. "I do not want to waste our time doing a search for nothing. Shall we just toss this and call it a day?"

Hyorda responded, "While I do agree that this is a waste of time, we all know our job is to investigate everything that comes before the council. Now I am too old to go traipsing around the realm just to see nothing. Hyleia, I believe you said the other day you have been busy with a new art piece you have been working on. Is that correct?"

Hyleia looked surprised. "Yes, Hyorda, I have been working on something. It is getting close to completion."

"Then I suggest, Joynox, you go and take a look around that part of the realm to see if there is any validity to this claim. You do not have a family or children to attend to."

Even though I knew this was part of the plan to get me out of the Realm, the words stung with truth. "Yes, you are correct, I have nothing much keeping me busy. I can go do a search."

"Then it is settled," Hyorda said, standing up. "I am weary and would like to go back to my chambers for some rest. Joynox, why don't you head out in the morning and try to be back within a fortnight."

"Do you really think it'd take him a whole fortnight to find nothing?"

"No, I don't, I think it'll only take him leaving Noygandia to see there is nothing more than birds in the sky. However, if he leaves and comes right back, no one will believe he did a thorough job checking into it."

I interjected, "Hyorda is right, Hyleia. If we do not take it seriously enough, the Klayn will stop having faith in the council and not trust that we are following up on their concerns. It has been a while since I had a vacation of sorts, and I have always enjoyed camping out. I will look at it as a business vacation then."

"Too bad Arnayx is still gone," Hyleia said. "You both always loved going camping throughout the realm together."

"Yes, I would have enjoyed his company," I said. "However, since this will be on official council business, it is best if I go alone."

"Then it is all settled," Hyorda said as they started to exit the room. "Be careful out there, Joynox. You never know, maybe a dragon is out there waiting for you!"

I could hear Hyorda laughing as they walked down the hallway. I turned to Hyleia and she said, "I feel like that was more creepy than when Hyorda is just silent."

"You and me both," I said, happy to see the plan Hyorda came up with working.

"Are you sure you don't want someone to go with you? I mean, I could pack some things and go."

"Thank you for the offer, but with two council members sick and me gone to search for the long-lost dragon, if you came with me, it would only leave Hyorda here to make decisions for everyone. That doesn't sit well with me."

"I couldn't agree more with you," Hyleia said. "I hope you have a safe little journey and enjoy the time away."

"Thanks," I said with a smile, "I am sure I'll be back with a lot of nothing to share."

When I got back to my office, Brydetor was gone. "Damn it," I said out loud.

"Damn what exactly?" I heard Hyorda say past my private office door. I stepped in and saw them sitting relaxed across from my desk.

"Nothing," I said, walking around and sitting down behind my desk. "I think things went well. I did not think it would have gone that smoothly, guess it is good luck to us that two had food poisoning."

"Luck, you call it?"

"What would you call it?"

"Strategy."

"Wait, you gave them food poisoning?"

"No, it was regular poisoning, but they thought it was from food."

"When? How?"

"The details of that are not important. Besides, the less you know the better."

"Fair enough," I said, raising my hands up at her. "Now I need to get to my house and pack just enough to not raise any suspicions. I don't think I'll be back in a fortnight."

"No, you most definitely will not," Hyorda said. "Once you fail to return, the rest of the council will be wanting to search your office and home for any insight as to where you've gone and why. Anything you cannot take with you that you need protected, put it all together in your living room tonight. I will pick it up shortly after you leave and hide it."

"Thank you," I said, surprised at the offer. "I really appreciate that."

"I am not as horrible as everyone thinks I am," Hyorda said. "It is just the roll I play. I have found over the years that it is much easier to have people fear you and never expect anything good from you than to be liked and have people disappointed in you when you do not live up to their expectations."

"Isn't it lonely though?"

"Very," they said solemnly, "though it has given me the opportunity to do things like this, to try to help heal our world instead of continuing to tear it apart."

"I wish I would have known this earlier," I said.

"Why? Would you have told me about Arnayx being Nyrieve's father?"

"Wait, how did you know that?"

"People assume because I am old I am hard of hearing or slow to move… It is best to keep it that way."

"That doesn't answer my question."

"When Nyrieve visited her father and they snuck out through that tunnel in his home, I was there on the other side, disguised, and listened. I could see the love he has for his daughters, both of them. I even could see the love he has for the other daughter of his wife. Arnayx has always been a good and honorable man, very similar to his grandfather."

"You and his grandfather, you were friends?"

"More than that for many years…"

"Then why?"

"Why didn't we tye? Because his family and my family didn't agree to it. My parents wanted me to be with someone whose family was more powerful and could lead the Klayn and take their spot on the council."

"But I didn't think you ever were tyed to anyone."

"I wasn't. After they turned down the person I loved, I then turned down every suiter they brought forward to me. It didn't matter who it was or from what family they ascended. If my flat-out refusals didn't work, then my attitude and demeanor was usually enough to push them away before long. Eventually my parents stopped trying, and I just enjoyed watching Arnayx's family line grow and change. When he left for a short time, when Nyrieve was born, I thought to myself, *Good for him. He is following his heart.* Even if it didn't work out for him and Osidya, they at least had the chance to try, even if it was only for a short time. And a wonderful thing came out of their union, the Bringer of Peace."

"So many people underestimate you, Hyorda," I said. "I am sorry I was one of them."

"It is okay, Joynox," they said with a smile. "In the end, I am doing what I choose."

"When this is all over," I said, "and Nyrieve brings Iryvalya back together, I would like it if you would be part of my family."

Hyorda looked confused and then stunned. "I… I do not know what to say, Joynox… That is a very kind offer, and if you make it back safe and the council doesn't figure out my proclivities to use against me, it would be my honor."

I stood up and walked around my desk and gave Hyorda a big hug. I could feel them tense up at first, but then slowly relax and hug me back.

146

"Now, now, you need to ease up on the mushy stuff with me and go get yourself packed to head out," they said, patting my back.

"I will do that," I said, righting myself. "Would you like an escort back to your house?"

"No thank you, I have a few things I need to finish up here. Just do me a couple favors."

"What is that?"

"One, before you leave Noygandia, tell that handsome assistant of yours that you do have feelings for him too. I have seen the way you have looked at each other for years. I do not think you ever allowed yourself to even imagine a life with anyone else in it, but I think the two of you could have a really good chance together."

I smiled, thinking of the idea of spending time with Brydetor away from this office, maybe cooking together in my home or traveling to see parts of Iryvalya. "I will do that, Hyorda. And what is the other thing?"

"When you see the Bringer of Peace again, please tell her I really do have old elf artifacts I think she would find most interesting. And I can promise they are not cursed, as you had thought they could be."

"I am sorry I thought that of you," I said softly.

"I'm not," they said. "It is how I needed to be seen. Oh, and one last thing before you leave, Joynox."

"Yes?"

"Volnyri!"

∞19∞

NYRIEVE

"Ny, it has already been over a week we have been here," Koyvean said. "I know you want to help Rowzey, but we do have the other matter to attend to."

"I know," I said with my head buried in my hands. "I just don't know what I should do…"

"I understand that, but there doesn't seem to be anything else we can do," she said. "Domi tried to figure out a way to save her, but even she is stumped."

"I thought for sure there would have been something in my pack from Lydorea that would have helped Rowzey. I feel like I have failed her. She wouldn't have needed to escape the Fire Realm if it wasn't for me."

"You know that isn't the case," Iclyn said, sitting next to me. "Rowzey would have gone anywhere and everywhere you went, Ny. You were like her own child, and there is nothing that would have kept her from going where you went."

The door to the house we were staying in slammed open. "I think I have an idea to maybe save Rowzey," Emryleia shouted as she rushed into the room.

"What?" I asked eagerly.

"I think if we can somehow get Rowzey back to the Spirit Realm, one of the dragons there must know of a way to help her."

"But how do we get her back to the Spirit Realm?" I asked.

"Like you did, Ny, portal her back there."

"But I don't know how to portal with someone," I said.

"Domi should know, shouldn't she?"

"She would, but she is basically in hiding from the other Valyas."

Emryleia sighed. "I just thought if it could save Rowzey, it'd be worth the risk."

"I know, and I thought that too, but I feel like we need Domi as well. I just, I don't know what to do or think."

"I'm going to go find Domi and see if there is another way to portal Rowzey or

148

something," she said. "There has to be something we can do."

Emryleia rushed back out the door. I stood up and walked to the door. "I am going to go spend some time with Rowzey. I'll be back in a while."

I opened the door and crossed over to the house Rowzey was in. I slowly and quietly opened the door and peeked inside. No one else was in the house for once. Typically there was always a pixie or ten flitting around the room. Right now it was just Rowzey, and as I stepped inside the room, her eyes opened and met mine.

"I'm sorry, Rowzey, I didn't mean to wake you."

"I's wasn't sleeping, Ny," she said. "I's was just thinking about the last time I's was here with yous in Troxeon."

"When I was born?"

"Yes," she said. "I's remember the hate and anger Rievenya was feeling. I's could sense it coming off of her like waves on the shore. She was taught to hate from an early age."

"But she changed her mind in the end…"

"No, yous changed her mind, Ny," she said, patting my hand.

"I was only a baby. There wasn't anything I could have done or said then."

"And yet, here we are," she said. "I's know yous have further to go with your journey, and even if yous bring our world into peace, yous will have more life to live."

"We don't know that, or anything, for that matter," I said. "There is too much unknown… I don't know if I can get the people of the Klayns to agree on something, especially with it coming from some mixed-blood elf. I always knew I'd likely never convince the leaders of the Klayns, but without the people listening, why even try? It feels like this is all for nothing."

"Ny, I's need yous to do something for me."

"Anything, Rowzey. What is it?"

"There is a place on the island here I's want yous to visit. The pixies are aware of the spot's existence, but that is it. I's am sure the Valya might know too, but it's not a place I's ever shared with another."

"Why do you want me to go to this place?"

"Yous will know when yous get there," she said, placing something in my hand.

149

I turned my hand to see a small stone with a spiral carved into the middle of it.

"What is this?"

"It is an enchanted iryrock. There are many stones like this around Iryvalya, and it's said if yous come across one, it will help guide yous."

"What does that mean?"

"I's always thought it was like a good luck charm, but it's so much more than that, Ny. It, like the irybugs, are messages from Iryvalya herself. We's might not always understand what it is trying to tell us, but eventually yous figure it out. This one in particular is special. It will take yous to a place I's spent a lot of time at. When yous are there, yous will get an opportunity to talk to those yous thought yous have lost. One day, yous will be able to go there and talk to me."

"Are you saying this will lead me to a place where I can speak to the dead?" I asked, confused.

"No, I's am saying this will lead yous to a place where yous can communicate with those who have passed that want to communicate with yous."

"What is the difference?"

"Not all those who have passed want to communicate with those left behind. And I's don't know if that is by their choice or because maybe they have moved on or changed energy forms... No one really knows until yous pass."

"Couldn't you just ask one of them that have communicated with you?"

"They won't answer that question... though I's have asked for years... The only thing anyone ever says is that the next step isn't scary, it's just the next step."

"Who is it you want me to go communicate with, Rowzey?"

"Whomever is there wanting to communicate with yous. Please, go now before it gets too dark. Everyone will think yous are still in here with me and leave yous be. I's will try to give yous as much time as I's can to spend some time there."

"How does the iryrock work?"

"Hold it in yous hand. As yous walk, the stone will get warmer if yous are going in the right direction. If it gets cooler, try a different way. Go now, please, Ny. I's need to know yous were able to find this place before I's—"

"Do not say it, Rowzey. We are going to figure out something to help you."

She smiled weakly at me. "I's know yous all will do everything yous can. Go... please."

I leaned over and placed a quick kiss on Rowzey's forehead, took the stone and left the house.

I slowly spun around until I was facing the direction to go deeper into the jungle from where we came into the village, and that was when the stone started to get warmer. I took off quickly in that direction and the warmth of the stone kept constant. I followed the pathway for about thirty minutes and then the stone began to get cooler. I stood still and started turning to the left of me and the stone began to warm up again.

"I guess I'm going off the path then," I said out loud to myself. I checked to make sure Klaw was in position and ready if I needed it and then took off in a light jog toward the direction the stone indicated.

It didn't seem like I was running for long when the trees started to part and in front of me was a pathway that looked as if it was built out of crystals in every color I have ever imagined and then some. There were crystals growing up out of the ground on either side of the pathway. The further I walked, the taller the crystals became. Once they were taller than me, I could see ahead a small spring with trees, plants and flowers all around it. In the middle of the pond was a small patch of land with moss growing all over it. As I stood next to the pond, I looked around and admired the beauty of everything. The crystals growing everywhere and the nature of trees and vines growing next to them. It was so beautiful here. I could hear the water moving. As I looked, I could see water flowing down one of the larger crystals and it feeding into the pond.

The water looked like there were rainbows dancing across the surface. I couldn't tell if it was some sort of optical illusion from the surrounding crystals or something else. There were two larger stones in the pond that led to the little island of moss in the middle. I stepped across them and sat down on it. I ran my fingers across the top of the soft green moss. It felt cool and almost energetic as I traced my fingertips around it.

I closed my eyes, trying to take in all the sounds and smells of this place. I

151

wasn't sure if I really would be able to talk to the dead here, but if this was a place Rowzey wanted me to find, I was glad I was able to do that for her before she was gone.

"Nyrieve?" a familiar voice said to me. I quickly opened my eyes to see sitting on top of the water someone I never thought I'd see again.

"Knarfy?" I said as tears welled up in my eyes.

"She finally shared with you this place, I see," he said, smiling, his face looking just as I saw him last.

"I can't believe you are here!"

"I am and I'm not, Ny," he said. "It is far too complicated to explain, but one day, hopefully a long, long time from now, you will understand it yourself."

"I am so sorry I wasn't there for you when you passed," I said. "I love you and I have been so worried you didn't know it, that I didn't say it enough and that me not being by your side when you died, you might have thought I didn't care."

"Oh, sweet girl," he said, "I know you love me, I always knew. Even now I can feel that love you have. You take it with you everywhere you go, the love for me, for Rowzey, Kylyan and all the family and friends that are in your heart."

"I am so glad you knew… know…"

"It is both, but I understand what you are trying to say."

"Was there something I could have done to help you, Knarfy?"

"No, Ny, it was just my time to go. In the end, Nyvilliry."

"The only guarantee in life is death?" I asked.

"You are very smart, Ny. You listen and remember. Nothing much is as important as remembering something. Things, people, moments… these are what help us to build a life worth living."

"Have you seen Lydorea?"

He sighed. "I did… She isn't here anymore."

"Where did she go?"

"She moved on… She said she knew she has done and prepared for everything she was worried about and moved forward."

"Forward to where?"

"Another one of those things that wouldn't make sense to you now."

"Why haven't you 'moved forward'?"

"I can come here and still see my Rowzey from time to time, though I know she thinks she is getting ready to pass on as well now."

"How did you know that?"

"It is complicated, Ny, but our energies are tied and tethered to one another in life and in death. I can feel her energy and it is fading, slowly, but fading."

"It is my fault, Knarfy," I said, feeling the hot tears pouring now from my eyes.

"No, it is not," he said. "Rowzey came here not long ago, with the help of Call and Ayllac, and she told me everything that had happened. She was so proud of you, for standing up to the elves, and she believed that you had escaped the volcano. I knew you had; otherwise, I would have been sure to meet you while passing. I wouldn't ever want you to be alone in that moment."

"People have died because of me, Knarfy, and now I don't know if… Wait, you would know if someone was gone? Are Baysil and Kaleyna there with you? Did they pass on?"

"You caring about others is just one of the things that make you such an important leader, Ny. I do not have all the answers you want, but what I can tell you is both of them are alive right now."

I took a deep breath and held it for a moment and slowly let it out. "Thank you, I have been so scared… I am still scared, but they are alive… I'm not too late…"

"Yes, they are."

"Thank you, Knarfy," I said. "Thank you for coming to me and telling me that. I wish I could hug you."

"Me too," he said. "I need to go, Ny. There is another here who needs to speak with you. I know one day I will see you again and give you the biggest hug I can muster, but if you get the chance to visit me before that happens here, I would really enjoy that. You are good, Nyrieve. You've always been good. I love you, and please, tell Row that I love her."

"Row?" I asked, realizing he meant Rowzey after I said it, but he was already fading away.

I looked around and saw the sun was beginning to fade behind the moon. As it slowly became darker, the crystals began to glow beautiful shades of green, blue and purple, like the irybugs.

Where Knarfy had appeared, a darker shadow started to form and turned into a strikingly beautiful elf. Her hair was long and thick with large curls. It took me a minute to see the hair was mostly a dark red with many small individual curls of light gold throughout. She looked at me and tipped her head to the side as if checking me over to see if I was the person she had meant to see.

"Nyrieve?" the elf asked, sounding formal.

"Yes," I said. "Who are—" Her widening smile stopped my words.

"I have waited so long for this moment…"

"You have?"

"You do not know what day it is, do you?" she said in a sweet yet raspy voice.

"It is… I mean… I seem to have lost track. Things have been a little…"

"Hectic for you?"

"Yes," I said, still confused. "What day is it to you?"

"Why, it is your Leaf Day. You are nineteen now."

I thought for a moment, from the traveling to Troxeon and the time here trying to help Rowzey, I had completely forgotten my Leaf Day. "I guess it is… How did you know?"

"It was a very special day for me, for a few different reasons."

"What reasons are those?"

"On this day, I made a decision that would forever change my life as I knew it. Some might think I was being selfish, and others might think I was being selfless, but either way, I believe I was doing the right thing. And with you here before me now, I know it was the right thing. While your eyes have changed with the new color, they are still the same. Let me see your wrist please."

I knew right away what she was wanting to see. I held out my right wrist to her and saw her eyes widen when she saw the spiral marking.

"It is darker than I remember, but then again, you were just born when I saw it last."

"Just born?"

"Yes, I was there."

"Who are you?"

She smiled again. "I always thought you'd figure that out right away, but then again, I thought that you would have had your mother in your life more than you have."

"My mother?"

"Yes, I did not foresee her being the type of person she ended up becoming. I hope my absence from her life did not cause that, but the truth is we become who we are meant to be. I didn't always know that before. I always thought I was one type of person and would always be, but in the end, I was someone different, someone I am proud I became."

"And who is that?"

"You haven't figured it out yet?"

I shook my head no, not knowing what else to say. The elf looked familiar and yet like no one I had ever met before.

"Today is your Leaf Day, my sweet Nyrieve, whose name is part my own. Today is also the anniversary of my passing. A special day we share together and one I would not change for anything."

I stared blankly at her and suddenly something clicked. "Are you saying you're... I mean, you are my..."

"Who do you think I am?"

"Aunt Rievenya?"

"Yes, Happy Nineteenth Leaf Day, Nyrieve!"

⳥20ⳃ

NYRIEVE

I didn't know what to say. I just sat there looking across the small distance between Rievenya and myself and wishing I could somehow hug her.

"Nyrieve?" Rievenya asked.

"Yes, I am here, kind of. I am just very surprised and at a loss for words."

"I can imagine," she said sweetly. "I have waited a very long time for this moment. I didn't think it would happen, but Rowzey assured me that one day she would make sure to bring you here. I am sad that she wasn't able to come with you though."

"She has fallen ill from an injury, and I cannot figure out how to help her."

"You cannot, Nyrieve, because you are not of dragon's blood. I believe what ails her could be helped by another dragon."

I looked at her. "Why would you think that?"

"Oh, call it intuition. Sometimes, things like this can only be fixed by your own bloodlines, those who might know you better than you can imagine."

"Thank you," I said softly.

"I didn't help Rowzey," she said. "I am just offering some advice that might help her."

"No, no, not just for that," I said, "but for giving up your life for me."

She smiled softly. "I just wish I wouldn't have cursed you in the first place, then perhaps we'd both be alive today."

"Why did you save me if you were the one who cursed me?"

"I believed my parents my whole life, even when things didn't seem to make sense. Because why would parents ever lie to their child or try to steer them along a path that wasn't good for them? I thought they were right, that you being born could cause more problems for my family than a possible solution. I thought Osidya was acting out of blindness in her love for your father at the time. And maybe she was, but that didn't mean that you were not someone who should be wanted and loved for who you are, not what you could bring to them or anyone else."

"Was it only because I was mixed-blood they wanted me dead?"

"Yes," she said softly. "They are a product of their environment, I'm afraid. They listened to those around them, other people on the Pyrothian Council, and believed you being born could jeopardize their position and power."

"Power..." I said. "Is that all the Klyan leaders care about? Power over others? Can they not see yet that all they are doing is slowly causing the elves to go extinct?"

"You are as smart as I hoped you'd be."

I chuckled. "I don't think I am all that smart, but I try very hard to be observant."

"You are also humble," she said, her smile getting bigger. "Not a trait your mother or I were really taught."

"No, I do not think that is something my mother will ever be."

"How did your interactions with Osidya go?"

"Not well," I said flatly. "She seems quite angry with my existence and that I, well, I used your name in front of the Pyrothian Council and, well, upset her a lot."

"How so?"

I bit my lip, thinking of how bad this might sound to Rievenya. "I announced that I had found out who my mother truly was, and I named you."

"Me?" she gasped with her eyes getting bigger.

"Yes, Osidya was expecting me to name her and then use that to her advantage to try to turn me to take the side of the Pyrothian Klayn."

"That sounds like something my parents would have trained one of us to do, if it would somehow help elevate the family name."

"She was very angry with me," I said. "But I just, I didn't want to be pushed like that or be so closely aligned with her. I am sorry if that was wrong to do."

"I am not upset with any of that, Nyrieve," she said. "I am just sorry that my sister was not the mother you should have had. I know you had others to watch out for you, but it is not quite the same. Though, I had a mother that didn't care about anyone but herself and how she appeared to others, so maybe it was for the best."

157

"Maybe," I said.

"Can I see your hand," she said.

I was confused for a moment, and then remembered I was wearing the ring she had given to Rowzey to give to me. I held my hand out to her and she smiled even bigger.

"I almost forgot what it looked like," Rievenya said. "I had loved wearing it so much."

"I have loved wearing it as well," I said. "Someone gave it to you, right?"

"Cyndorin," she said softly.

"Had you been tyed?"

"We were going to. We had been making plans to get tyed to one another, but…" She took a deep breath and then let it out slowly. "But he was killed in an attack."

"I am so sorry, Aunt Rievenya," I said, imagining the pain she must have felt. It made me think of Kylyan and how we just decided we want to get tyed as well.

"Thank you, Nyrieve, but it was a long time ago and I have had the opportunity to get some closure for that."

"Is he here? With you?"

"In a way," she said. "Again, it is really complicated to explain how things work after we move on from the realm you are in, but there is more to us than just this."

"That makes me feel better knowing something lies beyond when we die."

"It does, but it can be different for each person. Some want to remain close to those still alive, but others are ready to… to not, is the simplest way I can explain it."

"Why did you stay nearby?"

"You, of course," she said, smiling again. "I had hoped that one day I would get to see you and talk to you. I am very grateful that Rowzey made this happen, though I am sorry for what ails her."

"Me too."

"Have you found love, Nyrieve?"

I smiled. "Yes, I believe I have."

"What is their name?"

"His name is Kylyan."

"That is a strong name. Is he an elf or other?"

"He is an elf, a mixed-blood like me."

Her smile became bigger. "That makes me so happy."

"Why is that?"

"I don't know if you have figured it out yet, but our bloodlines do not extend very far anymore because of the limits placed on the Klayns."

"I did, actually, when I visited both realms, I noticed a shortage in children and figured it had to be in part to the limiting of possible partners."

"You are so very smart, my dear," she said. "I am very proud of the elf you have become."

"Thank you. I just hope I can convince the rest of the elves about this and hopefully they will help fight back against the councils."

"I hope you can too, Nyrieve. There is another thing I wanted to discuss with you. Something you might have been told, but I am guessing it is more likely that you have only been told just a little bit about your family's heritage."

"What is that?"

"Before the Pyrothian Elves and the Lumaryia Elves there were just elves. There were issues over things like lands and other more simple items, but what truly broke the two Klayns apart was a couple who were both of great powers. One had more skilled powers with fire and air, while the other was—"

"Stone and water?"

"Yes," she said. "You pick up on things quickly."

"It just made sense."

"There was a big fight between them, because at one point there was a royal family that ruled things in Iryvalya. They worked with the Valya to know and understand what was happening in the world. The two people, they were tyed to one another. One's name was Lumaryia and the other Pyrothian."

"The names of the Klayns?"

"Yes, it is where their names originated. These two people both loved each other fiercely and looked forward to having a family of their own to watch grow.

"They were the saygent of the elves. Their families were so happy to bring them together and combine the two different families into one and hoped it would usher in a continued peace when their children would create their own families and hopefully share their powers.

"The saygent would end up having no children. They tried, but it just did not happen. Each one blamed the other, both believing it had something to do with the other one's powers somehow hindering it.

"After years of ruling together peacefully, the inability to have children caused them to start hating one another, each thinking they knew what was best for Iryvalya and the elves. Both were wrong.

"Eventually they split apart, destroying the royal family and all it had represented. We descended from Pyrothian, and that's why we still had been referred to as royals, and titles of Your Highness sometimes."

"How did you learn all this?" I asked.

"When I was young, I liked to sneak off to the library and read everything I could about Iryvalya in hopes of being one of the next leaders as a Pyrothian Elf. My thought was, if I knew all the past mistakes that were made, I wouldn't repeat them. When I learned of what happened, I blamed the Lumaryia Elves only, because that is what I was raised to believe.

"I still believed it when I came to this island for your birth, and when I gave your mother the poison that would kill you. I had read in the different books about a Bringer of Peace. About a person who could unite the Klayns together, and thought it was wishful thinking or even a joke. Something to give the lower-class elves hope for a better life one day, but I was raised to know that only the deserving had a better life. Again, I was wrong.

"The moment I saw your beautiful little face and big violet eyes, I knew I had been wrong about so many things. Then I saw the mark on your wrist, and I knew you would be the Bringer of Peace. If it wasn't for Rowzey though, you would have died. She reminded me that there was a way to save you from the curse."

"By giving your life in return?"

"Yes, and I am so glad I did."

"You are?" I asked, surprised.

"Oh yes, Nyrieve, you are giving more hope to Iryvalya than it has had in hundreds of years. You are making people think about each other and not just themselves. That is what a true leader is. A true saygent."

"I am not sure I want to be a 'saygent'," I said.

"I understand that, but just the same, you truly are."

"It doesn't really change anything though. Not everyone will care or want to listen to me."

"I know, but I think there is a way to help open up people's eyes to listen to you."

"How?"

She told me of a plan she had thought of over the years, an idea that had even crossed my mind once or twice, but not something I ever thought would work. Rievenya believed that it had merit and could work to help gather supporters to turn against the Klayns and become one people again.

"This is a crazy idea," I said. "It will put so many at risk."

"Yes, it will. But without the risk, we cannot hope for the reward."

"I know, but…"

"But you are worried for those you care about, and that is good. You should always think of others and weigh that against actions you feel need to be taken. Sometimes people will be upset or even hurt, but it is always important to consider the many over the few. For far too long the few have ruled over the majority and it hasn't worked. Perhaps this will work."

"I hope so, Aunt Rievenya."

She took another deep breath. "The hour is getting late, and I am sure those you traveled here with will be looking for you."

"Can I ask you something before you leave?"

"Anything at all."

"When I traveled to the Leaf Day Tree, I found my leaf, and it was covered by your fallen leaf. Do you know how that happened?"

She tilted her head to the side. "I do not know that, Nyrieve, but it makes me happy it did. I wish I was there, able to help you and protect you."

"You have. Without you, someone else would have tried to kill me. You made the ultimate sacrifice to ensure my existence. I cannot be more grateful for that."

"Can I ask you one favor, niece?"

"Of course," I said, curious. "What is that?"

"One day, even if it is many years from now, please come here again and see me once more. I would love to see you and know you have gotten the chance to live your life the way you wish to, and if you have children, I'd love to learn about them. Knowing our family line, as bad as it might have been for a while, became something so much better."

"I promise you, Aunt Rievenya, I will come back."

"Thank you, and one more thing. The next time you see my sister, tell her 'Embers says you need to listen and follow her namesake.'"

"Embers?"

"A nickname she had given me once as children, because no matter how much I might have cooled off after an argument, I would still have 'Embers' burning, waiting to be reignited."

"I will do that. Thank you again, Aunt Rievenya, for everything."

Slowly she began to fade away like mist. I didn't want her to leave. I wanted to talk to her more, but I knew I needed to get back. I quickly got up, stretched my legs out and then ran all the way back to the village as quickly as I could.

When I reached the village, it was dark, minus the glow from the moon. I don't know how I found my way back so quickly without getting lost, but I just trusted my instincts. I looked around, thinking that something felt wrong. There were no pixies flitting around, and I couldn't see or hear any of my friends. I quickly went into the house we had been staying in. Everything was there as it was when I left, but no one was to be found.

Quickly I ran across to Rowzey's house, hoping she or someone would be able to tell me what happened. Inside the small house was Rowzey and all my friends along with many pixies staring at me.

"What is going on here?" I asked, out of breath.

"Did yous honestly think I's could ever forget yous Leaf Day?" Rowzey said with more energy in her voice than she had earlier.

"I... I honestly had forgotten until a little while ago."

"Well, Ny," Emryleia said, moving past Iclyn, carrying a small cake, "we would never forget!"

For a while we all just quietly enjoyed the cake. It was delicious, but not quite as good as if Rowzey had been able to make it herself.

"Did yous enjoy yous walk, Ny?" Rowzey finally asked.

"I did. I learned a lot, actually."

"I's thought yous might."

"And now I have a plan, a way to help us convince the elves to want to follow us and hopefully maybe some of their leaders will too."

"How is that?" Emryleia asked.

"It is a two-fold approach. First is by providing truth to everyone, and the second is showing a united front to provide people with the knowledge that joining us means they will never be alone."

༉21༈

NYRIEVE

"Rowzey," I said, hoping to wake her without startling her.

"Yes, Ny," she said, slowly opening her eyes.

"I wanted to talk to you about who I talked to."

"And who did yous talk to?"

"Knarfy came to me first."

Her smile got bigger. "I's thought he might."

"And then Rievenya."

"That is who I's hoped would talk to yous."

"She had some ideas that I think will help us, the Nomydrac," I said. "And she had an idea for you."

"Oh?"

"She thinks your injuries cannot be healed here, that you need to have help from someone with dragon blood."

Rowzey took a deep breath. "That is what I's have thought as well, Ny, but I's knew this would be a safe place and a place yous needed to come to before it was too late."

"I wish you would have just gone back to the dragons, Rowzey. Your life is more important to me."

"It wasn't just that simple either, Ny," she said. "I's didn't have a way back to the dragons without more people finding out about them. I's couldn't take that risk."

"Well, I have figured out a way to get you back to the dragons so they can help you."

"How?"

"I talked with Domi and she knows another Valya that thinks like her and is tired of not being able to act when they see something happening. They have agreed to portal you back to the Spirit Realm."

"Who?"

"Takyri."

"Ah, I's remember them. They seemed nice enough, but quiet. Are yous sure they can be trusted?"

"I am, but also it is the only chance we have to save your life, Rowzey."

"When will they take me?"

"Once we are done talking. Domi already filled Takyri in on what is going on and what we need to do. They are going to portal you back to the Leaf Day Tree and then get you to Eyree as soon as possible. They have already got a message to Aurilya, and she is going to meet you there."

"But what if I's..."

"No, Rowzey, we are not doing that, because you will get back there and get the help you need and you'll be fine. And one day, a long time from now, you will be cooking things for my kids and telling stories about how you were portaled back to the Spirit Realm."

"I's hope yous are right, Ny..." she said, patting the top of my hand. "I's just have to let yous know though, in case, for my own sake, I's love yous, Ny. Yous have always been like my own daughter and I's am so very proud of yous. This is not a path yous should have had to go down, but I's am glad I's could help every place I's have and I's hope I's can still help more."

"I love you too Rowzey and I appreciate everything you have done for me..."

"Yous have more to say, Ny. Say it."

"I need to ask a favor of you."

"Yes, I's will."

"Will what?"

"I's will convince the dragons it is time to be known and that they need to show full support behind yous, no matter what that might mean for them or the rest of the elves."

"I do not want anyone's blood on my hands, but I don't know if we have much of a choice anymore."

"I's agree, and it is time. We have waited long enough to come out of the shadows and fight for our world as well. If there are Valya that can see it's time to stand up for what's right, then the dragons can too. Yous will have all of the dragons' support. Aurilya will ensure it. I's promise yous that."

"Thank you so much, Rowzey," I said, giving her a big hug. "Just please, promise me you will do everything you can to get well."

"I's promise yous, Ny, and I's will promise yous when yous need it, the dragons will stand by yous side."

⋘⋙

"Call, thank you so much for everything you and Ayllac have done for Rowzey," I said, wishing I could give them both a hug, but knowing I would crush them if I even tried.

"We are always happy to help the Bringer of Peace," Ayllac said, flitting over to stand next to her twin brother.

"I am glad I could see you both before I left," I said.

"I was just gathering some supplies for you to go to the Blackened Forest," she said. "I provided everything to Iclyn and Emryleia. You should have enough food and other necessities for this next part of your journey."

"Thank you so much. Are you both going to remain here on Troxeon?"

"For now," Call said. "But I imagine in the near future we might be making a trip elsewhere."

"If there is ever anything we can do for you, let us know," Ayllac said.

"How would I get a message to you?"

"Just put it out there. Speak out loud that you need us, and Iryvalya will ensure we'll know," she replied.

"I will do that. I really do look forward to seeing you again. Hopefully it'll be under different circumstances."

"We hope so, Nyrieve, or should we say future saygent?" Call asked.

My eyes widened as I quickly looked around, and Iclyn's and Emryleia's eyes got as wide as mine, but they said nothing. Koyvean just stood with a smirk on her face and Domi's face was expressionless.

"I do not know if that is really a good thing to call me. I am not literally a saygent..."

Call smiled and said, "Did you know that, once, a very long time ago, saygents were not really of a specific bloodline? They actually were initially chosen by the people, and saygent was a title they were given. After centuries of different saygents, many people became comfortable with just letting the descendants of those saygents continue to rule. Some of those descendants did amazing, while others not so much."

"I didn't know that."

"I think you will be a wonderful saygent, Nyrieve," Call said.

"As do I," Ayllac said.

Em and Iclyn looked at each other and said in unison, "Us too!"

"You all are crazy," I said.

"We can just put a pin in this conversation, I think," Koyvean said. "Besides, to get this girl to be saygent, we need to win the war, so to speak."

"I agree," I said. "We need to get going to the Blackened Forest."

"One last piece of parting advice, Nyrieve," Ayllac said. "Trust your instincts, even if they go against everything you are being told or think you should do. Things in the Blackened Forest are not always what they seem, and you need to trust your gut over the things you see and hear."

"Thank you, I will try to remember that."

We gathered our belongings and headed towards the beach. When we finally arrived, I saw five small boats waiting for us. The pixies told us they were called kayaks. I had seen some like this before in Cliffside, but never really had the chance to use one for a long period of time. Each of us climbed inside one of the kayaks and pushed off with the paddles. I had never been so far away from land in a single-person boat like this and was feeling a little nervous with each paddle push away. Nervous about Rowzey, what we might find in the Blackened Forest, and mostly about not wanting to let so many people down.

We continued toward the Blackened Forest in silence. Just listening to the paddles splashing in the water. Every once in a while I would glance down into the water, amazed by how clear it was and the sea life that was visible below.

After at least an hour of paddling, I could see a dark haze in the distance. "Is that it?" I asked.

"Yes," Domi replied. "It shouldn't take much longer to get there if the waves and wind keep in our favor. When we arrive, we might want to make camp for the night on the beach. It'll be dark before too long."

"I agree," Iclyn said.

"Same," I said. While I was curious to explore the forest, I also would prefer to do it in the light.

As we approached the island, I noticed that even the beach sand was black. I had never seen a blackened beach like that before. I knew that this wasn't going to be the only thing to surprise me on this island.

When we got as close as we could inside the kayaks, we jumped out and pulled the boats as far onto the beach as we could.

"I think we should tie them off to some of the trees," I said.

"Why?" Iclyn asked.

"In case the tides shift or the waves come crashing in due to a storm," I said, grabbing some rope from the compartment in the kayak. "It looks like there is some rope in mine. Check yours, everyone."

"There is some in mine too," Koyvean said. "I do like the way you're thinking, Ny, very smart. I will tie everyone's kayaks up. You all go ahead and set up a camp for us."

It didn't take long to get some wood from near the edge of the forest to make a fire, and we each set up a blanket to sleep on. We sat around mindlessly talking about things we saw in the water, stories we had heard about the Blackened Forest, things we were missing, like pillows.

After we ate, we all decided to get some rest, and we'd each take a turn keeping watch. Koyvean offered to do the first watch, as usual. I lay down and listened to the waves crashing on the beach and drifted off to sleep.

CRULO

I woke up hearing the waves lapping against the shore. It was still slightly dark out, so I knew I couldn't have been asleep for too long. I looked at the embers cooling where the fire was, and I realized no one else was around me. The blankets were all there, but they were empty. I looked around. Everyone's stuff seemed to be gone, and I couldn't see a trail left by anyone. The kayaks were still tied to the trees, so I knew no one had left by those.

I didn't dare shout out, because wherever they went, I didn't think it was by choice. One of them would have woke me, I was sure of that. I didn't see anything or anyone else on the beach, so I decided the only thing I could do was to enter the Blackened Forest. I didn't think it was wise to head in while it was still so dark, but I really didn't have a choice.

I grabbed my pack and slung it over my shoulders. I reached down and took the latch off of Klaw to make it easily accessible if I needed it. I walked over to the small clearing by the beach and headed into the forest.

I made sure each step was quiet and direct. I didn't want to stumble and draw any attention to myself. Who knows what animals might live here, or even scarier yet, what people. Animals attack for food or fear, but people… they have more reasons, or even scarier, none.

The deeper I went into the forest, the more light came from the sun. The moon must have been moving away, but as it did, I noticed it was getting foggy. From what I could see, the trees appeared to be all black at first, but I stepped closer to one to examine it. It wasn't quite light enough out to see clearly, but I could swear there were thin lines of colors throughout the trunk, almost like veins. When I looked closely at one of the leaves, I noticed the same. It was black, but the veins were different colors. Some leaves were all one color, but others had multiple colors or shades all over them. There wasn't a pattern I could figure out, but it was beautiful.

As I kept walking, I noticed the trail had more twists and turns that didn't make sense. I didn't think I could be going backwards, but I couldn't tell if I was going forward anymore. Every once in a while I would stop and just listen, trying to see if I could hear anyone or anything to tell me what way I should be going.

Ahead of me was just more fog, and now, it seemed like there was even more behind me. I looked around. I couldn't see more than about two feet in front of me. I decided standing still wasn't going to help me, so I just kept walking in the direction I figured was forward, watching each step as there were roots and vines across the path I needed to watch out for.

It felt as if the sun stopped coming out and I couldn't see far enough above to see if there were clouds or something else going on. The air felt thick with water. Suddenly I felt drops of water hitting me. It must be a storm that was covering the sun. It wouldn't help me track anyone, but it might cover the sounds of my movements.

I decided to keep moving forward, and then I saw it. I squinted my eyes to try to see it more clearly, but I couldn't with the fog. I instinctively started to walk fast towards the little blue light I saw. It was on the ground, but it was moving impossibly fast. I had to run to keep up enough to see where it was going. I could feel branches smack up against my arms and pull my hair. I wasn't on the path anymore. I was stumbling over vegetation, trying not to lose the little light.

Somehow this light would surely help me find my friends. It had to. The rain was pouring now. I could hear my boots squish in the mud as I ran, but I didn't stop. I wasn't thinking clearly. All I knew was I needed to reach the light.

That was when the light stopped moving, so I stopped. I watched the light as it moved around slightly side to side and then it disappeared. I slowly walked towards where it had been, but there was nothing there. I leaned down and felt around on the ground, and noticed a small stone next to me. I picked it up and felt a strange texture to it.

For the most part, it was smooth and had rounded edges. In the middle of it, there was dirt and mud, but I could feel it was somehow not part of the stone. I felt around and was able to touch a small puddle of water. I put the stone in it and rubbed away the sediment on it, and where it had been left behind a carved out spiral. It was so delicate feeling and yet strong. I took the stone and placed it in my pocket. It looked a lot like the stone Rowzey had given me to lead me to the place I saw Knarfy and Rievenya, but I wasn't sure it was the same.

I stood up and looked around. The rain was still coming down, but it felt lighter now. I walked forward towards where I thought the light might have been and stood to listen again. That was when I knew I wasn't alone. Somewhere out in the rain, there was something moving. I couldn't see it through the hazy fog, but its movements were clear. It sounded like it was up in one of the trees, perhaps a bird or other creature, or perhaps an elf or fairy. Either way, I didn't think it was wise to stay where I was.

Forward seemed to be my best option, so I silently moved as quickly as I could. I wanted to get as much distance between me and the sound as I possibly could. The sound began to fade and eventually disappeared, and as soon as it did, I noticed yet another light moving ahead. It wasn't the same color as the last one. This one was a light purple color, but it was about the same size and had a similar movement pattern to the blue one. I quickly started to follow it, thinking it had to lead me to someplace better than this.

It seemed to speed up and move quickly. I could tell it was climbing over things I easily stepped over, so it had to be small. I wondered if it was a little bug, something quick and nimble. As I got closer to it, I started to notice more little lights ahead. They were every color I could ever imagine and even some that looked like more than one. They were not all moving, some I ended up walking past, as I just kept following the little light ahead. The little lights were all around me now. It was as if they were lining the pathway ahead so I knew where to go. I thought it could be a trap, but my instincts told me to keep going, so I listened.

The little light began moving faster and faster, so I started to run. Then the little purple light glided away from me. I ran harder to catch up and suddenly found myself going face first into a body of water.

☙22❧

Baysil

"As you requested, I have had Kaleyna moved to another location and far away from Miaarya," Osidya said as she sat back down across from me. Though this time I wasn't tied down to the chair, which I thought was odd.

"Thank you, Osidya," I said. "Have you thought more on what we discussed?"

"Yes, yes," she said, waving her hand at me in annoyance. "I have thought about it, and while I am not sure if I believe everything you have told me about Nyrieve, and Rowzey of all people, I do find it very suspicious the way she just disappeared, so it at least leaves room to reason you might be telling the truth."

"I have no reason to lie to you anymore," I said. "I am full of shame for the information I have given to you, and I can only hope that you will keep your word to me."

"As I said before, I have been able to move Kaleyna. Fyra thought it was best as well, seeing how everyone seems to be tiring of Miaarya and her obsession with Kaleyna. Once we moved her in the night and Miaarya found out, she went a little crazy thinking she somehow had any pull with the council leaders. She has been banished from the council and their meetings now, and with any luck she'll get tired of not being needed or treated as someone important and find her way out of the Fire Realm or just perish… I'd be more happy with the latter, to be honest. She lies so much that I honestly do not even think she realizes it anymore. I don't think I have ever met someone who believes their own lies more than that fairy does."

"I don't know if she believes them, but she is really good at convincing others to, usually."

"Well, unlike you and your Nomydrac, we Pyrothians do not easily fall for lies and trickery like that."

"Have you given any more thought to what we talked about with your hatred for Nyrieve?"

I saw her body stiffen for just a moment before she started leaning back calm and casually. "I have, and there is some merit to what you said."

"Oh?"

"Yes, I went through some of my old journals, even before I met Arnayx, and seemed to be of a different way of thinking back then. It was sometime after I arrived back in Prax, after the child was born and my sister died. I think it was a few months after that, my writing about the child changed, quite quickly too. I cannot figure out yet what the link is, but I am trying to find it."

"If you would ever want my help, I could—"

"Do you honestly think I would allow you to rummage through my private diaries?" She laughed.

"Sometimes it is hard to see something right in front of you if you are too close to it."

She stared at me for a long time before speaking. "I know what you are saying is correct, but my initial reaction is to cause you some great harm. Logic is telling me that isn't what I need to do, but I am not understanding the strong reaction."

"That, to me, sounds like something is forcing you to have a specific reaction to anything that has to do with Nyrieve."

"Perhaps..."

"Is there something I could say to convince you to trust me?"

"It is not likely, but I will think on it over dinner," she said. She stood up and knocked in a pattern on the door. It opened and two elves brought in a tray each of food that they set up on the table off to the side of the room. The food smelled so good, it was almost making me sick with hunger. The table was set up for two people to dine.

"Who is joining you?" I asked after the two elves left and shut the door.

She tipped her head to the side and squinted her eyes at me. "Do you really think I would have some sort of dinner date here with you watching?"

"No, I just... Is someone coming to take me back to my cell?"

She rolled her eyes. "The food is for you and me, Baysil. Come on now."

"Oh, I didn't, I mean, thank you," I said, feeling the aches in my stomach even harder.

"Come sit and eat," Osidya said as she crossed the room and sat down and started to eat.

I quickly and carefully got up, feeling the slowly healing bruises all over myself. I sat down at the table. The chair was so padded that my body didn't seem to protest the movement. The food was so delicious, but I couldn't tell if it was because it was simply good or just the first real food I had eaten since Nyrieve's fall into the volcano.

"Is the food to your satisfaction?" Osidya asked as she slowly and deliberately cut each item into a tiny piece to place carefully in her mouth.

"Yes, thank you," I said, muffled through big bites.

"You do not need to rush, Baysil. If you do, you will likely get sick. Take your time and eat your fill."

"Can I ask you something?" I said, trying to slow down. I knew she was right, and I didn't want to have this food just come back up on me in a little while.

"Yes, go ahead."

"If you do not think hard on it, just answer right away without thinking…"

"Oh my word, Baysil, just ask the question and I will answer."

"Do you want to see your daughter harmed?"

"No," she said quickly and then looked confused. "I mean… I thought I did…"

"Did your family have any fairies that were close or maybe worked for your parents?"

"Many Pyrothian families had fairies as servants in their homes while I was growing up," she said, seeming to like the change of topic.

"Ah… I think I know what might be causing your internal conflict, Osidya."

"And what is that, Baysil?" she asked, sounding skeptical and condescending.

"I have known many fairies who have been able to create potions and charms that can cause someone to spill their deepest kept secrets or influence them to either avoid things or hyperfixate on them…"

"And this is what you believe happened to me?"

"It is possible."

"You believe this curse of sorts has been put on me for the last… nineteen years," she said, furrowing her brow, as if the thought of how much time had passed since Nyrieve was born wasn't possible.

"I do, though I am not positive how."

"How would your fairy friends do this?"

"Sometimes it would be a potion that could be drank or even eaten. Other times it would be an item that was enchanted or cursed, depending I guess on its usage."

Osidya just sat in silence looking at her neatly cut-up plate of food. "What kind of item?"

"I have seen it be a ring, a decorative carving, a clothing item even."

"A family heirloom perhaps?"

"That is definitely within the realm of possibilities."

"I see…"

"But for it to work, usually it has to be something that is constantly nearby or worn if it isn't ingested."

We both sat without speaking. Osidya was just staring down at her plate, while I continued to slowly eat everything off of mine.

"Thank you for the food," I said genuinely.

"Oh," she said as if awaken from a daydream, "you are welcome, Baysil. You have proven yourself to be a loyal person to my daughter and those she appears to care about. While I do not understand why exactly, you seem to be proving yourself honest to me, though I am sure there is an ulterior motive."

"The only motive I have is the same I had before coming to the Fire Realm in the first place."

"And that would be what exactly?"

"To help your daughter unite our world in some sort of peace."

"Do you honestly believe that forcing elves to bow to the ideals of everyone else in Iryvalya is making us united?"

"No one wants anyone to bow down to others and not have ideas or thoughts of their own."

"Oh no? Then what is it your precious Ny plans to do?"

"Nyrieve is smart enough to know she doesn't know everything, Osidya. She knows that everyone has a different idea of what peace means to them. The idea would be to allow different areas to decide what works best for them, but allow everyone to have a voice and freedom to live in a place that works better for them without fear of punishment."

"Really? My child came up with all that on her own?"

"No, she didn't. No one did. It was a group effort of discussing how we can help the people of Iryvalya, so everyone has the same rights and freedoms. While there should be leaders, there should also be safe ways to challenge them and be able to provide new ideas that can help each community as a whole."

"Did you know that my family descends from earlier saygents of Iryvalya?"

I was surprised by her quick change of subject but figured it'd be best to follow along. "I didn't. I knew that your family comes from royal bloodlines, but not specifically saygents."

"Yes, a long time ago my family was in charge of Iryvalya, making sure it was prosperous and good to its people."

"What happened to them?"

"Someone became jealous of what they had and the power they possessed, so they decided to overthrow them. It worked seamlessly, because that family was all too trusting of those born below them. They allowed those who should not have power to grow and cause dissent amongst the other leaders appointed by the saygent. Had they squashed those people down immediately, we would still be running Iryvalya and there would be peace."

"Do you really believe that, Osidya?"

"How dare you talk to me like that? Do you think we are friends? Do you think you know anything about my family and my life to speak so familiar to me?"

"To be honest, I feel like I know part of you... at least that small part of you that your daughter seems to take after."

"She takes after me? Is that a joke?"

"No, not at all," I said, choosing my words carefully. "Nyrieve is not like most elves I have met. She is very curious and has many questions. You, though, are more steady and come with more answers than questions."

"And how is that anything like me then?"

"Nyrieve is passionate about wanting to help bring Iryvalya back to a peaceful time, same as you stated the world would be if your family would have stayed in charge."

"You seem to be splitting hairs on that one, Baysil. It is close, but not the same."

"I don't see it that way. You said the world should have stayed how it was, your family in charge and peace kept. Nyrieve wants to bring peace to our world, which is what you must want to a degree if you think your family should have stayed ruling to keep the world in peace."

"I still think it isn't close enough to say we are similar in any way, but I will concede that you have made a point, even if it is the tiniest possible."

"When you were younger, and you went off to have Nyrieve, what was it you wanted?"

"Wanted for who?"

"Yourself."

"I don't remember."

"Don't you?"

"Nope."

"Osidya, you are a very smart elf. I know you can think back to that time and remember your hopes and dreams, and if not, I am sure rereading your journals would have reminded you."

She rolled her eyes at me like a young child would have and crossed her arms over her chest. She even slouched down in her chair, which was nothing like I had ever seen. Typically she would be sitting upright, formal, and never losing her composure.

"Osidya, please, it is not like I will ever get to leave this place or tell anyone what you say to me. And even if I did, no one would believe me over you."

She looked at me through her squinted eyes. "You do know I could have you killed now if I so chose?"

"I do. Though I imagine Fyra would not be thrilled with losing me, even though I have no useful information to provide to her."

"And you think you have any useful information for me?"

"Perhaps, but none of it will mean anything if you cannot remember back to how you use to look at the world and what you wanted for the future of your child."

She stood up abruptly and walked over to the door. She opened it and whispered something to the guard outside. She then slammed the door shut and sat back down, but not at the table with me.

"I have lost my appetite, Baysil," she said. "Go ahead and finish your meal and leave me to sit in silence."

I slowly ate the food in front of me. I savored each and every bite as if it might be my last, because I knew it actually might be. Once I was finished, I looked at Osidya, who was still just sitting and looking off into space. I didn't dare move from the table, as I didn't want to disturb her, so I sat in silence waiting. I just didn't know what I was waiting for.

Eventually the stillness of the room was broken by a loud rapping on the door.

"Come in," Osidya yelled.

I quickly prepared for someone to come and get me, but instead a young elf walked in carrying a basket. They set it next to Osidya's feet, bowed, and walked back out of the room, closing the door softly behind them.

She looked over at me. "You are done, I take it?"

"Yes, thank you again for the food," I said, unsure of what she was expecting from me.

"Good, now before I change my mind, take these and see if you can figure out where and how things changed," she said as she pointed to the basket.

I slowly got up and walked over to her. I looked down at the basket on the floor. Inside were books, about seven I could count. "What are these?"

"My bloody journals from before and after Nyrieve was born. Perhaps you can figure something out within them to see if I was changed or if I am just who I am."

"You trust me to look through these?" I asked, shocked.

"Well, if I don't like your answers after you read through them, I guess I will just go with the backup of killing you."

"But Fyra wanted me alive."

"Actually that is not true... Over a month ago she stated you and Kaleyna were no longer of any use to her and said you could both be tossed into the volcano with Nyrieve. I, however, told her I thought there was more information we could obtain from you both and that we could use each of you as bargaining tools if we found the need. That annoying Miaarya agreed with me and helped convince Fyra. Now Fyra is too busy with her current project to care."

"What is her current project?"

"That is what you ask? You don't thank me for sparing your life?"

"I am grateful for that, Osidya, thank you... However, I am more concerned about what Fyra might be planning and how it could harm others."

"You truly are a good person to your core aren't you, Baysil? I can see why my daughter kept you around as counsel for her. But I do not think you need to worry yourself with Fyra right now. She believes that Nyrieve is dead. She has decreed it to all the Pyrothian Elves and told them there is no longer a concern about the future of our Klayn."

"Why is that?" I asked.

"Apparently at some point Fyra became pregnant. She won't say exactly by whom, but there were plenty of people that could be the possible father. She has it in her head that this child will be the next ruler of the Fire Realm and her eyes are only focused on that. The council seems to either believe and agree with her or..."

"Or?"

"Or they realize she has become as crazy as we already knew her to be and they are looking for options."

"What kind of options?"

"To rid the Pyrothian Elves of her or ensure her child rules. Could go either way. I have heard both arguments during meetings with various council members."

"What do you suggest in the meetings?"

"I am not dumb, Baysil. I do not suggest anything. I merely listen and provide information for both the positive and negative of each suggestion presented. It keeps me in a safe space, for now."

"I did not think you were dumb, Osidya, not even a little."

"Good," she said, standing up, "I will have my servants bring you in a cot to sleep on and food on a regular basis. I will be back in a day or possibly three. When I return, I will expect you to have insight on what you have found."

"What about Kaleyna?"

"She will be moved to another room, one with a bed and without someone whispering nonsense into her dreams. It won't be lavish, but she will be safe."

"Thank you, Osidya."

"Don't thank me just yet, you have a mission of your own to complete, and I do hope this won't all be for naught."

"I will try to figure it out as quickly as I can," I said, feeling a bit nervous.

"Good," she said as she stepped out the door. "Otherwise I will not have any more use for you, and no reason to keep you from going into the volcano as well."

ଔ23ଛ

STORYTELLER

"The sauce is perfect!" I exclaimed. "Dad would be proud of you!"

"Thanks, sis," he said. "They are always on my mind it seems, especially now with the festival of the Battle of Ash and Air only a couple days away."

"Me too..." I said.

"Are you okay?" he asked, sitting down next to me and setting a plate of savory-smelling spiced bread next to my plate.

"With this food, how could I not be?" I asked, taking a still-hot piece and dipping it into the sauce and taking a big bite. I closed my eyes, remembering the smell of the bread and sauce along with the taste. It was bringing me back to when we were children traveling around Iryvalya. No matter where we went, the one thing that usually remained the same was the food.

"Dad really was a great cook, wasn't he?" I asked.

"Yes he was," he replied somberly.

"I'm sorry."

"We both miss them, but they both lived as they wanted to and after a long and happy life together..."

"I honestly sometimes wonder how it was they both passed in their sleep at the same time cuddled up together..."

"Me too."

"Did you ever wonder..."

"If they somehow planned it?"

"Yeah."

"I did for a while, but I do not think either one would have left us if they had a say in anything."

"That is the conclusion I came to as well..."

"I do miss them though."

"Each and every day."

We both smiled and hugged each other. "At least we still have each other, right?" he asked.

"We always will."

"You have me too," Zozinyal said, walking into the room with a big smile on her face.

"We are happy we have you too, Zozo!" he said, giving her a side hug.

"I have an idea I wanted to share with you both," she said, grabbing a plate of food and sitting down at the counter with us.

"Will I end up with my head shaved this time?" my brother asked.

"No, Cuzzy." Zozo laughed. "We wouldn't want to do anything to that long dark red hair of yours that you love more than anything."

"It is not that and you know it!" He laughed. "But it did take over a year to grow even enough to need to trim it."

"Yes," I said. "He was gifted with that beautiful color of hair, but unlike me, his is not nearly as thick and luscious!"

"Not everyone could take after Mom and her beautiful hair like you have!" he said, still laughing.

"I will say, Cuzzy, you do have quite the amount of hair. How long is it exactly?" Zozo asked me.

"If I don't keep it back with a braid, it is almost to my knees... I was thinking I might trim it up for the festival. And I was thinking I would wear one of Mom's outfits too."

"Aww, that is so sweet, Cuzzy, but why cut your hair?"

"I don't know, something feels like it is just in the air. It's almost a tingling feeling in the atmosphere, you know, like right before lightning starts?" I said.

"I feel it too, sis," he said.

"I think I know what you mean," Zozo said. "And that kind of leads me back to my idea."

"What is it?" I asked.

"We have helped with this festival for as long as I can remember, first helping our parents with it and then eventually us taking it over," she said. "My thought was maybe after this year, because it is the two-hundredth anniversary, what if we say this is the last year we will be putting it on?"

"What?" I asked, surprised.

"I know, it is a lot, and our parents have entrusted us to keep this going, but I was thinking, we all deserve to enjoy our lives without having to do this each year," she said.

"Uhm, you don't do this each year, Zozo," my brother said sharply.

"And neither have you, Cuzzy," she shot back.

"Both of you stop it," I said.

"You have been doing it each and every year since your parents passed, Cuzzy, and I think it is time we allow the next generation to take over."

"If I am really honest with myself, I am tired. I love helping keep the memories alive of everyone and what some fought and died for, but…"

"But what?" Zozo asked.

"I do not want to force this upon our children. If they want to do it, great, but I just do not want this to consume them like it has us."

"What are you suggesting?" my brother asked me.

"I think we need to form a council of sorts, one that has family members on it to ensure everything we have been doing is preserved and continues, but then maybe an adjacent council that is volunteers who want to learn the history of the Battle of Ash and Air and help teach it to others."

"It sounds like you have been thinking about this longer than just moments from Zozo's suggestion."

"I have been… I am older now, and love seeing all my children and grandchildren growing up around here, but I would love to leave here from time to time and…"

"Live?"

"I have lived plenty, Zozo," I said. "And I have lived a very full life. I just feel like… I am ready to retire."

"Retire?" they both said in unison.

"Yes, stop working and doing all the things I have been doing, and maybe do some of the things I miss and love doing."

"I believe Mom and Dad would be so proud of you!" my brother said with a smile.

"Really?" I said, surprised. "I thought everyone would be upset with me..."

"You need to live your life, Cuzzy!" Zozo said. "You have been putting everyone else first for many years, at least since your parents passed away. I think it is time you do things for you!"

"I know my partner would love to travel some more... but they have been so supportive of me doing this all these years, and even beforehand."

"Wysh knew the family you came from when you met! I remember telling them before you were tyed that joining our family wasn't for the weak. Not with parents like ours or the extended family that comes with it."

"I didn't know that," I said, "and Wysh still went along with getting tyed to me?"

"Love, of course." My brother laughed. "You and Wysh have had such an amazing life together. You raised wonderful children and in turn grandchildren, a couple of your own and some from the manor... You have brought so much love to Iryvalya. Our parents and I couldn't have hoped for a better life for you, but I think it is time for you to enjoy the rest of your lives and put trust in those you've raised and those who have supported all this."

"I think so too... I do think I should discuss it with Wysh before making things, you know, publicly known," I said. "Maybe if all goes well, I can announce it at the festival. That would give a year for people to get used to it before the next festival."

"I love that idea for you, Cuzzy," Zozo said. "And I would hope that both of you would want to do some traveling with me as well!"

"We'd love to," I said.

"Me as well, Cuzzy," my brother said, smiling.

I looked around the room as my brother and Zozinyal kept talking about the food for the festival. I could remember one of the first times I was ever in this house.

I was so young still, but my mother wanted me to know how important this building was and how it brought so many people together for centuries before and her hope that it would do so for centuries more.

I couldn't help but wonder if she would truly be proud of me for quitting my duties to the festival. I love so much about it, and helping educate the youthful elves, fairies, and more about our history and why our world is like it is today. Explain why there are crumbled buildings full of dust, large grave sites for the many lost, and the statues that were made to honor those who gave their lives trying to fight for peace in our world. I know I would never forget these things. Mom and Dad made sure we knew all the stories, the good ones that provide continued hope and even the bad ones that when I think of them I still shudder wondering how my parents survived so much chaos.

"You okay?" Zozo asked, tapping my shoulder.

"Yes, I am fine. Just thinking about... everything."

"That's a lot of things." She chuckled. "When will Wysh be here?"

"Tomorrow," I said, excited to wrap my arms around them and tell them my plans.

"Where have they been?"

"Traveling to find some more things for the festival. I am not sure what exactly, as we usually always end up having everything we need, but they have a mind of their own and it's one of the many things I love about them."

"Then tomorrow you shall let them know, and soon, very soon, you can make the announcement at the festival," my brother said.

"Yes, I think it will be right... I do have an idea though..."

"What is that?" Zozo asked.

"I think my eldest daughter would be ideal for continuing the tradition of organizing the festival. Her sister is so busy with, well, everything else, but she has always been very interested in learning the stories about Rowzey, the Nomydrac, and of course the Bringer of Peace. I think she will be perfect to take over my position, but only if she wants to. I am going to check with her first though. If she is interested, I'll announce it too that she will continue my work."

"I think Lowyll will be fantastic as your replacement!" my brother said.

"Me too!" I said, standing up. "I think I will go talk to her now about it. Then when I talk to Wysh, things should be all ready to move forward."

"You know, sis, you doing this is following what Mom always said about hope and being the spark."

"How do you figure that?" I asked.

"Your child is the continuation of keeping the memories alive of so many, and with that, you and your children are being the spark!"

❧24❧

NYRIEVE

The pounding from my head woke me up. I tried to open my eyes, but it stung to open them. I realized I was wet and still in water. I wiped my eyes as carefully as I could. There was dirt and other debris all over my face, and I imagine my eyes as well. I forced myself to sit up, feeling the water pouring out of my hair and down my back. I reached around and found my waterskin and opened it, pouring water carefully on my eyes. I blinked as much as I could to clean them out. Finally I could open them without them burning. It was dark again. How long had I been laying here in this puddle?

I looked at my hands. They were all wrinkled up, so I must have been in this all day. I reached up and felt my forehead where it hurt and pulled back some sticky blood. I must have hit it when I fell into the pond, but how did I get turned over and not drown?

I took a small drink from the waterskin and put it back. I was hungry, but I needed to figure out where everyone else was. I put my hands down into the mushy, muddy water to push myself up and felt something hard underneath my left hand. I dug around it to loosen it up. Finally I was able to pull it out of the water. It was covered with mud, and weeds had grown around it. I used the water to clean off most of the mud and used Klaw to cut off the persistent weeds encasing it. It was almost in the shape of an egg, but the size of my hand. I knew it couldn't be an egg because of how hard it was.

As I sat staring at the egg trying to see what it could be, I realized the little colorful lights I followed started to pop up all around me. In the water and on the land. They were moving so quickly, but not like the irybugs.

Something seemed so familiar about all this. I know it did slightly when I was chasing the lights, but I couldn't remember what or why. As I sat still with my bent knees out of the water, one particular light moved closer and closer to me. It was a soft teal light, like out in the middle of the sea. It appeared to be swimming closer to me, and that was when I remembered my dream. Were these the same things I dreamt about?

The tiny teal glowing turtle swam closer to me and climbed up my pantleg and rested on top of my knee and stared up at me. It was one of the cutest things I had ever seen in all of Iryvalya. It was the size of a grape. I looked back at it, wondering how to communicate with it, but then it seemed to answer my question without my asking. As it stared up at me, it began to flash its light. It was in a pattern of some sort, but not one I understood. I slowly reached down with my still-empty right hand and gently petted its back. It seemed to enjoy it, because it began lighting up more brightly and flashing quicker. Suddenly it jumped off of me and started to swim away. I just sat staring at it, but then it turned around and swam back to me. It nipped onto my pant leg and started to pull it. It wasn't able to move me at all because it was so small, but I understood it wanted me to follow it.

I carefully stood up and slowly walked to the edge of the water and climbed out. I saw so many little turtle lights all around me, I wanted to make sure I was careful and didn't step on one. As I followed the tiny yet very fast teal turtle, I made sure to shuffle my feet as I walked, to make sure I didn't accidentally step on one of the hundreds of glowing and flashing little lights around me. It was as if they were lining the pathway the teal turtle was heading down.

I kept an even pace to not get behind the turtle, but not to get too close in case it stopped quickly. As I followed it, I placed the egg-shaped item I found into my pack through the top opening. I had no idea where this thing was leading me, but I just felt it in my gut that it was where I needed to go.

I tried to pay attention to the direction we were heading, but the moon was covered tonight by clouds, so I couldn't see much beyond the glow of the fast-moving turtles. Some of the lights seemed to glow bigger than the others, and the bigger lights didn't move quite as quickly as the smaller ones. I imagined that those might be larger and older turtles, but I couldn't be sure in the darkness. I thought with them glowing, I would be able to see the turtles' outlines better, but when they would glow, it was almost like a haze was around them, so I mostly could only see the light they gave off.

The teal turtle started to slow down, and when I looked farther ahead of it, I saw a little cottage with a campfire outside of it. The cottage itself looked old and worn, but the fire was obviously not old, and I slowed down to look around to make sure I wasn't heading into more danger.

"Nyrieve!" I heard an unfamiliar voice shout out to me.

From behind a tree next to the cottage a figure began to emerge.

"Who are you?" I asked with Klaw already in my hand.

"Do you really want to know, or would you rather fight me?" the deep male voice replied, sounding playful.

"I do not prefer to fight, but you seem to know me and I do not know you, so that leaves me more concerned," I said, keeping my voice steady.

As I stood still staring at the person still hidden in the shadows by the trees, I noticed the small teal turtle rushing up to the person and running in circles around them. He bent over and allowed the turtle to climb onto his hand and petted it carefully, then sett it on his shoulder.

"Our friend here trusts me. Why do you not?"

"Until I know who you are, I cannot be sure if you are someone I can trust."

"You don't remember me, I see," he said, stepping closer to the fire, allowing me to see him.

He was taller than me and very thin. He didn't look like he would be very strong, but that could be the point. I stepped closer on the opposite side of the fire to see if I could get a closer look while trying to keep enough distance between us in case I needed to run.

"Something about you seems familiar," I said honestly, "but no, I cannot place where I might know you from."

"Let me try something," he said playfully. He knelt down to the ground and looked up at me. His pure black eyes immediately brought the memory back to me.

"Alabynes?" I asked.

He smiled up with that same smile I saw in the memory I watched when he wrote my name on the scroll. His long black hair was pulled back in a braid. His skin had looked a dark gray before moving closer to the fire, and now it was a light gray, changing as the Valyas' always seem to do. "I had hoped you wouldn't forget."

"What? I mean, where… I mean… how did you get here?" I asked, confused by all my questions wanting to come out at once.

"Oh, I have been here for a very long time, Nyrieve. I have been here, waiting for you."

"Me?"

"I had hoped that one day you would come, perhaps looking for me or something else."

"I didn't know you were here," I said.

"No one did," he said, "but I am glad you found me anyway, at least with the help of our little iryturtle friend here."

"Iryturtle?"

"Yes, they are native to the Blackened Forest, at least, they are now. I remember once a very long time ago they were all over Iryvalya, but now they seem to only be here… unless things have changed since I got here."

"How long have you been here?" I asked.

"Here, like the Blackened Forest, not that long, maybe… seventy-five years."

"Not that long? That is a pretty long time to me."

"Time moves differently for the Valya than everyone else. To me, it feels maybe like a year or two to you."

"A lot can happen in just a couple of years."

"This is true, and I remember documenting so many things when I still was a watcher. But for us… we live much longer and see so much happen that time just doesn't move the same way for us."

"That must be nice."

"Yes and no," he said. "I have seen much change in a quick amount of time, to me. But I have also watched wars battle on and so many people die for such horrible reasons."

"Like what?"

"For a time, these little guys," he said, petting the small iryturtle on his shoulder, "somehow became a point of obsession. Similarly to the irybugs, these little creatures come from Iryvalya herself and they work to help keep balance in our world."

"How were they an obsession?"

"Some creatures that lived in Iryvalya believed that somehow the iryturtle was some type of ruler for the world. That if they were to appease and make the iryturtles happy, they would have gifts of some sort bestowed upon them."

"That sounds strange."

"Yes, it was, especially for them. They didn't understand why these creatures would constantly bring them things, like food, jewels and coins. While they enjoyed the food and sparkly stones, they did not have any concept of money or power. They exist only for the betterment of our world. Not for others to get extra things because they are nice to the iryturtles."

"How did it stop?"

"It was another war..." he said sadly. "In the end, what was hurt the most were the iryturtles. When the iryturtles were unable to do what the people wanted, they at first thought they were not worthy. So they would try hard to make the iryturtles happier, and while they were happy little glowing creatures, and who wouldn't be with all the fresh fruits and vegetables they received, they couldn't grant someone's wishes."

"You said creatures and then people. Which was it?"

"Ah, you caught that... both. At the time, they were a form of people, but if you had seen them, you would have thought them to be more creature than person."

"I see... Is that like the Koneyotta?"

He tipped his head to the side and smiled. "Yes, similar, but not from the same line of people. The Koneyotta were from before the fairies and elves, and as time passed and things evolved, the Koneyotta became what are now the elves and fairies."

"I do wish we wouldn't have lost the ability to fly..." I said, remembering the wings on the Koneyottas from the memory I watched.

"Yes, that was such a shame, but the bigger and more upright you all became, the less the wings could carry you. So eventually more and more were being born with tiny wings that didn't move, until none at all were born with wings."

"What happened to the people who were obsessed with the iryturtles?" I asked curiously.

"As in life, some of the people believed they received their wishes, just because things in life happened to work out for them. Others did not, and became angry and vengeful, not towards the iryturtles, but towards those who were getting the things in life they wanted. Those getting their wishes, so to speak, told the ones who didn't that either they were not worthy or they didn't believe enough in the iryturtles, and that was why they were unhappy."

"Oh, that must not have gone over well."

"No, it did not. There were battles, and people believing the ones the iryturtles deemed worthy would win, but in a battle over iryturtles being able to do something they simply could never do, everyone lost. Eventually that race of creatures caused their own extinction. The iryturtles did not like what had happened in the world and did not want to be a part of something like that again, so they migrated from place to place until they ended up here in the Blackened Forest. They picked this place because the island seems to have a life of its own. I haven't quite figured out how it works, but it is almost as if the island has ways to protect itself."

"Is that why you ended up here?"

"Maybe," he said. "I don't know for sure, but when I came here, it felt right. It felt like a place I could hide out until you could find me," he said. "Now, would you mind putting Klaw away and sitting with me by the fire? There is much for us to discuss."

I slowly slid Klaw back into its sheath, but kept it unhooked for easy access, just in case. "I would like to talk to you, but I do need to find my friends I came here with."

"They are fine."

"How do you know?" I asked, surprised.

"Once you all arrived on the island, I knew. The iryturtles led me to your campsite. I knew you needed to find your way to me, and not the other way around. I recognized Domi right away as a Valya like me, and awakened her to advise her of the journey you needed to take. She agreed after much argument and debate. She definitely is not like the Valya were when I lived in the Spirit Realm, but it made my heart happy to see her wanting to do the right thing over just being a watcher of the world."

"Where are they?"

He glanced at the cottage behind him. "In there, kind of."

"Kind of?" I asked.

"It looks like a small cottage, but it isn't. It is the entryway into a tunnel system that travels about a mile deeper into the island."

"And what is at the end of the tunnel?"

He smiled. "How about we take the long way there and I'll show you."

"Why the long way?" I asked, concerned.

"Because it is a beautiful evening, and I do not wish to spend it walking through a tunnel when you have yet to see all the beauty the Blackened Forest has to show you."

"Okay," I said. "However, I do expect a little more explaining along the way of what you are doing here."

"I'd be happy to."

I kept my hand near Klaw as I started to follow him deeper into the forest. I wanted to trust him, but also needed to be cautious in case this was a trap. Part of me thought it was crazy to follow him and just trust he would take me to my friends, but what other choice did I really have? I didn't know this island at all and apparently the iryturtles wanted me to find Alabynes. I had questions for him, but for now, I would follow him and hope for the best.

ᎶᏬ25ᏰᏯ

NYRIEVE

As I followed Alabynes, I tried to watch all around me. I thought that it would be a good idea in case I needed to run or take cover, but then as the sky slowly started to get lighter, I noticed so many beautiful things around me. The plants were black for the most part, which I expected for a place called the Blackened Forest, but what I didn't expect was to see so many beautiful and amazing colors hiding throughout the blackened plants.

At one point I stopped when I noticed a small flowering plant next to the path we were walking on. I kneeled down, and when the sun peeked out from the clouds, I could see that the black wasn't fully black exactly. The closer I looked, the more I could see that what looked like black on the petals was shimmery and beneath it a mixture of colors.

"It is pretty, isn't it?" Alabynes asked, kneeling down beside me.

"I have never seen anything like this," I said, still amazed. "It is as if there is something trying to hide the beautiful colors of the plants, but in itself is equally as beautiful."

"It is just another one of Iryvalya's many secrets, I guess," he said, standing back up.

I looked up at him. The sun was peeking through again and shone directly on his face. It was almost hard to see his facial features because it looked like his skin was constantly trying to blend with a background that kept changing.

"Why does your skin do that?" I asked.

"Do what?"

"Keep shifting in color... I know the Valya do that to blend in to not be seen, but when I am talking to Domi, hers usually stays the same."

"Oh, am I?" he said, seeming surprised. "It might be because other than you and your friends, I haven't interacted with other people."

194

"You mean in all the years you have been here, no other people have come to the Blackened Forest?" I asked, not believing that would be possible.

"No, no, there have been many people who have come to the island over the years, but I never interacted with any of them directly," he said simply.

"Why? I would have thought you'd have gotten lonely over the years. I think I would have been."

He just smiled down at me and offered me his hand. I slipped my hand into his and was surprised by its softness and his strength as he quickly pulled me to my feet. I took a moment and brushed off the dirt from my knee and started to follow him down the small pathway.

"Alabynes, can I ask you something?"

"You can ask me anything."

"How old are you?"

He laughed loudly. "To be honest, Nyrieve, I am not completely sure anymore. I don't know of anyone as old as I am still alive, but than again, I have been here for a long time."

"You might have people you knew still alive," I said.

"Perhaps, but time is a strange thing for me..."

"How so?" I asked as the path turned us towards a thicker wooden area.

"How about we sit here for a minute, and I can try to explain. I am getting older, and I need to take breaks from time to time," he said, gesturing to some downed tree logs covered in a blackened moss. I touched the moss and looked at my hand. There was nothing left behind, so I sat down.

"It's okay, my head is still hurting and I could use a moment to drink some water. Would you like some?" I asked, offering him my waterskin.

"What a fascinating invention. Did you craft this yourself?"

"No," I said, smiling. "A dear friend of mine did. She is actually why I am here in the Blackened Forest in the first place."

He stared at me for a moment, as if he was trying to remember something, and he said, "Lydorea, right?"

My eyes widened with surprise. "How did you know that?"

"I remember observing someone once who was here searching for something, and they mentioned the name Lydorea many times. Things such as 'Lydorea had said it would be here' and 'We should have taken her and brought her here to find it' and 'He killed her already; bringing her body wouldn't have helped.' I had thought at first this Lydorea had sent them, but then I could tell they were working with someone who must have killed her."

"Do you remember what they looked like?" I asked.

"No," he said with a frown. "I'll be honest, they were the first people here in so many years, and when I realized it wasn't you, I wanted to remain hidden."

"I can understand that."

"Now let me try to explain time for me here," he said. "I believe, if you recognized me, you have entered memories before, haven't you?"

"I think so," I said. "I was never able to ask those whose memories I have been in if it was true or accurate."

"I can understand that. It is hard to verify the unverifiable."

"That it is."

"I too have the ability to visit memories, my own, others I know, and even some I never met."

"That must be interesting to do."

"Yes, and for a while I would resist the temptation to do that. I didn't know how long I would be here waiting for you. But as time pressed on, it did become lonely here. Not hearing voices speaking back, it can make you go a little mad. To combat that, I started visiting memories. First I would only visit my memories from the past, and while that was nice, I knew everything that would happen, so it no longer was interesting to me. I started to allow myself to sleep and enter different memories, ones I didn't know and ones that now I wish I never entered. But these memories helped me pass the time. Sometimes I think I could have been lost in these memories for years at a time, so to know how old I am is confusing for me, because I lost years being in someone else's memories."

"That sounds both wonderful and sad. Wonderful to have a way to pass the time, but sad to lose yourself like that as well."

"That is accurate."

"How was it that when we arrived on the island you weren't lost in a memory?"

He smiled gently at me. "The iryturtles would always wake me up when I needed to come back. Anytime someone arrived on the island, they would nip at me until I awoke and was able to hide from the people. When you and your friends arrived, they did it again, and I was able to see you were the one I had been waiting for."

"In the memory dream I had, I saw you, and you wrote my name on a scroll. How did you know to do that?"

"I hadn't been a Valya very long when that moment in time occurred. I was quite young and it was probably my second or third time watching on my own, writing everything down. I remember watching what happened at the Spirit Tree, and while I was there, I had a flashback to a memory dream I had when I was very young. And suddenly it felt as if that memory and what was happening was the same. Like I had dreamt of the future and not just a memory. In that memory I remember everything as it was, except you were standing there watching the Koneyotta. At the time, I was confused by your appearance, as most of the people of the world were Koneyottas. You looked different from them and yet similar. I knew you were not from the time we were in nor anyone from the past I had ever seen, and my only guess was you would be from the future."

"That is a pretty good guess, but that doesn't explain how you knew my name to write it on the scroll."

"During the memory, while you were standing next to me, you couldn't see that behind you in the trees a large grouping of irybugs began to fly around. It was as if they were trying to reach you but couldn't. I am guessing it was because you were not really there. As you stood watching the death of one of the Koneyottas, the irybugs began to fly in a pattern, over and over the same quick pattern. So I drew the pattern they were making on the scroll, and that is when you looked down at it and recognized what I drew. I knew I was supposed to see you and you me. I didn't know what I drew was your name. It was merely what the irybugs were drawing, or I guess spelling out to me."

197

"You had no idea it was my name?"

"Names were not written the same way back then. I believe during that time the Koneyotta drew symbols and pictures for names. I thought it might be a future language, and I apparently was right."

"It just seems too strange to be real," I said, feeling somewhat skeptical.

"I can understand that, Nyrieve, but Iryvalya tries to help our world along in ways that she can. I am sure at times you have seen signs from Iryvalya that might have seemed like something you could consider a coincidence, and yet you knew deep down there was more to it."

"You are not wrong there, but I try to understand everything I can with reason."

"As do I," he said, patting my knee gently, "but sometimes Iryvalya sees us going the right or wrong direction and tries to encourage us somehow. For many centuries I ignored that day and what happened, but I never turned that scroll in. I knew it was something different, but I wasn't ready to admit it. Over time, as I saw the world change from the Koneyotta to the elves and fairies, I remembered that day, and began researching to see more about who this Nyrieve could be. That is when I remembered when I saw you, you bore the mark that was spoken of, the mark of the Bringer of Peace."

I didn't know what to say. It all sounded honest and possible, but how could Iryvalya bring us together like this over the course of centuries? If Iryvalya could do this, then why would our world be as broken as it is right now?

"You are questioning so much, Nyrieve. I can see it across your face. What are you wondering?"

"Why would our world get to this state if Iryvalya could encourage people to do the right thing?"

"Have you ever eaten an amazing dinner and found yourself so full you knew you shouldn't eat another bite, but you go on an eat more, leaving you to fill ill?"

"Of course," I said.

"That is the way of all creatures and people. You know what you should do, or at least know what might be the right things to do, but nothing in the world will force you to do that. You have to make those choices on your own. And not because

Iryvalya will force you to make those choices or kill you or something. It's because you know it is right. You know that it is what is best for the greater good of the world and its people. You do the right thing because it is the right thing, Nyrieve, not because you have to but because you want to do the right thing. You want to make the world a better place because you know how it would make most people's lives better for it. You also know that it will upset others and will cause harm on some level, but again, it is the right thing."

"I'd like to think I try to do the right things when presented with the options before me."

"And you have. Otherwise you would not be here with me," he said, gesturing around us.

"Why do you think Iryvalya brought us together then, Alabynes?"

"Maybe she saw I was someone young enough as a Valya who could hold on to the secrets of the world that might be helpful for you. Maybe because I am dumb enough to hide out in a forest for years waiting for you to arrive... Truthfully, I am not sure."

"Then why would you do all this?"

"What is the point of our lives, Nyrieve?"

"I don't know," I said, confused at his response.

"Most of the time, when we pass on, we are remembered for a short time, and only those who truly do something great or horrible are continually remembered. Otherwise, everyone else just lives their lives and, sadly, over time is slowly forgotten."

"So you are doing this to be remembered?"

"No, not at all. I think the point of our lives is to make things better for future people. And how can we do that if we stand by and watch people destroy our world and the happiness of others? As a Valya we were always told to never get involved, never interfere no matter what. Even if we could help or make it better, and I don't agree with that. I liked the idea of someone coming along and bringing a peace the world hasn't known for so long. I wanted to be a part of something greater and better than myself, and even if this didn't work out, at least when I pass, I will know I tried."

"Do you truly believe I have the ability to do that?"

"I think Iryvalya does."

"Why do you say that?"

"When those people came speaking Lydorea's name, they were looking for something. Something others had come looking for as well. Do you know what I am talking about?"

"Yes," I said, "I think they were looking for the same thing I am here to try to find."

"Clyr?"

Surprised, I responded, "Yes, do you know where it is?"

"Once I had learned what they were looking for, I started to look from time to time when I wasn't lost in memories. I searched the whole island. Every rock I could find, I turned. Every bush I searched under. Each tree I climbed, and I never found it. I honestly thought it was either never brought here in the first place or someone had found it long before I arrived."

"Then we made the trip here for nothing," I said, devastated. How could I get the Klayns' people to trust me if I didn't have Clyr to prove I was telling the truth?

"I wouldn't say that," he said with a sly smile.

"No, I mean I am glad I found you as well, but I really was depending on finding Clyr."

"That is not what I meant, but thank you. I am glad you found me as well."

"Then what did you mean?"

"How did you hurt your head, Nyrieve?"

I looked at him, confused with his changing of topics. "I hit my head when I fell into a pond. It knocked me out."

"What did you hit your head on?"

"I am not sure, when I woke and tried to get up, the pond was soft and mushy, nothing hard enough to hurt me."

"No?"

"Well, there was a rock I found," I said, still confused.

"Everything was soft in the pond but this lone rock?"

"Yes," I said, starting to feel annoyed.

"And you have the rock, don't you?"

"How did you know that?" I asked.

"I am a watcher. It is what I do."

"Yes, I have it. I placed it in my pack."

"Take a look at it, Nyrieve."

I sighed as I grabbed my pack and opened it. The rock was still sitting on top of everything. It wasn't wet anymore, but there was still some mud on some spots. I turned and showed Alabynes the rock, and he put his hands up in protest.

I looked closer at the rock. It had patterns on it that I had thought was just mud at first. Upon closer inspection, I could see there were things carved into the rock. It was a pattern of spirals all connected and intertwining with each other.

"What kind of rock is this?" I asked him.

"Nothing I have ever seen in all my years here in the Blackened Forest, Nyrieve."

I turned it over again and again in my hands. It was heavy like a rock, but it felt different somehow. As I traced my fingers over the spirals, I could see small faint lines of light starting to show. It was as if the rock was responding to my touch. The light looked silvery and sparkly. I showed it to Alabynes and he traced one finger across the rock as I did and nothing happened. So I tried it again, and once again the little lights showed up, following along the pattern of my touch.

"What could this be?" I asked.

"I have no idea, but if I were to guess, I would say that you found Clyr... or at least whatever Clyr is hidden inside of."

"How is it possible that I would find it by falling into a random pond and cracking my head on it?"

"How did you come to fall into this pond?"

"I was following..."

"Following?"

"I was following one of the iryturtles and couldn't see where I was going and fell in."

"Like I said, Iryvalya has her ways to lead us to things. You fell and hit your head. I quickly flipped you over so you wouldn't drown, but I left when you started to awaken."

"You did?" I said, surprised. "Thank you, but you're—"

"Not supposed to get involved, I know, but I couldn't let you drown. You are here to help us, so I will help you as much as I can."

"Do you really think this is Clyr?" I asked, looking down at the rock.

"As I said, I searched every place on this island, even all the ponds, and never have I seen this rock. You were meant to find it, and the iryturtles helped you, albeit not in the best way, by you smacking your head on it."

I traced the rock again, watching the light. "We need to get this to Iclyn. She knows how we can open it and has what we need."

"We are not far from your friends. They are just over that small hill down the path."

"Really?" I asked, surprised they'd be so close.

"Of course," he said. "I promised you I would bring you to them. I just wanted a few more moments alone with you first."

"Thank you for your help, Alabynes," I said, standing up and putting my pack back on and holding the rock tightly in my hand.

"It is my pleasure, Bringer of Peace."

"Let's go see Iclyn and the others. I am sure they are concerned by now."

"Yes, let's go. I will also prepare some food for dinner tonight, and then I can provide to you all the scrolls I have collected and kept over the years."

"You have them here with you?"

"Yes, they are records for you to help with your cause of sorts."

"I can't wait to read them," I said, eager to try to open this beautiful rock.

"Then let's head to my house."

ೞ26ೲ

NYRIEVE

A house? More like a small castle. The forest was still thick as we approached the house, as Alabynes called it. It looked so old and was crumbling in some places. It was built out of large gray bricks. It appeared to be multi-storied, but I couldn't tell exactly how many levels there were. There were a couple of towers on each side of the building, presumably to keep watch for whoever was approaching. I would guess when it was built and thriving in its glory days, the wooded area was less thick and likely pruned back.

There was black ivy growing all over the building. I had seen tons of ivy growing up in Cliffside, but never black or with leaves large enough to cover my entire face. I could see that on the edges of the ivy, the leaves had bold colors on them as well. On the ground in front of me was a freshly fallen ivy leaf, not as big as my face, but fully the size of the palm of my hand. I could see the veins of the leaf through the shiny black shimmer. It looked like it was orange and green throughout, not a combination I would have expected, but it was beautiful. I carefully slid it into one of the pockets of my pack and continued with Alabynes.

As we approached what I believed was the entrance, which was big enough for horses and even a carriage to go through, I noticed a second door. It was at least double the size of the door we were about to walk through. I wondered what or who exactly that door was made for, especially being so large.

"Alabynes," I said, "what would they have needed a door that size for?"

He smiled at me. "You know of dragons, correct?"

"Of course, but I would have thought they transitioned into a person shape before going into the *house?*"

"They could have, but perhaps during the time of construction, they wanted to make it so the dragons could decide for themselves. Besides, could you imagine a better surprise to any attacker than to find a dragon inside the house you are trying to breach?"

"Can't say that I can," I said, smiling, picturing someone caught off guard by a hidden dragon. Especially now, when most of the world still thought they didn't exist anymore.

Alabynes opened a normal-size door in the middle of the large door in front of us. I didn't even see it carved into it. "How did I not see the small door inside the bigger one?"

"Not everything is always as it seems, is it?" he asked, stepping through the doorway.

"I guess not," I said, following closely behind.

As I stepped through the doorway, I could see a perfectly kept courtyard with a large carved white fountain. The stone of the fountain looked like it had crystals or something in it, as it sparkled in the sunlight. The only thing that was growing in the courtyard were a few trees and the black ivy, but even that looked well maintained, and nothing like the outside.

"Why does the inside look so well cared for, but not the outside?"

"I have been living here for a while and have taken some time to clean up the inside. Although I cannot take full credit. I have had some helpers," he said, pointing to the fountain.

I took a step closer to see many of the tiny iryturtles swimming in the fountain. I looked at the trees and ivy and was able to see more lying out in the sun on the blackened leaves.

"Do the iryturtles ever get bigger?" I asked. "I remember seeing much larger regular turtles in other places in Iryvalya."

"They used to. They do vary in size now, but not very large. Hopefully, though, one day they will again thrive and grow. It seems since they came here, they do not tend to grow much larger. I think the largest one I have seen was about the size of my hand. I am not sure what made them stop growing."

"They are adorable being so tiny though."

"Yes, they are," he said with a smile. "I think we wil—"

"Nyrieve!" I heard Emryleia shout as she came running down some stairs on the other side of the courtyard.

"Em!" I yelled and rushed to give her a hug.

"I am so glad you made it. I was beginning to think we needed to start coming to find you, and what did you do to yourself? Your head!"

I laughed. "I'm okay now, I think. Alabynes has been filling me in on some things, and—"

"He didn't hurt you did he?" she asked, her eyes darting back at him and placing her hand on the staff strapped across her back.

"No, no, no, he hasn't harmed me. That was apparently my doing… or Iryvalya's… or the iryturtles… It doesn't really matter, because it was an accident."

"Iclyn will want to see you right away and get that cleaned up. It doesn't look like it is bleeding anymore, but she will know for sure if you need any stitches."

"Where is everyone else?"

"Iclyn is in the conservatory looking through the unique herbs and flowers there. She believes some of them might be handy for helping Prydos, in case…"

"That would be good," I said, not wanting to imagine him and Kaleyna never reuniting again. "It is best to make sure we can care for him, and any others that might have been cursed like he has been."

"That was our thoughts too."

"Are Domi and Koyvean in the conservatory as well?"

"No," she said, taking my hand and leading me in the direction she came from. "Domi kind of disappeared, but she said she was going to, so I guess that is a normal thing for her?"

"As a Valya, she definitely has the powers to do that," I said, glancing back to make sure Alabynes was following behind us.

"That is what Iclyn said. Koyvean has been walking the grounds and checking the towers, to make sure no one followed us and I imagine to keep an eye out for you."

"Sounds like Koyvean," I said, making sure to take notice of the intricate carvings in the handrails, the steps, the walls. It was amazing to see so many things with such beautiful accents on them. It was mostly ivy carved into everything, but they were delicate and not overpowering. Each of the small vine ends were twisted into a spiral. It was so beautiful.

We walked down a covered stone bridge to the conservatory. Other than a few pillars along the sides, it was open with large cutouts. Below was what looked like an outdoor ball room, also in perfect shape. In the middle of the dance floor was a single large ivy leaf with a stem that ended in a spiral. This place felt like something out of a dream, where a princess would live and throw lavish parties and have many suiters lining up just to ask her to dance. I smiled at the imagery in my head, wondering what something like that would look like. I had been to balls, but never one without something to always be worried about.

"Nyrieve!" I heard Iclyn exclaim when she saw me. She rushed over and immediately began checking my head, "What happened?"

"I fell and hit my head on something," I said, taking out the egg-shaped rock.

Her eyes widened and looked back at me. "Do you know what this is?"

"I think so," I said.

"What is it?" Emryleia asked. "It looks like a weird carved dirty rock."

"I think it holds Clyr inside of it," I said, watching Em's face light up.

"Could it have really been that easy to find?" Iclyn asked, furrowing her brow.

I rubbed my head and said, "It didn't feel that easy to me."

"Oh, Ny," Iclyn said, "I am sorry, let me get your head cleaned up first."

"I think all of me could use a good cleanup." I laughed, looking down at my mostly dry and muddy clothing.

Iclyn took some cloth from her shirt and dipped it into a small flowing fountain on the wall, then she slowly and carefully wiped my head where it connected with the rock. "It is a pretty nasty cut, but it is not deep and does not look to be infected. I don't think you will need any stitches either. Em, could you take Ny to one of the rooms Alabynes has provided for us and show her how she can wash up? I will come see you when you're done and bandage you up. I have some questions for Alabynes about some herbs here first."

"I think I know how to clean up," I said with a chuckle.

"Oh, not in this place you don't," Em said as she took my hand and led me through the conservatory and down a long hallway.

Everything looked clean and almost new, but there was no way this place was new, especially from the outside appearance. "Did you all help clean this place when you got here?" I asked.

"No, it was like this. Iclyn and I wondered about it, and Koyvean did some searching and testing of her own and she believes it has a charm of some kind placed on it. I mean, if you set something down, it stays there, but it doesn't seem to collect dust or anything," Em said. "Look over there, do you see that sunbeam coming down?"

"Of course."

"But did you notice you do not see any particles floating around in it?"

I looked again, and it was just a sunbeam, nothing floating around inside of it like you'd normally see. "That is the strangest thing," I said.

"There are also no bugs in here, not one spider or anything. I mean, I am not complaining about that, but still so strange."

"That it is…" I said, looking around more closely as we walked the corridors. There were more beautiful patterns carved into the walls and floors, mostly all ivy leaves with spirals. I noticed some of the trim around different hallways and doors were different. Some had what looked like maple leaves on them, and on another I saw dragons carved. "Em," I said, stopping for a moment, "look at this doorway. Do you know what those are carved into it?"

Emryleia stepped closer to look and said, "I am not sure, Ny. It looks like some sort of statue."

"I think those are gargoyles," I said, surprised.

"They could be. I never met one before."

"I did, back in the Stone Realm. They were very nice people," I said, starting to follow Em again down the hall.

"That is amazing that you have been able to meet so many different people."

"It is," I said. "You know, it looks like this place might have been built for entertaining people from all over. Maybe these were each carved to show representation for all the people of Iryvalya."

"I wonder if Alabynes would know, or maybe Domi…"

"Where is Domi? I thought I'd have seen her by now."

"I am not sure, to be honest, I think she portaled some place… I hope she's okay."

"I'd like to think that Domi is pretty good at taking care of herself, and she definitely knows how to hide."

"Here we are," Em said as she opened the large door to a beautiful and lavish-looking bedroom.

"I don't think I have ever seen a room so big and bright with light," I said, looking around.

There was a large four-post bed in the middle of the room. It was covered in velvet blankets and many soft pillows of different shapes and sizes. There were bars connecting the four posts around the top, and sheer cloths draped around the whole top of the bed. There was so much sunlight shining down on the bed, and when I looked up to see why, I was surprised to see a large window above the bed. There was a large looking glass leaning up against the wall. It was framed in silver that had carved vines climbing all around it. Along the furthest side of the room was an open balcony, with only sheer curtains held back that moved slightly with the breeze floating in.

"I do not think I have ever seen a room more beautiful…" I said, still in shock.

"Each room we have seen is similar to this. I am not sure how, because it feels like each room is much bigger than there is space for them to be."

"It is like Lydorea's charm for my pack. It can hold so much more than what it looks like it should."

"I wonder if Lydorea descended from someone who had been here once."

"Or maybe someone who lived here and helped create this place."

"There is a large tub over here," Em said, pushing aside a large curtain. It was in a small space off the room, and it had another window on the ceiling and other openings around the top of the room. In the middle was a large purple stone tub. There were strange handles and levers next to it that I had never seen before.

"How do I get the water to fill the tub?"

"Alabynes had to show us," she said. She pulled down one of the handles and moved another lever and water started to pour down into the tub from above like soft rain.

"That is… just wow, I've never seen anything like this."

"Right? I don't know how I'll go back to heating up water on the stove for a bath again!"

"Same…"

There was a bench to the side of the tub with large fluffy towels and at least ten different bottles of soaps and perfumes.

"What you might want to do is rinse off with the… uhm, I don't know what to call it, so I guess the raining water, and then if you look in the bottom of the tub, there is the drain and plug. I'd just put in the plug and soak for a while. Whatever the tub seems to be made from keeps the water warm. Makes me want to go take another in my room."

"Where is your room?"

"If you go outside your door, mine is next to yours on the right."

"Okay, and one more thing, how do I turn the water off?"

Em walked over and showed me how to maneuver one of the levers to turn the water off or even make it warmer or cooler. I couldn't believe this was real. "I feel like I am in a dream, Em, like how could a place like this exist and no one know about it?"

"I have no idea, but I will enjoy it while I can," she said with a smile. "If you want to clean up and take a nap or something, go ahead. I am going to go make something for dinner for everyone. Apparently Alabynes had been stocking the shelves with some things over the years, plus with what we brought I should be able to come up with something."

"Thank you so much, Em, I don't know if I can sleep, but I think I'll at least feel better once I am clean."

Emryleia left the room, closing the doors behind.

I quickly undressed, placing my clothing in a pile to not dirty up the room any more than I had to. I slowly stepped into the tub and let the water pour over me. I grabbed a couple of bottles and sniffed each one to figure out what to use to clean what. I found something that smelled of mint, which seemed like it could clean well, so I used it to wash my hair. There was so much dirt and so many little things from the pond that fell down and went into the drain. I took more of the mint and used it to scrub the dirt off of me. I smelled a couple of other bottles and found one that smelled like lilacs in the spring. I used that to hopefully soften my hair back up from the mint. Once I felt I was as clean as I could get, I checked the bottom of the tub and all the debris seemed to have gone down the drain. Then I put the plug into the bottom of the tub and sat down. The water filled up around me. Its warmth felt like a big hug. I sat with my knees up to my chin and hugged myself.

This was a place that I thought Kylyan would enjoy. Maybe if things went well, I could bring him here. I missed him, but knew he should be safe in Aquyleya, and he could keep my family safe too. If he were here, I don't think he would have been okay leaving me alone on the beach to find my own way and maybe I wouldn't have followed the iryturtles and found what I hope is Clyr. Though I would have loved for him to have seen one of the iryturtles himself. I smiled at the thought of coming back here one day with him.

I noticed the tub was getting full and pulled the lever Em showed me. The water raining down stopped and the room was silent other than my movements in the water and birds singing outside. It felt so calm and peaceful, it almost was too calm, but I wanted to enjoy it for however long I could. I knew we wouldn't be staying here long, so I might as well soak it up, so to speak.

After enjoying the warmth of the tub for what had to be at least half an hour, I pulled the drain plug and watched the water quickly disappear. I stepped out of the tub onto a soft rug and grabbed a couple of the fluffy towels. I didn't know how they could make a towel fluffy like this, but it was amazing. I wrapped one around my body and put my hair up in one too. I wandered back into the main bedroom and lay down on the bed, looking up into the sky. I could see big fluffy clouds overhead slowly moving and changing as they passed. My eyes started to feel heavy and I struggled to keep them open. Eventually I gave in and let the sounds of the birds and breeze whisk me away to sleep.

⍟27⍟

JOYNOX

Getting eaten alive was not the way I thought I would die. Then again, I didn't really think much about my own death. I was always more worried about everyone else and their lives. Now that I was standing here about to die, all I could think of was all the people I had loved and cared for over the years and how I wished I had told them all what they really meant to me. For too long I had shielded others from my true feelings... No, that was a lie. I had shielded myself from taking a chance and possibly getting hurt or finding utter happiness. This was my own fault, being here about to die alone.

The large serpentlike dragon was moving around me. It was long and dark with black scales everywhere except its underside that was a whitish silver. There was no way to get away from it. The feathers on its head moved back and forth as it tightened around me closer and closer. Down its body I could see five larger feather plumes with colors inside of them. If it wasn't for the imminent death that was awaiting me, I would have marveled at its beauty and grace as it moved.

Finally it quit moving closer and just brought its face closer to me, almost examining me. I could see its eyes as it stared down at me. They were soft pink and honey-like colors swirled. I wanted to scream, I wanted to run, but there was nowhere to go.

The dragon sniffed me and stared at me again, tipping its head to the side. It was as if it couldn't decide if I would be a tasty dinner or a disgusting snack.

"Please don't eat me," I kept saying over and over again.

Out of nowhere the dragon began spinning around and a swirling grayish smoke seemed to cover everything. I knelt down and covered my head the best I could.

I started to feel the heat of the sun on my back and glanced out of the corner of my eye to see the smoke was gone. I looked up, and standing in front of me was a woman, and she was naked. I quickly took off my jacket and handed it to her and looked around for the dragon.

"Be careful, miss, there was a dragon here a moment ago," I said, still checking the skies and hills around us.

"The dragon is still here, Joynox," the woman said in a sweet voice.

I looked at the woman, now covered in my jacket, looking back at me. "Where is it?"

She laughed. And then she kept laughing.

"What is so funny?" I asked, getting annoyed. I still could feel my heart pounding from almost being eaten and didn't find anything happening worthy of laughter.

"That is the question you ask me first?"

I looked at her again. She had long wavy hair that went past her waist. It was a light yellow at the top that faded down to a dark pink at the bottom.

"Who are you and how do you know my name?"

"Those questions make more sense. I know your name because Hyorda provided it to me. They said you would be here eventually."

"And who are you?" I asked, annoyed.

"My name is Aurilya… but if you prefer, you can just call me Dragon," she said with a smile.

"What?" I said, confused. "You… no you couldn't… Wait, you mean to tell me you are… you're the… the dragon?"

"I know you haven't met one before, but I thought elves would have at least been more educated about the history of my people than you are."

"I knew you… I mean dragons, could shift into a person form, Hyorda told me that, but I guess I didn't think it could be so quickly."

"Again, none of you are educated properly on dragon history or biology."

"I didn't know until a couple of months ago that dragons even still existed, so excuse me for not being up to par with the knowledge you expected of me."

"Fine, fine," she said, "I am tired from my travels, and I need to eat and rest before we leave here."

"Uhm…" I stuttered, not knowing what to say next.

Aurilya took a deep breath and let it out loudly. "I need sleep. Do you have something I can use to sleep?"

"I have a sleeping sack you can use," I said.

"What kind of food do you have?" she asked.

"I have some breads, cheese, and water."

She curled up her lip at me. "No meat?"

"I haven't been able to catch anything to kill for its meat…"

She then rolled her honey-and-pink eyes at me. "Wait here, I think I killed something when I landed… It was an accident, but might still be food."

She took off up the hill where I saw the dragon—well, I guess her—land before coming towards me. She was exceptionally quick moving, especially without any shoes on. It was only a few moments when I saw her coming back down towards me, carrying a small carcass.

"What is that?" I asked, trying to figure it out by looking at the mangled body.

"It looks like a boar," Aurilya said, tossing it to me, and I almost dropped it.

"What do you want me to do with it?"

"Don't you know how to clean one to cook it?"

"Uhm, I know how to do it, but I have never done it before," I said, embarrassed.

"Does Hyorda know what kind of elf she sent to me?" she asked seemingly no one.

"I might not be great at skinning animals, but I am pretty good at other things," I said defensively.

"Fine, I will clean it, but can you cook it?" she asked, trying to not sound super annoyed.

"Yes, I can cook it," I said.

She took my knife and cleaned the meat away from the rest of the body and handed me the knife back bloodied. "Look, I am not trying to be mean to you, Joynox, but I have been traveling for a while and I am very tired. Can you please cook this for me while I get some rest? And please feel free to eat some yourself, I

213

just… I am sorry, I just really need some rest."

"Yes," I said, "I can do that for you. Here, take my sleeping sack and get some rest. I will try to get this cooked up right away for you."

"No rush, I will need a few hours rest," she said as she opened the sleep sack and climbed in. She put the blanket over her eyes before she said, "After we eat and it is dark, we will be leaving the Water Realm. I hope you don't have motion sickness. I hate having to wash that off my scales."

Did I understand her right? Would I be riding a dragon? No, I knew I would be leaving the Water Realm, but Hyorda didn't say I would be… flying out of here! How does one ride a dragon? There has to be a way. I mean, Hyorda told me of how she had flown on dragons before and how fun it was, but me? I didn't think that would be something I would ever be doing.

⚬🙰⚬

Aurilya ate like no one I had seen before. She just grabbed with her hands and ate as much boar as she could hold. I was slightly disgusted because of how I was raised to always be clean and proper, but I was also very impressed with her lack of restraint. Maybe I had been inside Noygandia too long and been led to always think our way was the way. Even though I wanted Iryvalya to be a better place and more accepting, this showed me I had a lot to learn and needed to work on my own acceptance of others as well.

"Thank you, Joynox," she said when it seemed she was getting full.

"I hope it is to your satisfaction," I said genuinely.

"In dragon form, I wouldn't have bothered cooking it, but in this form, I have learned to enjoy things cooked more. And whatever it is you added to it to enhance the flavor was delicious."

"Oh, thank you," I said, surprised she noticed. "I just found herbs around the area and added them with some salt and dried spices I had brought with me."

"Whatever they are, it was just what I needed. Don't tell Aunt Rowzey, but yours was almost as good as hers." She chuckled.

"I would never suggest any food was better than Rowzey's. I only met her once,

214

but I learned right away food was very important and close to her heart."

"Yes, it is almost like it's her children." She sighed after swallowing her last bite of food. "Though I can't blame her. When you are good at something, you enjoy being known for it."

"True," I said.

"What questions do you have for me, Joynox?" Aurilya asked bluntly.

"Questions?"

"Yes, about where we are going, how we are getting there, and anything else."

"I don't really know anything other than what Hyorda told me," I said honestly.

"What did she tell you?"

"That I would come out into the Water Realm and someone would make contact with me, I would travel somewhere to help Nyrieve somehow, and that I might not be able to make it back here if Nyrieve wasn't successful in uniting our world," I said somberly.

"Okay, so she only told you the glossed-over version, good to know. I honestly do not have a lot more insight into everything that is being planned and maneuvered around Iryvalya. I know my part, and that is about it."

"What is your part, Aurilya?"

"I was to meet you here, take you to the Air Realm where you will meet up with your counterparts from the Fire Realm."

"Counterparts?"

"Those from the Pyrothian Klayns and the Drayks that also want peace in Iryvalya."

"I... I didn't know there would be... I think that is more surprising to me than seeing you as a dragon and thinking you would eat me."

"Eww, eat you?" she said, scrunching up her nose.

"I am gross to you?" I asked, surprised once again.

"People have never tasted good to me... not sure why, but I have only met a few dragons that enjoy the taste of elves or fairies or what have you."

"I guess that is a good thing for us, fewer chances for a dragon to eat us..."

"Well... eat you. You're correct, it doesn't mean we do not bite heads off or

215

chew them up and spit them out."

"Great, that really made me feel better."

"Wasn't my goal to make you feel better, just to be honest and provide what I know... at least what I am allowed to share."

"So there is more that you know and will not share with me?"

"It's not my place. Perhaps when you meet up with the Nomydrac and they feel it is appropriate to do so, they will fill you and Fire Realm counterparts in on more of the plans. What I do know and can say, there is currently a lot of moving parts within this plan. Not everyone is aware of what they others are doing, but between everyone, if it goes the way everyone is hoping, perhaps there can be peace in Iryvalya without having to shed blood."

"You sound like Nyrieve. Have you ever met her before?"

Aurilya became quiet and tipped her head to the side and thought for a moment before answering me. "I have... and similar to the regards in which you hold her father, I hold Nyrieve in as well."

I sat there thinking about what she said. First, how did she know I held Arnayx in any regard... and then it hit me, Hyorda told her. "I am sorry for that."

"Sorry?" she asked.

"It is a hard thing to care so much about someone who... is not able to care for you back in the same way."

"That it is... but, also like you, I want her to be happy, even if that is not with me."

"I feel the same, and as Nyrieve is Arnayx's daughter, I want all the happiness in the world for her. She has already been asked to sacrifice so much, just because of who she is."

"Yes, I agree. At one point I wanted to steal Ny away, so to speak. Take her where no one could reach her or harm her again. But that is not how the world works, and if there is any chance for her to have true happiness, even if it is not with me, I have to support her to get that chance."

I nodded, knowing that exact feeling. "Nyrieve is lucky to have you in her life then, Aurilya, even if it is only as a friend."

She nodded back to me. "So are you ready to get out of the Water Realm?"

"I won't lie, I am nervous."

"You have ridden a horse before, right?"

"Of course," I said.

"Imagine that is what you are doing… just a much larger horse… and one that can fly up into the clouds."

"That isn't making me feel better," I said.

"If it helps, I have never lost anyone who has rode on me before."

"It helps, but how many riders have you had?"

"Less than ten."

"That really doesn't make me feel better then. Had you said a hundred, maybe…"

"You only have one life, Joynox, and wouldn't it be oh so grand to tell people how you have ridden on a dragon?"

"No one will believe me." I laughed.

"Well, once it is known throughout all of Iryvalya we dragons are still here, they might."

"I guess we will see, won't we?"

"We definitely will, Joynox."

It was more amazing and terrifying that I could ever imagine. Once I climbed onto the back of the dragon form of Aurilya, I knew I would never be the same. She took off in what seemed to be a gentle manner. There really wasn't much to hold on to but some of the long feathers. I was surprised at how strong they were and how hard I could hold on. I tried to remember to loosen up when I didn't need to hold so tightly. When we took off, it was just as the moons were moving across the suns, so there was enough light to see all of the Water Realm. The hills, the mountains and all the rivers and streams. I could see the lake over the top of Noygandia. It was breathtaking. To see the place I spent the majority of my life from this view made it look so much smaller. I always thought it was a large city full of so much life, but watching Iryvalya pass by as we flew out over the sea, I realized how small we were in the grand scheme of everything.

Maybe this was part of the problem, we couldn't see Iryvalya for what it really was. A home to everyone, not just us. I couldn't stop looking at new things I'd never witnessed before. There were birds I had never seen before flying not far from us. Aurilya kept as high as she could without freezing us both, or at least just me, and tried to keep to the clouded areas, but even with that I could see so much. There were so many little islands all over the seas. Some looked like people lived there and others as if no one had ever set foot on them.

I felt something I never really felt before. Free. I felt truly free and filled with wonder. It seemed so silly that in all my years of wanting to do the right thing and help the right people, I had never really thought about what I wanted. Now I knew what I wanted.

I wanted to help bring peace to Iryvalya, so that meant helping Nyrieve. And I always wanted to do that because it was the right thing, but now I had another reason. Now I wanted peace so I could have this… freedom. I wanted to see all these places we had flown over, explore and find new things and meet new people, and the one person who I honestly thought about as I saw these places was Brydetor. I knew he would love to see places like this and explore them with me. I had spent too long ignoring my feelings out of fear of being hurt again, but that wasn't living, it was merely existing. I wanted to live, and I wanted to share the time I had left with someone who I longed to see each day and someone who knew I could be a stubborn person. I just hoped I was not too late with Bry. I should have told him these things before I left. But I promised myself that if we made it through this, I would tell him how much he meant to me and that I wanted to travel all over Iryvalya with him. I didn't really want to be on any council anymore. I didn't want to be stuck inside an office and in meetings.

My heart felt full right now. I didn't know if it had ever been like this. I hoped it would stay. I hoped we could help Nyrieve bring peace to the people of Iryvalya. The one thing I did know, especially after this adventure, I would fight and give up my life if I must to allow all the people of Iryvalya to feel this kind of internal sense of peace and freedom.

⊂ざ28ઔ

BAYSIL

"You are saying I was cursed?" Osidya said softly, rereading the pages I showed her in her journals.

"That is my belief. If you read prior to you leaving for Troxeon, you were elated and wanted to have this baby. You even seemed to hint at the idea of running away with Arnayx to have Nyrieve and raise her in secrecy."

"I don't remember writing any of this. I can see it is my handwriting, but I don't remember... How could I forget some of these things?" she asked.

"I am not sure," I said, worried she would be upset that I didn't have more answers for her.

"I remember going to Troxeon, but it feels like a fuzzy dream. I knew Arnayx and I argued about what we were going to do with the baby... but I thought it was because we didn't want it... The journal entries before, during, and after Troxeon are the opposite of what I remember. It is as if someone was able to go in and change the way I remember things. In reading this, it is almost like I remember both stories, but I don't know which to trust."

"From what I read, it doesn't look like you started to think differently until about a month after you arrived back in Prax. When Rowzey took Nyrieve away, you and Arnayx stayed in Troxeon for a couple more weeks to give your body time to heal before the journey. You both seemed to want to figure out a way to get back to each other and find Nyrieve. But suddenly you started writing about how you never cared about him and it was only a physical attraction for you and the baby was never supposed to happen. It is like something started to rewrite your memories."

Osidya just sat there poring over the pages in the journals I marked for her. I did not want to interfere with her processing of this information, because she could just as easily turn on me and have me killed. I just hoped that somewhere inside of her, her actual memories would try to come forward and she'd see that she did not always have such hate for her daughter.

"Baysil?" Osidya said, breaking the silence.

"Yes," I asked nervously.

"Did you find anything in the journals of something that changed or… I don't know, just something that we can point to as what forced me to change?"

I opened up one of the journals to a page I had marked and handed it over to her. She surprised me by reading it aloud.

Today would have been my sister's Leaf Day. Embers would have loved to have seen all the people who showed up to support our family and share their memories of her with us. Mother and Father used any time no one was around to remind me it was my fault she was dead. I will always be to blame for her death, they told me, and that it was a blessing that my child also died because Embers's other killer deserved death as well. If they ever find out the truth, I believe they will kill me. I must never speak of it to anyone. Perhaps one day things will change and Arnayx and I will be able to reunite with our daughter and help her learn to be better than those her father and I came from. Mother and Father also gave me a gift of sorts. They said it belonged to Embers, but I don't ever remember seeing her wear them. It is a small set of earrings with red gemstones to wear at the midpoint of my ear. They were very pretty, but I didn't want to remove the ones I was wearing that Arnayx had given me. When I showed hesitation, Mother got very angry with me and practically ripped out my old earrings and put in the new ones. My ears have felt almost like they were burning since, but I am guessing that is because of how aggressively she removed my old ones. If it doesn't stop burning, I'll go have it checked… Happy Leaf Day, Embers. I will always love and miss you.

"Embers?" I asked, to clarify.

"Embers was the nickname I used to use for Rievenya. She didn't like me calling her that much around others, but when we were little, it was all I called her. As we got older, I quit. I don't know why I wrote it here like that though…"

"Osidya?" I asked, taking a deep breath.

"What?" she asked, sounding slightly annoyed with the feelings she was having.

"You are still wearing those earrings."

She snapped her head up and looked at me with her head tipping to the side.

"So? What of it? Are you trying to steal them from me? They are mine!"

My eyes widened at her overreaction to my statement. "I do not wish to have them, Osidya."

"Then what about them?"

"It is after this journal entry that what you wrote started to change. You became more angry and hateful towards the memories and the idea of your child."

"What is your point?"

"You really can't see the connection?"

"What connection?"

"I believe the earrings might be what caused your thoughts and memories to change. They could have been enchanted to cause it."

"But my parents gave them to me, and they didn't know that Nyrieve survived."

"Do you honestly believe that they couldn't have read one of your journals or that someone might have known she was alive or that they didn't know but didn't want to take any chances on you wanting a life with her?"

She sat there rereading the journal entry over and over. I could see her mouthing the words and shaking her head. "I don't know, Baysil. What you say makes sense, but even as I say that, inside of me something is telling me you are wrong and you have to be wrong."

"Do you trust me?" I asked, not sure what her answer would be.

"I don't know if I can," she said, looking sad and lost. I had never seen her looking anything less than in control and sure of herself.

"Let me remove the earrings. I will place them on the table next to you. Then take some time and see if anything changes. If it doesn't, then maybe I am crazy and this is just how things are... but if I am right..."

"Then maybe I will start to feel different?" she asked, sounding like a hopeful child.

"Maybe. It really cannot hurt to try it. It is not like I can steal them and get away. You still control the guards and can have me killed at any moment."

She looked at me, studying my face, and finally nodded to me and turned her head for her ear to be accessible. I gently stood up and crossed over to her. I touched the first earring, and touching it felt similar to getting stung by a jellyfish. It hurt, but wasn't so painful I couldn't move quickly and remove it. The second earring felt the same, and as soon as both were set down on the table next to Osidya, the stinging feeling slowly dissipated.

I sat back down and watched Osidya as she softly rubbed both of her long pointy ears where the earrings had been. She looked over at me and said, "Something feels different... It is almost like... I am not sure how to describe it..."

"Take your time. There is no rush," I said calmly, while eagerly wanting to rush her to see if it made any difference.

"Do you know the feeling when you are swimming in water, and you can hear voices but they are not clear?"

"Yes, I have had that before."

"I feel like I just brought my head above water and everything now sounds silent."

"Silent?"

"Yes and no... I can hear you. I can hear the pages of the journal turning, but... it is like there is no longer this constant staticky noise that is angry and yelling at me."

"And when I say the name Nyrieve, what does that make you feel?"

She thought for a moment. "Sad."

"Sad?"

"Yes, normally I would feel anger and hate, but I feel sad."

"Sad is a valid feeling."

"But I also feel a form of disgust for the name and yet it feels different, not like it did before... It is more of a hollow disgust, like it is there and I feel it fully, but it doesn't make sense."

"That is good, Osidya," I said, giving her a faint smile.

"How is it good? My thoughts are contradicting each other..."

"If you read through your journal, you didn't immediately begin to hate your daughter. It was a slow transition. I think removing the earrings will allow you to start to feel your true thoughts and feelings, but I don't think it will just happen right away. It took years for you to grow in your hatred of her and anyone not like your parents. I think it is safe to say it might take you years to get all the anger and misinformation fully out of your head."

"So now I will just be walking around with mixed feelings about everything and not knowing what the right thing is?" she asked, sounding panicked.

I tried hard not to smile, but I couldn't help it, and from the look in her eyes she was getting pretty annoyed with it.

"I am sorry to smile, but, Osidya, that is something that most people deal with each and every day without a curse or charm. Nothing in the world is simply black and white. Most people live in the gray area between, so it is a daily struggle for most of us. For an example, on one hand, could we kill off all the elves and stop more wars? Yes, we could, but there are so many good elves, so that would kill them too… If you want good things in the world, you need to be part of the good and help others be part of the good as well…"

"This is just too much right now… I need to get some air and think on all of this," she said as she stood up and crossed over to the door and opened it. She looked back over at me with a confused look on her face. "Aren't you coming with me?"

I looked back at her in disbelief and asked, "You want me to come with you?"

"Yes, you know what is happening more than I do right now, so let's go," she said, sounding frustrated.

"Do you need to restrain my hands or anything first?"

"No, I am in charge of you, and for some stupid reason that I do not understand, I trust you," she said. "Now let's go before I change my mind!"

I quickly got up and followed Osidya out the door.

CঙৎঞO

I followed Osidya down dimly lit hallways and up spiraling stairs. I tried to memorize the way we were going, in case I needed to run, but after a while I had to give up. There was no way I would be able to figure out a way to get out of here, especially without Kaleyna. I could not leave her here with Miaarya and Fyra. They already seemed to have broken her down and I didn't want any more harm to come to her.

After what seemed like a half hour, we emerged into a house. It was similar to the one we stayed in when we first came here. It looked like it was owned by a high-ranking family. Everything was new-looking and nothing seemed out of place. There wasn't much light, so I couldn't see any viewing crystals on the shelves or anything, but I believed we had to be in Osidya's home.

She kept walking forward and opened a large glass door that led out to a massive balcony. There were a few chairs strewn around, but the best part was the view. I hadn't seen the outside in months. The air smelled so clean and sweet. The night sky was darkened by clouds but was still beautiful to see again. I could feel tiny raindrops hit me every so often, but not enough to really call it a rainstorm. I could smell the rain mixing with the dirt. I always loved the smell of the air after it rained. I closed my eyes and just breathed in as deeply as I could over and over. I didn't know how long I would get to enjoy this, so I wanted to make sure I enjoyed every moment.

"What is your story, Baysil?" Osidya asked me.

"My story?" I replied, confused.

"I know everything you told the guards and Fyra, and even some of the things you told Kaleyna while in your cell, but I want to know, why did you pick this path? Why did you decide to follow Nyrieve?"

"I decided that long before I ever even knew her name, Osidya."

"Why? Why is that? What is so amazing about her that she beckons people to follow her without a care for tradition or loyalty?"

"Because it isn't all about her. It isn't about following this one person who is supposed to unite our world. It is about wanting our world to be united. It is about wanting a better world for future generations to enjoy and take care of. She represents the idea of hope, and because she fits all the things listed in the prophecy, people will follow her."

"Do you believe in the prophecy?"

"I'm not sure… but I believe the idea of wanting a better world. I believe that we should all be able to coexist without war and killing. I am not against a leader for

224

the people, but it should be a person who is willing to listen to everyone's ideas and wants. Not all of them can be filled, but to know someone is taking the time to really hear you is a powerful thing."

"I remember as a child hearing the adults talk about this prophecy," she said, talking quietly and slowly. "I thought it was just a children's tale at first. Then as I got older, I thought it was a stupid story to scare elves into doing what our parents told us to do... When she was born and bore the mark of the savior... I was so upset."

"Upset at what?"

"I was upset that I brought a child into this world only to be forced to try to do the impossible."

"Do you still feel that way?"

"Yes, no one should have a burden like that placed upon them."

"You are right, and Nyrieve and I had many conversations about just that. She understood what was expected of her. She knew that she did not really have a choice, but she truly did. She had many chances and opportunities to leave. She could have run away with friends and maybe never been found. She could have lived a life in hiding and not always putting her own life at risk."

"Why didn't she?"

"I think it is because she knew that if she didn't follow this path, someone else would have to, and she knew how it felt with the weight of this on her shoulders and she didn't want to place it on someone else's."

"You make her sound like an unusually selfless elf."

"She is, Osidya. She is a good person at her core."

"When she met with her father, because I know she did, how did he treat her?"

"How honest do you want me to be?" I asked, unsure if she could really handle the truth.

"I did not bring you out here with me to feed me stories. Just answer the question."

"He treated her... Well, the opposite way you did."

She smiled, and it looked genuine. She took a deep breath and said, "I am not surprised. Arnayx was always a good man. He always wanted to have a family and settle down… I guess that just wasn't meant for me. My parents would have never allowed me to just be a wife and mother. If I wasn't making our family name better, I wasn't worth anything."

"That is a lot of pressure for anyone."

"Yes, it is…"

"What is it you wanted in life?" I asked.

"Me?" she asked, surprised. "What did I want in life?"

"Yes, what would have made you happy?"

"I don't think anyone has asked me that in over nineteen Leaf Years," she said solemnly.

I let the silence fill the air between us. I didn't want to push her for an answer, because that might make her more angry. Especially if those earrings were cursed, there could still be lingering thoughts going on.

"Baysil," Osidya said, "when I was young, I wanted power. I wanted to make my parents proud. I had always thought I could achieve being the next saygent of Iryvalya. My family held that title so long ago, I wanted to get it back and make them proud. Then as I became older, and I saw the truth of how our people were and what they were capable of, all I wanted to do was escape and have a family that just loved me for me. I dreamed I would make my sister run away with me, and she and I would find our happiness together. Maybe we'd both end up with people we love and have children who could be as close as she and I were."

"That sounds like it could have been a good life…"

"Once Cyndorin was killed, my sister changed. She wasn't hopeful anymore. She just did as she was told without question, like she was unable to have thoughts of her own. I think that was when I realized I could never leave without her. I couldn't let her become the thing my parents had forced me to become now in my life."

"I am sorry that she lost Cyndorin and that you in turn lost her…"

"I didn't lose her though… My parents put her in a position to destroy my happiness, and in the end, she gave up her life for a child I ended up hating and wishing was never born. I thought Nyrieve was to blame for the death of my sister and me not being able to ascend higher in the council. I know many people knew I had a child, though most thought I lost it, but it was still enough for me to be looked at as if I was tainted."

"I honestly cannot imagine how hard that must have been for you."

"No one knew, but more so no one cared. I tried to talk to my parents, especially in the days after returning home from Troxeon. I honestly think that is why they gave me the cursed earrings. It made me shut up and not speak about things they didn't want to hear. As much as I don't feel the same hate as I did, I can still feel it lingering in the back of my mind, like I should still hate… but I guess it doesn't matter anymore. I never achieved what they wanted me to, and they died disappointed in me."

"If you don't mind me saying, from what you said about your parents, I do not think there would have been something you could have done to achieve the kind of respect and praise you had hoped for from them."

We stood out on the balcony, not talking. I could hear the crickets in the distance, the sounds of the night coming alive. I missed being outside, and I hadn't fully realized it until now. My eyes stung and tears flowed gently down my face.

"What is it?" she asked me.

"I missed being outside," I said.

"I'm torn on if I should be understanding or laugh… I don't like how I am feeling so confused," she said, rubbing her forehead. "I feel like my brain is being controlled by two different beings."

"A suggestion then. When you are not sure which to do, think about which one would possibly have been the choice your parents would have wanted, and then do the opposite."

She laughed lightly. "I see your point, Baysil… I will try to do that."

I smiled at her, hoping she would really try to be a better person, and this wasn't some sort of trick.

"Now I have something I need to tell you, and you are not going to be happy about it, but it wasn't my choice," she said.

"What is it?" I asked, my stomach starting to turn.

"Fyra is coming here tonight or tomorrow morning to collect you. She already has Kaleyna ready, but she needs you as well."

"Needs us for what?"

"Apparently she is planning on cleaning you up, making sure your wounds are all healed before she tries to barter with the Nomydrac."

"Barter for what?"

"I am not sure. I have been told she wants them to give their allegiance to her and the Pyrothians, and I believe her intent is to have that solidified before she gives birth, which I was told will be soon. I do not see how she can do that, but she has it in her mind right now she can."

"So you bringing me here was only to set me up for Fyra?"

"Yes and no… She was going to come for you either way, but I convinced her to give me some time with you first…"

"Time with me for what?"

"The real reason was to figure out what was going on with me, but I couldn't tell her that. She believes I have interests in you."

"Interests?" I asked.

She sighed. "Yes, I lied to her and said I have never bedded a fairy before and wanted to do so before she takes control of you. She agreed, because I believe she liked the idea of me taking you against your will."

"And do you plan on doing that?"

"No, of course not, I don't do things like that… I might be… whatever I am, but for some reason over these past months, I have come to respect you and what you say. You have no hidden agenda that I can see, and I want to believe you when you say my daughter will unite Iryvalya."

I took a deep breath and looked out to the distance. "I think we might be on the right track, Osidya."

"Why do you say that?"

"Look," I said, pointing out in the distance. There was a small group of irybugs flickering around, moving towards us. They floated around for a few moments and then left. "If you don't trust in me, trust in Iryvalya and trust in your daughter."

"I don't understand what is happening, but I will do what I can to help you, Baysil. You and… my daughter."

For some reason, and I didn't know why, I believed her. I believed she really would do what she could to help Nyrieve. I just hoped I was right.

∽29∾

NYRIEVE

"How is it we have been here for a week already?" Emryleia asked. "It feels like we just got here."

"I know," Koyvean responded, "but we can't stay here much longer."

"I know," Emryleia responded sadly.

"I am not excited to leave either," I said. "I feel like this place is so far away from everything else going on in Iryvalya. Like time forgot about it, and it has just existed out of the reach of everything."

"You're not excited to leave and see Kylyan?" Iclyn said, walking into the conservatory.

"Of course I am," I said with a smile. "I just wish I could bring him here to see this place."

Koyvean chuckled. "You think he'd love all the fanciness of this place?"

"No, not the fancy part. I don't think he'd really care much about that, though I know he'd enjoy some parts of it. But I think he would love how peaceful it is here, and he would love the rain bath thing!"

"I can see that," Domi said, walking in silently.

"Domi!" I exclaimed. "Where have you been?"

"Here and there," she said softly.

"What does that mean?" Iclyn asked. "You have been gone for days. I didn't know if something happened to you."

"If it had, I am sure Alabynes would have let you all know."

"How would he have known? He's been here the whole time," I asked.

"Valyas can usually sense when another of us has passed."

"Then how come none of you knew he was still alive?" I asked her.

"He was alive much longer than the rest of us, so we didn't feel him come into the world, his presence was just always there. I imagine when he passes on one day,

I'll feel it and it will be like losing something you didn't know you had until it was gone."

"How is it possible he has been alive so long?" I wondered aloud.

"I have a theory," Koyvean said.

"What?" Emryleia and I said in unison and smiled at each other.

"I believe whatever spell or charm is placed on this castle protects those in it from time passing."

"How do you figure that?" Iclyn asked.

"I tested my theory. While I was out scouting, I found a little bug that looked like it was about to die. It appeared something might have crushed it. I brought it into the castle, and while it did not get better, it did not get worse and die."

"That doesn't really prove it," Iclyn said.

"No, but when I brought it back outside of the castle, it quickly died. It is the only thing I can figure that makes any sense."

"So this place, for some reason time doesn't move?" I asked curiously.

"It would explain how Alabynes is still here. He said he spent most of his time in the castle. While he has aged, according to things he said, that can be attributed to the time he spent outside the castle looking for that," Koyvean said, pointing to the egg-shaped rock I was holding.

"Well, we think it is holding Clyr, but we won't know for sure until we can get it open," I said.

"I thought Lydorea's blood was supposed to be able to open it," Em said.

"It is, but we only have a small amount of it here," Iclyn said.

"Iclyn," I said, "we have spent days searching around the island for something else that could possibly be Clyr or holding Clyr. I do not think that there is anything else we'll be able to find. Besides, I believe the iryturtles led me to this. I don't like that I had to crack my head on it, but it has to be it."

"I know, I just…" she said.

I walked over and put my arm around her. "I know, Iclyn, it is one of the last things Lydorea gave to you and one of the last things you promised her you'd do. If you use the blood, weather it works or not, it is done and I think you will feel like your ties to Lydorea are done."

Tears welled up in her eyes. "I just am not ready to be done and move forward."

"And you of all people know that Lydorea would want you to move forward. She wouldn't have wanted you stuck in this limbo of just holding on."

"I know, Ny, I am just really struggling with it."

"If we don't open this and find Clyr, we need to start planning another way, and we do not have much time left," I said.

Iclyn closed her eyes and took a deep breath. "Fine," she said, "let's try it and find out if it works."

Iclyn took the rock from me and walked over to the table where she kept all her supplies. She reached inside and seemed to be searching around for a bit. Part of me wondered if she was doing it on purpose to take just a little more time.

Eventually she pulled out a small crystal vial filled with a dark red liquid. "Here it is," she said. "From what Lydorea told me, it shouldn't take too many drops to break the curse."

Iclyn set the rock back in my hands, then she opened the crystal vial and carefully let seven small drops of blood drip onto the rock. At first it just started to flow down the rock, but then I noticed it wasn't just moving downwards, it was spreading out all over the rock, but deep inside carved crevasses you could barely notice. Eventually the entire rock had Lydorea's blood on it, yet it didn't ever drip onto my hands. It was like the rock was holding it close to itself.

The rock started to get warmer, and I could feel something moving inside of it. There was some sparkling silvery light that began to emit from the rock. It looked like the rock was cracking apart and the light was coming from inside trying to get out. It began to shake more and more violently, almost to the point I thought it would shoot out of my hands, but it didn't. The silvery light became brighter and brighter. It was almost too blinding to look at, but I couldn't look away.

Suddenly the rock shattered apart in my hands and parts fell to the floor. Left among the broken rock was a teardrop-shaped gemstone covered in Lydorea's blood. I looked up at Iclyn and asked, "Is the blood supposed to be on it like this?"

"I don't know," she said. "I think the gemstone was attracting or pulling the blood to break apart the rock."

I walked over to the fountain next to the wall and gently washed the blood off the gemstone and then dried it off on my shirt. Once it felt clean, I really looked at it. It was a teardrop shape like I thought, and the stone inside was wrapped in a silver band with a closed hook on top. It was already made to be worn on a chain. I guessed someone else once wore it around their neck. I took the pendant over to the window and let the sunlight shine down on it. I knew immediately when I saw it what kind of gemstone was used.

"It's a rainbow moonstone," I said, surprised.

"Like your ring?" Emryleia said.

"And your earrings?" Koyvean asked too.

"Yes, and like the stone in the top of Klaw," I said. "How is this possible?"

"The rainbow moonstone holds more magyc and power than most know," Alabynes said, walking into the room.

"But how likely is it that all these things would be the same?" I asked, confused.

He smiled at me. "I don't know the answer to that question, Nyrieve, but it is one of the quirky things that seems to happen in Iryvalya, and I enjoy it for what it is."

I didn't understand how it could be all these gemstones that I had were the same, it just didn't seem likely. "I feel like there is more to it than that," I said.

"It could be," he replied, "but that answer I do not have."

"You have given me a lot of other answers this week Alabynes, letting me read through the scrolls you have kept. I don't know if I will ever be able to understand all the things you showed me, but so far you have been completely honest with me, so I believe you when you say you do not know."

"I don't know if I do," Koyvean said, looking at Alabynes with distrust.

"I don't think there is anyone you really trust, is there, Koyvean?" I asked with a smile.

"If only there were a few thousand of those amulets to pass around Iryvalya, then maybe we would always know people are telling the truth free of persuasion," she said.

Emryleia walked over and looked at the beautiful rainbow trapped inside the amulet. "Until someone tries this, none of us will know if it is really Clyr and if it works."

Iclyn walked over to me, bringing with her a silver necklace. Without taking it from my hands, she simply slipped the chain through the loop on the amulet and let me hook it on myself. "The main purpose of Clyr was to protect the wearer from curses, charms, or any other form of mind control. Telling the truth though, that is a choice of the wearer. What you want, Koyvean, is a truth stone."

"Back before we left for Lynawn, someone gave me a truth stone. Rowzey had fixed it into a ring for me, but it never seemed to work much after she gave it to me," I said, looking down at the simple ring.

"Did you ever take it off or anything?"

"No, I didn't," I said. "I just figured maybe the charm on it wore out or something."

Domi walked over and took my hand to look at the ring. "It looks like it was cracked. It could have happened when it was being set in the ring, or perhaps you fell or were injured at some point. If the stone is broken or fractured, it doesn't work anymore."

"Oh, that would explain it then, I guess. I know I have fallen many times since I started to wear it."

"Did you know that this island is covered in truth stones?" Alabynes chimed in.

"It is?" I asked.

"Yes, the iryturtles seem to love to dig them from the ground and place them around the island. They are all quite small, but fascinating."

"Alabynes," Koyvean asked, almost sounding excited. "Would you be able to show me where I can find some of these stones?"

"Of course I can," he said. "Would you like to go find some now?"

"Yes," she said. "If that is okay with everyone? I have an idea and I want to collect as many as we can carry."

I smiled. "I don't have a problem with it."

"Me neither," said Iclyn.

"Okay, Alabynes and I will be back as quickly as possible," Koyvean said, leading Alabynes quickly out of the room.

"Now," Emryleia said, "how do we test this Clyr thing?"

"I don't know," I said, taking the necklace and hooking it around my neck, letting the teardrop amulet rest on my chest. When it touched my skin, I felt something warm push throughout my body. It left a tingling sensation to where I almost lost my balance.

"Ny?" Iclyn said, taking my arm to help steady me. "Are you okay?"

"I think so," I said, able to stand up again. "It just… I don't know how to explain it. When I placed Clyr on my chest, it felt like a rush of warmth and sensations throughout my body."

"I guess it is working then," she said, letting my arm go. "Shall we try to make it work?"

"How?" Em asked. "We don't really want Ny to be cursed or anything, do you?"

"No, but I could try an influence spell on her, maybe see if that forces her to like or do something she wouldn't normally do."

"But to try it, you'd have to do it with Clyr on and test it again to see if it works without it on as well," I said.

"I think I can do that," Iclyn said. She quickly moved around the conservatory and placed five different items on the table in the middle of the room. I walked over to see what she placed. It was a blackened leaf with green veins, a bright red rose bud, a dark brown mushroom, some white seeds, and a pinch of dirt.

"Okay, how does this work?" I asked.

"I am going to recite an incantation and see if you do what I try to make you do," she said. "But before I do, I will tell Domi and Emryleia what I am going to try to make you do."

Iclyn walked over and whispered first in Domi's ear and then Emryleia's. I couldn't hear her, which I thought was good, because I was not sure I wanted to know what she was going to try to make me do with these things.

After both nodded to her in understanding, Iclyn began to chant something I couldn't make out. It was in a fairy language I had heard her and Lydorea use when they didn't want people to hear their conversation. As she was speaking, I could feel a tingly sensation coming from Clyr. It wasn't overly strong, but it was just there where I could feel it.

Once Iclyn was done speaking, we all stood there and looked at one another. "Are you done?" I asked, confused.

"It should have worked by now," Iclyn said, seeming surprised. "Now, if you can, take Clyr off and we can try it again."

I hesitated to take Clyr off, because it felt so right next to my skin, but I knew this might be the only way to know if it was really working or just all in my head. I took Clyr off and set it on the edge of the table next to the five items.

Iclyn started to chant the same thing she said before, and I felt myself grabbing the mushroom and ripping it into little pieces. I then took the rose bud and pulled each petal off of it and placed them in a circle around the destroyed mushroom. Then I grabbed the white seeds and dirt in separate hands and sprinkled them both overtop of the mushroom pieces. Finally I took the leaf and gently laid it on top of the pile in front of me.

Both Domi and Emryleia looked surprised at me, and Iclyn just smiled, saying, "She was right, Lydorea was right. Clyr existed and we were able to get it for you, Ny. She was right!"

I smiled back at Iclyn. "She was always right, wasn't she?"

Iclyn smiled and cried at the same time. "I did what she asked of me. She wanted me to help you, help you find Clyr, and I have been able to honor her wishes, Ny. I didn't let her down."

"Oh, Iclyn," I said, grabbing her into a big hug. "You never let her down!"

Iclyn hugged me back, and when she let go she was smiling. She reached over and grabbed the necklace and hooked it around my neck again. I didn't get the same feeling throughout me again, but I could feel the amulet when it touched my skin give what felt like a spark. It was where it was meant to be, and I had no plan of ever taking it off.

"I think when Koyvean gets back, we should get going," Domi said.

"Where should we be going to?" I asked.

"While I was gone, I did some… watching, and there have been changes and movements in both Klayns. They are looking at mounting an attack on you, Nyrieve."

"But where? And when?" I asked, "Do they know we are here?"

"No, they don't know where you are, but somehow they learned of where your family was hiding and planned on moving there to get them in hopes of flushing you out. I talked to some other Valya that think like me, and they have rushed to help move everyone from Aquileia to the Air Realm."

"The Air Realm?" I said, surprised. "Why there?"

"The majority of the dragons are there and they are able to stay hidden until it is time for them to be revealed. It is also close enough to travel to the Stone Realm too, to gather anyone else that we might need to help us. The main ones planning on attacking Aquileia are the Pyrothian Elves, but it seems like they are working with some of the Lumaryia Elves as a form of backup. From what we can tell, a couple of the higher-up leaders are willing to work together to bring you down, for now."

"But how do they know Nyrieve is alive?" Em asked.

"They are not positive that she is, but they figure if they attack or kill her family, if she is alive, she will come after them, where they believe, they are aptly prepared to fight and win."

"How long before everyone will be in the Air Realm?" I asked, worried about Kylyan and my family.

"It should already be happening. Sudryl has also offered to help move them in a way that should keep them from being detected."

"How?" I asked, feeling panic starting to well up inside of me.

"He and his people were able to craft most of Aquileia, Nyrieve. Between what Emryleia showed them with her magyc and their own, I can only imagine what they will be able to create to get them to safety," she said calmly.

"Okay," Iclyn started. "Then we need to get a move on as well. I will go get Koyvean and Alabynes and tell them we need to head out by first light tomorrow."

"Tomorrow?" I asked, thinking we should be leaving right now.

"Yes, Ny, tomorrow," she said. "We need to get to the Air Realm, and going by boat won't be the quickest way there, will it?"

"No, but then how are we going to go back?"

"Domi," Iclyn asked, "is there a way you can portal us there?"

"I would if I could, but if I did that, the other Valyas will notice and might tell Jagula. I do not trust her," she replied.

Iclyn shouted something that must have been a curse word, but not in a language I knew.

"I have an idea," I said.

"What?" Iclyn said, pacing back and forth.

"Domi," I said, "you can portal to the Air Realm without much issue, right? Especially if you go there and stay for a while."

"That is true," she said, tilting her head to the side.

"Then can you portal there and have one of the dragons come here to get us and bring us to the Air Realm?"

"I should be able to do that, but what about if the dragon is seen, since the Klayn warriors are on their way."

"Have them fly by night, and we will wait here until they arrive. Then they can be careful and maybe fly in a direction that might take a little more time but will keep them from being seen."

"I can do that. But why do you want me to stay there?"

"Because, if for any reason we're too late to get there, then you can portal everyone you can to safety."

"Where would that be?" she asked.

"I don't know, but I am trusting that either Kylyan or my parents might have an idea of a place to hide."

"I will do that for you, Nyrieve," she said as she started to walk out of the room.

"Wait," I said. "Did you say they are bringing their warriors?"

"Mostly their warriors, but in truth most of the people are not actual warriors. They are just part of the Klayn and being forced to fight for their leaders."

"Good," I said. "I want as many of their people there when this all happens. I want them to see they have a choice between the life they have lived and a life of peace and freedom."

"I believe you will be able to give them that, Nyrieve," Domi said. "I will go now and get someone to come collect you all as soon as possible."

"Thank you, Domi," I said.

She simply nodded, and before stepping out the door, she said, "Volnyri."

⊂ß30⊷

NYRIEVE

"What are we supposed to do while we wait for a dragon to come get us?" Iclyn asked, pacing around the conservatory.

Emryleia laughed. "I am guessing whatever we want, Iclyn. I know it is a stressful time, but us sitting here and worrying about it is not going to make the time pass any quicker."

"I know, I know," she replied, still pacing.

"Iclyn," I said, grabbing her attention enough that she stopped and looked at me. "I think we should go over some contingency plans."

"For what?" she asked, squinting her eyes a little at me.

"In case the things we are trying to do, you know… don't work," I said.

"No," she snapped. "They will work, they have to."

I closed my eyes and thought for a moment. "If you are unwilling to help me, Iclyn, then I will set something up without you and your input."

She stared at me with her mouth gaping open.

"I am not trying to be rude to you, Iclyn," I said, "but I need to know some things will be taken care of for me, if I am unable to do them myself."

"Like what?" she hissed at me.

"Like who is going to help hide or protect Kylan and my family? I need to know going into all of this, that if I do not make it out, they will be taken care of, or at least helped to have a chance of having some sort of life past me."

"Ny, you shouldn't be thinking like that," she said, sounding softer.

"I cannot lie to myself and think that everything will work out the way we want it to. We have been doing this for long enough that we know that most things do not go according to plan. It's great to have an idea of what we are going to do, but to believe whole heartedly that what we think is going to happen is exactly what will happen is naive and dangerous for others who are counting on me to bring peace to

Iryvalya."

"Do you honestly think we are going to fail?" Emryleia asked, sounding nervous.

"I don't think we will fail, but I don't think everything will go exactly as planned," I said. "The best I can say is I am cautiously optimistic."

"Cautiously optimistic?" Em asked rhetorically. "Maybe that is what we should say instead of Volnyri…"

"Look," I said, trying to get them to understand. "After I fell into a bloody scalding lava-shooting volcano and truly thought I was going to die, my thought wasn't that I failed the prophecy, it was what about those I love and care about? What would happen to them or how would they survive if anyone blamed them for me? Even after I awoke in the Spirit Realm, those were the questions that continued to haunt me and keep me more alert. I have people I love very much and want to ensure their safety to the best of my ability. Why is that so wrong?"

"It isn't, Ny," Iclyn said sullenly as she sat down next to me. "I don't think about things like that anymore. I used to, before Lydorea…"

"I know, Iclyn, but there are still things to live for, and you know she would want you to keep going," I said, placing my hand on top of hers. She took my hand in both of hers and squeezed them.

"I know you are right," she said, "but I feel empty and lost without her. She was my rudder, Ny. She led us everywhere we went, and without her I am just moving. It could be forwards, it could be backwards, I don't know. All I know is that I want revenge for those who caused her harm and nothing else feels like it is as important."

"I understand, I really do… but she wouldn't want you to live that way," I said.

"You don't know that," she snapped.

"Yes I do," I said. "You know the pack she gave me, right?"

"The one with all the herbs and stuff she collected for you?"

"Yes, that one. That is not the only things that were in it."

"Oh?"

"She wrote me a couple of letters… and she has one that she wrote for you, but she doesn't want me to give it to you just yet."

"What?" she exclaimed, dropping my hands. "You have a letter for me from Lydorea and haven't given it to me?"

"Iclyn," I said, "please listen to me. You knew Lydorea better than anyone, right?"

"Of course."

"Did you trust that she knew the best for you?"

"Yes."

"Then trust that when she wrote to me not to give it to you until a certain time, there is a really good reason for it."

"Have you read it?" she asked.

"No, it is sealed, and I have no desire to go against Lydorea's wishes. I am doing exactly as she instructed me to do."

Iclyn became silent. I let her sit and think things over for a while before asking her, "Do you trust me, Iclyn?"

She looked at me with the two shades of gray swirls in her eyes, and said, "I do trust you, Nyrieve... Otherwise I wouldn't be here. I just... I miss her so much... more than anything or anyone else... I would give my life for only a moment with her again."

"I know you would," I said, giving her a side hug, "and if there was a way to bring her back, I would. The only thing I can do is honor her and her wishes and trust that she knew what would be right and best."

"I know you are right," she said. "I just... I would have thought by now it wouldn't hurt as much. The pain is the same in my heart today as it was the day she was killed. And yet time moves forward. I live each day, I breathe, I fight, I sleep, I eat, and there is a part of me that isn't there. It's like a phantom limb. Part of who I was... who I am, is missing."

"I don't know loss like that," I said, "but I can imagine that is how I would feel if something happened to Kylyan."

"I truly hope you never know this feeling, Ny... but you are right. We are here trying to help the living, and that is what Lydorea wanted. To help the people of Iryvalya, elves and fairies alike." She took a deep, quivering breath. "I promise you

242

that if something does not go right, we will do everything we can to protect your loved ones."

"You know that includes the both of you too, right?" I asked.

Em and Iclyn smiled at me. Iclyn said, "We love you too, Ny, and I promise we will try to help everyone we can."

Emryleia nodded in agreement.

"Thank you," I said.

"What is going on in here?" Koyvean said as she sauntered into the room.

"Just going over some contingency plans," I said.

"I love making backup plans!" Koyvean said eagerly.

Iclyn, Emryleia, and I all laughed.

"We know," I said. "And that is why I am leaving it to you and Iclyn to set up alternative options to get everyone we can to safety. I do not want my parents to come with us where we will meet up with the Klayns, but I do not think I will be able to keep Kylyan away."

"I agree," Koyvean said. "Kylyan will not want to leave your side, and I believe you will want him there as well."

"I do want him there, but I am worried for him as well."

"Of course, Ny," she said, "but I believe having him by your side will also help you think more clearly."

"What do you mean?"

"When you are confronted with the people who have almost killed Rowzey, killed Ghily, and have done who knows what to Baysil and Kaleyna, you need to be able to keep your head clear and ready to make decisions. If Kylyan is there, I am less worried about you taking a more… drastic approach."

I laughed. "Do you really think I would act rashly?"

"I know I would."

I sat there thinking about what it would be like to have Fyra in front of me right now. What would I want to do? Would I be able to put aside what she has done if she was willing to agree to peace? Could I allow her to live out her life in the freedom that she tried to take away from everyone? I want to say that I would, that I would want to look past that for the greater good of Iryvalya and the people. But if there was no one to stop me, would I cause her great harm? I honestly didn't know the answer.

I looked at my friends here with me and said, "We have gotten to a point where we have a whole new possible world for us all on the horizon. I want to believe that I would make fair and just decisions for the betterment of our world… but I honestly don't know if I would."

"And that is why I think you need Kylyan there. You need someone there that you want a future with to look at and hold your rage back enough that you can see clearly and think of everyone and not just how you feel. What has been done to you is more than most can handle, and yet you keep showing up with a kindness and grace that I could have never had. But perhaps, if I had someone like your parents or Kylyan, perhaps I would think more before I acted."

I smiled at her. "Thank you, Koyvean… You are right. I need him by my side to keep me grounded and thinking about what is important. He will be thanking you, I can bet."

"No need," she said. "I just speak the truth. I have found life is much easier living in truth and honesty in the long run, even if it seems to make some people uncomfortable at times."

"I am glad you do," I said.

"As far as your family is concerned," Koyvean stated, "I have a plan on where I can move them to. It is not as beautiful as this place here, but they will be safe and well cared for. That I can assure you."

"What about Kylyan?" I asked.

She took a deep breath and sighed. "If he is by your side if things go all sideways, we will be limited on our ability to get him away and to safety."

"I will be by your side too, Ny," Em said. "I will do everything I can to make sure Kylyan gets to safety and I will arrange things with Koyvean to get him to where ever your family is being sent."

"Thank you," I said to all of them. "It means the world to me to know they all at least have a chance to live beyond all of this if things don't go as we hope."

"Now we need to talk about something more pressing," Koyvean stated.

"What now?" Iclyn sighed.

"I went to find some of the truth stones..." she said. "I found some, but we have a small problem."

"What is that?" I asked, not sure if I wanted to know.

"Come with me, and I'll show you," she said, turning and walking out of the room.

We all jumped up and followed her down the halls and then to the platform at the top of the stairs where she had stopped.

"Look down there," she said, pointing in front of the large fountain.

"Oh my..." I said, my eyes starting to dry out from how wide they were opened.

On the ground in front of and around the fountain were several hundred small truth stones, but that wasn't what was surprising. Mixed amongst the stones were at least fifty tiny iryturtles crawling all over the rocks and appearing to lay eggs. The eggs they laid were no bigger or smaller than the truth stones.

"What are they doing?" I asked aloud to no one in particular.

"I think I know," Alabynes's voice shouted up to us. He was down at the bottom of the steps, so I didn't even notice him there.

I quickly ran down the steps to meet him. "What do you think they are doing?"

"They only started doing this after we poured all the truth stones onto the ground," he said. "I am guessing they want to go wherever the stones go."

"The iryturtles or the eggs?" Em asked from behind me.

"Both," he replied. "I saw them do something similar once many, many years ago. They wanted to try living elsewhere, back out in Iryvalya."

"Did it work?" I asked.

"No," he said, "because I never ended up leaving..."

I walked down past Alabynes and walked over to the pile of stones and eggs. I knelt down and picked a couple up in my hand. I couldn't tell one from the other. I checked another spot and again couldn't tell them apart.

"How will this work? We need the truth stones to help the people of Iryvalya to know we are telling the truth, but we can't just hand out a... I don't know, like a hundred iryturtle eggs to people unknowingly," I said.

"I don't think they will be in eggs for very long," Alabynes said.

"What do you mean?"

"In the rest of Iryvalya, most turtles, both land and sea, lay eggs that take about eight to ten weeks to hatch. That is the same time here with the iryturtles. However, as we have figured out, time moves differently here than it seems elsewhere."

"You're saying the iryturtles only lay their eggs inside the castle grounds?" I asked.

"It would seem so," he said. "At least for as long as I have been here. I have not seen them laid anywhere else in the Blackened Forest before."

"How long do you think they would take to hatch?" I asked.

"I would estimate that within a fortnight of being here, they will hatch. You could always check each one before giving them out to people though."

"How? They all look the same," Emryleia said.

"You will need a very bright and powerful crystal that you can hold the egg up to and see the iryturtle inside of it. I am sure someone could enchant one if needs be, but by then you should be able to see the size of the iryturtles shell maybe get bigger. I wish I could be of more help."

"But won't the truth stones break the eggshells?" I asked him.

"You would think so, but I have never seen anything able to break one of the iryturtle eggshells before. They will survive, that I can promise you."

"Koyvean," I said, "do you think we can get all of these loaded into a bag or tarp of some kind to haul with us?"

"That shouldn't be a problem," Iclyn responded for her. "I have one of Lydorea's old larger sacks. I believe it will hold everything there."

"Are you sure about that?" I asked.

"Your pack from her, did you think it could hold as much as it does?"

"You have a point," I said, looking at the hundreds of stones and now eggs too.

"This will work," she said. "I know it will... I am cautiously optimistic."

I laughed at her joke. "I will trust you then to figure that out," I said.

"Good," Alabynes said. "Now that this is all sorted out, Nyrieve, I have something I want to give you. Could you please come with me to the library?"

I looked back at the others, and they all looked as confused as I was. "Okay, Alabynes, I will follow you there."

ᦉ31ᦉ

NYRIEVE

I followed Alabynes into the large library. We had been in this room many times this week, and I doubted I would ever stop being amazed. The walls were covered in floor-to-ceiling detail-carved bookcases. On each wall was a ladder that you could roll from side to side so you could reach the higher books. Each section had different carvings around them. When I asked Alabynes about them, he said he believed when this place was originally built, each section was to represent a different group in Iryvalya. I figured that was the same reason different areas of the castle also were carved to represent different groups.

"I know we've been in here a lot, Nyrieve," he said.

"You can call me Ny, Alabynes. I think we know each other well enough by now," I said lightly.

"Thank you, Ny," he said with a smile. "I wanted you to come in here today because I have one more scroll that I haven't shown you yet."

"The one you wrote my name on?"

"Yes," he said softly. "I wasn't sure if you noticed that, because you never asked about it."

"I knew you hadn't shown it to me, but I believed that it was for a good reason, such as you lost it or it was damaged."

"No, no such good reason I am afraid," he said, walking over to a bookcase that I hadn't spent much time investigating.

"Then what was the reason?" I asked, watching him go through the books, and when he finally seemed to find the one he was looking for, he gently pulled on it. The book didn't come off the shelf, but instead made a faint *click* sound and he was able to pull the whole bookcase forward, showing a hidden room behind it.

"I wanted to be sure you were… I don't know really. I have been holding on to this for so long, it was as if I was afraid of losing it," he said, stepping into the dim room first. He quickly used magic and lit a small brazier filled with an oil of some sort. The flames danced in the brazier and made beautiful patterns on the walls.

"You do not have to give it to me, Alabynes," I said, looking at some of the really old-looking books and papers in the room.

"I know, Ny. However, I do need you to see it," he said as he rifled around some papers in drawers of the only desk in the room. As he pulled his hand out, I could see a small blackened key. He walked over to the bookcase furthest away from the entry and pulled down what appeared to be only the binding of books that were connected to one another. Behind that was a carved wooden door. He stuck the key in it and opened the door. I could see there were numerous items inside it, but he only reached in and pulled out a very worn and old scroll. He then closed and locked the door back up, pushed the false books back in front of it, and tossed the small key back in the drawer. Alabynes then turned to me and held out the scroll.

I carefully reached my hand out to him, and when the scroll touched my hand, it felt like a zap of static electricity. I pulled my hand back initially, but then reached back and took it into my hands. I looked down at the scroll and saw my name written on it, just as I saw in my dream.

"Do you know how it was possible for me to see that dream and for you to see me as well?"

"I do not, Ny," he said. "Nothing like that had ever happened to me before or since."

"It still amazes me that the irybugs basically gave you my name..."

"That is even more curious to me," he said, "but while I was there watching the Koneyotta and writing down what was happening, I started to notice what looked like a haze of some sort. Eventually you came more into focus and I ended up watching you as much as I watched the Koneyotta. I thought it was a strange anomaly, but surely something that could be explained to me by another older and wiser Valya. I tried to pay not much attention to it and just write what I was seeing. This had also been the first time I had witnessed someone killing another Koneyotta."

"Is that what happened when the one pulled a leaf from the Leaf Day Tree?" I

249

asked. "Were they taking someone else's life?"

"Yes, that is exactly what was happening. The one was begging the other not to do it, telling them they would find another way, but the one knew the only way to get rid of someone for good was to remove their leaf from the tree. In removing someone else's leaf, their life was ended as well."

"That is what I thought had happened, but I wasn't sure. Why did they feel they needed to kill the person in the first place, especially if they knew they were going to die doing it?"

"At the time it didn't seem like something important enough to concern myself with, because as you know, our reason for existing is to watch and observe but not be a part of it."

"But who made that rule?"

"What do you mean?" he asked, sounding perplexed.

"You and Domi keep saying a Valya is only supposed to watch and record the history of Iryvalya. And I agree that the Valya are the best at doing so, because I do not know of any other beings that can do what you all do, but what made you all feel that is what you must do?"

Alabynes looked confused and unsure of what to say. "Ny, it is just the way things have always been."

"Right," I said, still curious. "I understand that is how things have always been, but like everything else in Iryvalya, things and people change. I am just surprised that doesn't seem to be something the Valya do... well, except for you, Domi, and a few others."

He stood there seemingly thinking things over in his head.

"I am sorry, Alabynes," I said. "I didn't mean to distract from the reason you brought me to see this scroll."

"Oh, yes," he said, snapping back to the current moment. "When the Koneyotta were talking, I could gather the killing was because there was a rogue person trying to divide their people. They thought by killing this person, it would stop the division and that peace would return. Sadly, it only did the opposite and ignited more division and fights, leading to the Koneyotta dividing themselves.

Eventually the two factions ended up becoming elves and fairies."

"Domi had told me about that when we were in the Spirit Realm… It is still so strange to think we both come from the same people…"

"Yes, and when they were divided, things changed for both. The elves seemed to be more powerful than the fairies, but the fairies were far superior in their knowledge and skills of healing and helping."

"That is… just wow. I knew that we all had to come from the same people, but to know that what I saw happen caused the divide is kind of sad. I wonder why I dreamt of that though and saw you there."

"I think you were supposed to see that for centuries Iryvalya has been dealing with similar things as you are today. One wants to lead, or at least doesn't want to listen to another. It is something that has been working against the peace of Iryvalya since time began."

"Do you think that means there is no point for me to try to unite the people of Iryvalya?" I asked.

"No, not at all," he said. "I think you were meant to see that and meet me to learn what happened, so you know a couple of things. One would be that even killing someone does not always change the path that is before us. No matter how hard we try to steer something in another direction, sometimes it is just not possible. The second would be that it's important to know where you and your people come from. While the Pyrothian and Lumaryia Elves are all elves, they are more than that, They, like the fairies, are all Koneyottas, which means they are one people. It shouldn't be divided like it is."

"I agree. I grew up thinking I was a fairy and was happy with that. When I learned I was actually an elf, I was confused and slightly ashamed because of all the problems they had caused. Now I realize it is okay to be either. One isn't better than the other. It is just the individuals that are good or bad."

"Exactly, Ny," he said. "When I saw you there so many years ago, at least for me, I couldn't understand, of all the memories I had witnessed, why that specific one. Then as I watched life over the years, I realized because it is your destiny to bring not only the elves together but the elves and fairies."

"What do you mean?"

"The fairies were attacked over and over and almost completely wiped out. They have as much right to be here and live in safety as the elves."

"I agree with you," I said, thinking things over. "I guess I just always assumed that when all the fighting was done, we would all live in harmony, but I guess I didn't think about how some elves and fairies might not think that is the best way."

"Correct," he said. "I think you need to make sure when you start leading all of the people of Iryvalya, you make sure that both the elves and fairies are equally represented."

"I agree, and I know some pretty amazing fairies that I think would be willing to help me make that happen."

"I think that would make Iryvalya a much better place for all."

"Yes, but not just the two," I said. "We need to make sure each group of people is represented and get to be a part of how the order of our world will continue, so we can try to keep a division like this from happening again."

Alabynes smiled warmly at me. "I cannot express to you, Nyrieve, how wonderful it is to hear you say that, especially without someone trying to tell you what you should do. I believe you really are the one the prophecy was written about."

"Thank you, Alabynes," I said. "I hope I do right by all the people of Iryvalya."

"I think you will," he said as we both heard a loud noise from the courtyard.

Alabynes quickly closed the hidden doorway and we both rushed out to see in the middle of the courtyard a naked person with long wavy light purple and silver hair. She turned around towards me and smiled. "Volnyri, Your Highness."

"Volnyri," I said, still shocked at the naked woman in front of me.

"I am Wyndrynali," she said with a strong, powerful voice. "I believe I am your ride."

"My ride?"

"Oh, yes," she said with a smile. "I am a dragon, but I changed from the form when I landed."

"Oh, okay. That explains the…" I said, gesturing to her.

"Yes, my nakedness," she said with a smile.

"We didn't expect you so soon."

"When I received the call, I wasn't actually very far from here, but I flew nonstop, so I am a bit tired. And I hoped I could rest before we leave, and eat too, of course. It is a long journey to Vylerynmyst, and I wanted to make sure I was able to rest enough to get us there without many stops."

"I don't believe I've ever heard of that place," I said.

"It is a small village in the Air Realm," she said. "I don't think you had the opportunity to visit it when you were in the Air Realm last. Besides, it wouldn't have been interesting then because it had been abandoned."

"Is it far from the Lyvional Forest?" I asked.

"Not very far, but because it had been abandoned for so long, the Nomydrac felt it would be a good location to get everyone to. Less likely for unwelcome guests."

"Ah," I said. "Okay, well, how about we get you something to wear and then some food, Wyndrynali."

"Thank you," she said. "I would like that. And please, just call me Wynd."

"Of course, Wynd," I said.

"Thank you, Your Highness," she said, bowing her head.

"And you can just call me Nyrieve or Ny," I said.

She smiled and bowed her head again. "Yes, Nyrieve."

CR80

After getting Wyndrynali some food and something to wear, she took to one of the rooms to sleep and rest for a while.

We discussed how everyone should prepare to be ready to leave as soon as Wynd let us know she was ready. Iclyn said she wanted to get some more herbs from the conservatory. Koyvean declared she was already packed and prepared. She somehow had gotten all of the truth stones and iryturtle eggs into the large enchanted pack that Lydorea had made for Iclyn. Emryleia said it wouldn't take her long to get her things together and rushed off to her room to gather everything. I went to my room to make sure everything I brought was packed.

As I grabbed my hairbrush and looked around the room, I realized everything was now in my packs and stuffed the brush inside. I cleaned up the room as best I could, and thought again about how much I would love to bring Kylyan here one day. I could see him enjoying some of these lavish comforts, even though I know on some level it might make him uncomfortable.

I walked out onto the balcony and looked out over the Blackened Forest. It was so beautiful and unique. I wished I could save this view in a crystal or something. I could look out here for days and weeks and never get tired of seeing it.

I heard a light knock on my open door, and I turned to see Alabynes standing there looking sad.

"What is wrong, Alabynes?"

"I am struggling, Ny," he said. "I want to go with you, but I know it isn't my place to be there."

I smiled at him. "Thank you for wanting to come and wanting to help bring Iryvalya back to a more peaceful existence, but I don't think you leaving here would be a good idea anyway."

"Why is that? Do I look too old or weak?" he asked, sounding slightly offended.

"Not in the least," I said, walking to him and giving him a hug. "You are very capable, but if for some reason I fail…"

"I don't think you will," he said confidently.

"Thank you, I hope I don't fail either, but if I do, I believe someone needs to stay here to help safeguard the iryturtles. They are a part of Iryvalya that needs protection. I know some are apparently coming with us to the Air Realm, but this is the home they have known for so long. If our plan falters, I would like to know they will be protected and safe."

He nodded. "I can do that for you, Ny. I know that isn't the only reason you don't want me to come though."

I half smiled at him. "If you leave here, Alabynes, you will begin aging again. You already said you were quite old when you came here, so who knows how long you would last away from this place."

"I know," he said solemnly.

"Besides, you are important and need to be protected. You have so much information over your years as a Valya as well as things you have learned in that library. I believe knowing our past can help shape our future. If we don't remember the things that happened, especially the bad, we are likely to repeat those things, and if we have you here with the stories and information, we surely have a better chance at doing things right moving forward."

"I understand what you are saying, and I will do that, but I do wish I could be there by your side."

"I appreciate that, but like we have discussed, I think I have a good group of people that will be able to help me."

"I do agree…"

"What else is bothering you?" I asked, knowing there was more to it.

"I…" he stammered. "I have lived on this island for so many years, and it was fine. I had a purpose and a reason. I have fulfilled that and now… I don't want to be alone anymore."

I gave him a gentle hug. "You won't be for long, I promise. I will come back to see you, and I would love for you to meet some people."

"Do you promise, Nyrieve?"

"I do promise," I said. "Who knows, maybe we can throw a celebration ball here one day."

"A celebration of something would be grand."

"Yes, it would," I said.

"Very well… I am not good at saying goodbye, so I am going to go off and wander away from the house for now. And I will just say, I hope to see you again soon, Nyrieve."

"I hope to see you again soon too, Alabynes. Thank you so much for all your help and insight."

"Always, Bringer of Peace."

I smiled at him, still never knowing how to respond properly to that title. "Volnyri, Alabynes."

"Volnyri, my saygent," he said as he rushed out of the room before I could ask what that meant.

෬32෯

NYRIEVE

We had been walking for over half the day when we finally started to approach Vylerynmyst. The flight here with Wynd took only one full day. She was much faster than the other dragons I had ridden before, but this was the first time I had ridden on a Fire Realm dragon. She was so much larger in dragon form than the others, so maybe that was why she was faster as well. I was pleasantly surprised to see there were not many spikes running down her back where we had to sit, but was saddened to learn it was from an injury many years ago. She would say nothing more about it, and I didn't want to press her. She flew us so high in the sky that from the ground we must have looked like a bird. We made a couple of stops for Wynd to rest and for us to stretch out before taking off again. Her body was covered in large scales that looked silver, but when I looked closer, they were really a soft lavender color. She truly was beautiful in both forms.

Wynd had landed us far away from Vylerynmyst, and when I asked why, she had said it was in case anyone managed to spot us, they wouldn't know exactly where we were heading. She changed into person form and borrowed a dress from Iclyn to cover up. She didn't want to wear shoes from any of us, telling us she preferred to feel the ground as it was beneath her feet.

She had led us towards the village and had us wait for a couple of hours. Once the moons had taken over the suns and the world was darker, she led us onto the pathway directly towards the village. I had stayed in the Air Realm long enough to think I knew how most of the villages would look, but I was so very wrong.

As we got closer, the path changed from a hardened dirt road into a beautiful curving wooden path. At first I couldn't figure out why they made it out of wood, but the night sounds soon let me know the pathways were more than they seemed. They were bridges. Everywhere we walked, we were on top of a water source that was covered in plants and flowers, making it seem almost like normal ground coverings.

Once we started to approach the homes, I noticed more spaces where I could actually see the water with the moons' glow dancing on top of it. There were large trees that grew out of the water, their branches hanging over the homes and the bridge walkways. There were soft glowing little lights strung around on the trees along the way and the homes. They were all built on stilts above the water, and each had a few steps up from the walkways. I guessed in case there was flooding, the water wouldn't get into the homes at least.

Some of the houses looked like they were built into the trees and some others stood alone but underneath the large tree canopy above. There were a couple of houses that had no lights on inside, and we just walked right past them. Ahead was a grouping of houses that looked like they were connected to each other by little bridges between them.

Wynd stopped and turned towards us. "I am going to go in and let them know we are here. Please wait out here."

"Why do we need to wait?" Iclyn said.

"If I am not back outside to get you within ten minutes, then I want you all to head back the way we came and hide. Perhaps try to figure out a way off the Air Realm. Because the only reason I won't be right back out would be because the village has been compromised and you are not safe."

"Thank you, Wynd," I said. "We appreciate you looking out for us."

She nodded and walked further up the pathway to a large house. It was made from planks of wood, with large curved windows that had thin curtains covering them from the inside. There was moss and ivy growing over parts of the roofs and walls. There were the typical fireflies dancing in the trees and above the water. I kept my hand on Klaw, just in case, but took a moment to close my eyes, listening to all the sounds around us and breathing in deeply the smells of the village. I could smell the water mixed with the plants growing out of it and the sweetness of the flowers still blooming despite being well into the harvest season.

I opened my eyes and looked around, wondering how this place could look so old and yet new at the same time. It was as if it was also untouched by time, similar to the castle in the Blackened Forest. I wondered if the people who built the castle also built this village.

It had not been the full ten minutes before Wynd opened the door and gestured for us to come inside. We all started to walk down the pathway to the door when someone suddenly pushed past Wynd, almost knocking her over, and ran straight towards us. It was harder to see them as clouds just began to cover the moon and I couldn't see their face as they rushed at us. My hand was holding Klaw tightly, ready to use it, when the clouds parted and I saw the sparkling eyes of Kylyan.

He ran right to me and picked me up in a tight hug, spinning me around. It felt so good to have his arms around me. I had missed him so much, but I didn't realize just how much until I was in his arms with my feet dangling down while he held me close.

Kylyan stopped spinning and looked at me with a smile. I couldn't help but smile back with a huge grin. He then slowly brought his face close to mine and gently pressed his lips to my forehead and then my lips. I could almost feel an electrical pulse when our lips met.

"Okay, okay, you too," Emryleia said. "I think for safety we should get you both inside!"

Both Kylyan and I smiled while still kissing, and then we both started to giggle. He squeezed me tight once more before slowly placing me back on the ground, making sure I had my balance before letting go.

"Did you miss me by chance?" I asked him.

"Was it that obvious?" he asked with his beautiful smile.

"Just a little," I said, putting my thumb and index finger close together, showing a small amount, and then winking at him.

"Only a little bit? That just will not do," he said, picking me up again and kissing me more passionately. Heat moved throughout my body and knew that feeling of being home just because I was next to Kylyan again.

"Hey, hey, hey," I heard my father say from the doorway ahead, "you two knock it off and get in here. We would all like to get a hug!"

I laughed as Kylyan put me back down again and winked at me. I turned and rushed ahead to Arnayx and gave him a big hug after I raced up the few steps. "I missed you too, Dad!"

"We are so glad you made it safe," he said, squeezing me tightly. "Now let's everyone get inside. We have food for you all and beds ready."

"Thank you," I said, stepping inside the house. Suddenly Dymma had her arms around me, followed by Cleo. It felt so good to know they missed me as much as I missed them. It was an amazing feeling to know I had a family I could call my own. It didn't make my chosen family of friends any less, but growing up as an orphan, I had always dreamed about this and was so happy to be experiencing it. Then, in the next moment, I realized that Kaleyna was missing out on it and my heart sank.

"What's wrong?" Clyo asked, looking worried.

"I just wish Kaleyna was here to feel the love I am feeling from you all."

"We do too," Clyo said, "but that is what we are working towards, right? Getting her back."

"I know," I said. "I just feel guilty."

"Ny," Emryleia said, "it's okay to miss her and hold space for what she's going through, but it doesn't mean you cannot enjoy and appreciate what you have in front of you right now."

I smiled at my friend. "Thank you, Em, I am so happy you are here and with us. I know we have spent so much time together since reconnecting, but I still really missed you while you were gone too."

"I missed you too," she said. "Life would get busy and crazy, and I would think about you and everyone from Cliffside, but it wasn't until we weren't able to spend time together I really realized how much I missed being around you."

"I feel the exact same… On one hand it feels like we were apart for so long, and on another, with the way we are connected, it felt like no time at all…" I said.

"Exactly!" Em said, giving me a big hug and stepped back. "Okay, someone said something about food, and I don't know about the others here, but I am tired of just old bread and dried meats!"

"Hear, hear," Koyvean said. "I am ready for fresh anything to eat."

I looked around the room and asked, "Where is Domi?"

"She keeps coming and going," Kylyan said. "She said it has something to do with checking in on what is happening with the Lumaryia and Pyrothian Elves. She has been giving updates to all the Nomydrac that are here."

"How many are here?" I asked.

"Each of the houses you saw and the ones you probably didn't are full of your supporters, Nyrieve," Arnayx said.

"Oh wow," I said in shock. "I saw at least fifteen houses…"

"There are over thirty houses here," Clyo said. "You have a lot of support. We just hope it'll be enough."

"I hope our plan will be enough, and maybe we won't have to battle," I said, trying to be optimistic.

"Let us hope that the Klayns are wiser than we think they are," Iclyn said. "Now, let's enjoy some of the food, I'm starving!"

"Definitely," Em added. "What is that I am smelling?"

"It is my aunt's recipe," Kylyan said.

"Your aunt's?" I asked, smiling at him.

"Yes," he said. "When I was a kid, she kind of disappeared. I didn't understand then, but she was being searched for by the Klayns for getting tyed to a fairy. Little did I know, she was hiding out here!"

"Oh, Kylyan," I said, smiling. "That is amazing! She is here now?"

"Yes, and she can't wait to meet you!"

Kylyan took my hand and led me to the kitchen, while everyone else went to start eating in the large dining room. From the outside I could tell the house was large, but from the inside, it seemed so much bigger. The kitchen was separated from the rest of the house by a few steps up and a window that opened into the dining room. A neat way to pass food through to the other side. Standing over the stove was a striking woman. Her sky-blue hair had thick dark purple streaks throughout it. The blue was straight and cut just below her chin, and the purple was a little longer than the blue and in perfect curls.

"Aunt Patryvla?" Kylyan said. "I would like you to mee—"

"Oh, Nyrieve!" she said as she rushed over to give me a big hug. She was a little bit taller than me and smelled like fresh pastries.

"Hello," I said, feeling an almost overwhelming sense of family and togetherness.

"I am so glad to meet you, child," she said, stepping back and taking my hands in hers.

"I am very glad to meet you as well."

"And I am glad you both are meeting, and you both are here right now!" Kylyan said, smiling.

"Now you go get something to eat, Nyrieve," Patryvla said. "We have plenty of time to get to know one another, but I know you have been traveling for quite a bit and I am sure some fresh home-cooked food will do you some good."

"Thank you so much, Patryvla," I said. "I am quite hungry and tired."

"And please, just call me Aunty," she said. "I imagine we will be family soon enough from the way Kylyan talks."

I could feel my face blush, but I wasn't sure why, maybe because we hadn't fully discussed telling people our plans to get tyed one day. "Thank you, Aunty," I said, as Kylyan gave his aunt a kiss on the cheek and led me back down to the dining room to eat.

There was plenty of food for everyone and then some. It reminded me of Rowzey's cooking. They were not the same, but there was so much love put into this food, just like Rowzey always did.

I hoped Rowzey made it back to the Spirit Realm and was healing. I really wanted to talk to Domi to see if she knew anything, but I didn't dare say much about Rowzey just yet. I didn't want anyone worrying or perhaps make people worried that without Rowzey the dragons might not back us up. I believe they would either way, but I should make a point to talk to someone with the dragons about it, just not right now. Perhaps Wynd could tell me who would be best to talk to. I'd make a point to ask her later when there were fewer people around.

I felt like I ate more than I would typically eat in two days. The food was so delicious and fresh, I just couldn't stop. However, once I did, I found myself nodding off at the table while everyone was talking about our adventure to the Blackened

Forest and what we found there. I could see Kylyan's eyes light up hearing about the castle and the iryturtles. I couldn't wait to show him one… well, once one of the eggs hatched.

It wasn't long after that my father and Clyo suggested I get some rest. I felt horrible to leave everyone, but I knew they were right. Even though there was so much to discuss, I just wasn't able to keep my eyes open any longer.

Kylyan said he would help me to my room. He quickly grabbed my pack from the front room and rushed back to show me to the bedroom. I held on to his arm as we made our way up two flights of stairs and then walked through a door to an outside bridge that went to another building that was much smaller than the rest. While walking across the bridge, I took a moment to breathe in the night air and listen to the frogs and crickets and just smiled.

"What is it?" he asked me quietly.

"It just feels… I don't know, I just feel like I am where I am supposed to be right now," I said. "It was wonderful seeing my family, some of the Drayks, and getting to meet your aunt, it is just… I mean, if this was any other life, I would think things were normal and we were maybe getting closer to not having to part again or something… I don't know, I am overly tired and probably speaking crazy."

He smiled at me and said, "Wait here a moment, please."

He quickly rushed to the little house we were headed to and in a minute he was back without my pack. He must have realized I noticed that because he said, "I placed your pack in the room there. That is where you are staying. I just had to get something as well."

"What did you have to get?"

"Well, since you left to go to the Blackened Forest, all I could do was think about you and us, and I talked to your father at great length and we discussed my intentions and expectations of you…"

"You talked to Arnayx about all that?" I asked, laughing. "That must have been fun."

"Surprisingly it was, Ny," he said. "He cares a lot about you and learning how he never forgot about you and always hoped to find you one day… it made me realize that if I have to, I would wait for you for as long as it took."

"Wait for me to what?"

"To be able to be tyed to me, start a life together, maybe one day a family."

"You know I would love for that to happen," I said, feeling so lucky to have someone who cared so much about me. I felt almost unworthy of it.

"But I also know you have a destiny ahead of you that I cannot and will not get in the way of. If I can be there by your side, I will, but if you need to go and do things and I must stay behind and wait…"

"Yes?" I said nervously.

"Then I will wait until the end of my days for you, Nyrieve," he said as he got down on one knee in front of me. He slowly pulled a small carved wooden box out of his pocket and opened it up.

Amongst the bright moonlight and hanging lights all around us, I could see it had a ring inside. It was a bright silver-colored band and in the middle was a square, sparkling, clear stone. On each side was a smaller blue stone that was also square.

"What is this?" I asked, tears welling up in my eyes.

"I want to ask you if you would want to get tyed together? It doesn't have to be today, or tomorrow, or even a year from now, but just someday."

"Are you sure?" I asked, not able to stop smiling and crying at the same time.

"There have been so many catastrophes in our lives, Ny, and before another catastrophe, I want to ask you to spend our lives together, through good and bad and everything in between."

"Oh, Kylyan," I said as I dropped down to my knees next to him. "Of course I will!"

"I love you, Nyrieve Vynlync," Kylyan said as he slipped the ring onto my left hand. It fit perfectly, and from the coolness of the metal on my skin I could tell right away it was Iryvalyan steel.

"I love you, Kylyan," I said, kissing him and then hugging him close to me.

He stood up and picked me up with him and spun me around on the bridge. "You have made me the happiest elf in all of Iryvalya!"

"Not possible," I said, laughing. "I am the happiest elf!"

"We have our whole lives to argue about this," he said as he lifted me up and carried me into the small house to spend the night together cuddled up in each other's arms, and there was no other place I wanted to be.

≪33≫

NYRIEVE

"Oh, Ny!" Emryleia said, grabbing my hand. "That is one of the most beautiful rings I have ever seen! I am so happy for you!"

"Thank you, Em!" I said, unable to hide my own excitement and happiness.

"How did he ask?"

"On the bridge last night heading to my... well, our room."

"That is so romantic..."

"It was," I said.

"Where did he get the ring though?"

"He said his Aunt Patryvla gave it to him shortly after he got here. She said it had been Kylyan's great-grandma's and she thought that it should be his."

"It is really pretty. Does it represent anything or is it just pretty?"

"Kyl said that his aunt told him that the two blue stones represent two people and the one in the middle represents the joining of their lives together into something beautiful."

"That is so sweet. I like that idea. Uhm, I don't want to overstep, but where are Kylyan's parents? I mean, are they still alive? Because I would have thought they would have been the ones to give him a family ring," Em said.

"The last he had heard from them was they were with another Drayk group up in the Stone Realm. They were trying to help everyone who was hurt during the attacks on Cliffside. His aunt said because she was the older sibling it had gone to her, and her children were older than Kylyan, and already tyed to people and didn't need it."

"Oh wow, that is amazing of his parents to be doing that, but dangerous as well," she said. "And also really nice his aunt wanted to pass it to him and by that, to you as well."

"It was very kind of his aunt. Regarding his parents, as long as I am not there right now, they should be safer at least. The trouble mostly seems to follow me."

"Yeah, nothing like us here having the Bringer of Peace around to keep us on our toes just in case!" She laughed, winking at me.

"I hate that any of you are at risk just because of me."

"You do know that it really isn't just because of you right?"

"What do you mean?"

"Most of us are here to support you, but it isn't just you. It is what you represent and that you want for us all to have the freedom and ability to live our lives in peace. That is what we all want, and when you were born, well, you drew the short straw, so to speak, and happen to be the amazing person who represents us all."

"You are right, I know it isn't all about me, but it's about the ideas and dreams we have for our futures."

"Nope, but sadly the Klayns seem to only focus on you," she said. "They see you as the figurehead, the one who represents us, and think if they can get rid of you, our thoughts and dreams will just go away. And to be honest, I don't think that will work anymore. Trust me that I do not want any harm to come to you, Ny, but if it did, I do not think the rest of us would just slide back into the shadows and hide. It is too big now. Too many people have stood up to the Klayns and they don't want to go back to how it was."

"That is good to know, because there is a good chance I won't survive this."

"Don't say that!" She scowled at me.

"The odds are not overly in my favor for this, Em," I said softly. "I am not looking to die. I plan to fight as long as possible, but I also know what can happen. If I can convince the people of the Klayns that we only want to live in peace with each other, we have a good chance."

"Especially with dragons on our side!"

"True..."

"What is it?"

"I am hoping Rowzey is okay... that she made it to the Spirit Realm, and they could help her. I hate not knowing."

"I know," she said, giving me a hug. "I think she will be okay, I really do."

"I hope so."

"Now, let me see that ring again!" she said, taking my hand. "What are the stones?"

"The large square stone in the middle is what Kylyan called a diamond. I had never heard of it before, but Kylyan said that it is a very old gem that was mined centuries ago. The two small squares on each side are sapphires."

"It is so simple and yet elegant," Em said.

"The metal is Iryvalyan steel," I said, looking at the ring. "Do you think I should not wear it though?"

"Why wouldn't you wear it?"

"Then people will know my and Kyl's intentions, and it'll put him at greater risk."

"Nyrieve," Emryleia said, raising an eyebrow at me, "do you honestly believe that it is not known throughout Iryvalya that Kylyan loves you?"

"I didn't know all of Iryvalya would know that, especially as some places do not seem to know I am still alive."

"That isn't true anymore," Domi said, coming up behind us without making a sound.

"Domi!" I said, rushing to give her a quick hug. "Are you okay? And what do you mean?"

She gently hugged me back. She then smiled kindly at me and said, "I am doing well, Nyrieve. I have been checking in with some fellow Valyas to make sure things are lining up as we anticipated."

"And?"

"So far, so good," she said. "Our connections in all five realms are working together quickly to prepare for... well... battle."

"Battle?" I asked. "When? Where?"

"Here, in the Air Realm," she said. "And when... from what we can surmise, within a fortnight or less..."

My heart pounded hard in my chest. I always knew there would have to be a battle of some sort, but I didn't know it would be so soon.

"Why do you think it will be so soon?" Em asked.

"There has been movement from the Water Realm and the Fire Realm. Word has spread that you were seen alive, and both Klayns have prepared their warriors to head here."

"Their warriors?" I asked, remembering what she told me about their warriors before.

"It's as we talked about before. Warrior isn't a good depiction of who they really are. While there are some well versed in fighting, most of them are just the people of each Klyan being forced to fight for what their leaders want. Though from what we are hearing, they are bringing a lot more people than actual warriors."

I shook my head thinking of all the innocent people being forced to fight against their will. "All of this has to end..."

"And it will," Em said, "when you are victorious."

"I agree," Domi said. "It is time for the age of madness to end... at least for a few centuries I hope."

"Wait, how do they know I am alive?" I asked.

"Apparently there was someone among the people living in Aquyleya. They shared the information to both the Pyrothian and Lumaryia Elves."

"How did they share it? I thought Sudryl said the place was locked down."

"It was... However, Miaarya was more clever than we gave her credit for." Domi sighed.

"Huh?"

"She put the curse on Kylyan and Prydos, as you know, but apparently she didn't think Kylyan's would hold up as well, so she entrusted Prydos with something that works like your mirror journal. He was able to send messages to her, but she could not respond."

"He told her I was alive and where we were?"

"Yes and no," she said. "We do not know if he knew he was telling her where you were or he thought he was just writing in a journal. That part is unclear. He did write that you were alive, but he wasn't able to write where you were. Something with the protection spells on Aquyleya didn't let him give up the location."

268

"Where is Prydos now?" I asked. "Kylyan said they had been able to give him the charm to sleep, and that they were bringing him here. Could he have awoken and told her where to find us?"

"No, he is still under the sleep charm. However, prior to him getting the sleep charm working, he either overheard something or had good insight as to where we would move you all next. Though I do not think it would take a genius to figure out the only unoccupied places you could be would be either the Air or Stone Realm. Logic would dictate it is not safe for you to go back to the Stone Realm after they already attacked it once, so the Air Realm would be the most logical choice."

"So it was not good planning for us to come back here," Emryleia said.

"I disagree," Domi said. "This is what is destined to happen. Might as well not run from it anymore."

"Easy for you to say," Em said.

"It's not really," she said, "but how long can we do the cat-and-mouse game of hiding from them? A few months, maybe a year? Eventually this will happen. This, though, they are not prepared for."

"Why do you say that?" I asked, pondering it all.

"They still do not know of your secret weapon, and as long as that is in your corner, you have the upper hand."

"The dragons?" I asked.

"Yes, the dragons," she said. "And the truth is, I think once the people of Iryvalya know what the Klayn leaders have been keeping from them, they will not be likely to trust anything they say again."

Emryleia and I both nodded in agreement.

"Do you know if Rowzey was able to get to the dragons in the Spirit Realm?" I asked.

"She was," Domi said. "They are still trying to save her. She was very badly wounded, and while they think they might be able to save her, she might not be able to shift back to dragon form again."

"Oh no," Em said.

"What?" I asked. "They have to be able to help her. If she loses her ability to fly… it'll be all my fault."

Domi cocked her head to the side, looking at me, confused. "Did you harm her yourself, Nyrieve?"

"No, you know—"

"Did you tell her to jump from the balcony or where to fly to?"

"No, I—"

"Then you really should quit trying to take credit or blame for others' choices. You did not harm her, you did not want her hurt, she knows that. We all know that. I know that if you had the ability to take all this on yourself and ensure that no one else could get hurt, you would do that, and so does anyone else who has ever truly known you. You need to stop doing that. Everyone who is following and supporting you are doing it of their own free will."

I couldn't think of what to say. She was right, but everything in me still blamed myself, something I had always done for everything. Even as a kid, I believed it was my fault my parents abandoned me. I thought it was my fault when Kaleyna fell and sprained her ankle while we were playing on the cliff top, and even now I believed everything bad was my doing.

"I think you stunned her to silence," Em said to Domi.

"That would be a first," Domi said with a smirk.

"Did you just make a joke?" I asked Domi.

"It would seem that way. I guess you and your friends are rubbing off on me."

I smiled. "I'd say I am sorry, but I am not supposed to anymore."

"Exactly!" they both said in unison.

"So… what do we do now?" I asked.

"Let us go tell the others what is happening," Domi said. "Then we will go from there."

We walked in silence to the largest building in the village, where most everyone had gathered again for food. Kylyan's Aunt Patryvla had been making communal meals for everyone since they arrived. It was so kind of her to do that and unite everyone.

After waiting long enough to see everyone sitting, I stepped up on top of one of the dining tables in the great hall and addressed everyone.

"Volnyri, everyone," I said, working hard to keep the shaking out of my voice. "I am sorry to interrupt you all during your meal, but I have some information to share with you all. I was just informed that both the Lumaryia and Pyrothian Klayns are heading toward the Air Realm as we speak. Our exact location here has not been revealed. However, it is close enough that we need to prepare for imminent battle. I need the Nomydrac to send messages to all of those who can make it to the Air Realm within a fortnight to come here to our aid. We need as many able warriors as we can get. It is my hope we can resolve everything without fighting, but from what I have seen with my own eyes, I do not think that will be completely possible. Make no mistake, I will be right there on the front line with you all. I will not cower or leave everything up to others to fight for me. What I do need for you to do, though, above all else, is protect the people of Iryvalya. That does include those who still call themselves Pyrothian or Lumaryia."

I heard groans and anger start amongst my people and knew I needed to explain more. "Not all of these people are the enemy. They are being told what to do, and many of them, if they do not comply, either forfeit their lives or the lives of those they love. We cannot blame someone for wanting to live and see their loved ones alive. We need to focus on the leaders that are not willing to concede that their time to rule is over. Once, there were leaders of Iryvalya they called saygents who didn't try to force their will upon its people but listened to all their people and tried to do what was best for everyone. That is what we need now. These leaders would be chosen by the people to help everyone, not just work towards their own agenda. And if those people no longer represent what the people want, then new leaders would be chosen. This is what we must work towards, not just for us, but for all the people of Iryvalya. That includes many of those who are heading towards us right now to fight. They have as much right to live in this world in peace as we do. I will not force anyone to fight on my behalf or for this idea we have, but if you want to fight for hope, then I need you to do whatever you can to help us prepare. We need more weapons, we need food prepared, we need medical supplies and so much more."

Iclyn stood up. "I will do whatever I can to help, Nyrieve. You are the Bringer of Peace that was prophesied to come, but you are also the leader I choose to follow. Volnyri."

Many others followed suit, standing up and stating they would follow me. My heart filled with so much support I thought it would burst. We took turns discussing plans and things each person could do to help. Each time someone volunteered to assist with something else, I felt more hope for our future.

After an hour or so, everyone seemed to be quieting down and ready to head out to start working on their projects. I decided I needed to make one more announcement.

"Thank you all for everything you have said and volunteered to do today. There is one more thing I wanted to make known." Everyone's eyes fixed on me, I looked around the room until I saw my family sitting with Kylyan among them. My heart fluttered at seeing them all together. "For a long time I have been afraid of... so many things. The biggest was losing those I care about. So I put off so many things because I thought it would be better or easier if I did that, maybe be able to keep them and myself from being hurt, but I cannot do that any longer. While I know it isn't a secret that there is someone I love very much... I am very happy and excited to announce that last night, Kylyan asked me if I would get tyed with him, and I of course said yes."

Everyone cheered and clapped, and I heard Kylyan's aunt shout, "This is cause for a celebration! I will make a feast for everyone in two nights' time!"

I could see Kylyan's face blush red with everyone looking at him, but his smile only grew as he stared back at me. My father and Clyo both hugged him close and Dymma jumped up and hugged him as well. It felt like an almost normal moment. A time to share with those you care for about something wonderful, but it wasn't a normal time by any means. But I wanted everyone to know, if something happened to me or Kylyan, that this was the person I loved above all else and who I wanted to share the rest of my life with.

Now I just hoped I would get that chance to do so. Maybe we'd be lucky and make it through all of this... Maybe we'd get to have the life we wanted together, have a family of our own one day... Right now in this moment, I had something I hadn't allowed myself to have in a long time, even if it was foolish… hope.

༼34༽

NYRIEVE

"It is going to rain today," I said, looking out the window of the room Kylyan and I were sharing.

"Do you think that will stop my aunt from cooking up a feast for everyone?" he asked playfully.

"From what I know of her so far, I don't think anything would stop her from doing something she's put her mind to."

"Then you know her pretty well," he said. "So then what is bothering you? It can't just be the rain."

I continued to look out as little raindrops started to fall and splashed into the water below us. It was so peaceful and beautiful. I was excited to celebrate today, but the anxiety was building inside of me.

"Ny?" he asked, sounding more concerned.

I turned and looked at him sitting on the edge of the bed and smiled at him. "It's nothing, Kyl," I said, taking a deep breath. "Just trying to think of what I could possibly say or do to stop the fighting without people losing their lives."

"And that is nothing to you?" he said, tipping his head to the side and squinting at me. "I know you feel like you have to save the world. That all of Iryvalya is depending on you and you alone, but it isn't just that simple."

"And yet it is still a true statement. If I didn't exist, would this all be happening?"

"We will never know, because you are here and you do exist. Besides, I believe in you, Nyrieve Vynlync. I know when the time comes, you will be steadfast and hold true to your ideas and hopes for Iryvalya. We practiced all day yesterday with knifes, swords, and hand-to-hand combat. You are physically ready for this. I believe you will be able to hold your own if it comes to that."

"I still can't get my powers to work right," I said, remembering how I was able

274

to only get a few inches off the ground yesterday.

"Do you think that if you could have levitated back in the Fire Realm none of this would be happening now?"

"Maybe…"

"Then that is why your magyc is stuck, so to speak."

"What is that supposed to mean?"

"Ny," he said, getting up and walking over to me. He placed his hands gently on my shoulders as he kissed my forehead. "Your powers are there and ready for you to use them as much as you need them. But as long as you are not trusting and believing in yourself and your abilities, you won't be able to tap into them."

"It's easier said than done, Kyl," I said, leaning in and giving him a soft kiss on his cheek.

There was a bright flash and a loud crack of thunder that forced me to spin around and look out the window. Kylyan moved up behind me and wrapped his arms around me as we both watched the rain starting to pour down faster.

"I promise you, Ny, you will be able to access your powers if and when you need to," he said, squeezing me tight.

"I hope you are right, Kyl," I said.

"Now here is a much more pressing question: Where should we have the tying ceremony?" he asked.

I couldn't help but laugh at him. "How do you figure that is a more pressing question?"

"Tonight we are celebrating our intent to get tyed. I am sure it will come up, which is sooner than the looming battle ahead. So I think that question might be asked first." He chuckled.

I held his arms as they stayed wrapped in front of me and squeezed him close. "You are right, that is more likely to be questioned tonight than the possibility of me fighting someone this evening."

"So… any special place you can think of where you'd want to do it?"

I honestly hadn't really thought that far out, so I was surprised when I heard myself say, "The castle at the Blackened Forest."

"Oh really?" he said. "It made that good of an impression on you?"

"I don't know why, but it feels like that place was made for celebrations and gatherings."

"If that is where you want to do it, then that is where we will do it."

"Are you sure? You've never even been there."

"If at the end of the day we are tyed together and we get to start building the life we want with each other, then I honestly wouldn't care if we did it in the middle of a mud pit."

I smiled, thinking of how lucky I was to have found someone that loved me as I was and that I loved just as they were. "I hope you know how lucky I am, Kylyan."

"Nah," he said, "I'm the lucky one."

"Can we call it a tie then?"

"You got it," he said. "Now I am supposed to go and help my aunt with a few things. Do you have anything to wear for tonight?"

"Just my normal clothes," I said. "It's not like I could pack and carry a trunk of ball gowns everywhere I go."

He laughed, giving me another squeeze and a kiss on top of my head. "Then just make sure they aren't covered in dirt!"

I rolled my eyes at him as he started to head to the door. "I'll see what I can figure out to wear to look pretty for you."

"You are always pretty, my lady," he said. "I will see you tonight. I love you, Ny."

"I love you too, Kyl."

He closed the door softly behind him and ran across the bridgeway back to the main house. I stood there for a long time watching the rain fall and trying to not think about anything other than what I was seeing, hearing, and smelling. The fresh smell from the dirt and the rain always smelled intoxicating to me. Gave me a feeling of rejuvenation and the hope for new beginnings.

There was a knock on the door, and before I could say anything, it swung open with Emryleia rushing inside and shaking the rain off of her.

"Come on in," I said sarcastically.

"I wasn't about to wait outside in the rain just to be polite!" She laughed.

"I am glad you didn't. You know you are always welcome where I am."

"As are you!"

"So what is going on?"

"Aunt Patryvla felt someone should come up and help you get ready for the celebration tonight, and I happily volunteered. Besides, I am not always great at doing my hair, so I thought you could help me."

"I'll help you and you'll help me, and we'll either both look amazing or we'll both look a mess."

"But either way…"

"Either way we'll both be in the same boat!"

"Exactly!" she said. "Is that what you are going to wear?"

"Oh my word, you and Kylyan are killing me with that!" I laughed. "As I told him, I didn't pack a ball gown."

"No, I wouldn't expect a ball gown, but…"

"But what?"

Em bit her lip and then said, "Okay, this is strange, but Iclyn told me to tell you to check your pack from Lydorea."

"What? Why?"

"She said she believed Lydorea might have put something in it for you to wear."

My brain thought about everything I saw in the pack and remembered the purple silk wrap dress. "She did!" I said. "I had totally forgotten about it."

I rushed over to the pack and placed it on the bed. I started to rummage through it, making sure not to poke myself again with the enchanted hair stick, and found the thick silk purple package. I pulled the ribbon off and opened up the silk wrapping.

Inside was not just one but two beautiful silk dresses. The light purple one had a small note card with my name on it, and the second, beautiful dark blue dress had a card with the name Emryleia on it.

"How did she know I would be here?" Emryleia asked me.

"I don't know," I said. "This is the first time I have opened it. I thought there was only one dress inside."

"Lydorea sure knew what would come to pass, didn't she?"

"She certainly seemed to," I said, wishing she would have only used her knowledge to keep herself safe and alive as well, to be here with us now.

"Let's hang them up so they get fluffed up a bit, and then we can start getting hair and makeup done," she said as she opened the pack she brought in with her. She pulled out a few brushes and makeup and laid them out on the bed. Seeing all the items spread out gave my heart a small pang. It all reminded me of Ghily and how much she seemed to enjoy doing hair and makeup. I would never be as good as she was with doing this myself, but I felt so grateful she took the time to teach me some things to do for myself. I really missed having her around with us, just one more reason all the fighting and bloodshed needed to stop.

"Is something wrong, Ny?" Em asked with her brow furrowed.

"No, just trying to remember how to do all the different things someone once taught me, but it does lead me to my question... Where did you get all of that?" I asked curiously.

"Aunty Patryvla gave it to me to bring up."

"Seems she is quite prepared for things as well," I said with a chuckle.

Neither Em nor I wanted to go crazy with fancy hairstyles or makeup, especially if it was still raining when we were ready to leave. I managed to put Em's hair into a long braid that went down to the middle of her back. I placed little pieces of flowers from the vase in the room. She then put mine in a looser braid, where some of my wavier hair was able to make it look more full and soft. We each put some makeup on using the looking glass that was also in the bag, and helped make sure neither of us looked like children getting into makeup for the first time.

Once we were done, we put on the dresses. Emryleia's was a shiny dark blue like her hair, and was form-fitted at the top and then slowly flared out and went down to the ground. There were sleeves that were split down the inside but covered the outer part of the arms. She looked like a princess in some sort of children's story.

I put my shiny lavender dress on, and it too was very similarly made. The only main difference was the sleeves on mine were made from some gauzy material, but in the same color as the dress. I felt almost like a little princess as I looked in the reflection of the window.

"Wow," Emryleia said. "You look amazing."

"You mean we look amazing, right?"

She smiled. "Yes, we do!"

"Em," I said. "Thank you so much for today, but also all the other days as well. You being in Aquyleya was kind of life saving to me. I honestly do not know if I would have been able to get through everything that has happened without you."

"I am happy to be here for you and help wherever I can. You were always like a sister to me when we were growing up. You and Kaleyna both were. I know I am not Kaleyna…"

"And she is not you, Em," I said, smiling at her. "One friendship doesn't make another friendship more or less valuable. There will always be a place in my heart for Kal, but there is definitely a huge place for you as well."

"I know," she said. "I feel the same way."

"And when Kaleyna is back, your friendship to me will be just as important to me as it is right now," I said truthfully.

"Thank you," she said. "That means a lot to me."

"Shall we get going to the main house?" I asked.

"No time like the present," she said. "Besides, the rain has stopped!"

We hurried over to the main house and found it full of so many smiling and happy people. It was wonderful to see and get to talk to the other Drayks I hadn't seen in a long time. Relonya told me how I looked so much more grown up since she last saw me. I was excited to see Louv made it as well. He told me how the other gargoyles had traveled to the Air Realm to show their support for us.

There was so much food, I felt that even Rowzey might have been surprised at how much Aunty had made. Everything was delicious. There was music being played in one of the rooms and it softly wafted throughout the whole building. There were so many people to talk to and hear about their journeys from last I saw them until now, and others who I just met telling me their adventures as well. I could feel my head spinning with so many different stories I wanted to remember. Kylyan and

Emryleia were both near my side throughout the evening, both helping take over some conversations when they seemed to just be able to tell I was getting overwhelmed. I couldn't be more appreciative of both of them and just hoped I could do the same for them.

As the evening wore on and most everyone had left, Iclyn and Koyvean cornered Kylyan and me to come to another house, as there was someone we needed to see.

We followed them to the house my parents and sister were staying in, and I was surprised to see Joynox sitting across from my father.

"Joynox!" I said, walking over to give him a hug. "What are you doing here?"

"I was sent by someone on the council to provide you with some information we feel you need, that hopefully can help sway at least the Lumaryia Klayn," he said calmly. "And it is so very good to see you again, Your Highness."

"Just call me Ny, remember?" I said with a smile. "Who sent you and with what information?"

"Hyorda," he said.

"Wait, Hyorda sent you here to help Nyrieve? That doesn't seem right," my father said.

"Believe me," Joynox said, "I wasn't expecting it either, but as it turns out, they have been working towards our goals as well, they just never told anyone... Well, except Rowzey."

"Rowzey and Hyorda know each other?" I asked, surprised.

"They are friends actually... Hyorda was the one who found Rowzey injured on the shores of the Water Realm and was able to get word to someone to help get her someplace safe, hopefully to heal."

"Rowzey didn't tell me that when I saw her," I said, confused.

"Where is Rowzey now?" Joynox asked.

"She is in the Spirit Realm, being attended to by... uhm, by her people," I said.

"By dragons?" he asked.

"How did you know that?" I questioned.

"Hyorda knew who and what Rowzey is, and they told me about it. I didn't know if I truly believed that dragons still existed, but after Hyorda lined me up a ride to get here with one, I definitely believe."

I smiled, remembering the first time I saw the dragons and could only imagine how shocking it was to Joynox.

"Wait," Arnayx said. "You've ridden a dragon, Noxy?"

"Yup, beat you to it!" he said back.

We went over the information that Joynox and Hyorda had gathered about the Klayns and how they had noticed the decreasing of magyc in the children and the continued decline in children being born. Everything tracked with what I had uncovered with Quwyst in the Fire Realm. Both Klayns had the same problems, but none of the leaders were willing to tell their people the truth.

By the time Kylyan and I headed back to the main house and our room, the sky was completely full of stars. We walked back hand in hand along the bridge paths, and every once in a while we stopped and just held each other close.

"I know I missed your Leaf Day, Ny," Kylyan said as we walked along the paths.

"It's okay," I said, surprised he brought it up. "I spent it with Rowzey, so that was pretty great."

"I am glad to hear that," he said, smiling as he took my hand and stopped us, "but I didn't want you to think I forgot about it. I have missed your last two now."

"And I have missed yours," I said, looking at his handsome face. "Maybe as a gift we can just promise each other to try to spend the rest of our Leaf Days together?"

"That would be the best Leaf Day gift I ever received, Ny," he said, smiling and kissing me softly on the lips.

"Me too," I said. "While I appreciate gifts, knowing I will get to spend the rest of my Leaf Days with you is the best thing I could have hoped for."

"If I haven't told you yet, my lady, you look absolutely beautiful tonight," Kylyan said as he kissed the back of my hand and started heading us back down the path.

"Oh, I think you have only mentioned that to me about a hundred times," I said, laughing.

"Then I haven't told it to you enough!" he said, taking my hand and twirling me around to the music nature was making. The water lapping at the edges of the bridge beams, the crickets and frogs singing. It was like out of a storybook. One of those tales of love triumphing over all and happily ever after.

As we crossed the bridge to our room, something shifted, but I couldn't place exactly what it was. The sounds were all the same, Kylyan was still smiling the same, but somehow, there was something amiss.

"Kylyan," I said as he approached the door, "something is… I don't know, off."

"What do you mean?" he said as he opened the door and we stepped inside.

As soon as I entered the room, I knew we were not alone. I looked over to the far corner, and inside the shadow someone was sitting in the chair. They leaned forward and I saw the light from the moon spill across their face. I reached for Klaw, still attached to my thigh through a pocket—thank you, Lydorea, for knowing the importance of pockets and quick access to a weapon.

"Hello, Nyrieve," a familiar voice said softly.

"Osidya?" I asked her.

"Don't you mean Mother?" she said.

∽35∾

NYRIEVE

"Perhaps I should call you Aunt Osidya?" I asked my mother, feeling annoyed at her presence, but for some reason I was not afraid.

Osidya took a deep breath and tilted her head back. "I did not come here to fight with you, Nyrieve."

"Then why would you have come here at all?" I asked, still not trusting her.

"Because I made a promise to someone I would come here and try to do the right thing."

"And exactly who was it you made this promise to?" I asked, noticing Kylyan purposely staying between my mother and me.

"Baysil."

"What?" I asked. "When did Baysil make you promise him anything?"

"The last time I saw him, which was about a fortnight ago now."

"He's alive?"

"Yes," she said flatly. "At least he was the last time I saw him… as well as your vexatious friend."

"Kaleyna?" I asked, my stomach doing flips, hoping this meant they were both still alive and well.

"Yes, yes, yes, that one," she said. "I do not see the… appeal of that one, but than again, I cannot tell how much of her personality is her or what that fairy has turned her into."

"Baysil has changed Kaleyna?" I asked, feeling relief Kaleyna was alive, but confused.

"Wrong fairy… I was meaning the one who is really good at pretending to be someone she is not… Miaarya."

"Kaleyna and Baysil are with Miaarya?"

"Not exactly," she said. "Are you going to stand there gripping your knife

283

waiting to pounce, or can we continue to talk like adults here?"

I slowly put Klaw back in its sheath but did not secure it. That way I could still grab it with ease. "I have put it away. Now talk."

She rolled her eyes at me like a child would, but then she seemed to think better of it and looked at me. "I am sorry for that. I am... I am trying to not be..."

"Be what?" Kylyan asked.

"I am trying not to be who I was," she said. "Now would you please sit down so we can talk."

I looked at Kylyan and he seemed to be waiting for me to decide what I should do. I looked at my mother and asked, "How do we know I can trust you? You must have taken liberties to get into this room tonight that would lead me to not trust you."

"Fair enough," she said. "I did use a charm to appear as someone else, but no one really seemed to notice me. Everyone was so excited for your pending tying that I was simply ignored. The only one who seemed to notice something was amiss with me was Koyvean. She is really untrusting of everything and everyone, isn't she?"

This made me realize that I had not seen Koyvean since the beginning of the celebration. "What did you do to her?" I asked, worried she would be dead.

"Nothing much really, just a slight poke with a sleep charm. I must say she looked quite surprised when it happened. I am sure she will be quite angry with me for a while. However, I needed to see you and I knew that if I was spotted prior to talking to you, I'd never get to come say what I needed to say."

"Where is Koyvean?" Kylyan asked.

"She is in the main house across the bridge. I put her in one of the rooms on a bed. She wasn't light in the least for such a slender elf. She must have a lot of muscles then," she said with a smirk.

"Kylyan, go find her and make sure she's okay, please," I asked.

"How can we trust her alone with you?" he asked.

Osidya started to roll her eyes again and quickly stopped. "Tie me up if you must, boy. I have no plans on hurting my child."

"No more than you already have?" I asked and saw what looked like pain quickly wash over and then fade across her face.

"I deserve that one," she said softly. "You can check me for any weapons and tie me to the chair if you like. I will not fight either of you."

Kylyan quickly patted her down and emptied any pockets she had. There appeared to be nothing else with her, no bag or pack she carried, and all the pockets on her were empty. Kylyan quickly took the sheet off our bed and ripped it into strips to tie Osidya to the chair. Once he felt she was secure enough, he came over to me and whispered in my ear.

"Are you sure you want me to leave the two of you alone?"

"I don't know if this is smart or stupid, but I need to know Koyvean is okay. I will keep Klaw on me and not get too close to her."

He looked at Osidya once more. "If you harm even a hair on Nyrieve's head, I will end you, Osidya, even if it is the last thing I ever do in this world."

"I truly do believe you, Kylyan," she said, "and maybe a year ago I would have welcomed the challenge... However, today I only wish to speak with my daughter."

Kylyan quickly went out the door, and I turned to my mother, who was looking at me in a way that seemed endearing but only made me feel more uncomfortable.

"You wanted to talk to me, so talk," I said.

"You look a lot like him you know," she said.

"Who?"

"Arnayx," she said softly. "He looks happy with Clyo. For many years I was angry at him for finding someone... but the truth is I was jealous. He found something I wanted for so long, and I thought I had found with him, but we weren't a good match."

"He said the same thing," I said, hoping my words would sting.

"He was right," she said. "I think we connected to one another because of our differences. It was new and exciting to meet someone the opposite of me. But in the long run, you cannot stay with someone just because you want to. I do not blame him for our inability to make it work out. We were and likely still are two very different people."

"I definitely agree with you there."

"But I am grateful for him, and that our union created you."

"I am having a hard time believing that, Osidya," I said. "I distinctly recall conversations that expressed the opposite sentiment."

"I know," she said. "I am sorry for that. I can't lie and say I didn't mean it at the time, but I did and didn't mean it... It is hard to explain..."

"Where are Baysil and Kaleyna?"

"They are with Fyra."

My heart sank. Fyra was crazy, and who knows what she would do to them.

"She isn't prepared to harm them as of yet," she said, seeming to realize my thoughts. "I know she is a horrible elf, but she believes that they are the leverage she needs to convince you to drop this effort to fix Iryvalya somehow."

"If I give in to her, she will just kill them along with me anyway," I said, walking to the bed and sitting down, making sure to keep far enough away that Osidya couldn't reach me if she tried.

"You are correct," she said. "I think Fyra would love to watch the whole world burn to ashes if she had the ability to then be the Saygent of the Ashes."

"Why are you here?" I asked, wanting to get to the point of this whole thing.

"Baysil helped me..."

"Helped you how?"

"There are reasons I behaved like I did throughout the years of your life... reasons that were not really my own, but I still did and said things I can never take back... The only thing I can do is try to do right by you now. And in my head it is still a struggle, but I am working really hard to listen to myself, my real self, and do what is right."

"You are not making any sense, Osidya."

"I know, I am sorry... Baysil helped me realize I had been under my parents' control for many, many years, and much of what I said and did were because of them."

"I thought they were dead?"

"Yes, they are," she said, "but that didn't stop the steps they took to control me."

"And what steps might those be?"

She explained to me how Baysil figured out the curse on the earrings and how the longer she spent without them, the more clear her head seemed to be getting. She claimed that it was still a struggle for her with making quick choices, so she was trying to think things through before making any decisions.

"How can I possibly believe you?" I asked. "You have to understand how crazy and convenient this sounds for you."

"Baysil confided in me some things he said might make you believe me…"

"What things?"

"He told me about the dragons… that you rode them from the Air Realm to the Spirit Realm… that you have seen the Leaf Day Tree and that my sister's leaf now covers your own…"

Everything she was saying was true, but how did I know it wasn't a trick of some sort?

"People can get this type of information from torturing someone."

"He said you would say that," she said with a smile. "He knows you quite well… He also cares for you very deeply. At first I thought perhaps he was in love with you, but after months of talking to him, I knew he really does love you, but like a daughter."

"Baysil has been like a parent to me these last couple of years," I said, trying to force back the tears threatening to spill from my eyes.

"I know," she said, "and I am glad you had someone there for you like that."

"You know," I said, "I want to believe you, that there was a curse and you are magycally now on my side and want to do the right thing, but logic and our history doesn't make me think that is possible."

She sat there for a moment, and then softly started to speak. "Nyrieve, you were the child I had always dreamed of having. I wanted a strong-minded daughter who wouldn't let the world force her into submission. When you were born and I saw the mark on your wrist, I knew I was going to lose you, either by someone killing you or you being taken away into hiding. I was so angry, but then you curled up in my arms and looked up at me with your big violet eyes, like your father's, and I knew you would be okay. I don't know how I knew it, but I did… I knew even if you had to be hidden away with Rowzey, you would be okay, she would make sure of it. That Iryvalya would do everything it could to keep you safe as well. I even understood that my sister chose to give up her life so you could live, even though it was her actions that put your life in jeopardy. It all made sense. I thought about how one day I could run away and find you, and we could live somewhere together. After my parents gave me those earrings… I felt my thoughts shifting. I was beginning to blame you for things that were not your fault, but I couldn't stop. All I could see after a while was all the horrible things I thought of you and wanted to happen to you… I still can remember those things like I did then, and feel the hate as real as anything else, but it also feels tainted somehow… almost like I was watching it happen, but it wasn't me controlling the words and thoughts I had."

"I of course want to believe all this, but honestly how could I?"

"I do not expect you to ever believe me," Osidya said somberly, "but I needed to at least come and try to provide you with the information I had… and while I know I owe you a lot more than an apology, I felt I owed it even more to Baysil, for helping me see more clearly than I have since you were born."

"What is it that Baysil wanted you to tell me or warn me of?"

"He said that when it comes time to make the final choice, to fight or give in, you must fight. You must never stop fighting for your own life and those who follow you. He believes that the Lumaryia Elves could agree with you, if they are able to understand what the future will be for them if they don't. He thinks they want something similar to what you want, but they cannot see it is the same. He said that there was a person in Noygandia that he talked to, that seemed to think similarly to you. It was a friend of your father's, but he would not tell me the name. I guess he didn't trust me fully…"

"I know who you are speaking of…"

"Good," she said, seeming genuinely relieved.

"Is that all? Was that everything he wanted me to know?" I asked.

"He wanted you to know him and Kaleyna were alive and that he didn't blame you for what happened. He was so happy when he learned you somehow survived the volcano. I was at the party in Prax… I had been hidden to the back of everything, as Fyra thought it would be a great punishment to watch everything occurring but not be a part of it all… When I saw you fall into the mouth of the volcano, I felt something… it was so conflicting. Part of me almost cheered aloud, but then deep in my stomach it felt like something stabbed me. It made me want to immediately jump in after you, and I couldn't understand why. I ran to where you went in, and when I looked down, I couldn't see you or anything part of you… I saw remnants of Jehryps… but I said nothing to anyone… I couldn't understand why everything felt so contrasting to one another."

"Should this make me feel better about all the things you have said and done to me?"

"No," she said loudly. "Nothing I did was right by you."

"Nothing?" I asked.

"No… you should never have had to grow up thinking you were a fairy, or that you were unwanted and unloved by your parents. Let alone everything I did and said to you when we met. Nothing I have done is forgivable, and I do not expect or want forgiveness."

"Then what do you want, Osidya?" I asked. "I am happy you have let me know that Baysil and Kaleyna are alive, and for your sake, I am glad you are not under some curse or something, but what am I supposed to do with this exactly?"

She looked down, looking truly defeated. We sat there in silence for a few moments before she picked up her head and looked at me. I could see tears streaming down her face as she spoke with a voice that kept cracking. "Nyrieve, you are my daughter, even if you choose to never claim me as your mother. And if you do not, I will respect your decision, because I have done nothing in my life up until now to deserve the title, let alone your affections. But I want to do the right thing. I don't know if I will be any good at it, or if doing it will end up getting me killed, but I have spent so much of my life doing as I was told, without question, even when I knew it was wrong. I want to live out whatever remaining time in my life trying to atone for my wrongs and help make things better in this world. I don't deserve it, Nyrieve, and I know it, but I want so much to be better and be a part of your life. I feel like once Baysil helped me see things clearly for what they really were, my life was starting all over and this time I had the choice to do the right thing."

I was at a loss for words, and I didn't know if I could trust this woman, but for some reason Baysil trusted her. Baysil told her things I know he would never tell. Even if he was being tortured to death he wouldn't have spilled this information.

"I want to believe you, Osidya, I genuinely do… but honestly it is a lot to believe."

"I understand," she said, sounding broken.

"But…" I said, pausing to be sure I really wanted to say what I was about to. "But if Baysil trusted you for some unthinkable reason, I should at least have the smallest amount of hope in you as well."

She looked up at me with her eyes wide with surprise. "Do you mean it?"

"I do… though much of my brain is telling me I am stupid to trust you, but I trust Baysil more than most anyone…"

"He was right about you," she said.

"Why do you say that?"

"When I told him this was a crazy plan, he said that you are smart enough to listen to both your brain and heart."

"He knows me well… and I hope that soon he can actually come tell me about the interactions you two had himself."

"As do I…" she said softly.

"Do you know when Fyra and her people should be here?"

She looked surprised. "I hadn't told you that she was coming with all her people yet."

"I have more people on our side than most of you realize, Osidya," I said, enjoying that I had the ability to surprise her.

"I am glad to hear that… I was about a week ahead of them leaving, so perhaps you have a week, maybe more but maybe less…"

"That tracks with what we have been told as well, so thank you for the truth."

The door to the room opened with both Kylyan and Koyvean coming in quickly.

"Ny," Kyl said. "Are you okay?"

I smiled at him. "Yes, I think so…"

"I am so sorry, Nyrieve," Koyvean said. "I thought she was someone suspicious, but I let my guard down enough that she bested me."

"It's okay, Koyvean," I said. "I am just glad you are okay. And I am sorry that she did that to you."

"I am sorry as well," Osidya said, sounding genuine. "I just needed the chance to speak with my… I mean, with Nyrieve."

"Everyone here knows who you are, Osidya," I said. "There is no reason to hide it anymore."

She smiled softly. "It has been a very long time where I was able to be honest about who I am."

"What do you want me to do with her, Nyrieve?" Koyvean asked.

"Let's get her untied, and then I want someone to have eyes on her at all times. I believe she is telling me the truth, but until I am positive, I do not want to take any chances. Do you have a problem with that, Osidya?"

"Not at all," she said. "I will do whatever it is you need me to."

"Kylyan," I said, looking at him, "while Koyvean gets Osidya squared away, would you join me in the kitchen for some tea? I'd like to discuss with you everything Osidya has told me…"

"Of course, my lady," he said, kissing my hand as he led me from the room.

As I started to step onto the bridge, I turned back to my mother and said, "By the way, Osidya… Embers told me to tell you that you should listen and follow her namesake…"

My mother's mouth opened in a gasp as she tried to ask me more, but I turned and kept walking with Kylyan to the kitchen.

⚝36⚝

NYRIEVE

"Everyone is here, Your Highness," Quwyst said.

"Are the protection charms seeming to hold?" I asked.

"So far so good," she said. "The village has been shrouded by the enchantment and no one will be able to ever locate it unless someone inside breaks it."

"Good, I need to know my family and those who cannot fight will be as safe as possible."

"Domi said she has people ready to portal them out if it comes down to it."

"Thank you, Quwyst... I don't think I would have been able to do all of this without you," I said, thinking over the last few days. I had spent some time with my mother, always with her guarded just in case. It was so strange to hear her speak kindly and sound genuine. I just hoped that it was the truth and not a big setup. But with her insights of Fyra and the information Joynox was able to provide us, I believe all our preparations would help us succeed today.

"I am just glad I was able to get here and help before..." she said, gesturing out to the coast where both the Pyrothian and Lumaryia Klayn legions were at the ready. They had agreed to one more set of talks after the sun was fully up but stated if it didn't go the way they wanted, it would be war... This was more what Fyra said, while the current leader of the Lumaryia Elves said they were more willing to work towards a peaceful agreement of sorts, which gave me a small glimmer of hope.

Somehow, I had hoped it wouldn't come to this, a battle or war, but deep in my gut I always feared this would be the only way for all of this to end or begin again. I did not want anyone to lose their life unnecessarily, and hoped me being able to provide the people of both Klayns with the truth that had been hidden for so long from them would help them decide to move towards a peaceful existence with one another.

"I am glad you were as well," I said, looking out and seeing the moon slowly

292

begin to move away from the sun. "I need a few minutes before I'll be down to meet with everyone."

"No worries, Your Highness," she said. "I understand. Koyvean and I have everything exactly like we discussed, and I will leave you time to prepare for what's about to come. I'll see you down there, and remember, you have all of us on your side. Volnyri!"

I watched her walk down the path along the side of the mountain and disappear out of sight. I was lost in thought about everything that was about to happen when I heard large crunching footsteps coming up behind me. I turned and looked at Aurilya in her dragon form approaching me.

"Are you ready?" I asked, knowing she could not speak in a way I could understand but that she could understand me.

She slowly nodded her head in confirmation.

"I know it takes too much energy to change form right now to talk, but I want you to know I appreciate everything you have done, Aurilya. I know it is because of you that Rowzey is alive and well and had the ability to have you get the word out to all the dragons to come here in support of... well, me."

I stood there thinking about Aurilya and how I knew at one point she wanted us to be more than friends. "Aurilya, I know you can't answer me, and maybe that is for the best, but I want to just say that even though I am in love with Kylyan and want to spend my life with him, you do mean so much to me. I love having you as part of my life and I truly hope if we succeed today, that you being around will continue."

Aurilya tipped her head to the side and slow-blinked at me, and then continued to look off in the distance. I hoped that meant she understood and felt the same.

We were standing at the top of the highest mountain in the Air Realm, looking out to see the edge of the sun starting to crest past the moon moving away. Most everything was still shrouded in the blue light of the moon. I could see the valleys in the distance with a winding river that was flowing calmly and peacefully.

Aurilya nudged me and gestured with her head into the forest off in the distance to the left of me. I could see a bunch of the irybugs fliting around each

293

other, making a beautiful dance with their brilliant light. I smiled, knowing it was another sign from Iryvalya herself that I was where I was supposed to be. When I looked down, I couldn't help but laugh just a little at the tiny iryturtles surrounding me in the grass. Ever since they hatched a few days ago, they had been trying to lead me in different directions. Sometimes I could figure out the reason, other times I had been left at a loss, but I figured maybe those times I just needed a walk, and they knew it somehow.

It was only yesterday that my journey with them led me and Kylyan here to this mountaintop. I knew there was a reason for it, and now here I was, able to look down and see in the far distance the large gathering of so many of the people of Iryvalya. I looked over to Aurilya and asked, "Are all the dragons prepared?"

She turned from me and looked out in the distance. I could see a few of the dragons swooping around in the dark. I could see their silhouettes moving about, but if I didn't know what they were, I could have mistaken them for large birds. Hopefully if the Klayns see them, they would think the same, though either way, when the dragons emerged with me shortly, there would be no question about their existence, let alone their loyalties.

As we stood there, I figured it was time to try once more what Kylyan, Emryleia, and I had been working on for the last few days. I put my hands out a little from my body and concentrated on feeling the air movement all around me. I let the tingling from my core push out to my fingertips. I took a deep breath, smelling the pine in the damp morning air. As I slowly exhaled, I traced a spiral out with my finger and felt the winds wrap around me and lift me into the air. My hair was billowing in the back but the braid on the top of my head helped make it so I could still see everything around me and was able to hold myself in place a few feet off the ground. I looked around and knew I had more control than I realized. I felt stronger and more powerful, wanting to lift up higher and higher, maybe even out to the dragons flying around. I took a deep breath and slowly let myself descend to the ground. I loved the feeling of my power and how strong it was, but I also knew that I couldn't let my guard down and get careless now. We had worked out a good plan for today, and I was not about to let it all go to waste just because of a rush of power.

"I think it is time, Aurilya," I said. She instantly changed the way she was sitting, allowing me to climb on her back with ease. Once I got settled and took a few more deep breaths, knowing this was it, the make it or break it moment of my life, I leaned down and whispered to her, "Let's go rouse the other dragons and see if we can perhaps bring Iryvalya out of the darkness and chaos it as known for far too long and bring peace back to Iryvalya."

She pushed off the ledge fast and hard, leaving the little iryturtles scurrying off. The irybugs moved into the air and began following us and dancing around me as Aurilya brought us over to the mountain peaks the dragons had been hiding out on. I knew Aurilya followed Rowzey's instructions to gather as many dragons as possible, but as I saw them start ascending to the sky, there were so many more than I imagined. All the different types from each realm united in helping us put an end to these centuries of meaningless war.

As we flew around waiting for all the dragons to take flight, I kept making sure I had everything I needed. Clyr was fastened around my neck and Klaw was secured to my thigh. I was as ready and prepared as I could be. I thought about the letters I had written to those I cared about that I laid out on the bed before we left. I hoped they'd never need to be read, but if they were, at least they would know how much they all have meant to me.

The sun started to get brighter with the moon pushing past it. I saw the dragons all surrounding us ready to hopefully put an end to the hiding and fear this world had come to know all too well. It was time. I leaned closer to Aurilya and said, "Volnyri."

She quickly shot up into the air, making a twisting pattern up and then started the descent back to the Air Realm. I knew she knew what to do, but feeling her power underneath me left my legs slightly shaking as they held onto her as tightly as they could. She dived down directly towards the gathered people and the large platform with the table set up for the leaders to have this one last discussion to try to settle this peacefully. I couldn't see who all was standing around the table with the force of the wind in my face. Through my squinted eyes I could swear I saw Baysil's and Kaleyna's hair colors, but as Aurilya swooped past the table, the only thing I could be sure I heard was gasps and shouting. Behind us over three hundred dragons flew around, making themselves seen and known. Those who could breathe fire did so out into the sky. One even managed to shoot out a ball of fire that landed on an unoccupied catapult, melting it to the ground in a couple of minutes. The people who had gathered around the platform seemed almost too scared to try to run away, but even if they had wanted to, they couldn't with the protection spells we put around the area.

I think Aurilya made a few passes by the table before she decided to land on the platform next to where the table had been set up. She landed with a heavy thud that jerked me around, but I made sure to hold on and not look like I was not in control. I took a deep breath and climbed off of her. I walked up by her head and thanked her. She in turn bowed down before me, then looked over at those at the table and let out a gut-ripping screech right before she bounded back up into the sky with the other dragons circling around all of us.

I turned to face the table as Kylyan walked up to me and bowed down. "My saygent," he said. We had practiced this, and each time, I burst out into laughter at the idea of this title, but the dragons insisted this would be a title that the elves should recognize as something important and agreed upon by the dragons. I wasn't sure why, but Aurilya claimed that was the only high-ranking title that dragons had agreed with back in the days before the wars and them going into hiding and felt this would be an appropriate nod to them supporting us today. When I looked at Kylyan, I was able to not laugh, because instead I dug my nails into my palm to keep the laughter at bay.

"Arise," I said to him. As he stood and offered me his hand, I took it and allowed him to lead me over to where the other leaders were standing in wait.

I walked steadily and sure-footed to the center of the table where my chair was placed. I looked around at the people here. I recognized everyone representing our interests and most of those representing the Klayns. I was wrong in my thoughts of seeing Baysil and Kaleyna, as they were nowhere to be seen. I could feel the anger building in me, as it was discussed and promised they would be here.

"Good morning, everyone," I said clearly for all to hear at the table and beyond.

Many spoke back the same sentiments, except for one. Fyra stood with her lips pressed tightly together, and I could read the anger that was all across her face.

"Before we begin," I said, "there was an agreement that Baysil and Kaleyna would be present this morning, and yet I do not see them here."

"They are here," Fyra spoke, sounding frustrated, "but I wanted to make sure you would keep up your end by showing up here before bringing them out."

"Then I would imagine you plan on bringing them out now?" I said flatly, not trying to hide my annoyance.

Fyra snapped her fingers and I could hear someone pushing people aside in the crowd around the platform. It was a tall and large Pyrothian elf who stepped up first onto the platform. When he stepped aside, I could see Kaleyna walking towards me and Baysil right behind her.

Kaleyna's overall appearance did not look much changed. Her hair was neatly pulled back into a long braid with beads strung throughout it. She was clean and well dressed. She looked far different from Baysil. His hair was grown out and messy. He had stubble all over his face from what looked like a poor shave from at least a week ago. The clothing he wore did not fit him and looked like it hadn't been washed in over a month. Baysil's face looked hollowed from not eating, where Kal's didn't. I could see healing cuts and bruises on Baysil, but again nothing out of the ordinary on Kaleyna.

It took everything in me not to run to them and hold them tightly to me, but I knew I couldn't.

"I do appreciate you bringing them, Fyra," I said without emotion. "However, I do not appreciate the way Baysil has obviously been treated."

"He wasn't as cooperative as Kaleyna was," a familiar voice shouted from behind Baysil. I turned my head to see Miaarya standing behind him with her short pink hair moving in the breeze.

"I see," I said. "As far as I was made aware, Miaarya is not on either of the councils, is that correct?"

"I don't need to be—" Miaarya started.

"I was not talking to you," I said, interrupting her.

297

"She is not a part of the Lumaryia Elves, Your Highness," Hyorda said. I turned and looked at this person whom Joynox spoke so highly of and hoped he was right, putting his trust in them.

"Thank you," I said, "and what say the Pyrothian Elves of Miaarya?"

"She is no concern of ours anymore," Fyra said with a smirk, her eyes darting to Miaarya.

"What?" Miaarya shouted at Fyra, looking terrified.

"Ah, I see," I said. "Koyvean, would you please have Miaarya removed at once and taken to be held and tried for all her many crimes against the people of Iryvalya?"

"Yes, my saygent," she said, signaling to a couple of Nomydrac to do as I instructed.

They quickly confiscated her and dragged her off yelling and screaming about how Fyra promised to protect her. While it was not a surprise to me Fyra breaking a promise, I was just a little surprised Miaarya had trusted her.

"You may all take your seats," I said, watching the Pyrothian guard force both Baysil and Kaleyna into their seats as everyone else sat down.

"I see you have some new allies," Hyorda said after they sat down and took a sip of water.

"Not so much new, as reemerged," I said. "Their loyalties have always been to Iryvalya, which now aligns them with me."

"The Fire Realm dragons should align with us then," Fyra said, sounding more and more like an insolent child.

"And yet they don't," I said, shooting her a glance. She scrunched up her face but remained silent for the moment.

"Now, we are here to discuss for the last time an agreement of peace between us all," I said as I walked around, not just addressing those at the table but all the people here. Each Klayn had their warriors ready and prepared to battle, but the way they looked at me told me they were not aware I would be engaging with them directly. "I believe that the people of Iryvalya, whether you are a Pyrothian elf, a Lumaryia elf, a mixed-blood elf, a fairy, a gargoyle, a pixie, a satyr, or even a dragon, you all have the right to live freely in a world of peace."

"This was supposed to be a discussion with the leaders, not our subjects!" Fyra said loudly.

"That is because you do not view them as people with the right to make choices about their own lives, Fyra," I said.

"They aren't. They are my subjects!" she shouted back, pounding her fist on the table. I could hear murmurs of frustration throughout the crowds around me.

"That is part of the problem, I think," I said. "Now, if you will please quit interrupting me, I shall like to continue addressing everyone here."

She started to say something, but the council member next to her touched her shoulder and whispered something to her that quieted her down quickly.

"As most of you know, I am Nyrieve Vynlync. I bare the mark of the one that was prophesized to be the Bringer of Peace. I don't know how or why this prophecy came to be, but for the last couple of years of my life, I have tried to understand it and figure out how I can possibly be the one to unite all of us as one people. Over this time, I have traveled throughout Iryvalya, meeting new people and learning about different traditions and finding most all of them are valid and deserving of existing in Iryvalya, with the exception of those trying to force others to submit to the will of the few.

"Throughout these travels I was taught about an enchanted pendant that is supposed to keep someone from having a spell placed on them or be influenced," I said, showing Clyr to everyone. "To prove this works, I would like Fyra to try to place a charm or influence on me, something simple, but enough to show you all I speak from my heart without anyone else's influence."

I looked at Fyra. "Could you please?"

"It would be my pleasure," she said happily and began to try to place a curse on me to light myself on fire. I tipped my head to the side, looking at her and realizing if she really could hurt me like this in front of everyone, she would without a second thought. It was crazy to set myself up for this, but hopefully a true show to others that I trust in Clyr. I felt Clyr tingle, blocking what Fyra was trying to force me to do, and heard gasps from the crowd when it didn't work.

"Thank you, Fyra, for that demonstration," I said with a smile. "Now, when you all arrived, you were given the option to obtain a small truth stone. Hopefully most of you took that opportunity." As I said that, many people held theirs up for me to see. I took a deep breath and continued, "One of the most valuable things I have learned in the last couple of years is the importance of honesty and truth. My goal was to show you with Clyr that I am not being influenced by someone else or under a spell of any kind. To show you the truth stones work, I will simply tell you a lie that will cause your stones to react. The lie I will tell you is right now it is the middle of the night, and the sun is not shining down on us."

Again, I heard gasps throughout the crowd of would-be warriors as their truth stones became warm and the clarity got cloudy.

"Now, these do not only work on me, but on everyone. The stones over time can crack and stop working, but they are genuine. Try it with each other for a moment."

I could hear people talking to one another and seeing that when they lied, the stones did just as I told them. Once it quieted down again, I addressed them once more.

"The reason I wanted to address the councils as well as the people of Iryvalya is simple. I want you to know the truth in what I am saying and what my goal is for Iryvalya. When I visited the Water and Fire Realms, I met many wonderful people there. Kind and caring, wanting nothing more than a better life for themselves and their families. Though one thing I noticed was the lack of families, and what I mean by that is children. I am sure most of you have noticed there are less and less children and even less magyc within the new generations that do exist." The crowds murmured with agreement. "I believe I have figured out the reason why this is happening... Elves were not meant to be separated like they are, into two Klayns and never mixing bloodlines with one another. We are one people, but when you start narrowing down the groups in which you can create families from, children become less and less healthy or optimal for being born in the first place. I do not feel everyone needs to have children. It is your choice if you want a family or not, but if that is something you do want, you should have the right and ability to do so. However, because of wanting to keep control over each Klayn, the truth has been hidden from most everyone for so long that the lies that were told at one point became the truth that they knew. Not all of the leaders in the Klayns were even aware of this being the cause, because they simply believed they were being told the truth."

"These are all horrible lies she is telling you," Fyra shouted from the table. The crowds looked at their truth stones that were shifting to cloudy and getting warmer. The people realized she was the one in fact lying. It felt like it was working, but I didn't want to get ahead of myself. Some might still fight for Fyra and the other Klayn if they were told to.

"I do not need to lie to any of you," I said to everyone. "The only thing that comes from continuing to spread these lies is more hate and death. These lies and disinformation that have been fed to everyone are what is wrong. We as a people have a right to know the truth and make decisions from there about what is best for us."

"What about the dragons?" someone shouted from the crowd.

"They have been in hiding for many, many years... Most of us were not aware that they were still alive and that they also have the ability to shapeshift into person form." There were again gasps and noises from the crowd. "They were tired of the fighting and did not wish to be a part of it any longer, so they started hiding and living amongst the rest of us to survive. They are now ready and willing to do what must be done to fight for Iryvalya and the freedom of its people, ALL of its people, not just the elves. The elves have ransacked this world and tried to make it all about them, but it isn't and no longer can be that way."

I took a deep breath and continued, "I have come here now today, before you all and your councils, asking that we learn to move forward in a way that is peaceful for everyone. We should be allowed to live and travel throughout all of Iryvalya, not just one realm or another and only if we follow the rules of the few."

"I have a question," Hyorda asked.

"Yes?" I replied, turning to face Hyorda, feeling a bit nervous to hear their question.

"The people here seem to be calling you by a new title, Your Highness. They keep calling you saygent. Why is that?" they asked with a blank look on their face.

"Thank you for asking that, Hyorda," I said, relieved. It was the question Joynox promised they would ask. "Back before the wars between the two Klayns, there were leaders who had been chosen by the people of Iryvalya to help lead and come up with solutions for problems. The person that was picked was called either the saygent or king. Typically their children would be trained to continue to do the work of their parents. However, it was not just a given that they would automatically take over. They still had to be chosen by the people. The title "saygent" isn't one of someone who is placed in charge by their bloodlines, but it is a job title that one earns by the desires and respect of the people of Iryvalya. When I discussed this with the Nomydrac, we all agreed that while I am the figurehead that is known, we should also vote for who should be the one to lead and move our world forward. The Nomydrac voted and chose me to represent them all as saygent. Now if we can all agree to work together towards peace, we will again vote as one people for someone to lead us, whether it is me or someone else, that person would take the title saygent for five years, when another vote will be had to either keep the same person in charge or pick someone else. This would also be done at other levels, such as leaders and representatives of the realms and even the different villages and cities. Each person should have a say in who represents them."

"I think that is a wonderful idea," Hyorda said as Fyra shot them a nasty look.

"That is not how it has been for the Klayns for many years," Fyra said.

"That is true," I said, "but we wouldn't be separated by Klayns or anyone else anymore. It would be the people as a whole."

"The Pyrothian Council will not agree to such disgusting ideals," Fyra said, standing up. "We are not scared of your stupid dragons or anything else. We came here to take over the ruling of this world, so you might as well start addressing me as saygent!"

Before I could speak, another person from the Pyrothian Council stood up and said, "You do not speak for all of us, Fyra."

Fyra turned quickly to the elf next to them who spoke, and from out of nowhere had a knife in her hand and held it to the elf's throat, nicking it. "I am your leader!" she shouted as she stood up with blood now on her hands. "You will all do as I say, or I will have all of your families drawn and quartered with their heads on a pike and you will not need to worry about continuing your bloodlines because there will be nothing to continue!"

It was silent for a few moments. I could see those dressed with Pyrothian sigils on their clothing looking around at one another. I decided I needed to pounce on this moment at once by saying, "Do you notice if your truth stones are saying if she is lying or not?"

Everyone looked at their stone and it was cool and clear, she was telling them the truth as she believed it to be. "It does not have to be like this. You and your families do not have to die for this war that wasn't ours in the first place. We do not want to fight you all. And you know with the dragons on our side, it will not be much of a fight. Even if I die during it, the rest of us here are not going to just go away and allow this world to continue the way it has for far too long."

Hyorda drew everyone's attention when they stood up. "While I have not discussed this with everyone on the Lumaryia Council, I feel with the information provided here today, we should be more than willing to start working together to make peace with the rest of Iryvalya. It has been a long time coming to move towards a peaceful existence."

The other members for the Lumaryia Elves all stood up and nodded in agreement. I looked at Fyra still standing and breathing heavy with a crazed look in her eyes.

"Do you honestly think this quanta'mu has the ability to lead the people of Iryvalya? She knows nothing of how the elves live and how we are the superior race. We need to be the ones in charge and make the decisions! If anyone should lead Iryvalya as saygent, it will be me!"

Before I could say anything, Fyra took her knife and quickly plummeted it at Kaleyna. Baysil quickly jumped up and blocked the knife with his own body, screaming out as the long blade sank deep into his back. Horrified, I started to run towards Baysil as Fyra grabbed Kaleyna as a hostage and began backing towards the center of the platform. I reached Baysil and he had blood pouring from his mouth.

"Baysil, stay with me, you will be fine. We have healers that can help you," I said, holding him.

"I don't think they can," he said, his face looking paler by the second. There was blood flowing from his back and spreading all over my hands and clothes.

"No, we just got you back. You can't die now, Baysil. We need you… I need you!" I said, tears flowing down my cheeks.

"Not anymore," he said hoarsely. "You have come so far, Nyrieve. I couldn't be more proud of you or love you any more if you were my own daughter." He looked behind me at Kylyan and said, "You both share a love like the one I shared with Maelyrra… Don't ever let it or each other go."

"Baysil, you need to stay with me. I love you too. You have to stay with me!" I shouted at him.

"Ny," he said in barely a whisper, "I'm ready, and you know this isn't goodbye."

"No, Baysil, you can't…"

He smiled up at me weakly, the blood still staining his face. "You can do this, my saygent. We all believe in you… Volnyri…"

He passed away in my arms. I looked at the face of the man who helped me figure out who I was and what that meant. He supported me in ways I never thought possible and now he was gone. I failed him. I had promised I would save him and Kaleyna, and I failed.

I couldn't think clearly anymore. I didn't care what we were here trying to do anymore. Fyra killed Baysil. She needed to die.

I jumped up and started walking to Fyra as she held Kaleyna close to her. I knew Kaleyna didn't seem like herself but hoped she could see what I was intending to do. Kylyan tried to grasp my shoulder, likely to stop me, but I shook it off and moved quicker.

"Em, take Kal," I shouted at Emryleia as I rushed towards Fyra. Emryleia had been sneaking up behind them and pulled Kaleyna to the ground as I grabbed Fyra and pulled her with me as I used the wind to lift us up into the sky.

She screamed and tried to cut me with the knife still covered in Baysil's blood. She managed to nick my left cheek, and I felt blood start to trickle down, but the way I had her held she couldn't move much more to hurt me or get free. It was only a matter of seconds before I realized how high up we were. It was high enough that there were dragons circling around us, keeping a close eye on what was happening.

The wind from my magyc was holding us pretty steady, but the wind from everywhere else had our hair billowing around us.

"Why did you do that, Fyra?" I shouted at her. "He was good. He only ever wanted to help!"

"He was a fairy. He served no purpose in my world!" she shouted back.

"This isn't your world anymore, Fyra! We all live here and have the right to live as free as anyone else. You know this is all over for you, right? There is no way you can come back from this. Your time as a leader and ruining lives is over."

"It is never over. Even if you lock me up, my child will avenge me."

I looked down at her flat stomach. The reports we had said she claimed to be with child. Did she have it already? There was no way she could have this flat of a stomach and be pregnant for as long as it was claimed.

"What child? You are not even pregnant!"

"Not yet! I will be pregnant once again and this time it will work!"

"This is the exact problem I was talking about, Fyra! If you wanted to have a child, there could be ways to help that happen, but it will never work like this!"

"You are wrong! I will, and me and my child will rule Iryvalya and ensure you and all your people are slaughtered!"

"Look down there. No one is fighting for you! No one is trying to get me to bring you back down safe! You are done, Fyra! This. Is. Over!"

"You are wrong! I have my own magyc and I will survive this and keep my claim!"

She fought me harder to get away. I kept holding, knowing she would plummet to the ground if she did. I started to descend back to the platform, and Fyra managed to get an arm free enough to stab me in the left side. I still held on to her, trying to get us both safely down, but then her hands got hot as she used her fire magyc to burn me. My skin was blistering where she held on to me. I screamed in pain, and after trying so hard to get us both safely down, I knew I couldn't. I let go of Fyra and

305

through the pain lost my ability to levitate. We both started plummeting to the ground and all I could remember was the feeling I had when I was falling into the volcano. I closed my eyes and took a breath and cleared my mind of panic and pain and instead felt the winds around me and pulled them to me to slow me down.

I landed hard on the platform, but I was okay. I opened my eyes and saw Fyra sprawled out on the platform in front of me. Limbs bent in ways that shouldn't be possible and blood slowly pouring from behind her head. I walked over to her to try to help somehow, but she was already gone.

Kylyan rushed to me and saw the blood coming from my side. He ripped my shirt open enough to see the wound and put pressure on it. The burns were covered by the blood still seeping out and stung.

"You're going to be okay, Ny. It isn't deep. We just need to get you to some healers right now," he said.

"No, I need to speak to everyone first. We need to make sure this is done and that we can move forward in peace."

"Ny, you are hurt. Everyone will understand if—"

"Kyl," I said firmly, our eyes meeting each other, "I need to see this through now."

He nodded at me and helped me stand up. He tied some cloth around my waist to keep pressure on the injury and slow the bleeding.

I walked to the edge of the platform. "It did not need to be like this. Fyra did not need to die. None of you need to die, but if you are not willing to work together, then we will fight."

Hyorda walked over to me along with all the remaining council members from both Klayns. "We all agree to move to peace. What say all of you? Volnyri!"

It was quiet for a moment and then the crowds started shouting over and over, "Volnyri! Volnyri! Volnyri!"

C3 37 80

NYRIEVE

"Could it really have been this simple?" I asked aloud.

"What do you mean?" Emryleia said as she helped me straighten up the room. After a couple of days recovering from the battle and the voting in of the leaders, the room was a mess. I was just happy I was able to hide all my goodbye letters before anyone saw them.

"Everything that was built up to this battle and it was just…"

"Just?"

"Just me killing Fyra."

"I find it almost amusing you think that everything that has happened was simple… Do you honestly believe that, Ny?"

"We had the dragons ready to fight. We had all the Nomydrac we could get, the protection charms we had placed for the Klayns to keep them from attacking one another, and even the gargoyles made the trek here for this… but it was over in only a matter of minutes it seems…"

"Not every great battle ends with the majority of the people in attendance dead. I honestly think the fact that there were not many people lost was a good thing. We have known and seen enough death in this world. Why force the Leaf Day Tree to lose more leaves if it wasn't necessary?"

"I know you are right… It lost enough with Baysil…"

"I am so sorry, Ny. I know he meant a lot to you."

"He really did…"

The door opened quickly, and I turned to see Kylyan's smiling face. "You're not letting her do any of the heavy lifting, right?" he asked Emryleia.

She laughed and replied, "She keeps trying to, but I won't let her!"

"Good!" he said. "You need to take it easy with your injuries."

"It's only a scratch!" I replied solemnly.

"Ny," Em said, "you were stabbed, burned, and fractured your leg when you landed."

"Meh," I said, "I didn't feel that when it happened, so it doesn't count."

They both laughed at me.

"Did you get a chance to talk to Iclyn?" I asked Kylyan.

"Yes," he said. "She said she is going to coordinate with some of the Valya to return Baysil's body to be buried next to his wife. I didn't know it, but he had her interred just outside of Cliffside."

"I am glad their bodies will at least be able to be together again," I said, remembering the small ceremony we held for him yesterday. He would have told me he didn't need something big, so I made it the small group of us that knew him the most. We retold many fun stories about him and jokes he liked to tell. I don't think he ever realized how many people's lives he touched and how so many of us looked up to him. There would never be a day that he was not missed.

We were finishing straightening up the remaining things in silence when there was a soft knock on the door. Kylyan quickly opened it. Standing outside the door was my father.

"Hi, Dad," I said. "Is everything okay?"

"Hello," he said. "Oh yes, everything is fine, Ny... I just..."

"What is it?"

"Well, I met with Hyorda, Joynox, and the leaders representing what I guess was the Pyrothian Klayn, and we had some thoughts..."

"Why were you all meeting without Nyrieve?" Emryleia asked.

"It wasn't out of disrespect for her in any way," he said, looking a little nervous. "Everyone is still happy that she will be the saygent, until she no longer wants to be or is voted out for whatever reason..."

"But?" I asked, thinking about how strange it was the day after Baysil died, all the people that were here, elves, fairies, gargoyles, dragons, pixies, and more all took the time to vote for me to be the person who leads our world. I still couldn't wrap my head around it. I think if anyone had asked me who I voted for they would have been shocked to learn it wasn't for myself. I couldn't think of anyone who could have run anything better than Baysil. He was always levelheaded and wanted the best for everyone in Iryvalya… so instead of writing down any name, I simply drew a spiral.

"There was a thought on your upcoming nuptials," he said. "I know you had said that you wanted to do it at the castle in the Blackened Forest. However, everyone was thinking it might be best to have it done here, before everyone departs. It could be something positive and reaffirming to many of you and Kylyan's love for one another. For a long time, the rumors were that you hated one another and then there was the nasty business of the curse that was put on him and Prydos… Apparently Miaarya has been shouting these things out to anyone willing to listen."

"She is such a wonderful little instigator, that one," Emryleia said.

"Yes, she is," I added.

"Ny," Kylyan said, "in the end, I want to do what makes you happy. If you want to wait until we can get to the Blackened Forest, I am more than happy with that, but if you want to do it adjacent to the coronation ceremony, we could do that as well and maybe have a celebration here, but then travel to the Blackened Forest for a… I don't know what it would be called…"

"That is called a vacation," Arnayx said. "Clyo and I took one after we were tyed. It was a nice little getaway, just the two of us…"

"Well…" I started, "first, it is still so weird to me were doing a coronation in the first place… That said, if I think about this logically it makes sense. It can also show the uniting of two mixed-blood elves and how it is okay for us and anyone else to be tyed to one they love."

"But?" my father asked.

"No buts about that part," I said.

"But there is a but about a vacation?" Kylyan asked smiling.

"Oh goodness, enough with the buts! There is no but… more like a however," I said with a chuckle. "I do want to go back to the castle in the Blackened Forest with you, Kylyan. However, I was thinking, since it has been a really long time since we have been able to be in one place with each other and the people we love, perhaps we could have an extended person vacation."

"What would that look like?" Em asked curiously.

"Instead of it just being me and Kylyan going away, we have our families come with us, and our friends who are basically the families we have chosen."

"Who would be included in that?" Em asked, raising her eyebrow and smirking.

"Oh geez, I don't know, maybe Rowzey, Iclyn, Domi, and even you!" I laughed. "Of course you would be invited to come."

She smiled and said, "Then I am interested in that option! I really liked that island and would love the chance to explore it some more."

"I think that is a wonderful idea, Ny," Kylyan said with a smile. "I would love to send an invite to my parents to join us there, since they couldn't get here in time for the coronation."

"I would love to have them meet us there. I honestly can't wait to meet them myself," I said. "Oh, what day did the other elected leaders decide for the coronation?"

"Tomorrow," my father responded.

"Tomorrow?" I asked, shocked. "So soon?"

"It is for a few reasons," he said. "Many of the leaders and people want to return to their homes to share the news of what happened here and start enjoying their new freedoms and setting up elections to elect the new leaders of the realms and such."

"What are the other reasons?" I asked, knowing there was more to it.

"I was able to coordinate with Aurilya to have Rowzey here by that day and Domi said that she will have some items here that might help with the coronation itself by then."

I looked at the faces in the room, staring at me and waiting for my decision. This was never going to be easy, being the person who made and enforced rules, but this was the life I had now chosen for myself, and I might as well start embracing it. I smiled and said, "I think that will work wonderfully. I think if we can do the ceremony for Kylyan and me before the coronation, that would be best."

"Why is that?" Kylyan asked.

"Because, for the most part, Iryvalya must be my priority and doing what is right for all the people, and I am okay with this, but being tyed to you is something I want, and it isn't for Iryvalya that I want it, it is because we love one another. So, I feel that we should declare our love to one another before I swear my oaths to Iryvalya. Then no one can question if you are okay with my role as saygent," I said, "and that will never not be weird to call myself."

Everyone laughed at me, but I didn't mind, so I laughed too.

Kylyan crossed to me and kissed the top of my head. "It would be my honor to be tyed to you just as you are, the love of my life. I want people to know that it is you I love and not the title that will be bestowed upon you, my lady."

"It is settled then?" Arnayx asked.

"It is settled," I said with a smile.

"Fantastic," he said. "I had figured you would go along with it. I am sorry and hope you are not mad at me for that, but Clyo and many others have already started working on preparations for everything."

I rolled my eyes and said, "Of course you all have."

"You typically do the right and reasonable thing, my sweet daughter," he said, "and speaking of daughters, Emryleia, Dymma said she would like to talk to you about something."

"I shall head over and talk to her straightaway," Em said. "If you need me for anything, Ny, just send word and I'll be here."

"Thank you, Em," I said, giving her the tightest one-armed hug I could. "I love you, my friend."

"I love you too!" she said, then she hurried out the door.

"Was there anything else you wanted to talk to me about, Dad?" I asked, seeing as he was standing there starting to look uncomfortable.

"Ah, yes," he said. "I uhm… well, Clyo has been able to get in and speak to Kaleyna…"

"How is she?" I asked, hoping she had improved. She didn't seem to have any emotional reactions while everything occurred, even Baysil being killed.

"The healers are saying that Miaarya had put some kind of curse or charm on her, and they aren't sure exactly how to fully reverse it. They have pressed Miaarya for ways to fix it, but from what she has told people it can only be fixed with time, though we can't be sure that is the full truth."

"What does that mean for Kal?" I asked, worried.

"We don't know when or if she will start to feel herself again. She has some inclination that what Miaarya told her were lies, but she is having a struggle to wrap her head fully around it. Surprisingly your mother has been helpful in trying to explain to her ways to see things more clearly."

"Osidya is helping?" I asked, surprised.

"Yes," he said. "I was surprised as well, but apparently Baysil had a pretty big effect on her, and she has said she feels she owes it to him to help Kaleyna see more clearly."

"What about Prydos?" Kylyan asked.

"After he was awoken from the sleeping charm and he was reunited with Kaleyna, he seemed to start thinking more clearly as well. I think he has some lingering issues like Kaleyna, but together they seem quite happy."

"When can I see her?" I asked.

Arnayx sighed. "I don't know, Ny. She has been through a lot, and when we talk about you to her, she doesn't seem hateful but becomes more despondent and uninterested in discussing you. It might take some time for her to come around."

"Oh," I said, not knowing what else I could say.

"If you would like, I could try to arrange a meeting for you both. I would need to check with Koyvean though. She is handling most everything for Kaleyna and Prydos out of caution they don't revert back to thinking like they did when they were cursed."

"I would like that," I said.

"Then I will ask that it be done," he said. "Now I will leave the two of you alone. I am sure you could use some more rest, my dear."

He came over and gave me a careful hug and kiss on the cheek and headed out to the main house.

"He isn't wrong," Kylyan said.

"About what?"

"You look so tired, Ny. Maybe instead of straightening up anymore, we could just cuddle for a while?"

"I'd love that," I said.

Kylyan helped me lie back on the bed and get comfortable. He climbed in next to me and pulled a blanket up over us. The window was cracked open and cool air flowed inside. I could smell the sweet grasses and trees surrounding us. I allowed the sounds of the water moving against the bridges and frogs to lull me into a much-needed nap.

〜

"Just remember, Ny, Kaleyna has been through a lot and she might not be exactly like you remember her to be," Koyvean said to me.

"I understand she's been through a lot," I said, believing she couldn't be that different from the person I had known my whole life.

"Okay," she said, sounding unsure. "She is in the room across the hall."

I took a deep breath before I opened the door and stepped through to see Kaleyna standing near the fire.

"Hi, Kal..." I said, feeling my voice shake as I looked at her and knew instantly something was different. Typically, I would have rushed to her and hugged her as tight as I could, but her stance told me not to even think about that.

"Hello, Nyrieve," she said softly. Her using my full name felt so distant and not at all like the Kal I knew.

"How are you doing?" I asked, not sure if I was ready for the answer.

"I am okay. Improving each day."

"I am really happy to hear that. I was so worried about you for so long. I never stopped trying to figure out a way to get you back."

"That is what I have been told."

"Kal?" I asked, stopping myself from asking the obvious question.

"I am not sure where to start with this," she said, giving me a long look. Her eyes were the same colors as they were last time I saw her, but they looked like they were heavy with great burden.

"Me either... This seems so strange, Kal. We have known each other our whole lives, but it feels like..."

"Like we are almost strangers now?"

"That isn't exactly what I was thinking, but I guess it kind of does…"

"We are strangers now," she said.

"Why do you think that?" I asked. "I know that this was the longest time we ever were apart, but we are still the same people we once were."

"I remember most everything from before the Fire Realm… but it is different. It is like another life I had, but it isn't my life anymore," she said. "Miaarya made sure that anything and everything good we had together has been somehow tainted."

"I am so very sorry for everything that happened to you in the Fire Realm," I said. "And now I wish I would have killed Miaarya when we had the chance to before we even arrived in the Fire Realm."

"It isn't for you to apologize for," she said. "I went into it knowing something could happen. I wasn't forced or made to do any of it. It was my choice to follow you."

"I know that, Kal," I said, feeling that big sticky ball forming in the back of my throat, making it hurt when I swallowed. "It is just, none of this would have happened to you if I hadn't been… well, me."

"You can't spend the rest of your life blaming yourself for the things that happened to me, to you, or to anyone else really. None of us can choose who we are. We all knew what the risks were, and we all made our choices."

"I know, but so many bad things have happened because of me or an association to me."

"Don't take that on yourself. You risked everything to save me and Iryvalya. You should be proud of everything you have done."

"It is hard to when I know there were too many losses, and too many mistakes made."

"You made the best choices you could with the information you had available at the time," she said simply. I noticed that there was not much inflection in her voice and her words seemed hollow. I believed she meant what she was saying to me, but there was no emotion in anything she said, as if she was reading from a book that held no special place in her heart.

"I just wish I would have done some things differently," I said. "Maybe then you wouldn't have had to go through everything you did."

"Perhaps," she said. "Maybe Prydos would not have been cursed, maybe Baysil would still be alive, maybe I would still feel… whole… The world is full of maybes, but I only want to focus on the here and the now moving forward."

"I think I can understand that."

"Can you?" she asked, tilting her head to the side as if studying my reaction.

"What do you mean?" I asked, feeling even more concerned.

"Because you seem to want to maybe talk and be like it was, and it cannot be."

"Why can't things be more like they used to, Kal?" I asked. "Just because we both have times we do not want to think about doesn't mean we can't move past them to be like we were once."

"Because we are not who we were. We've grown up, and now… we have grown apart. It doesn't mean the time we spent together was any less special, but it just isn't the same moving forward, at least not for me."

"Oh," I said, "I didn't realize that the things that have happened would have pulled us so far apart."

"I didn't think you would have, Nyrieve," she said, still flat in her responses. "Maybe if I would have only been tortured and beaten like Baysil it wouldn't have caused this, but Miaarya is very good at manipulation and made me think some really awful things about myself, about you, and everyone else I knew in Cliffside."

"I am honestly sorry to hear that," I said, feeling at a loss of how to respond.

"I know you are, but this is how I need things to be at this point. You are my friend, my sister even, but there are too many memories and events that have been twisted and confused in my head that I cannot always tell what is real and what is fake. Maybe one day it'll be different, but for now…"

"But for now what?"

"For now, Prydos and I are leaving."

I could feel my forehead furrow as I asked, "What do you mean you are leaving? Where are you going to go?"

"We haven't fully decided yet. He wants to be away from"—she paused, looking at me and everything around us—"all of it… everyone."

"Me," I said flatly.

"Yes, you," she responded, still looking at me blankly.

I nodded, feeling my heart breaking and the sting of tears trying to well up. As I stood there looking at Kaleyna, I dug my nails into my hands to keep the tears at bay.

"This isn't about you, Nyrieve. It might seem like it is, but it really isn't. It is about him and I needing to be away from everything and everyone that has brought us so much heartache as of late. Prydos and I both were forced to think the worst of you, and even though we both know logically it isn't true, our initial reactions to things are still trying to catch up. Maybe down the road one day, things will be different. I hope they are, but I just don't know."

"But, what about Clyo and Dymma?"

She sighed. "I know they will be upset about this, but again, it isn't about them either. This is what I need for me."

"You need to cut off everyone who cares about you?"

"If that is how you need to see it, then so be it."

"They are going to be heartbroken, Kal," I said, knowing how much they were both wanting to have their whole family back together.

She simply shrugged.

"When are you going to tell them?"

"I guess you can fill them in when you see them next."

"Wait, what? You aren't even going to tell them yourself?" I asked, shocked.

"We figured they would hear it from you or someone else. We do not want to make a scene. I have talked to both of them, and they seem to be in good spirits about everything, so I believe that it was best to leave things on a positive note with them in person."

"How could you do that to them, Kal? Even if you want to be away from me, it kills me, but I don't see why that would stop you from seeing your mother and sister."

"Again, it isn't about anyone else. Please quit being so dramatic and selfish,

316

Nyrieve."

"Me? Me selfish? I have risked everything for everyone. I was willing to lay down my life for you and everyone else in Iryvalya. You are the one just leaving everyone without even telling them why or saying goodbye!"

"It might not be goodbye," she said, tipping her head to the side again. "Who knows, maybe I'll come visit them in a few months... maybe a few years, who knows. But I will do it when I am ready to do it."

"There is nothing I can say or do that will change your mind, is there?"

"No, there is not."

I stared at my friend. She was such an amazing and beautiful person. I thought we'd grow old together and always share everything that was happening. Her beautiful face looked the same as it always had, and yet a look in her blue-and-purple swirled eyes and I couldn't see the same light that I used to. I wished I could fix this, go back in time and stop her from going to the Fire Realm. She should have stayed with Prydos back then, and maybe things would be different. But this was where we were, and apparently I was powerless to do anything... I was the Bringer of Peace of Iryvalya and I couldn't even help my friend.

"I am sorry, Kaleyna," I said, taking a deep breath, trying to keep my voice calm and steady.

"For what?"

"I am sorry for everything negative that has happened to you. I wish I could take it back and maybe stop you from going to the Fire Realm, but I can't. I cannot fix any of this and I am sorry for that. I won't try to convince you to stay or anything. I just want you to know something."

"Yes?"

"You have been an amazing friend to me and I am grateful for the memories we shared. I will always think back on them with fondness. I do hope one day you visit or reach out or something, but I will not pressure you to do so ever again."

"Thank you, Ny," she said, her voice sounding lighter. "And I hope after your coronation that you do not use your power as saygent to change any of this."

"Do you honestly think that little of me that I would force you to be my friend?"

She thought on it for a moment and said, "No, the logical side of things tells me that you wouldn't do that."

"I wouldn't, Kal. I promise you that…"

"Thank you, Nyrieve."

I could see her getting antsy and wanting this interaction to end. I looked at my old friend and said the only thing I could think to say, "I love you, Kal."

"I love you as well, Nyrieve."

"I will let you and Prydos get going," I said. "Could I give you a hug?"

"Of course," she said, putting her arms around me and giving me a hug. "I will miss you."

"I will miss you as well, Kal," I said. "And if you ever feel like it, perhaps once in a while drop a line just so I know you are okay."

I felt her lightly chuckle. "Yes, I will do that. Somehow my mirror journal ended up coming with us here. I will try to write in it from time to time if I feel it's appropriate, and please do the same."

"I will…" I said, unable to keep the tears from streaming down my face. "I can't let go and say goodbye."

"Then we won't say goodbye."

"Okay," I said, finally letting go of her. I stepped back, wiped the tears off my face, and said the last words I would say to her for a long time and hoped would be true, "See you later."

↷38↶

STORYTELLER

"I cannot believe another year has passed as we come to remember the Battle of Ash and Air," I said, looking out at the hundreds of people who had traveled to be here today. "Thank you for coming and helping to remember and honor all those who lost their lives throughout the years of war and battles that plagued Iryvalya. It wasn't known at the time, of course, we would continue to discuss and remember the events of that day. The battle that took place and came close to changing the path that we get to walk today.

"I know many of you have come just for the celebration and to enjoy the freedoms that we sometimes take for granted, but please, while you are here in Cliffside, remember all the things that not just the Bringer of Peace sacrificed to ensure all of us the freedoms we have, but all those who helped her along the way. Anytime Saygent Nyrieve was asked after the Battle of Ash and Air about what she did for Iryvalya, she was quick to make sure the people knew it wasn't just her who brought this freedom to Iryvalya, it was so many others along the way who helped her. From the gargoyles to the dragons, she would say that each person who did something to help move our world forward deserved as much recognition as she did."

Everyone began to clap and cheer. I remember when my mother would say similar things during these celebrations, and the response was always the same. As a child it made me excited and cheer as well, but now as an adult who had overseen this event for many, many years, I just wondered if they really did understand the cost that so many paid for us all to be here today.

"Before everyone goes to enjoy the food and games, I wanted to announce that this will be my last year in hosting these celebrations. Over the years, I have enjoyed helping my mother and father plan these and then taking it over when they couldn't any longer. It is time for me to pass the torch to the next generation, and my daughter Lowyll will be heading up everything moving forward. I have no doubts that she will continue to make everyone proud of her, especially me."

Lowyll came up to say a few words of thanks to me and everyone who helped us get everything together for this, and also that she hoped she would make me proud with her efforts. As if I could ever be anything but proud of my children.

The celebrations went as perfect as they ever had. There were many people sitting around enjoying the fireworks show that was being put on. They lit up the sky, making Cliffside look like a place out of a children's story book. I wondered what it was like for my mother to return to this place year after year to celebrate and remember those who fought for our freedoms and those who lost their lives for just being themselves. I remember asking her if she liked coming back here year after year, and she told me once, "Most of the time I do enjoy coming back here. I have so many good memories, especially since your brother and you came along. I always knew this was a special place, but I also knew that it wasn't the place I was meant to stay. I think that is why I wanted to do the celebrations here. It gave me a reason to come each year to remember and celebrate."

"I think everything went perfectly," Zozo said as she sat down next to me.

"Yes, not too bad for my last festival," I said with a smile.

"Well, your last one you are doing all the work for at least." She laughed.

"True, I will have to come back and I'll enjoy seeing what Lowyll does for it next year."

"So, what is next for us?" she asked.

"Us?" I asked back.

"I hear your brother is heading out in the morning to see his family and wife. I know you have Wysh—"

"And you have Yndoximal waiting for you, I would suppose…" I said with a smile.

"How did you know about us?" she asked, looking surprised.

"Oh, Zozo, you have never been one to keep secrets from me. When I saw the two of you working together over this week, I could just tell you were happy and in love."

"That I am, dear Cuzzy!" she said with a big happy grin on her face.

"I am so happy to hear that. You both deserve to be happy!"

"But that doesn't answer my question."

"I suppose it doesn't," I said, taking a deep breath. "I think maybe we should plan a trip, you and Yndoximal with Wysh and me, and the four of us go on a trip to the castle in the Blackened Forest."

"Oh, I love that idea," she said happily. "It has been so long since we have been there."

"I know," I said. "I heard that there are a bunch of young iryturtles that would like to come over to some of the other realms. I figured it would be a good excuse to go visit and help them out."

"You never could say no to helping the iryturtles!" she said. "I love how even though you are stepping away from the festival, you are still trying to help different parts of Iryvalya."

"My mother said it best, I think," I said as I remembered looking in her beautiful eyes as she said this to me. "Ivynilo, I might have been the Bringer of Peace, but you and Joauxy are the keepers of the peace."

"Yes, I can see Aunty Ny saying that to you!" Zozo said.

"She never quit trying to help Iryvalya, even after the battle and her and father tyed. She would travel around trying to help right the wrongs and give hope to the people of Iryvalya."

"That is why she was saygent for so long. My mother always said that she was so proud of your mom when she finally wanted to step down as saygent and called for an election to have a new leader."

"I remember Aunty Dymma telling me that too. She said it takes a person with a pure heart and full of hope to know when it is time to allow others to finish the work you have started. Oh, and Aunty Emryleia always said that as long as Nyrieve was the leader for Iryvalya, we knew the world was a safer place, and then when she stepped down, Aunty Em made that crazy cake, what did she call it?"

"The Cake of Doom!" I laughed out loud.

"Oh yes, that was it!"

"She was always so much fun to have around growing up too!"

"They were wonderful women," she said. "They definitely set the bar really high for the rest of us."

"That they did," I said.

"Aunty Kal could be fun too when she would come for visits."

"Yes she was," I said, remembering hearing the stories of adventure they had as they grew up together. "I am always glad that near the end all three sisters were able to have a good relationship with one another."

"Me too," Zozo said. "I wish it would have been sooner, but better late than never, I suppose."

"Very true."

We sat in silence for a while watching the fireworks light up the sky. After they were done, we sat waiting for everyone else to collect their belongings and head back to their lodgings for the night. This was a tradition we did each year, but I remember when we were children, so many people would stop by us and take a moment to talk to my parents and ask questions about them or the other Nomydrac. When I was a child, I would sometimes get annoyed having people constantly stop and ask questions or interrupt our family time. As I grew older and my parents traveled around Iryvalya with us and showed us places that were still damaged from the wars, I realized how amazing it was that my parents helped bring Iryvalya to what it was today. My father would often remind me that it was just my mother who did it all, but when we were alone, my mother would confide in me that while she was the Bringer of Peace, she was also a confused and worried elf most of the time, and without those around her to help guide her and encourage her to keep going, she wouldn't have succeeded.

I looked out to the small island in the middle of the little lake and could see hundreds of little iryturtles lighting up as they scurried around. I remember the day we brought them here, to Cliffside. My mother said she thought the island would be a nice and safe place for them, especially with us staying in the small cottage from time to time to keep an eye on them. Part of me wanted to go out to that cottage tonight and sleep like I did as a child, but with passing the festival to Lowyll, it was only right for her and her family to stay there tonight. When her face lit up when I told her, I knew it was the right thing.

"Are we ready to go back to the manor for the evening?" Zozo asked me, sounding tired.

"I think so. It looks like everyone else has left."

We stood up and walked into the manor. I thought about my mother living here as a child thinking she was abandoned and unloved and now seeing how she was the most beloved and honored person still in Iryvalya.

As I sat down on my bed, ready to turn in for the night, I took out the letter my mother wrote me, and like every year on the anniversary of the Battle of Ash and Air, I read it to myself.

My Dearest Ivynilo,

It has been an amazing week and I wanted to thank you. You have been helping me with preparing for the festival to celebrate the anniversary of the Battle of Ash and Air and you have gone above and beyond what I have asked of you. I truly hope you know how utterly proud of you I am, not just for how helpful you are, but because of who you are. Both you and your brother have made your father and I so proud to be your parents.

I have watched you grow so much over the past year. Not only are you almost as tall as me, but your talents far surpass many of mine. I have never seen someone who loves to create beauty through art like you do, or someone who tends to and cares for the iryturtles the way you always have. You have worked hard to help find them homes in each realm, and every time you ask us for help in doing so, we can't say yes quick enough.

I love you so much, my sweet Ivy. I hope you never ever forget that. In my life I have been called many things... quanta'mu, fairy, mixed-blood, Highness, saygent, Bringer of Peace... Each one meant something to me, good or bad, but nothing has ever come close to the pride and gratefulness I have each and every time I hear you and your brother call me Mom. It is truly the highest honor I have ever had bestowed upon me and something that fills my heart with joy each and every time I hear it.

I know I taught you and Joauxy your whole life that after years of everything I had seen and had to do, that in the end the one thing that keeps us going and drives us is hope. Hope that tomorrow will be a better day, hope that next year will be better than this, and that our next generations will have so much more happiness than we could have imagined.

I know you both sometimes groan and roll your eyes at me when I tell you this, partially because I say it all the time, but never ever forget it: In Iryvalya, the smallest spark of hope can change the world… Be the spark! I am so lucky that I found that spark, over and over again throughout my life, and was able to recognize them. The people of Iryvalya coming together, your father, each of my children, and maybe one day grandchildren. You and your brother are my sparks of hope.

I love you so much, my sweet girl, always and forever. Thank you for being everything you are, because you are exactly who you should be!

Love, Mom

I folded up the worn little note and placed it back inside the blue journal covered in purple stars my mother entrusted me with, and then wiped away the tears I always got after reading it and said aloud, "I love you too, Mom, always and forever…"

❦39❧

NYRIEVE

"Are you okay, Ny?" Emryleia asked me for probably the tenth time in the last hour.

I smiled and said, "I think so, Em. It is just a lot in a short amount of time."

"If it makes you feel any better, the dress is beyond amazing."

I looked down at the beautiful gown and smiled at its loveliness. The dress was made from the softest material I had ever felt, and if held up to the light, it could have been transparent, but the way it was layered, it wasn't even a little. The top was pretty well-fitted and when Em tightened the velvety strings along the back, it definitely made all my assets look their best. From my shoulders down to my hips, it started as a pale green that shifted to a beautiful blue that went down to my knees before it shifted again into shades of purple that went all the way to the ground. There were many layers of the dress, making each ending layer look almost like a cascading waterfall. I had never seen such artwork in something someone would wear. Throughout all of the dress there were ivy vines stitched in an iridescent thread that seemed to change colors depending on the light.

Around the bodice there was also similar stitching of spirals where some were intertwined and others that went in their own direction. My shoulders were bare; however, there were cap sleeves on the sides of my arms that went down to the middle of my lower leg. It was mostly made out of the same material as the dress and matched in color locations with the rest of the dress. If my arms were held to my sides, it almost looked like they blended into the dress itself. Also on the top edge of the sleeve was a thin metal chain that I was told was Iryvalyan steel. I didn't know such a strong, hard metal could be made to look so delicate.

Hanging off the chains across the sleeves were five strands of the chain hanging down along with the rest of the sleeves. On these chains there were color beads and stones attached that had been carved and made to shine beautifully when the light hit them. When I asked about where the dress came from, no one would answer me.

I was promised that before I left to get tyed to Kylyan, someone would come and explain everything to me.

My variegated shades of green hair had been made into long wavy curls with parts woven in intricate patterns around the top of my head. It wasn't tight, but it was staying held in place. Emryleia had helped me get dressed and ready, even helping me with some of the makeup that Iclyn had brought in for me to use. I remembered how Ghily used to make my face look so beautiful without any effort, and I definitely had to do a lot more work to get it almost halfway as great as she could. I wished she was here for today, she, Lydorea, and Baysil and so many others, but I wasn't going to think on that too much today. There was so much to be grateful for today and that was what I needed to focus on.

"Where do you think this dress came from, Em?" I asked, glancing at the looking glass far more often than I usually would.

"I don't know, Ny, but it is as if this dress was made for you!"

"I's know where it came from, Ny," Rowzey's voice said as she carefully walked into the room we were getting ready in.

"Rowzey!" I shouted as I ran to her and hugged her closely. "I didn't think you'd be able to make it!"

"Do yous really think I's could miss the day yous are tyed?" she asked, hugging me back.

"If it was up to you, no," I said, stepping back and giving her a look over, "but with your injuries I didn't know how you were faring. Domi said she had been to visit you, but I know sometimes you put on a braver face than you need to."

"Are yous saying yous get yous stubbornness from me?" she asked, pretending to be appalled.

I laughed. It was so good to have Rowzey here. It made things feel more normal, or at least as close to normal as it could be.

"I's am sorry about Kal," Rowzey said solemnly.

"Thank you, but she made a choice to live a life that she feels is best for her, and I cannot fault her for that. Her life with Prydos is what she should live for and do what is best for."

Rowzey smiled at me. "Yous are a wonderful leader, Ny. I's think there is more hurt than yous are letting on, but what yous are saying is true. Her choice to leave with Prydos has nothing to do with yous, so try to not let it weigh down on yous like I's know it likely has."

"Thank you, Rowzey," I said, giving her another quick hug. "But I have not been letting it weigh on me too much. Besides, Emryleia has been here by my side through all of the things that have been happening and helped me prepare for today."

"Hi, Rowzey," Em said. "I am so glad to see you looking so much better than when we saw you in Troxeon."

"I's am glad to see yous too, Em," she said, giving her a big hug. "I's am feeling more and more like myself each day. Soon I's think I'll be able to shift again to my dragon form."

"I can imagine you've been missing that," Em said.

"Yes, I's have. This isn't the longest I's gone between shifting, but it's been the hardest one so far, seeing as I's no longer need to hide who I's am."

"So, Rowzey," I said, "you said you knew. Can you please tell me where this dress came from?"

"This dress was made for yous, of course," she said with a sly-looking smile.

"How and when was this made for me?" I asked, confused about who would have had the time to make it.

"I's did, of course," she said with a smile.

"When could you have made this?" I asked, shocked.

"I's have been working on it for years for yous. I's left it in the Spirit Realm when we traveled there, and I's was able to work on it again shortly after Domi got me back there to heal. I's did get a little help from Aurilya as well. She added the colorful beads down the sides. She said it was to represent all the people of Iryvalya, and how on the Leaf Day Tree each leaf is a different color and shade."

I looked more closely at the beads and realized I could see a bead that matched Rowzey's eyes perfectly as well as one that matched Baysil's eyes too. My heart skipped and my eyes stung.

"No, Ny!" Emryleia said with a laugh. "You cannot cry. We just got the makeup to look as right as we can!"

I started to laugh instead and took a deep breath. "Thank you, Rowzey, for this amazing dress, and I will thank Aurilya too when I see her."

"I's sure she'd like that," Rowzey said. "Now are yous about ready to get going with this? There is more people than I's ever seen in one place outside waiting for yous."

"Only on one condition," I said.

"What is that?" Rowzey asked.

"If you walk me down the aisle to Kylyan."

Her face brightened up and she said, "Oh, Ny! I's would love that!"

"Fantastic! Emryleia already agreed to stand up next to me during the ceremony with Kylyan."

"Who is standing for him?" she asked, knowing with Prydos gone that spot might not have been filled.

"His father," I said happily. "His parents were able to get here in time with a little help from a dragon we know."

"That is wonderful, Ny," she said. "I's look forward to meeting them after yous tying and tell them what a wonderful and kind son they have. I's am sure they must be so very proud of him."

"I think they are," I said. "I only had the chance to meet them a couple days ago, but they seem quite wonderful. They all talk a little bit louder than I am used to, but I think I could get used to it!"

Emryleia laughed. "You better get used to it. They will be your family too now."

After taking a few more moments to check ourselves in the looking glass, we were ready.

We headed out the doors of the house and down the wooden pathway out to a large clearing in the forest. As we headed there, I could hear music playing softly. There were stringed instruments and what sounded like a flute of some sort. When we got to the clearing, I could see there were long rows of wood benches. At the outer side of the benches there were trees that were covered in flowers and green vining plants. Across the tops, strands of green and purple flowers were draping down but not blocking anyone's view of the platform ahead where Kylyan was standing and waiting for me. He had the most beautiful smile on his face I had ever seen.

He was standing on the moss-covered platform looking so handsome in his fancy clothes. I knew he said he didn't overly love getting dressed up, but when he did, I just couldn't take my eyes off of him. Behind him was a large arch that also was covered in hanging vines and flowers. Everything looked so beautiful. Now I was kind of glad when my father suggested letting them get everything ready and let it be a surprise, because I was definitely surprised at all the beauty.

Emryleia went ahead and was standing down one step on the platform ahead with Kylyan's father standing on the same step but next to Kylyan. I was starting to really feel the importance and weight of everything as Rowzey and I slowly made it down the aisle to the front. There were so many people here, I couldn't imagine how all these people wanted to be here just to watch us being tyed to one another. As if I said something aloud to her, Em caught my attention, and because all others were looking at me, she made a silly face, sticking her tongue out at me. It made me smile and laugh and forget my nerves and focus on what mattered the most. In that moment, I was forever grateful for the ability to reconnect with Emryleia and I knew we had a friendship that would last the rest of our lifetimes.

Rowzey and I finally made it to the bottom of the platform. I turned and saw my father and Clyo standing with tears falling. Dymma was next to them, looking so happy and excited. Next to Dymma was Osidya. I was still surprised at her presence here, and the work she had been doing to try to be a better mother towards me. There were still times where I wasn't sure if she was genuine or if I could truly trust her, but in this moment, I was happy she was there to share in this wonderful day with us.

Kylyan stepped down and took my hand in his as Rowzey stepped back and stood next to my father. I let Kylyan lead me up the steps. They were firm but still a little unbalanced, so I was extra glad I turned down Iclyn's suggestion to wear the shoes with the tall heels. I was happy with my simple silver shoes that didn't make me worried I would fall.

Once Kylyan and I were standing at the top of the platform together, he took both of my hands and gave me a little wink, and all I could do was smile back an even bigger smile at him.

Hyorda came and stood at the back of the platform and brought the attention of everyone to them and began speaking loudly and clearly. "Today is a wonderous day we have all been lucky enough to get to be a small part of. These two elves have had more challenges thrown at them than most and, in the end, they still found their way back to one another and choose today to promise before you all their intentions to be tyed to one another."

Everything was beautiful and amazing, but it all seemed to go by so quickly. While Hyorda was talking about love and what it meant to be there for one another, all I could think of was how it was only a couple of years ago I didn't truly know who I was or what I wanted in my life, and now I knew the things that meant the most to me as well as what and who I wanted in my life.

After the hand-tying part was finished, Hyorda smiled and announced aloud, "I hereby state for any and all to see, these people are tyed to one another. You may seal your promise to one another with a kiss."

Kylyan and I both smiled as we leaned in and kissed each other. As we did, there were loud cheers from the crowd, and I could hear Emryleia cheering the loudest behind me.

Kylyan and I turned and faced the people and smiled as we started down the steps of the platform and down the aisle to the entrance of the forest into the area that was set up with tables for feasting and enjoying music being played.

Once people had begun to take their seats and enjoy the amazing food organized by Aunty Patryvla and apparently Rowzey as well, it started to really sink in that I was tyed to Kylyan and him to me. We had promised in front of our families we would always be honest and kind to one another and continue to choose one another each and every day. I knew that not all tyings worked out, but right now, looking at Kyl and seeing him smiling and laughing, I couldn't imagine there ever being a day or a moment where I didn't want this person in my life next to me sharing it all.

"I would like to make a toast," Domi said loudly for all to hear and voices stopped talking in mid-sentence. "I have been witness to many tyings throughout my life as a Valya, but I must say, none of them struck me quite the way the union of Kylyan and Nyrieve has today. Before, the ceremonies were often quiet and even sometimes secretive. I never knew that these events could be full of love and happy wishes for the couple as much as I have seen here today. I truly believe that this union is one that will last and be the kind of love that inspires others to strive for or even be written about. The Valya have never really engaged in relationships in the way most people do, but I believe that as we move forward in this new era of Iryvalya, things like that will all change for the better. With that said, I have been instructed that now that dinner has concluded, everyone who wishes to, please return to the ceremony area, where in a few moments Nyrieve's coronation will commence."

Everyone quickly stood and headed back over to where Kylyan and I were tyed. I took a deep breath. I knew this part was next, but I hadn't put as much emotion into it as I had about being tyed. Now all the thoughts and fears were starting to seep into my brain, wondering if this was something I could possibly do and be good at.

"Uhm, knock it off, Nyrieve!" I heard Emryleia say to me as she lightly smacked my arm.

"Huh? What?" I asked, confused.

"She's right, Ny," Kylyan started. "You need to stop thinking you will not be good enough for this. You were born to lead. You just hadn't been given the chance to before you were forced to. I believe you will be an amazing leader, and you know I will always have your back."

"Me too!" Emryleia said with a smile. "Kylyan and I will spend our lives holding that mirror up to your face to prove to you that you are good enough and worthy of people following you."

I laughed and cried at the same time. "Between the two of you, I do not think I will ever be able to think a negative thought about myself!"

"Exactly," they said in unison and then started to laugh because it was not intentional.

"Ny," Rowzey said, "it is yous time, dear."

"We will see you in there," Kylyan said.

"Wait, I have to walk in there alone?" I said, realizing I figured I would just walk in with Kylyan and not by myself.

"Yep," he said. "You must walk in there alone, and you can do it, because you are much stronger than you realize."

"Nyrieve," Osidya said, "I am sorry to interrupt you all, but I promised Baysil I would give this to you right before your coronation. He made me promise to wait till now."

She handed me the sealed note with my name on it in Baysil's handwriting, then she smiled and headed back towards the ceremony area. I looked at Kylyan, Emryleia, and Rowzey. "Should I open it?" I asked.

"If Baysil said you should, you should," Kylyan said, giving me a kiss on my forehead. "We will see you in there, my lady... Oh, I mean, my saygent!"

I smiled as I watched them all leave me alone in the middle of the clearing. It was starting to get dark, so I decided to quickly open the letter so I could be sure I could read it.

My dearest Nyrieve,

If you are reading this, then sadly I did not survive to see you crowned the saygent of Iryvalya. You might be wondering how I knew this was going to happen. Lydorea, of course. She and I had many conversations over the years, and I told her that I always wanted to see you become who you were born to be. The look on her face let me know I wouldn't get that opportunity, and I finally wore her down to explain what she knew about my future. She wouldn't give me all the details, but she did say I would live long enough to see you start to figure out that you are the true leader all of our people have needed for so long, and I am happy enough with that.

While I have no idea what happens after we die, I just hope that were ever we go, I will be reunited with Maelyrra and perhaps see you again someday.

I just want you to know I am proud of you, Nyrieve. Ever since I started to keep an eye on you back in Cliffside, I knew you were special and different than most. You cared more about how people felt than who they were or what they had. Your choices in life have always shown that mentality. You do the right thing not for a reward of some kind but because it is the right thing to do. I know you will continue to be like that throughout your life as well.

I do want you to also remember, trying to do the right thing for others does not mean stop taking care of yourself. Remember that you too deserve peace and happiness. I know you will be a wonderful saygent, and one day you will have a family of your own. Yes, that is a little spoiler Lydorea shared with me but made me promise to never tell, but it is something I wanted to share with you. I will not say when or how or with whom, though I think you already have the whom part figured out. You will be an amazing mother, Nyrieve, because you know what it is like to have an absent mother and one who has hurt you so much. I know Osidya is trying to figure out everything with that. I am sure she has told you by now about the cursed jewelry she was given. I am not telling you to forgive her or anything, but I will say, there are moments when she and I have talked that I caught glimpses of who she once was and who she could be again. I hope for her sake she does the work and gets the chance to know you, because she will miss out on so much if she doesn't.

Before you wear the crown, know that you have worked so hard for this. It isn't because you were born with that mark on your wrist. Anyone can have a mark and be foretold to be a hero. The only people who can genuinely achieve this is someone who is willing to do the right thing over and over again, even when everyone and everything around her tries to stop her. You, my dear, are unstoppable.

I am so very proud of you, Nyrieve. I always felt if I had a daughter, I would have wanted her to be like you. Losing Maelyrra robbed me of the chance to have a family with her, but over these past couple of years, I have felt I had the real chance to be a father, and I will always carry you in my heart like a daughter.

I am sorry I missed your Leaf Day. I know it passed while I was still here in the Fire Realm, but I thought of you that day and hoped that you were able to spend it with those who love you. If you ever get back to Cliffside, make sure to check in my old room, and hidden under the floorboards by the window is a blue book with purple stars on it. It is a journal I kept over the years of keeping an eye on you. Maybe it'll tell you things you want to know or maybe it will just let you know that you were always seen.

I love you, Nyrieve Vynlync, and so many more people do as well. Do not fear this next part of your journey. It will have its ups and its downs, but in the end, it will be a life worth living.

Hopefully I will see you again one day.

Volnyri, Saygent Nyrieve!

Baysil

The tears were streaming down my face. I grabbed a cloth from one of the tables and wiped my face the best I could without rubbing off all the makeup. I couldn't believe he was able to write all this to me while captive. I guess Osidya really had been trying to do the right thing. Maybe there was hope for us after all.

I tucked the letter into the hidden pockets of my dress, felt Klaw still sturdy on my thigh as always, took a deep breath, and headed back over for the coronation. It was dark, but as I wandered my way there, I started to see some light.

I knew that there would be slight changes for the coronation, but I didn't expect to see glowing crystal lights from the strands where the flowers were hanging above everyone. There, dancing around the platform at the front, were hundreds of irybugs. Their blue, purple, and green lights flashing and calling me forward. I looked down and all around my feet were iryturtles wandering and glowing different colors. I took another deep breath and started to follow the little iryturtles forward as they guided me back to the platform. As I walked forward, I looked at the people all around, so happy to see familiar faces from my journeys over the past couple of years. Louv, Leyhroi, Jynkins, Crymson, Marselyus, Draykorian, Jyngy, Sudryl, Tycori, even Reayondr. So many people, here to support this... to support me.

Standing on the platform waiting for me were Rowzey, Iclyn, Hyorda, Osidya, Arnayx, Louv, Domi, Call, and Ayllac. I took my time going up the steps to the top of the platform and waited to hear what I was supposed to do next. When I had asked before, everyone said I just needed to show up and that was it.

"Thank you all for joining us this lovely evening. We spent the day celebrating the union of Nyrieve and Kylyan, and now we will celebrate the crowning of our new saygent," Hyorda said loudly. The people responded in cheers, which I did not expect, and made me feel like I was blushing.

"A saygent has not been crowned for many centuries," Domi said, "but tonight, I am proud to present this crown to our new saygent, Saygent Nyrieve!" There were more cheers and excitement from behind me, but I could only focus on what was happening in front of me.

Domi stepped forward with a pillow. On top of the pillow was a small and delicate crown made from Iryvalyan steel. It was in the shape of a bunch of ivy vines, with their ends twisting into spirals. I didn't know why I thought it would be something big and clunky, but this was perfect. It was small but refined and regal. I could see little sparkles as it caught the light and could tell there were gemstones fixed throughout.

I kneeled down, and Domi placed the crown on my head. When she pulled her hands back, I could feel the weight of the crown and it almost felt like it got heavier, but perhaps it was just my thoughts of the weight of my responsibilities it carried.

I slowly stood back up, everyone in front of me smiling back at me. I turned around and looked at all the people gathered and felt overcome with gratefulness and pressure all at once. No one said I was supposed to do or say anything, but I felt like I needed to say something.

"People of Iryvalya, I am very humbled that you have chosen me as your leader. It wasn't fate that decided that, it was all of you. I want Iryvalya to be a place where everyone's voice matters and you feel safe enough to speak your minds. I also want it to be a place where within reason we are more tolerant of one another. I believe it is something that is possible, but we all have to want it and work for it. I promise as your saygent, I will always try to do what is right for all the people of Iryvalya.

"My life has taken me on a strange and exciting journey up to now, and I can only imagine it will continue to do so. My hope is that after a small amount of time with Kylyan, we will travel all over each realm and meet with everyone to get a sense of what is important to you and what resources you need. I would love to see the realms working together with one another to help fill needs and hopefully the same in return. If we can unite all of our people, I believe we have a wonderful chance at keeping peace throughout Iryvalya.

"I could not have made it to this point in my life without the help of many supportive people. If I had the time to list them all off and explain what they have done for me, we would be here at least until tomorrow evening. As I was walking up here tonight and seeing so many faces, it reminded me that the main thing I always tried to carry with me throughout all this was hope. Hope for a better tomorrow, hope for a better future, and what I learned from it all was that in Iryvalya, the smallest spark of hope can change the world... Be the spark!

"You have all been so kind and gracious with the tying ceremony today and now my coronation. Thank you for coming. Please go forward and bring kindness, empathy, and inclusiveness to all those you encounter. We are all Iryvalya.

"Volnyri!"

"Volnyri!" everyone shouted back.

"Everyone," Rowzey said loudly, "please head back to the dining area for desserts and more celebrations for this evening!"

Everyone quickly headed back to the other clearing. I stood on the platform for a few more minutes and looked around me. Dancing around me were the irybugs and the little iryturtles scurrying around my feet. It was a moment I would always hold sacred deep in my heart. I felt the power and love of Iryvalya around me and knew that I was not just destined to lead the people of Iryvalya, I wanted to.

I smiled as I opened my eyes and saw Kylyan standing halfway up the aisle smiling back at me.

"Are you coming?" he asked. "Your guests are waiting for you."

I nodded and carefully stepped around the iryturtles and ran to Kylyan, giving him a big hug as he picked me up and twirled me around. I held tight as he spun us around a few times. The irybugs had followed and were flittering around with us. A moment I wished I could have captured forever, but one that will always be in my memory.

As he stopped and helped me to get steady on my feet, he looked down at me and placed his warm hand on my cheek and leaned down and kissed me softly at first, and then his hand around my back pulled me in even closer to him and he kissed me deeper and with more passion than ever. I didn't want the kiss to end, but slowly he pulled back and said, "I best not keep them waiting on their saygent, my lady."

I laughed and we walked back arm in arm. The rest of the night was filled with laughter, music, and food. There was dancing and it was a beautiful thing to see elves of both Klayns dancing with one another, fairies dancing with gargoyles, dragons dancing with merpeople, and me dancing with everyone. It was the true picture of what I hoped my reign would look like, everyone seeing there was nothing separating us from being able to get along and be happy.

As the night started to come to an end, there were only a few people left still dancing or talking. I was dancing slowly with Kylyan as he held me close.

"What are you thinking about, Ny?" he asked softly.

"How if you were to have told me all this would happen a few years ago, I would have thought you beyond crazy."

"Why is that?"

"I never thought I could be someone others look to for anything, let alone someone to lead them. But now, here I am and I am happy with this life."

"What about being tyed to me?" he asked with a grin.

"That is the best part of today, Kylyan, knowing we will be together for the rest of our lives."

"That we will be," he said.

"And one day, we'll enjoy having a family of our own."

"A what?" he asked with a huge grin. "Do you know something I don't?"

"Maybe," I said, giving him a kiss.

"Maybe?"

"We'll take it one day at a time, Kylyan," I said.

I looked around us. All of our closest friends and family were standing, handing out glasses of my favorite drink, Pealyalt.

"To Nyrieve, the Bringer of Peace," Emryleia said.

"No, no, no," I said quickly, "to all of us and to us all bringing peace to Iryvalya!"

In unison we toasted and cheered aloud, "Volnyri!"

CRBD

Term	(Pronunciation)	Definition
Adularyin Mountains	(Ad-u-lar-e-in)	Mountains in the Spirit Realm
Alabynes	(Al-a-bee-nes)	Name – Male Valya
Aloyc	(Al-oy-sea)	Name - Death Elf
Aquyleya	(Aqua-lay-a)	Underwater City
Arnayx	(Are-n-axe)	Name - Male Elf
Aubryx	(Uh-br-icks)	Name – Elf
Aurilya	(Uh-rill-ya)	Name – Female Dragon
Aylavyri Tirips Mlaer	(Ay-lav-ur-e Tear-ips M-lay-Er)	Portal Phrase
Ayllac	(Aa-lack)	Name - Female Pixie
Baletzya	(Bale-eat-z-ya)	Name - Female Elf
Balthyza	(Ball-thee-za)	Name - Male Elf
Baysil	(Bay-zl)	Name - Male Fairy
Blackened Forest	(Black-ened Forest)	Island near Troxeon
Brydalwind	(Bri-dal-wind)	Meadow in the Stone Realm
Brydetor	(Bri-dee-tor)	Name – Male Elf
Callya	(Call-ya)	Name - Female Pixie
Cliffside	(Cliffside)	Village in the Stone Realm
Clyo	(Clee-o)	Name - Female Elf
Clyr	(Clear)	Amulet
Coreyum	(Kor-e-um)	Name – Male Elf
Crymson	(Crimson)	Name - Female Nymph
Crystoval Mountains	(Cryst-o-val)	Mountains in the Stone Realm
Cuzzy	(C-uz-zy)	Shorted name for cousin
Cyndorin	(Sin-door-in)	Name – Male Elf
Dalorvya	(Da-lor-vee-ah)	Destroyed Fairy village
Dazyen	(Daz-yen)	Name - Female Satyr
Demetryus	(De-me-tree-us)	Name - Male Gargoyle
Domi	(Dome-ee)	Name – Female Valya
Drayk	(D-ray-k)	Elf Rebels
Draykorian	(D-ray-core-e-an)	Name - Male Goblin
Dymma Loycuvr	(Dim-ah Loy-curve-er)	Name - Female Elf
Drycoro	(Dry-core-o)	Word for Destroy
Eldreyva	(El-dre-va)	Name - Female Elf

Elethya	(El-e-th-e-a)	Name - Female Elf
Elyzia	(El-eez-ee-ah)	Name - Female Fairy
Emryleia	(Em-re-lay-ah)	Name – Female Elf
Eritsong Woods	(Ear-et-song Woods)	Village in the Stone Realm
Everglyn Woods	(Ever-glen Woods)	Village in the Air Realm
Everlyfyur	(Ev-er-ly-fire)	Magycal Spell
Eyree	(Eye-ree)	Village in the Spirit Realm
Flurya	(Fl-u-ry-a)	Name - Female Elf
Fyleeza	(F-eye-lee-za)	Name - Female Elf
Fynnasla	(Fin-as-la)	Name - Female Fairy
Fyra Avdrak	(F-eye-rah Av-drake)	Name - Female Elf
Ghilyauna	(Gill-lee-au-na)	Name - Female Nymph
Gramzy	(Gram-Z)	Name - Grandma nick name
Grolyndiva	(G-row-lin-dee-va)	Word for a type of bread
Grydios	(Gr-eye-de-os)	Village in the Stone Realm
Gwyndal	(G-win-dal)	Name - Female Fairy
Hyleia	(Hi-lay-uh)	Name – Female Elf
Hyorda Gomylon	(Hi-or-da Go-my-l-on)	Name - Elf
Iclyn	(Ice-Lynn)	Name - Female Fairy
Irybug	(Eye-re-bug)	Name of bugs that light up
Iryrock	(Eye-re-r-ock)	Name of a spiral carved stone
Iryturtle	(Eye-re-tur-tle)	Name of turtles that light up
Iryvalya	(Eye-re-vale-ya)	World
Ivynilo	(Eye-vee-nill-low)	Moon
Jagula	(Jag-u-la)	Name - Female Valya
Jaryc	(Jar-ick)	Name - Male Elf
Jaxyon	(J-axe-ee-on)	Name - Male Elf
Jehryps	(J-air-rips)	Name - Male Elf
Jeseclyean	(J-ess-ee-k-lee-an)	Name - Female Fairy
Joauxy	(Jo-aux-ee)	Moon
Joynox	(Joy-knox)	Name - Male Elf
Jyngy	(Gin-gee)	Name - Female Elf
Jynkins	(Jink-ins)	Name - Male Satyr
Jytt	(Jet)	Name - Male Gargoyle
Kaleyna Tarsys	(Ka-lee-na Tar-sis)	Name - Female Elf
Kelvyhan	(Kel-vee-han)	Name - Male Fairy
Kivesyon	(Key-ve-sy-on)	Mountains in the Stone Realm

Klaw	(K-law)	Knife
Klyan	(Clan)	Group of people
Knarfy	(Nar-fee)	Name - Male Satyr
Koneyotta	(K-own-ee-o-ta)	Ancestor to Fairies & Elves
Koyvean	(Coy-veen)	Name - Female Elf
Krulyna	(K-roo-lee-na)	Name - Female Elf
Krystolena	(Cry-st-o-lee-na)	Name - Female Fairy
Kryvon	(Cry-von)	Name - Male Elf
Kyangol d'Siyang	(Kai-an-goal d'Sai-ang)	Magycal Phrase
Kylyan	(Kill-ee-an)	Name - Male Elf
Legatey Rodyron	(Le-gat-ee Ro-die-ron)	Name - Male Elf
Leyhroi	(Lee-roy)	Name - Male Satyr
Louvyordal	(Lou-vee-or-dal)	Name - Male Gargoyle
Lowyll	(Lowell)	Moon
Lumi	(Lou-mee)	Name - Female Elf
Lumaryia Elves	(Lou-ma-re-a Elves)	One of the Elf Klayns
Lydorea	(Lie-door-e-ah)	Name - Female Fairy
Lynawn	(Lynn-awe-n)	Island East of the Stone Realm
Lyndrea	(Lin-dre-a)	Name - Female Elf
Lynfavyta	(Lynn-fav-ee-ta)	Magycal Phrase
Lyvional Forest	(Li-vee-o-n-al)	Forest in the Air Realm
Lyosx	(Lie-o-six)	Name - Male Elf
Maelyona	(May-lee-o-na)	Name - Female Elf
Maelyrra	(Mae-leer-a)	Name - Female Fairy
Magyc	(Magic)	Magic
Marselyus	(Mar-sell-ee-us)	Name - Female Fairy
Miaarya	(Mee-are-ee-a)	Name - Female Fairy
Montryos	(Mon-tree-os)	Name - Male Fairy
Mylterias Cove	(Mal-tear-e-es Cove)	Village in the Stone Realm
Nedoryte	(Knee-door-tee)	Outcasted people
Nomydrac	(N-om-ee-dre-ake)	Group of people
North Sea	(North Sea)	The Sea in the North of Iryvalya
Northern Sun	(Northern Sun)	The Sun to the North of Iryvalya
Noygandia	(Noy-g-on-dia)	Town in the Water Realm
Nulya	(New-lee-a)	Name - Female Fairy

Nydian	(Nigh-dee-an)	Moon
Nykirys	(Nigh-key-rus)	Name – Male Elf
Nyrieve Vynlync	(Nigh-r-eve Vine-link)	Name - Female Elf
Nyvilliry	(Nigh-vil-eye-ree)	Old Koneyotta saying about death
Orbryton	(Oh-bri-ton)	Name – Male Elf
Oryliout	(O-rye-lee-oat)	River in the Stone Realm
Osidya	(Oh-sid-ya)	Name - Female Elf
Ossyr	(Oss-er)	Bird
Oumryn Nordyl	(Ohm-ren Nor-dial)	Name - Female Elf
Pairyn	(Pair-ing)	Romantic Relationship
Patryvla	(P-at-tr-ee-v-la)	Name - Female Elf
Peayalt	(Pea-y-alt)	Cucumber Lemon Water
Polyoux	(Pa-lee-ox)	Name - Male Elf
Prax	(P-r-axe)	Town in the Fire Realm
Prydos	(Pry-de-os)	Name - Male Elf
Pyrothian Elves	(Pi-row-thee-an Elves)	One of the Elf Klayns
Quwyst	(Qu-west)	Name - Female Elf
Quanta'mu	(Kwann-ta-moo)	Derogatory word for Mix-Blooded Elf
Reayondr	(Ray-on-der)	Name - Female Fairy
Relonya	(Re-lon-ya)	Name - Female Elf
Rhyon	(Rye-on)	Name - Male Gargoyle
Rievenya	(Re-vin-ya)	Name - Female Elf
Roliyom	(Ro-lee-ohm)	Name - Male Elf
Rowzey	(Row-zee)	Name - Female Dragon
Rydison	(Rye-di-son)	Moon
Ryucha Berries	(Rye-oo-cha Berries)	Berries that increase fertility
Sangrynaw	(San-gra-naw)	Bird
Saygent	(S-age-ent)	Title – Ancient Title of Elected Leader
South Sea	(South Sea)	The Sea in the South of Iryvalya
Southern Sun	(Southern Sun)	The Sun to the South of Iryvalya
Stovokow	(St-ov-o-k-ow)	Large Rabbit-like animal in the Spirit Realm
Strylea	(St-rye-lee-ah)	Giant Seahorse-like animal
Sudryl	(Sud-rile)	Name – Male Merman

Sunorlyna	(Sun-or-lena)	Name - Female Elf
Sweyton	(Sway-ton)	Name - Male Elf
Symiar	(Sigh-me-are)	Name - Male Fairy
Syngladen	(Sin-glay-den)	Village in the Fire Realm
Syviss	(S-ih-viss)	Name – Female Mermaid
Takyri	(T-ay-kai-re)	Name – Valya
Tycori	(Tie-cor-re)	Name – Goblin
Torgany	(Tore-gan-ee)	Name - Female Fairy
Trolls	(T-r-oul-s)	Creature's that use to live in Air Realm
Troxeon	(Tr-ox-ee-on)	Island
Twyn	(T-win)	Intimate Relations
Twynslag	(T-win-ss-la-g)	Derogatory word for Twyn'ing
Tye	(Tie)	Wedding
Tyed	(T-i-ed)	Married
Umlya	(Um-lay-ah)	Name – Female Dragon
Untyed	(U-n-t-eyed)	Divorce
Unvartory	(Un-v-ar-t-or-ee)	Word meaning attack
Valtalya	(V-all-t-all-ya)	Name – Female Elf
Valya	(V-ale-ya)	Watchers & Recorders of Iryvalya's history
Vestollo	(V-est-o-ll-o)	Word meaning Kill
Volnyri	(Vol-nigh-re)	Old Iryvalya saying
Voynder	(Vo-ander)	Name - Male Gargoyle
Vylerynmyst	(V-ill-air-in-m-ist)	Village in the Air Realm
Whyndal	(Wine-dal)	Name - Male Gargoyle
Windoberry	(Win-doh-berry)	Wine
Wyndrynali	(W-ind-dry-na-lee)	Name – Female Dragon
Wysh	(W-ish)	Name – Elf
Xetyna	(Ze-tee-na)	Name - Female Elf
Xylonia	(Zi-lone-ia)	Village in the Stone Realm
Xylota	(Zi-lo-ta)	Magical Berries
Xyvoltis	(Zy-vol-t-iss)	Word meaning War
Yndoximal	(Yen-dox-imal)	Name - Elf
Yorsot	(Your-s-ott)	Name - Male Elf
Zagnyon	(Zag-nee-on)	Name - Female Elf
Zendiya	(Zen-die-ya)	Name - Male Gargoyle
Zozinyal	(Zo-zin-yal)	Name – Female Elf

Zyjoyvi	(Z-eye-joy-vee)	Name - Female Fairy
Zyrontax	(Zi-ron-tax)	Name - Male Elf

Acknowledgments & Thanks to:

My family, Joe, Joey & Ivy, You three are what have made this world possible. I honestly cannot imagine my life without the three of you in it, let alone the world of Iryvalya. You all have been so supportive of me over these years with my writing, coming up with crazy book ideas, and even listening to me have arguments with my characters. When I think of how my books are geared towards having hope and bringing people together, it would have never happened without the three of you. You three are the spark in my life, you give me love, hope, joy, happiness and so much more. Thank you Thank you Thank you for being my family. I truly feel I have hit the lottery when it comes to you three. Thank you for being the spark! I love you all so much!

My amazeballz husband, Joe, I honestly don't know where to begin with this… You have stood next to me and showed me I could (and should) believe in myself. I honestly do not think these books would have ever happened without your love and support. I am grateful that each and every day we wake up and choose to love one another. I honestly could not have hoped for a better partner to go through this life with. You not only gave me love, you brought me a family and then expanded it with me. I absolutely love our life together and wouldn't change anything in my past if it ever meant I wasn't right here with you and our kids (Moon too). Thank you for going on this journey with me, and helping keep my feet on the ground. I also appreciate you pushing me out of my comfort zone and helping me grow as a person, an author and a mother. You are the person who came into my life and changed everything for the better, and I will always be grateful for you doing that. I look forward to spending the rest of my life with you and I am excited to see all the adventures we'll go on together. I love you always and forever! Ditto!

My son, Joey, my Joauxy! You have made me so proud of you, watching you on your journey. There were times when I couldn't stop worrying about you and what your future held, but I see you growing as a person who cares about others and wants to make a difference in the world, and I know if that is what you want to do and be, you will be able to do it. You are so creative, and I know that with your ideas and instincts you will go far in life. Anything you want to do or be is possible, because you are smart, strong, caring, creative, funny, and so much more. You deserve all the happiness your heart can hold, and I believe that those you chose to have in your life are some of the luckiest people in the world. You deserve the best and do not to settle for less! Thank you so much for welcoming me into your life when your Dad and I got married. Thank you for letting me love and care for you as my own. I know I didn't carry you into this world, but I do and always will carry you in my heart. I love you Joey, so very much, always and forever!

My daughter, Ivy, oh my sweet Ivynilo! I cannot call you my little girl anymore, when you are almost the same height as me, but you will always be my little girl, even when you are 60, it will still apply. I am so grateful each and every day that you came into my life. I always dreamt of having you, not just a baby, but you specifically. I dreamt of having a little girl who loved being creative with me and was kind, and you are the kindest and most caring person I have ever met. I watch you with your friends, and you truly care about each and every one of them, always wanting the best for them. You love without fear or restraint, but you hold boundaries well, knowing that you deserve love and respect in return. Thank you for all your ideas and suggestions for me when I have been writing, I could not have imagined IryValYa without you. I love seeing the creative ideas you come up with and cannot wait to see how you'll grow and all the magic you will bring into this world. Before you were born we didn't know how long we'd get to watch you grow, I am grateful and thankful each and every single day that you are in our lives and the world is such a better place with you in it. You are who I wish I could have been like when I was your age, and I feel honored to get to be your Mom and watch all the amazing things you have done and all the even more amazing things I know you will do! I love you Ivy, more than I'll ever be able to put into words, always and forever!

Moon, pss-pss-pss… you live the life of leisure, but you bring so much love and joy to our home. I swear there is no other like you nor will there ever be!

Frank & Rose, aka Dad & Mom, the two of you have been such a wonderful addition to my life. I was so happy and excited to join your family and still am. You both were always so supportive of my writing and gave me such positive and encouraging feedback. I remember the first time I met Dad and gave him a hug, it was like hugging a cement pylon and I didn't know if it would ever change. But I happily remember the last time Dad and you came to visit us before he passed, and before I could do anything, he came over and gave me the biggest bear hug, and it felt so amazing and that it came full circle. Mom, I swear you must be one of my biggest supporters, ever since day one you wanted to hear about my writing and gave me so much encouragement and help researching and bouncing ideas off of you. You always ask me about my writing and listen to me babble on about my characters, and you never once made me feel like you didn't really want to know these things. Thank you for letting me create a character with some of your traits, I truly think Rowzey is one of the most interesting and fun characters of the series! I truly cannot thank you enough for all the love you both have given me over the years. Thank you for being who you are and allowing me to be a part of the family. I love you both so dearly and always will.

Emily, there are so many things I want to say to you, and yet I do not think there are enough pages possible to write everything down. We have been there for each other through it all, good and bad, with pickles and without (those without pickles are some of the hardest ones), but always there for one another. Thank you for being the most amazing friend. You have never once made me feel like I was a bother to you or annoying, even when I know I can be. I have loved spending time with you at the retreats, with our families together and when it's only the two of us just us doing our thing, just like we did back in the day hitting up the mall! Whenever I think back on the beginnings of our friendship, the main thing I always see and hear in my head is your big smile and amazing laugh. You bring a contagious positive energy with you every time we are together, and I love it! I am always here for you and always will be, you'll never have to question that. I love you and your family so much, and grateful to you each and everyday Em! Thank you for being such a huge support to me with my writing and letting me bring a piece of you into my world, Emryleia! Love you always, cuz you're stuck with me forever!

Adriana G, you are such an inspiring and supportive person. I feel so lucky to know you and get the privilege of calling you my friend. Throughout the years of my writing, each time we have talked you have always been so supportive and encouraging. Thank you for that and for being one of the most caring and kindest people I have ever known. Much love and light to you always! Love you!

Aeriel B, you helped me so much with the first two books and I cannot thank you enough. I appreciate the feedback and support you have given me over the years! Thank you so much! Love ya!

Alby B, thank you so much for meeting with me and providing me so many great suggestions and feedback. I appreciate it so very much. You are a talented writer, and I feel very privileged to know you!

Belinda E & Megan S, we met through a mutual friend and love of a tv show, and from there got to know each other and support one another, even if only through the internet. I am very thankful for the support you have both given me as a writer and a friend. Love you both!

Beth J, you had started your writing journey before I did, and were always so helpful with me trying to figure out everything. I am so grateful for your advice and encouragement throughout the whole process! Thank you for being such a wonderful friend! We've known one another since forever, even learned to drive together, and I love that we still have connections to share as we keep growing up! Love ya!

Betsy H, you have helped me get to the finish line of finishing my third novel. You have helped me see myself in ways I never thought possible. I can see myself as someone who is worthy and deserving of all the good things that come my way and still be humble and appreciative of all these things. Thank you for your continued guidance and support, I appreciate it so much more than words can ever express. Thank you so so very much.

Carol & Al H, you both are such amazing and wonderful people. Thank you for all your love and support over the years! I am so grateful to you both! Love ya!

Chelsea S, you, like your mother, always leave me in awe. You are such an amazing human and even more amazing mom to a bunch of other amazing humans! I love seeing your family's growth over the years and feel lucky to get to catch glimpses here and there. You also were such a huge supportive person when we found out about Ivy's heart, because you been down the road and knew all the possible challenges we faced. You are truly a person I look up to. Thank you for being you and being such a wonderful supportive person of me and my books! Love ya!

Christine B, there were times in my life growing up when things we all skewed and I couldn't see past the minute ahead of me, but I remember in your class you once told me I needed to remember to look ahead and not get lost in the moment. Those words helped me multiple times over the years and I will always appreciate that. Your strength and support of others is unmeasurable, those who know you are so lucky. You have always been an amazing teacher and librarian. Thank you for all that you do and helping so many kids find the books that resonate with them, perhaps like me they will one day write the stories that want to get lost in!

Christy EK, we were brought together in such an unconventional way, but a lot of the strangeness of our lives was so normal for us. Like most friendships we had our ebbs and flows, but at the end of the day, I am so grateful for our friendship and connections. Whether we were performing our own dance routines in my living room or listening to music in the camper in your yard, we always found ways to enjoy life and time together. I have always admired how you were always true to yourself and what you like, you had so much more confidence than I ever did. I was scared of figuring out who I was, but I always wanted to be more like you and just be who I was. Thank you for the last 40-ish years of memories and friendship, love you!

Crystal R, Girl, I don't even know where to start! Our friendship has had so many wild and crazy moments, and each one I am so happy to remember, even the flooded tent! You are such an amazing person who has more energy than I ever had all combined and you bring that with everything that you do. You always know how to make me laugh and smile and always make me feel like I was something special. Thank you for being exactly who you are! Love ya!!

Debra W, Karla Y, & Nicole R, the three of you helped start me back onto the path of my writing. I remember you all encouraging me almost every day at work to write more. While I didn't end up finishing the original story I had started writing with you all reading it, I know it was with your encouragement that I started to write again and opening myself up to possibilities of being a "real" author. I cherish the time we spent together and miss you all so very much. Much love to each one of you!

Deranged Doctor Design, you have repeatedly brought the world of Iryvalya and Nyrieve to life for all to see and allowed me to share the vision of my world to all. Thank you so much for all your talent and hard work. Each of you there I have worked with have been so professional and amazing, thank you so much!

Elise K, I knew you were amazing before we even met, but just how amazing was not fathomable. You have been able to capture a part of me that I never truly believed existed. I was so nervous before I sat and posed for you, not because of you, but because of me. In a moment all the nerves went away and all that was left was you and me with a lens in between us. It felt like I was just hanging out with a longtime friend who knew all the right things to say at the right time, and that feeling over the past 4+ years hasn't gone away. Each time I get to shoot with you I am nothing but excited to see what you are going to find and what different side of me will shine through. We have also gone beyond the lens and became friends, and it is a friendship I genuinely treasure. You bring such an intoxicating energy with you, that it is impossible to be anything but happy to be around you. Thank you for showing me the side of me I didn't believe existed and helping me learn to really love myself in every different side of me. Love ya, you and Devon!

Erin H, B2, you are such awesome and caring friend. Your support of my writing has always meant so much to me. I loved the year you came and helped us at GR Comic Con and even bought elf ears to wear. You always know how to brighten up each room you enter and bring joy everywhere you go. You honestly have such an amazing and powerful energy that attract people to you, and I am lucky to be someone who you don't seem to mind buzzing around! We will always have Vegas and so much more! Can't wait to make more memories with you! Love ya!!

Frances & Jack R, you were the only set of grandparents I ever knew, and I sure was lucky to have you both showing me so much love and support throughout my life. I am so sad that you are both gone now and that my kids never really had a chance to get to know you as I did. You both did so much for me growing up and even as a young adult, and I never could fully express how much that meant to me. Thank you for loving me like you did. Thank you for encouraging my reading and always making sure I had another book to read, those things helped me on my journey to be the author I am today. You both will be forever missed and never forgotten. I love you both so much and hope that you are proud of me wherever you might be.

Gary G, you were such an amazing teacher to me. I remember that year was the first year I was put in advanced reading and read the whole Laura Ingalls Wilder series and we even made homemade butter in class. You helped me see my passion for reading was a good thing. In your class we had a story competition that I won one of the categories, and it really made me want to be a writer. I might have put it off for far too many years, but eventually I went back to my passions and followed my dreams. Thank you for being a part of that and my story!

Jennifer Lyn B, the amazing confidence you have given me through your amazing artistry! Your talent knows not bounds and you have worked your magic helping me achieve a look and confidence I always wanted to try! You also are just a truly amazing human being who I feel very fortunate to get to call my friend.

Jessica G, girl, you were a much-needed friend when I first moved and I was so happy and grateful we found each other! You made the days so much more bearable and the evenings when we hung out were the best! You were always there for me when I needed you and hopefully, I was able to be there for you too! You are an amazing person and I'm lucky to be your friend! Love ya!

Jill B, you helped me get through sometimes I wasn't sure I could, and your constant support and encouragement helped me get to where I am today and I am very appreciative of all you have done.

Jim & Rose E, as a whole your family was always like my second family growing up. I always felt safe and welcome in your home. I remember over the summer's Rose taking us kids to the library so many times, where we were participating in the BookIt program! I might have been that kid that was annoying for always wanting to come over, but you never made me feel that way, and I appreciate that so much. Thank you for just being you and always making me feel like I was welcome and a part of the family. I love each and every one of you (J,R,J,C,&J)!

Jodi C, you have been such a big supporter of my books and giving me the little nudges I need to keep writing! I also need to give you a huge thank you for not only enjoying my books, but taking the time to share my books with others, it means so very much to me!!! You are awesome!

Julia F, you left this world way too early… There are not many memories of high school without you in them. We had our differences but were there for each other. Our vacations together, our listening to music in the playhouse, going for drives once we could, so many sleepovers, and so much more run through my mind when I think of you. While time moved us around, and our conversations lessened, they never fully went away. I am so grateful when you called me after you found out you were sick, we were able to talk about the things we never had before and could appreciate one another on a whole new level. I never wanted to see you pass, but the love that I saw pouring out for you just showed how many lives you touched and how you will not be forgotten. Wherever you are now, you should rest easy in knowing how much you are missed and loved.

Kelley M, it is crazy how much things change and yet they stay the same. While distance can sometimes be inevitable, the memories will always remain and be kept in a special place in my heart. I will always wish you nothing but joy and happiness and look forward to a day to catch up. Love ya.

Kim H & George RR M, the day I was in Santa Fe to see you both was a game changer for me. While I was so excited to see two of my favorite authors, it was also the day the world of Iryvalya came to me. Sitting in the theater waiting for the interview between you both to start was where a story about a mixed blooded elf who was supposed to save her world popped into my head. I remember writing the ideas that were coming to me as fast as I could on my Blackberry, hoping this wasn't a memory of another book I had read once. I remember asking a question about writing and you both were so kind and encouraging to me that when I went home, I thought for the first time I could actually write a book myself. Here I am eleven years later and now just finished my third book from this series. I am grateful for that day and while you did not give me the idea of my books, you gave me the inspiration and encouragement I needed to write my stories, thank you both so much!

Knarfy… you are thought of, spoke of and missed each and every day. You will never be forgotten by those who knew and loved you so much…

Kris K, you have been a wonderful big sister to me ever since I joined the family and I feel beyond lucky that we had the opportunity to get so much closer when we lived nearby. Even with distance, the love and friendship will always be the same. Love you!

Laurie K, in your class you showed me that it was okay to like things that were not the typical or most popular. Because of you I began reading Edgar Allen Poe and watching Vincent Price movies, and both are still in my top 5 of artists. My tastes expanded and I do not think they have ever really stopped. I love finding new ideas and styles and I know you started me on that journey. Thank you!

Lisa Gilliam, for your continued insightful edits and suggestions that help polish Iryvalya into the magical world that it is today. Thank you so much!

Marci B, you are the best thing that I ever found in a yahoo chat room! You are one of the strongest women I have ever known. You fight fearlessly for those you love and do the right thing. You are an inspiration not only to me, but so many others. I wish I had half the courage and strength you possess. Thank you for all your encouragement over the years and know it has always been appreciated! I love you!

Mia/Amy D, while I know the contact is gone and many things have been said that cannot be unsaid, I am still grateful for the friendship we had once and the encouragement we gave to one another, especially when it came to our writing. I wish you so much success and happiness in your life.

Micheal K, you and your beautiful soul came to me in a time I felt so alone and unaware of who I was. You brought me into a world I had always respected but never had the chance to be a part of, and because of it I felt I found my people and was able to find more of myself. I am in such awe of you and everything you have accomplished in your life and so very VERY proud to call you my friend! Love you!

Mike & Auna R, you are two wonderful people who I am so happy came into my life through Joe. I'm super grateful for Auna sharing her water glass to help bring Ivy about! LOL And Mike talking to me about interesting ideas for characters in my books! Both of you have been so kind and supportive of my writing, even coming to help at the booth at GR Comic Con. That means so much to me, and I will always be grateful to you both! Love you both!

Mike, Linda & Paula G, you and your family always made me feel so welcome and loved. With you I had a little sister and another set of parents who I always knew I could go to if I ever needed something. I will never forget our family vacations together and all the memories inbetween. I am forever grateful for all the love and support I received from you over the years. Thank you so much, I love you all!

Missy D, you are an amazing person who has been there for me and my family in ways most could not understand or appreciate, but I do! It is crazy how our friendship came to be, but I wouldn't change anything. I love the laughs we share and fun we have together! Thank you for all your support! Love you!

My Inner Child, kid, have come a long way. You never believed in yourself and wanted so much to have people believe in you. You have that now. You have people who believe in you and show up for you in ways you never thought were possible. But the best part is you have slowly come to believe in yourself. You not only wrote a book, but you wrote three books in a series! You read so many of those growing up and never allowed yourself to believe you could do something like that, but you did it. When you started with your first book, your far reaching goal you never thought you could do was write three books, and you did it, all within a 10 year span! I am proud of you! Your dreams never went away, they just were hiding and now most of them have all come true! You are me and I am you, and I wish we could have been told we could do all the things we dreamed of doing and drowned out all the noise that held us back, but the only voice we really needed to hear telling us that was our own. I am sorry it took us so long, but better late than never. I am so glad we didn't give up every time we were so close to it. Your journey is far from over, and I am excited to see what we will accomplish next!

Nieces & Nephews, (Micheal, Jessica, Spencer, Ally, & Christopher) I love each and every one of you so much and am beyond proud to be your Aunt. You are all such amazing unique and different people, and I truly hope you know that, never forget it, and live your lives to the fullest! I love each of you!

Micheal Z, you are such an awesome nephew, I don't know many others who can enjoy sending some of the weirdest meme's to each other like you do! You have been there for me in times where I really needed it, like right before Ivy was born and Joe was out of town, you helped me with so many things and I will always be so grateful for that, and will provide the "Bangin' Pasta Salad" whenever it's requested!). We love having you and the fam visit us whenever possible and look forward to the next time! Love you!

Jessica Z, you are a beautiful and talented woman, and I wish you all the joy and happiness your heart can hold. Love you!

Spencer V, you are such a strong and intelligent man. I love hearing about the things you are into and seeing you smile! I hope that you keep chasing the things that bring you joy! I am proud of you for following your heart and knowing who you are. Love you!

Ally V, you have so much talent and creativity that has always impressed me, not to mention one of the sweetest smiles ever! I hope that you continue to do the things you love and that bring you happiness! Love you!

Christopher K, I loved getting to know you better while we lived near each other. We always loved having you over and hanging out with us. You are a smart and hard worker, and I know you have the drive to follow your dreams and enjoy your happiness! Love you!!

Patricia B, I remember as a kid ALWAYS loving getting to come to your home or having you come on family vacations with us. You always made me feel like I was a special person and loved. Now as an adult, I am even more grateful for all your love and support of me in so many ways. I hope you know you are and always be in a special place in my heart and my families. Thank you for being such an amazing Aunt and loving us like your own. Love you so much Aunt Patryvla!!!

Rachel B, our kids' friendship, brought us together, and I'll always be grateful for that. You are such a wonderful and caring person. You have always made me feel like you were eager to hear me talk to you about my characters and their personalities and offered insight as well. Thank you for your friendship and support over the years, I know it'll just keep growing! Love ya!

Readers and Fans... without you, there really would not be more than one book... when I have heard from you in reviews or in person about my books and what you liked, or who you related to, those were the things that pushed me to keep writing and continuing the world of Iryvalya. Thank you so much for enjoying my world and being a part of it!

Rick & Yola V, my big brother and sister, I love you both very much and appreciate you both so much. It is crazy how fast time goes, because I can remember like it was yesterday how Rick and I would get lost in the woods or play chess or standing up next to you at your wedding. While we have moved in different directions (living in different places and such), I know no matter what happens, love is always there. Love you both!

Rosie C, you have brought the voice of Nyrieve, Rowzey and more to life, and it brings happy tears to my eyes when I hear it! I am so grateful for all the work you have done to do the voice work for Bloodlines and look forward to working with you again on the others! Thank you!

Rowzey… as always, it is and always will be the sauce! Thank you for this amazing journey!

Sarah/Harleen H, you and your supportive spirit blows me away each and every time! You are one of the biggest cheerleaders for your friends that I have ever seen in my life. You light up the room with your smile and beautiful soul! I am so grateful for you and your friendship. Never stop being the amazing person you are, because you, my friend, are truly one of a kind! Love ya!

Sherry R, you have been such an amazing and supportive person to me, especially these last few years! I always look forward to getting messages from you and look forward to hanging out! Thank you for being you, a sweet, caring, loving and compassionate person! I'm lucky to get to call you family! Love ya!

Squad Bettie, you are more than just a group, you are womxn that help support and lift each other up. Throughout my writing, this group has helped fill me with courage and strength. Thank you all and I wish nothing but happiness for each one of you.

Susan C, we have known each other and been friends for more years than not, and I love that we were able to reconnect and share our love of writing together. You are a strong and amazing person, and I am so grateful for your support and encouragement. I look forward to our continued friendship and supporting each other's writing journey! I am so proud of what you have accomplished already with the GRLitFest and cannot wait to see it grow! Much love to you!

Tina M, your guidance truly helped set me on the path for writing and finishing my books. I remember when I told you my goal was to write three books, and I am so glad I get to share with you that I reached my goal, and you are a part of me getting here. Thank you for everything you helped me with, I am always and forever grateful.

Thrive (Amanda, Julie, Liz, Melissa & Sierrah), finding you has given our family the balance it needed outside the home. You all have provided our child with an environment that allows her to be who she is and know that she is amazing exactly like that. Having this balance has taken so much stress and fear off of me that I was able to relax and be able to really write again. I am so thankful for you and all that you have brought into our world.

Thrive Caregivers, you are such an amazing group of people who have welcomed me (and my family) and show such amazing love and support. The morning meetings have been amazing to connect and support one another. Also many of you have been supportive of my writing and encouraging with me, and for that I will be forever grateful!

Tabitha W, we have known each other for over 3 years now, and sometimes I feel like I have known you forever. I cherish our conversations so much and always look forward to seeing your adventures and catching up on just the day to day things. You are truly an amazing person and I am so grateful we came into each other's lives! Thank you for being such a great friend!!! Love ya!

Tracy K, no matter what has happened in life, I have and always will consider you my sister. You have listened to me when I have needed to vent and I hope I have been able to be like that for you as well. You are an amazing Mom and Friend and I am forever happy our paths crossed when they did and we were able to stay in touch over so many years! I love you!

(Vivian) Alice S, sadly I only got to have you in my life for eleven years, and it was not enough. I remember sitting in your living room seeing all the pictures on the walls, the squeaky floors as I'd walk around and hearing your unique laugh that always made me smile. I remember thinking of how I wish I could have known you when you were younger, thinking I would have loved to have been your friend. Every time we'd visit you'd give me a bag of things you'd pick up for me at the local "dime store", as you called it. There were many different things in there, but mostly it was books and personal things of yours with little notes as to what they were. I read through all the books and kept all the pins you gave me, because they always meant so much to me. I am so sad that my family never got the chance to meet you and learn where I got a lot of my stubbornness from. I think of and miss you often and hope you always knew how much you meant to me and how much I love you still.

Wana Mama Wild Women, you women are so beyond amazing, caring, compassionate, fierce, loyal, funny, strong, and so much more. We all came together for different reasons but left with bonds and friendships that I believe will last a lifetime. Thank you for listening to my struggles and making me see that I am valued and deserve good things, just as you all are and do too! I look forward to each and every time we get to see one another! Thank you all! I love you!

Zoey Z, you are such an amazing, strong, smart, beautiful and caring person, and I love hearing you and your cousin laughing and playing together, even when it's just online. You honored me beyond words when you dressed up in costume as Nyrieve, that is something I never thought would happen and it truly is one of the highest points of my career. I'm so proud to be your Aunt! Love you so much "Zozo"!

With Much Gratitude, there have been so many people in my life that have brought me so many different emotions and memories. Some good, some bad, some easy and some hard… I draw from all of these emotions when I write and appreciate these moments in time that have helped me as a writer write even better… and those of you who have supported me, even just by sharing my book online… thinking of you and so appreciative of you… Acacia F, Adrian S, Amity T, Amy T, Andrea H, Alyse W, Beth D, Brian T, Cara H, Carol V, Cathleen V, Cathy R, Cherri D, Chris M, Christie H, Christopher W, Cicely W, Cristy M, Cruzita L, Danielle M, Dara S, Darcy L, Dee B, Emily S, Geri S, Heather J, Heather W, Holly G, Ikuko B, Jaci S,

Jade C, Jayna M, Jeff H, Janelle K, Jenn B, Jenna Z, Jennifer A, Jennifer J, Jennifer S, Jenny D, Jeremy H, Jeremy R, Jessica C, Jessica D, Jessica P, Jill D, Jill V, John B, Jonna J, Josie D, Joyce H, Judy W, Karen V, Katherine H, Kaylie S, Lacey F, Landa O, Lauren R, Layla B, Lee M, Laena/LowKii, Lindsey D, Lisa B, Lisa M, Lisa S, Liz F, Loretta C, Luke K, Maggie R, Mandy S, Marianne W, Marisol H, Marynes P, Matthew W, Melissa P, Melissa T, Melissa V, Nathan B, Nicholette D, Pamela C, Rachel R, Renata A, Ruth M, Sandi S, Sal S, Sara B, Sam BR, Seka P, Sonia M, Tami Λ, Tara F, & Tasha Band so many more… if I forgotten a name, I am so sorry, I really tried.

Anti -Acknowledgments

(Those who were not helpful or supportive)

School Counselor – you told me that I shouldn't bother with doing ACT's or SAT's and trying to go to college because I wasn't smart enough. When I told you I wanted to be a writer, you told me not to bother because I wasn't good enough. I know I am not the only person who you talked to like that, and I am saddend to think there were others like me who believed you. But today, I am a college graduate and have now written and published THREE novels. I did not push myself to go to college or write because of you, I did it because of me and finding people who believed in me and helped me believe in myself.

Bullies (there are too many of you to write about each one separately) – all of you took time out of your life to make me feel pretty worthless or ugly or unworthy of good things in life, and each one of you wasted that time in the end. Yes, I was hurt when these things were said or done against me, but in the end they didn't work. I might not be the most beautiful person ever or the smartest or even have an ounce of sporting ability, but what I do have is compassion and empathy, even for each of you. They say only hurt people hurt people, so in that, I hope you all have been able to heal and grow and no longer carry the hurt you had that caused you to hurt others.

Others – I have been told by a few over the years "I hope you have a child like you one day, and you'll see what it is like", and I want you to know, I did just that. I had a daughter who is very similar to me, very creative, full of imagination, caring and so much love to give so many, and you know what? It is the easiest thing in the world to love her just as she is. Which made me realize that I too wasn't hard to love.

About the Author:

LeAnn Kelley is the author of *The Tales of Iryvalya* series, including:

Bloodlines

Crossroads

Horizons

LeAnn is a storyteller known for weaving fantastical worlds rich with detail, heart, and characters readers are drawn to journey alongside. She has been writing since childhood—often trading her allowance for books and dreaming up realms of magic and mystery. Though she holds a degree in Psychology, her true passion has always been storytelling. That passion was sparked into action after meeting one of her favorite authors, Kim Harrison—a moment that reignited her creative fire and gave rise to the world of Iryvalya.

A West Michigan native, LeAnn was raised just outside of Grand Rapids in the small town of Lowell and now lives nearby with her husband, daughter, their rescue cat Moon, and a lively flock of chickens. From a young age, she dreamed of creating her own fictional world—one filled with immersive landscapes, heartfelt character journeys, and a touch of magic. Heavily influenced by authors such as Laurell K. Hamilton, J.R.R. Tolkien, Suzanne Collins, and George R.R. Martin, she brings those dreams to life through richly imagined realms that invite readers to escape, reflect, and return for more.

Outside the pages of Iryvalya, LeAnn enjoys hiking, kayaking, traveling, and soaking in the energy of nature. She is also a dedicated advocate for CHD (Congenital Heart Defect) awareness—a cause close to her heart since her daughter was born with CCTGA.

"Every heart warrior I have met is more of a superhero than any I've read about in comics or seen in movies."
—LeAnn Kelley

Reading and writing have always been her sanctuary. Today, she continues to expand the world of Iryvalya while encouraging others to pursue the stories waiting inside them.

"I have always wanted to create worlds and characters with my own words. It may have taken me many years to get here, but dreams do not expire if you keep chasing them. Never give up on yours!"
—LeAnn Kelley

www.ingramcontent.com/pod-product-compliance
Lightning Source LLC
Chambersburg PA
CBHW050030030726
47506CB00001B/196